JUN

O9-AHW-012

Praise for

IF THE SLIPPER FITS

"Filled with romance, breathtaking passion, and a dash of mystery that will leave you wanting more."

—*Night Owl Reviews*

"A dash of danger and a dash of fairy tale in the form of a very special pair of shoes add to the romance plot, filling out *If the Slipper Fits* nicely." —*Romance Junkies*

"Cinderella knew it was all about the shoes, and so does master storyteller Drake as she kicks off the Cinderella Sisterhood with a tale filled with gothic overtones, sensuality, sprightly dialogue, emotion, an engaging cast, and a beautiful pair of perfectly fitting slippers."

—*RT Book Reviews* (4 stars)

"I was enchanted with this story as Olivia Drake took the residents of Castle Kevern *and* this reader on an emotional, delightful journey. A magical fairy tale deserving to be read and read again!"

—*Once Upon a Romance*

Praise for Olivia Drake's Heiress in London series

SCANDAL OF THE YEAR

"The final installment of the Crompton sisters' trilogy is as charming, sweet, humorous, and poignant as any of Drake's previous books. Marked by her fine storytelling and engaging characters, this volume stands alone, but fans familiar with the series will revel in the conclusion." —*RT Book Reviews* (5 stars)

NEVER TRUST A ROGUE

"Olivia Drake will keep readers coming back for more."
—*Publishers Weekly*

"Drake is a consummate storyteller who cleverly blends intrigue, suspense, and sensuality into a pulse-pounding mystery, à la Amanda Quick. Give yourself plenty of time to savor this fast-paced, non-stop delight of a book."   —*RT Book Reviews* (Top Pick, 4½ stars)

SEDUCING THE HEIRESS

"This book has it all: a fabulous hero, a wonderful heroine, and sizzling passion. Read it and watch the sparks fly!"   —Christina Dodd

"Guaranteed to seduce readers everywhere. This book is something truly special, an unforgettable story filled with passion, intrigue, and sweep-you-away romance."
—Susan Wiggs

"This decadent Regency romance is carried along by a spunky heroine and sumptuous descriptions of upper-class life . . . there's enough glitz to keep readers coming back."   —*Publishers Weekly*

"Drake entices readers [and] twists the traditional with an unconventional heroine and a bad-boy hero that readers will adore."   —*RT Book Reviews*

"Drake takes what could be a been-there, read-that story of a scheming scoundrel and a headstrong hoyden, and weaves a tale of wit, seduction, secrets, and sensuality that's as vibrant as it is refreshing."
—Michelle Buonfiglio's Romance: B(u)y the Book®

Stroke of Midnight

OLIVIA DRAKE

St. Martin's Paperbacks

This is a work of fiction. All of the characters, organizations, and events portrayed in this novel are either products of the author's imagination or are used fictitiously.

STROKE OF MIDNIGHT

Copyright © 2013 by Barbara Dawson Smith.

All rights reserved.

For information address St. Martin's Press, 175 Fifth Avenue, New York, NY 10010.

ISBN: 978-1-250-00209-9

Printed in the United States of America

St. Martin's Paperbacks edition / June 2013

St. Martin's Paperbacks are published by St. Martin's Press, 175 Fifth Avenue, New York, NY 10010.

10 9 8 7 6 5 4 3 2 1

The London Gazette, *5 April 1838*

On this day ten years ago, a terrible crime was perpetrated upon Her Grace, the Duchess of Knowles. In the dark of night, whilst Her Grace attended a soiree in Mayfair, a robber crept into her mansion in Grosvenor Square and purloined several valuables from her private chambers. The most spectacular of these was a necklace containing the Blue Moon diamond, a gemstone so large and perfect that it is priceless, for none other like it exists in the world.

A fortnight later, after an intensive hunt for the criminal, a set of earrings belonging to Her Grace was discovered by Lord Copley in the possession of an unscrupulous gentleman named Martin Falkner. When his lordship attempted to apprehend the villain, Mr. Falkner brutally attacked him with a knife, thereby evading capture and disappearing along with his eighteen-year-old daughter. Despite the offer of a handsome reward, the Blue Moon diamond has never been found . . .

Chapter 1

She had no reason to fear the constable.

Holding fast to that thought, Laura followed the burly officer through the graveyard. The cloudy afternoon cast a gloomy pall over the rows of headstones and wooden crosses. A few of the mounds had been carefully tended, though many others showed signs of neglect. Rough masculine laughter came from one of the gin houses in the surrounding slums. It was the only sound besides the squelching of the constable's boots on the sodden ground and the patter of her own footsteps.

Though any woman in her circumstances might feel a bit nervous, Laura had more reason than most to be wary. She reminded herself that the constable could have no notion of her true identity. A decade had passed since she and her father had fled London. She had been someone else then, leading another life under a different surname. A lady garbed in silk and jewels rather than the drab commoner she was now.

No one in this vast city knew her anymore. Miss

Laura Falkner, toast of society, was as dead as the poor souls in this paupers' cemetery.

The constable glanced over his shoulder, the dark sockets of his eyes boring into her. "Almost there, Miss Brown."

Laura kept her face expressionless. Had a stray curl escaped her bonnet? She hoped not, for the police surely had a description of her that included mention of her distinctive tawny-gold hair. "You've done more than your duty, sir. If you'll point me in the right direction, you can be on your way."

" 'Tis no trouble to take ye there. No trouble at all."

His insistence increased her disquiet. He continued onward, his large head moving back and forth to examine the gravestones. What was his name again? Officer Pangborn. She had not wanted an escort, but he'd insisted that no decent female should venture alone into these crime-ridden stews.

Laura had acquiesced only because a refusal might arouse suspicion. She had taken a risk in going to the police in the first place. But she'd needed to learn more about her father's recent death and also to discover the site of his final resting place.

Papa!

The wind tossed a spattering of icy raindrops at her face. Shivering, she drew the cloak more securely around herself. After so many years in the sunshine of Portugal, she had forgotten the damp chill of an English springtime. Or perhaps it was just that she'd suppressed the memory of her old life before she and Papa had escaped into exile.

Now he lay dead. Murdered by an unknown assailant in an alley near Covent Garden. The shock of it still numbed her. News of the attack had arrived while she'd been tending the garden outside their little cottage in the mountains of Portugal. How contented she'd been that day, trimming the camellias, weeding the arum lilies, while having no inkling of the disaster that was about to shatter her tranquility. Then a boy from the village had delivered a letter from the London police stating that one Martin Brown lay severely injured, that her address had been found in his pocket. She'd departed in a rush, traveling for many days over land and sea, only to learn that her father had succumbed to his wounds shortly after the letter had been posted.

Laura swallowed past the painful lump in her throat. At their last parting, Papa had told her he would be gone for a fortnight on business—she had presumed to Lisbon to buy and sell antiquities, their only source of income. Instead, he must have boarded a ship to England. *Why?*

Why would he go back to a place where he would be tried and hanged if captured?

"There 'tis, Miss."

Constable Pangborn stopped near the low stone wall that marked the perimeter of the cemetery. The middle-aged officer had muttonchop whiskers and the bulky build of a prizefighter. He had been out on patrol when he'd found Papa lying sorely injured in the alleyway. Now, as he pointed his wooden truncheon at a nearby grave site, his speculative gaze remained fixed on Laura.

Her skin prickled. She couldn't shake the sense that he knew more about her than he let on. Had Papa in a delirium on his deathbed revealed his real identity? Did this officer believe she'd been her father's accomplice in the jewel theft that had rocked society ten years ago?

She warned herself not to make wild assumptions.

More likely, Pangborn's interest in her was of a carnal nature. Over the years, she'd had ample experience in discouraging such lechers.

Laura leveled a cool stare at him. "Your assistance has been very helpful," she said in polite dismissal. "I shall bid you good day now."

His thick Wellington boots remained planted in place. "I have me orders, miss. I'm to guard ye from harm."

"The sergeant bade you only to escort me to the cemetery. You've already done more than enough."

"There be drunkards and thieves roaming these stews, ready to pounce on a wee creature such as yourself. I'll see ye home—and that's that."

Home was a cheap lodging house in an area nearly as wretched as this one. Yet Laura would sooner risk the walk alone than let this man learn her temporary place of residence. If the constable really did harbor a suspicion about her true identity, he might search her portmanteau and find the news article about the decade-old robbery that she'd clipped from an English paper. Then he would have proof that she was the notorious Miss Laura Falkner.

She dipped her chin in a pretense of humble acceptance. "That's very good of you, sir. If I may, I should like a few minutes alone now. Kindly await me at the entrance gate."

Constable Pangborn scowled as if gauging her sincerity. Then he gave a curt nod and marched away, glancing back several times over his shoulder. The breeze carried the far-off sounds of conviviality along with a fishy stench from the nearby Thames.

She watched until he reached the gate before lowering her gaze to the grave site. Weeds already had sprouted on the freshly turned mound. A small square of stone lay flat on the ground, and a name was chiseled into the surface: MARTIN BROWN.

Heedless of the damp earth, Laura sank to her knees in a billow of gray skirts. Tears blurred her eyes as she reached out to trace the crude letters with a gloved fingertip. "Papa," she whispered brokenly. "*Papa.*"

The harsh reality of his death struck her anew. She hunched over the grave, weeping, no longer able to stem the tide of sorrow. He had been the very best of fathers, full of good cheer and wise words, concerned more for her happiness than his own. He had treated her as an equal and schooled her as the son he'd always wanted. He didn't deserve to have suffered such a brutal end—or to lie forgotten in a pauper's tomb. His memory should be honored with a fine marble headstone carved with haloed angels and a loving tribute.

And it should bear his true name: MARTIN FALKNER.

With trembling fingers, she plucked out the weeds and tossed them aside. Someone here in London had destroyed his good reputation. Someone had deliberately planted evidence to make him appear guilty of stealing the Blue Moon diamond. Had her father returned to England to track down the villain? Why had he done so without telling her?

It must have been the quarrel they'd had over that news clipping.

When Papa had brought home the broadsheet and she'd noticed the small article, it had resurrected her buried anger over their forced flight from England ten years earlier. She'd spoken bitterly about the injustice of their exile. They had exchanged sharp words over her wish to restore their standing in society. But when his expression had turned melancholy, she'd regretted her mistake in bringing up the topic and had hastily reassured him of her contentment. It had been only a day later that he'd set out on his fateful journey . . .

Across the cemetery, a bulky form started down the path, arms swinging purposefully. Constable Pangborn!

The prospect of leaving the grave site wrenched her heart. Yet Laura dared delay no longer. Leaning down, she whispered, "My dearest Papa . . . good-bye."

She sprang to her feet and made haste to the stone wall. Since it stood no higher than her bosom, the barrier should be easily climbable. Hitching up her skirts, she found a few toeholds and hoisted herself to the top. Hard work and mountain hiking had strengthened her limbs, one more reason to be thankful she was no longer the fragile debutante.

"You there!" Pangborn shouted. "Stop!"

Dear heaven, she'd been right to mistrust the officer.

A bramble hooked her hem, causing a brief delay. Laura yanked herself free and scrambled over the wall. As she landed, her shoes slid on a mound of damp leaves. Her arms wheeled as she caught her balance, only just managing to stay upright.

She risked a backward glance. The constable had left the path and sprinted on a straight course over the graves. The scowl that darkened his whiskered face sent a chill into Laura's heart. There could be no doubt he meant to arrest her.

As he neared the wall, she plunged into the maze of narrow streets.

Chapter 2

She ran until her lungs burned. The lanes twisted hither and yon between ramshackle tenements of soot-stained brick. People watched her with dull curiosity: a costermonger pushing his cart, a slouched old woman sitting on a wooden crate, ragged children playing tag among the piles of rubbish. Here and there, drunkards lolled in doorways, some sleeping and others staring bleary-eyed as she flew past.

Running footsteps echoed in her wake. Several times there came a shout, "Stop her!"

None of the locals complied. They were either too weary to put forth the effort or too reluctant to lend aid to the police.

Laura thanked God for small favors. She clutched up her skirts to avoid tripping. Her bonnet blew back to dangle from its tied ribbons behind her neck. There was no time to make repairs, not with Constable Pangborn less than a block behind her.

He moved with the speed of a bull charging a matador. But Laura had an agility and strength born of determination. She refused to be named an accomplice to a crime her father hadn't committed. Even if she was acquitted eventually, she would languish in prison for months while awaiting a trial. She had no money to pay for a legal defense, no friends or relatives to whom she might turn.

She simply *must* evade capture.

Turning a corner in a burst of speed, Laura glanced about for a hiding place. She ducked into a darkened alley littered with refuse and reeking of foul odors. There she crouched behind an old barrel until the officer ran past.

Her heart pounded wildly. She forced herself to tarry for a moment before cautiously peering out into the dirt lane. Overhead, strings of laundry flapped in the breeze. No one peered out of any windows on this quiet side street.

Pangborn was gone—but he wouldn't be for long.

As she stepped out of the alley, something moved in the corner of her eye. She spun toward it, her fingers clenching into fists. But it was merely a cat prowling through the shadows. The creature bounded up onto a windowsill and vanished through a broken pane of glass.

Walking swiftly, Laura doubled back and took a different route through the rabbit warren of streets. All the while she kept a sharp watch for the constable. Pangborn likely knew every nook and cranny of these slums. That made it all the more imperative to increase the distance between them.

A slattern in an upper window called out, "Need a bed, Goldilocks? Pretty thing like ye'll 'ave yer pick o' customers."

Ignoring the woman's crude invitation, Laura hurried onward as she replaced the bonnet, tucking every blond strand out of sight and tying the ribbons securely at her throat. For good measure, she raised the voluminous hood of her cloak over her head. It wasn't much of a disguise, but it would have to do.

Reaching a crossroads, she paused to get her bearings. Several lanes branched off into identical gloomy byways. Dear heavens, which way would lead her to safety? She was utterly lost in this labyrinth. No, not lost . . . it was late afternoon, and that faint brightness in the cloud cover must indicate the west.

She veered in that direction, hoping it would lead to better neighborhoods. Would Pangborn have given chase if his sole purpose was seduction? She doubted so. That left her with only one logical conclusion. Somehow, he suspected her true identity. He must believe she knew what had happened to the stolen diamond.

In the eyes of the police, she was as guilty as her father.

Laura reached a main thoroughfare teeming with drays and hansom cabs. Finally she could feel safe among the many pedestrians that thronged the foot pavement. She fit in well with these commoners who were intent on their own destinations, women with market baskets, maids toting parcels, workmen gathered by a street seller of meat pies.

Her stomach growled at the succulent aroma. She'd eaten nothing since breaking her fast with cheese and a crust of bread that morning, nothing while she'd waited for hours at the police station. Beneath the cloak, her precious few coins jingled in a hidden pocket of her gown. After the expense of the voyage, she must guard her savings. Heaven only knew how long the money needed to last her.

But first things first. Her sense of place had been hopelessly muddled by the chase through twisting streets. Where exactly was she? This area looked vaguely familiar.

In her youth, she'd spent a portion of each year in London. Her world back then had consisted of shopping trips to Regent Street, carriage rides in Hyde Park, and social events at the finest homes in Mayfair. There also had been occasional forays beyond those rarefied boundaries: visits to Astley's Circus, St. Paul's Cathedral, or the Tower.

A scene blotted out the present.

She sat in an open phaeton, her gloved fingers grasping the reins of a pair of matched bays . . . Alex had his arm around her as he taught her how to manage the frisky horses . . . she loved the feel of his strong body next to hers . . . even more, she loved it when he bent his head to brush his lips over hers . . .

Someone in the crowd jostled Laura. Jolted back to reality, she spun around with a gasp, half expecting to see the constable.

It was merely a fishwife who aimed a glare over a hefty shoulder. "Move along, miss—'tis n' place to lollygag."

Laura realized she'd come to a halt. As she resumed walking, her thoughts dwelled on that long-ago carriage ride. The scent of male cologne lingered in her mind, as did the warm pressure of his kiss. The absolute clarity of the memory rattled her. Ten years ago, she had relegated that naive romance to the dustbin of history.

Alexander Ross, the Earl of Copley, had betrayed her in the worst possible way. He had attempted to arrest her father for stealing the duchess's jewels—

without giving Papa the benefit of the doubt, without even *considering* that someone else might have planted the jewels in Papa's desk. Laura's desperate pleas on her father's behalf hadn't made a bit of difference.

Bitterness filled her throat. She wouldn't think about Alex. He meant nothing to her now. Nothing at all.

Laura marched briskly past dingy shops selling everything from tobacco to medicines, groceries to old clothing. At least now she knew her location: she was heading west on The Strand, a wide thoroughfare that cut through the heart of London.

Papa had been attacked not far from here in Covent Garden. Had he been the random victim of a robber? Or had her father *known* his assailant? The question nagged at Laura like a sore tooth. Had he traveled to England for the purpose of finding the villain who had wronged him—only to pay for that confrontation with his life?

Deeply unsettled, she trod onward without any clear destination in mind. If she couldn't rely on the police, then whom *could* she trust? Her former friends and acquaintances undoubtedly viewed her as a pariah. She had no living relatives—there had only been her and Papa. She was on her own now, a rudderless raft in a vast sea of humanity.

She had come to London with the intention of nursing her father back to health. The news of his passing left her with the sharp ache of loss. The most prudent course of action would be to return to her little cottage in the mountains of Portugal. There she could eke out a living by selling her watercolors of flora and fauna. Yet something inside her resisted the notion of departing on the next ship.

If indeed Papa had been murdered, she could not allow his death to go unavenged.

It had long been her wish to clear his name by rooting out the villain who had set him up as a jewel thief. She would have done so already had not her father begged her to drop the notion as being too dangerous. The topic had come up several times over the years, most recently when she'd spotted that little article in *The London Gazette* commemorating the tenth anniversary of the spectacular crime.

Now he was no longer alive to stop her.

A sense of purpose revived Laura's flagging spirits. There were several people in society who might have had reason to ruin her father—and her, as well. The trouble was, how could she question them? It wasn't as if she could pay a call on any fine house in Mayfair. She was *persona non grata* to the ton . . .

Of a sudden, Laura noticed that the store fronts had become more posh. The signs were gilt-framed, the windows displaying goods of the finest quality. Tall buildings with columned fronts lined the broad, curving road with its elegant carriages and coaches. Footmen carrying parcels trailed after ladies in costly gowns and feathered hats.

Pausing beneath a marble colonnade, she realized that her idle wanderings had brought her to Regent Street. Though perhaps it had not been happenstance. Perhaps she had been drawn here by the allure of the forbidden.

Caution told her to retrace her steps. It would be foolish to risk being spotted by an acquaintance from her old life. Her presence in London must not be known before she'd had time to make plans and determine how best to solve the mystery of her father's death.

Yet she hungered to view the window displays. To indulge in the pastime that had once been an integral part of her life. To relive the happy times when she had strolled here with Alex. Would it not be wise to study the latest fashions so that she might prepare herself for whatever lay ahead? She would, after all, have to blend in with society.

The temptation proved too powerful to resist.

Adjusting the hood over her head, she lowered her chin in the manner of the lower class. In her drab dark cloak she'd be taken for a maidservant out on an errand for her mistress. Laura started down the foot pavement, taking care not to meet the eye of any of the ladies or gentlemen promenading along the street.

Her own eyes swept their clothing in surreptitious glances. How hopelessly outdated was her much-mended attire. The skirts now were considerably wider, the sleeves more voluminous than when she'd made her debut a decade ago. Living in the mountains, she'd had no reason to keep up with the latest styles, let alone pay for new gowns each season.

But oh, how she would love to enter these shops and order an entire wardrobe without a care for the cost. To once again feel the cool slide of silk against her skin, to set a beribboned hat at a jaunty angle on her upswept hair. She paused in front of a display of fans, admiring the carved ivory sticks and painted folds. How lovely it would be to snap open the fan and peer flirtatiously at an admiring gentleman . . .

The bell above the shop door tinkled as a trio of ladies strolled out in a waft of expensive perfume. They were too young to recognize her, so Laura saw no need to make haste as they gathered into a little flock of gossipy hens.

"Did you *see* the frightful hue of her lace?" said the plump one with brown sausage curls and rosy cheeks.

"Quite," replied a bucktoothed girl in pink muslin.

"I vow her laundress must have soaked it in bile to create such a putrid yellow."

The third girl screwed up her narrow, horsey face beneath a hat with too many feathers. "Her father earned his fortune in coal, so what else can one expect but deplorable taste?"

Laura pitied the unknown subject of their tittle-tattle. How well she remembered the spitefulness of debutantes who were competing to make the best marriages. It was an aspect of society that she didn't miss.

As the three lapsed into giggling, Miss Sausage Curls let loose a squeal. "Oh, my heart! You'll never guess who just walked out of the boot maker."

The toothy blonde heaved a romantic sigh. "Lord Copley! I daresay I may swoon. He seldom attends parties—Mama says it's that unfortunate scar on his cheek."

"Well, *I* think it makes him look dashing," Miss Horse Face said, then added in a hiss, "He's coming this way! Form a line, ladies. Such an eligible gentleman mustn't be allowed to pass us by."

They linked arms and preened at someone behind Laura.

Laura stood paralyzed. All rational thought fled her mind. Lord Copley . . . Alex. *No. No, no, no!*

She didn't dare turn around. Nor could she walk forward. The three girls in their voluminous skirts filled the entire footpath, even blocking the entrance to the fan shop.

Weighing her limited choices, Laura huddled inside her cloak. How close was he? Could she dart across the street in time?

A glance in that direction compounded her bad luck. A large coach was parked at the curbstone. How had she not noticed it before?

Like something out of a fairy tale, the cream-colored vehicle had gilded wheels and a team of matching horses. No coachman sat on the high perch—which meant that the owner of the conveyance must be in one of the shops. A groom held the horses. His back was turned as he chatted up a pretty maidservant.

Laura needed a quick place to hide. With a compulsion born of panic, she made haste to the coach, opened the door, and stepped inside.

Chapter 3

She drew the door shut at once, enclosing herself in a shadowy interior that smelled faintly of lilacs. Laura had a quick impression of plush dark cushions and gold appointments before her gaze riveted to the window. By good fortune, the brocaded green curtains were drawn, which afforded her ample concealment.

Crouching on the floor, she peered through the narrow parting of the curtains. Not a moment later, a tall gentleman in a formfitting coat of cobalt blue strode into view. He tipped his hat while the three youthful gorgons practically fell over themselves curtsying to him.

Alex.

Laura's breath knotted her lungs. The sight of him after all these years struck her like a blow to her midsection. The cocoa-brown hair, the broad muscled build, the arrogant stance of those long legs—she absorbed it all in one searing glance. His presence set her ablaze with an intensity of emotion that could only be pure vitriol.

How she despised the scoundrel!

He aimed that familiar crooked smile at the trio and engaged them in conversation. *Eligible*, one of the girls had said of him. So apparently he hadn't married Lady Evelyn, who'd once been Laura's chief rival for his affections. A pity, for he deserved the witch.

Laura could imagine the smooth banter he directed now at his adoring audience. Clearly he hadn't changed one iota. Rogues like him never did.

She had learned that truth the hard way. Long ago, she had been as young and foolish as those girls. She hadn't realized the fickleness behind his charm until the final, terrible meeting between them.

She had been heading downstairs for breakfast when the sound of male voices drew her to Papa's study. That deep, distinctive tone belonged to Alex, and she thrilled to the unexpected prospect of seeing him so early in the day. Was it possible he'd come to ask Papa for her hand in marriage? Oh, she hoped so! She could scarcely breathe for the tangle of love and longing in her heart . . .

Then Laura froze in the doorway, unable to believe her eyes. Alex was twisting her father around to face a wall of bookshelves. Papa didn't resist; his craggy features bore a look of dazed shock. With a length of cord, Alex proceeded to tie her father's hands behind his back.

Horrified, Laura rushed toward the two men. "What are you doing? Stop that at once!"

She thrust Alex away, seized the cord, and tugged at the knot. He caught hold of her wrists. "Forgive me, Laura. I'd hoped you wouldn't have to witness this."

"Witness what? Why are you treating Papa like . . . like a criminal?"

"*I was seeking notepaper and pen to leave a message for you a few moments ago when I spied those earrings in his drawer.*" He nodded toward a pair of large, bluish diamonds sparkling atop the desk. "*They're so distinctive, I recognized them at once. They were stolen from the Duchess of Knowles, along with the Blue Moon diamond necklace.*"

Laura stared in disbelief at the precious stones, unable to fathom how they'd come to be here. The robbery had been the talk of the ton for the past fortnight. "*You must be mistaken. My father is not a thief.*" *She grasped her father's coat sleeve and implored,* "*Tell him, Papa! Tell him that you didn't steal those earrings.*"

His gray eyes clouded with bewilderment, he shook his head. "*I've already done so, my dear. But he won't believe me.*"

"*Someone else left the jewels here. To make you look guilty of the crime.*" *She spun toward Alex.* "*You must listen to him, help us find out who did this. Please, the least you can do is to give him a chance.*"

Those dark eyes held hers for a moment as if he were wrestling with an inner dilemma. He glanced away, and then looked back at her. "*I'm sorry, but he'll have to be taken to Bow Street for questioning. The magistrate will decide how to proceed.*"

She could scarcely believe Alex was the same man who'd amused her with his charming banter, who had kissed her so tenderly and made her ache with desire. "*And what will happen to Papa then? He'll be found guilty on your testimony. He'll be sentenced to die.*"

With the bleak chill of a stranger, Alex re-
garded her. "That remains to be seen. In time, I
hope you'll realize that I've no other choice.
Please try to understand, I'm obliged to do my
duty."

As he turned away to secure her father's
bindings, she realized with a cold knell of shock
that Alex cared nothing for her father—or for
her. He wouldn't shed a tear even if Papa were
to swing from a hangman's noose. A frantic fear
choked her throat. She couldn't let this happen,
she mustn't. In wild desperation, she snatched
up a penknife . . .

Laura took a deep breath to clear her mind of the
vivid memory. Even after the passage of a decade, she
still felt a sense of sick betrayal at Alex's unwillingness
to trust in Papa's exemplary character. The earl had not
been interested in finding any other explanation for the
presence of the jewels. He had treated her father as a
common thief who was subject to his lordly judgment.

She glared through the crack in the curtains. If
only it weren't a vastly stupid thing to do, she'd relish
flinging open the coach door, witnessing his startled
expression, and giving him a severe tongue-lashing in
front of everyone on the street. Many a time she'd
imagined that confrontation, planning in her mind
precisely how she would cut him to shreds with sharp
words in retaliation for his treachery.

But not now when he could thwart her plans. The
Blue Moon diamond was still missing. If he learned
she was back in London, he'd likely haul her off to the
police station and accuse her of being her father's accomplice.

Gripping the edge of the window, Laura willed

him to turn toward her. She felt a morbid curiosity to view the scar on his cheek. Contrary to the report in the newspaper, *she* had been the one to attack the earl with a penknife, not her father. Alex must have lied about that because he'd been too humiliated to admit that a mere woman had bested him . . .

"You might be more comfortable on the seat, my dear."

The disembodied voice came out of nowhere. Laura yelped, spinning in a crouch and half losing her balance. Bracing a hand on the floor, she glanced wildly around the gloomy interior.

As if by magic, a person appeared to be sitting in the shadows of one corner. Her eyes adjusting to the dimness, she discerned a slender woman garbed in a rich dark gown that blended with the leather upholstery. A veiled hat adorned with a diamond aigrette hid her features from view.

There was something vaguely familiar about that regal tone. Who was she? Laura didn't intend to stay long enough to find out.

"I-I'm terribly sorry . . ." Recalling her pretense of being a servant, she adopted a working-class accent. "Beggin' yer pardon, m'lady. Didn't see ye there."

"Apparently not."

The woman's cultured voice held a note of dry amusement that made Laura blush. What must she think of Laura's peculiar behavior?

"I mean ye no harm. I'll be on me way now." She scrambled to the opposite door, intending to exit on the street side in order to avoid encountering Alex. But when she tried the handle, it was locked. "Do ye have a key?"

The lady reached a dainty, kid-gloved hand to the door. Instead of unlocking it, she opened the curtains with a flick of her wrist, allowing a flood of dull daylight to penetrate the interior of the coach.

Laura immediately averted her face.

"I presume," the lady said sternly, "you've a good reason for not wishing to depart by the way in which you entered."

Laura considered how to reply. She didn't know which would be worse, to be recognized as a fugitive who was wanted in connection with a jewel heist or to be thought a common pickpocket who'd taken refuge here after filching someone's coin purse.

"'Twas me husband," she fibbed. "We quarreled an' he was chasin' me. Drunk on gin, he is. Makes him fly into a rage."

"I see. Then it is quite imperative that I spirit you away from here as quickly as possible."

Laura risked a glance at that veiled face. "Nay! I daren't involve ye, m'lady. He . . . he might do ye a harm."

"Nonsense. I've two stout footmen and a coachman for protection." At that moment, the vehicle rocked slightly. "Ah, there they are now, back from fetching my parcels." Leaning down, the woman took Laura's gloved hand and patted the back of it in a motherly fashion. "So you see, my dear, you've no cause for alarm. You are quite safe with me."

Uneasy, Laura withdrew her fingers. "'Tis very kind o' ye, m'lady. But—"

"I will hear no more objections. Pray take a seat now. Right beside me, if you will."

The firmness of that voice brooked no disobedience. Laura found herself rising from the floor and gingerly settling onto the squabs. How luxuriously soft the cushions felt, how pleasant it was to rest after walking for hours.

But she mustn't be lulled into relaxing.

Was Alex still outside, chatting up the girls? To her frustration, she couldn't see from this angle, for the curtains on that side were still partly closed. In a moment she would have to step out and take her chances. The trouble was, he had always been a very observant man. She would have to hope that the hood sufficiently hid her features . . .

The coach jerked slightly and then settled into a gentle rhythmic swaying. The other window revealed that the vehicle had started down the street. Her stomach clenched in alarm. Where were they heading? Had she merely traded one perilous situation for another?

"M'lady, please, ye must let me out at the next corner."

"Nonsense, you're clearly distraught. And I daresay it is time to end this silly pretense."

"Pretense?"

The veiled lady caught firm hold of Laura's chin and tilted it to the window, scrutinizing her in the daylight. "Ah. I knew you were no common servant. And it appears my first impression was correct. You are indeed the notorious Miss Falkner."

Laura's heart pounded. She had a wild notion of making a lunge for the unlocked door and jumping out onto the cobblestone street, never mind that the coach had picked up speed.

"Ye're mistaken."

"Am I? It is a particular trait of mine that I never forget a face. Perhaps you will remember me as well."

In one smooth motion, the lady swept the black netting up over her hat, revealing a lovely countenance with lushly feminine lips, high cheekbones, and shrewd violet eyes. Though not a young woman, she had dark hair untouched by gray and an ageless beauty that struck a faint chord of memory in Laura. It took a moment to dredge up the name from the mists of the past.

Lady Milford. One of society's premier hostesses.

Pinned by that astute gaze, Laura refused to quail. She would simply have to brazen her way out of trouble. And she *was* in trouble, for there could be no doubt this woman knew all about the still-missing diamond necklace. The famous crime had rocked society and dominated the newspapers for weeks even before Papa had been accused by Alex.

The rudiments of a plan took shape in her mind. Perhaps . . . just perhaps there might be a way to use this twist of fate to her advantage.

"I confess you're correct, Lady Milford," she said, throwing back her hood and abandoning the charade. "I remember being introduced to you briefly some years ago."

"It was in a receiving line during your debut ball. You were an exceedingly lovely girl, the nonpareil of the season."

Laura was all too conscious of the contrast between that social butterfly and her present appearance. She mustn't feel embarrassed for a circumstance not of her own doing. "My situation has been vastly altered since then, as I'm sure you know. I am no longer welcome in the best homes." She bowed her head in not-quite-feigned humility. "Pray forgive me for pretending to be someone else, my lady. I have no husband, drunk or otherwise. It's just that . . . I feared I'd been recognized on the street, and I didn't know where else to conceal myself."

Laura saw no need to confess that it was Lord Copley she had been avoiding. That near-encounter was still too raw in her mind. To see him again after all these years had rattled her equilibrium.

Lady Milford regarded her with cool hauteur. "Subterfuge seems to come naturally to you, Miss Falkner. After all, you have been in hiding for many years."

Laura refused to flinch. "Yes. Until a short time ago, I was living in Portugal."

"And your father? Has he, too, returned to London?"

Though she had been expecting the query, Laura felt a catch in her throat nonetheless. "I'm afraid . . . he died quite recently."

How difficult it was to voice those words. She had hoped to play on her ladyship's sympathies and now found it required no effort at all to make her eyes swim with tears. Blinking, she groped unsuccessfully in her pocket for a handkerchief. "I know what you're thinking, my lady. That he only received his just due, and that he didn't deserve to live. But you're *wrong*. Papa didn't steal the Blue Moon diamond. I swear he didn't. He was utterly innocent of the crime."

Lady Milford pressed a dainty folded square of linen into Laura's hand. "My dear, there were jewels belonging to the Duchess of Knowles in his desk."

"I don't know how they came to be there—nor did he." Laura dabbed at her cheeks. "If he'd possessed the diamond necklace, we might have sold it and lived handsomely off the proceeds. But all these years, we have been living as *paupers*."

Lady Milford frowned slightly. "I'm sorry for your distress. It is clear there is more to the situation than I was aware." The coach gave a slight jolt, and then came to a stop. "We've arrived home. You will tell me the whole story over tea."

Chapter 4

Laura considered it an encouraging sign that Lady Milford allowed her a room in which to freshen up. At least she was trusted enough not to pinch the silver or pocket a trinket from one of the many beautiful items on display. She only prayed that her own instincts were correct, that Lady Milford had not tricked her by sending a messenger on the sly to Bow Street Station. The woman simply *must* be persuaded to give Laura the assistance she needed.

As a white-wigged footman led her back down the central stairway, she absorbed the splendor of the soaring, two-story entrance hall. It seemed like forever since she'd been inside such a fine house. She had taken such luxury for granted in her youth, for it was all she'd ever known. Her father had had a distinguished lineage that linked him to some of the best families in England. Consequently, she and Papa had been welcome in the highest circles of society.

As an only child, her mother having died in childbirth, Laura had been the joy of her father's life. He'd taken great pleasure in her debut, purchasing an extensive wardrobe for her and making certain she was introduced to the most eligible young gentlemen. Those days seemed like a dream to her now, a fantastical fairy-tale world of balls and shopping and flirtations. How carefree she'd been, how silly and self-absorbed. At the time, Laura had never imagined how swiftly it could all come crashing down on her.

In one fell swoop she and her father had lost everything. They'd had to flee the country when he'd been falsely accused of thievery.

Not that she regretted the years living in the cozy cottage in the mountains. She had come to prefer having only one servant, a village girl to assist with the more difficult chores like hauling water and washing clothes. In hard work Laura had found contentment, her days filled with tidying the small rooms, weeding in the garden, or cooking the meals, and her evenings spent reading by the fire with Papa.

A knot filled her throat. That simple life, too, had been swept away by a caprice of fate. She had returned to England to save her father's life, only to learn of his untimely death. Now she had a new purpose: she must somehow restore his honor in the eyes of the ton.

There was only one way to do so. She must find the real thief who'd stolen the Blue Moon diamond.

The footman left her in an airy sitting room that was decorated in subtle shades of rose and yellow. A fire burned on the grate beneath a mantel of carved white marble. Gilded chairs and chaises were grouped for intimate conversations.

Having arrived first, Laura wandered to the tall windows that overlooked a pleasant display of greenery interspersed with beds of blooming roses. A stooped-shouldered gardener clipped the boxwoods into symmetrical shapes. It was all so civilized, so perfect, so

English that despite the long years of absence, she felt right at home again, as if she'd never left.

At a sound from the doorway, she pivoted to see a mob-capped maid wheeling in a tea cart. Lady Milford entered a moment later. "By the hearth, please," she instructed the girl, who scurried to obey.

Laura was struck anew by the woman's beauty. Lady Milford glided forward, the slenderness of her waist enhanced by a violet muslin gown that matched her eyes. It was difficult to guess her age, for she bore no resemblance to the fusty old matrons of society. Laura recalled hearing whispers of a long-ago scandal attached to Lady Milford's name, something about her having once been mistress to a son of King George III. Her stately manner certainly brought to mind royalty.

"Do join me, Miss Falkner," her ladyship commanded as she picked up the silver urn to pour the tea.

Laura gratefully accepted a steaming cup, and then sat down to stir a lump of sugar until it melted. She tried not to be greedy on being offered a plate of dainty sandwiches. But in her famished state, she felt too faint to care for appearances. Nothing had ever tasted more delicious than those thin slices of fresh-baked bread spread with soft white cheese and spiced by watercress.

Only after eating several and then reaching for another did she notice Lady Milford sipping a cup of tea without partaking of the food. "Pardon me," Laura said, drawing back her hand. "I didn't mean to have more than my share."

Lady Milford smiled slightly. "My dear girl, I insist that you eat your fill. No guest will starve in my house. Besides, you will need fortification to relate this story of yours."

Was it her imagination, or did her ladyship place a slight emphasis on the word *story*?

Laura couldn't blame Lady Milford for harboring doubts about Laura's honesty. The evidence against her father was quite insurmountable. Yet if Lady Milford could not be convinced of his innocence, then Laura's hopes would be dashed.

Her teacup rattled as she placed it in its saucer. "I can only reiterate what I told you already, my lady. My father swore to me that he knew nothing of the robbery—and that was proven by our lack of funds. I assure you, he was an honest man. In all our years together, I never knew him to steal so much as a fig from a neighbor's tree."

"How did the jewels come to be in his possession, then?"

Laura lifted her shoulders in a helpless gesture. "I . . . don't know. Perhaps the police were asking questions and the robber needed to pin the blame on someone else. Perhaps someone held a grudge against my father and wanted to ruin him. Since it happened so long ago, we shall likely never know."

Laura kept her suspicions about the perpetrator to herself. Until she could sleuth for more information and confirm that her father had indeed been murdered, she preferred not to involve her ladyship. Besides, she didn't trust Lady Milford not to warn the persons in question. These aristocrats would close ranks and protect their own.

"Why have you not gone to the police?" Lady Milford asked.

Laura thought it best not to complicate matters by mentioning Constable Pangborn and the chase through the slums. "I was afraid . . . I might be arrested."

"Why? *You* were never accused of thievery."

"Surely you know that I'm tarred by the same brush as my father. And the Blue Moon diamond is still missing, my lady. It's only logical that I would fall under suspicion since they no longer have my father to accuse." Laura strove for a forlorn expression, not a difficult task given the day she'd had. "Besides, they will consider me an accomplice for the way I lashed out at Lord Copley."

Lady Milford arched an eyebrow. "According to the newspapers, your father struck Lord Copley. Are you saying it was actually you?"

Laura froze, wishing she could erase the inadvertent confession. But it was too late for a retraction. And it would hardly help her cause to be viewed as a wild termagant who'd attacked a peer of the realm with a penknife.

Clasping her hands like a supplicant, she leaned forward to look Lady Milford in the eye. "Please understand it was an act of desperation, my lady. His lordship was attempting to apprehend my father and take him to Bow Street. I couldn't allow Papa to be thrown into prison. He would most certainly have been sentenced to hanging—for a crime he didn't commit."

A pregnant pause stretched out as Lady Milford pursed her lips. "I seem to recall that Lord Copley had been paying particular attention to you. There was talk of a marriage between the two of you."

Laura stiffened. "Youthful folly, nothing more."

She burned to denounce Alex as a bully who'd cared nothing for her father's good character or her own pleas for mercy. But those harsh words, however well deserved, would ruin the docile image that she needed to foster.

In a subdued tone, she added, "My old life is long

gone, my lady. Though it was lost through grave injustice, please be assured that I harbor no ill will toward anyone. The past cannot be changed, I can only accept matters as they are and look to the future. And now that my father has been laid to rest, I must make my own way in the world."

"You've no other family?"

"No, my lady. I have been hoping that I might find a kind, decent person in society to hire me, perhaps as a companion. Unfortunately, given my damaged reputation and having no previous employers to write a reference for me, I'm in rather a pickle."

Laura paused. Was she being too obvious? She could read nothing in the enigmatic expression on those perfect features.

As desperately as she needed to secure a position that would allow her some means to move about society, Laura didn't want to overplay her hand. A letter of recommendation from Lady Milford certainly would open closed doors. But it wouldn't be written if her ladyship became irked by Laura's presumptuousness.

Lady Milford set aside her teacup and rose to her feet. "You will wait here for a moment."

Offering no explanation for her actions, she glided out of the sitting room. Laura was left with only the hissing of the fire for company. Her ladyship couldn't have gone for pen and paper; Laura could see those supplies resting on a dainty desk against the wall. She waited on pins and needles, wondering if she would be tossed out on her ear. Perhaps Lady Milford intended to fetch a footman to escort Laura to the door.

The more she thought about it, the more plausible that scenario sounded. She imagined the encounter from Lady Milford's perspective—to have an uncouth fugitive burst into her coach, to bring her home only to see her eat all the tea sandwiches, to be made to listen politely to her sob story, including a confession that she'd maimed a peer of the realm. To top it all, the shameless hussy had all but insisted that her ladyship compose a counterfeit reference.

Yes, Lady Milford might well be intending to evict her—or even to summon the police.

Laura jumped to her feet. She ought to depart right now and spare herself further trouble. Yet a sense of desperation made her hesitate. Wasn't she allowing pride to overrule common sense? If she walked out now, she might never have the chance to discover who had stolen the Blue Moon diamond. She might never clear her father's good name. For Papa's sake, she must humble herself and beseech her ladyship . . .

Her musings came to an abrupt end with the reappearance of her hostess. Lady Milford was alone, much to Laura's relief, and she was carrying something in her hands, something that glinted a deep rich red in the late-afternoon light. Reaching Laura, she bent gracefully to set it on the floor in front of her.

Laura looked down to see that there were actually *two* things: a pair of low-heeled dancing slippers. Covered in exquisite crystal beadwork, the shoes were fashioned of the finest garnet satin. They were so gorgeous she could scarcely take her eyes off them.

She blinked in wary confusion. "My lady?"

Those violet eyes held a hint of mystery. "It would please me greatly if you would try these on."

"But . . . why?"

"It's an old pair that I've owned for quite a long time. Rather than allow them to gather dust in my dressing room, I thought you might be able to use them—provided, of course, that they fit you properly."

Laura felt an unpleasant jolt. Was *this* all the help she could expect from Lady Milford? A pair of castoffs that Laura would never even have occasion to wear?

Flushed with mortification, she wanted to kick them away. Everything in her rebelled against being viewed as a beggar in need of charity. To add insult to injury, she was being offered something that was utterly impractical to a woman in her circumstances.

She wanted a letter—not *shoes*.

Lady Milford stood watching, the faint smile on her lips indicating her pleasure in the gift. Instantly Laura regretted her own ingratitude. The woman was only trying to be kind. Having never experienced a life of penury, Lady Milford didn't even realize the absurdity of her bequest.

Oh, well, perhaps the slippers wouldn't fit.

Good manners made Laura resume her seat and tug off her practical brown leather shoes. She was conscious of their scuffed and worn appearance as they thumped to the carpet. Before Lady Milford could notice the much-mended state of her plain white stockings, Laura quickly wriggled her toes into the fancy slippers.

To her surprise, they enclosed her feet as if fashioned expressly for her. She turned one foot to and fro, admiring the elegance of the garnet satin and the sparkle of the beads. A shower of pleasure rinsed away all her troubles. She had forgotten how wonderful it felt to wear pretty things. Perhaps it had been necessary for her to lose everything in order to truly appreciate such a luxury.

Rising from the chair, Laura took a turn around the sitting room, her steps light. She no longer noticed any weariness from her long trek through the city. Rather, she felt awash in a soul-deep desire to dance all night, wrapped in the arms of—no, not Alex—a handsome, *trustworthy* gentleman who would court her with polite respect.

"They're perfect, my lady," she said. "How remarkable that we should wear precisely the same size."

"You should rather regard it as a blessing," Lady Milford said, a certain enigmatic satisfaction to her expression. "You will do me a great favor by taking the shoes."

"That's very kind of you." Laura lifted her skirts and regarded the shoes with wistful regret. "Though perhaps there's someone else who's more deserving of them than I am. I've really no place to wear something so lovely."

"Quite the contrary. You'll need the proper attire for balls and other society events." Surveying Laura up and down, Lady Milford tapped her chin with a dainty fingertip. "I believe a wardrobe allowance can be arranged. One cannot have a ragtag appearance when serving as companion to a dowager."

Laura's eyes widened. "Companion? To whom?"

"To a dear acquaintance of mine. She's become a trifle forgetful in her old age, and her nephew recently mentioned the need to hire a nurse to assist her." Lady Milford's face again took on an inscrutable quality. "I rather think *you* will be perfect for the post."

Chapter 5

"I don't wish to be a bother," Lady Josephine apologized as she inched her way down the grand staircase with the help of a cane. A striped yellow gown hugging her round form and a silk turban wrapping her gray hair, she brought to mind a benevolent gnome. "You needn't feel obliged to help me, my dear. Such a lovely girl as you surely has more important things to do."

Laura gently cupped the woman's arm to steady her. "There's nothing more important to me than your comfort, my lady. That's why I'm here."

Lady Josephine flashed a sunny smile. "You *are* a peach, Norah. I've very much enjoyed your stay with me."

"Laura, my lady."

"Upon my soul, how silly of me to forget your name! It's certainly no way to treat a houseguest."

Laura bit her tongue to keep from explaining again that she wasn't a visitor, she was a paid member of the staff. The information would go in one ear and out the other, just as Laura's name also was forgotten more often than not.

Nevertheless, she had grown quite fond of the elderly woman in the four days since her arrival. Lady Josephine had been starved for company, if her constant chatter was any indication. Widowed and childless, she had no immediate family except for a nephew and a niece who apparently didn't bother to visit very often.

Nearing the bottom of the stairs, Laura tilted her chin down to peer over the cheap spectacles perched on her nose. She had purchased the eyeglasses in a secondhand shop as a means of disguise. The only trouble was, they blurred her vision and required her to spend most of the time looking over the rims.

In this cluttered house, it was important to see where she was going. The entrance hall held an impressive array of bric-a-brac: oversized vases on side tables, alabaster statuary in niches, even a full suit of armor that most fashionable Londoners would have consigned to their country seat. Numerous age-darkened portraits hung on the walls, and the air smelled rather musty—as if the place had not been aired in half a century. Laura itched to put things in better order. But when she'd tried to move several extra footstools out of Lady Josephine's bedchamber, Mrs. Samson, the hatchet-faced housekeeper, had forbidden Laura to alter anything, insisting that the mistress preferred everything exactly as it was.

Laura had her doubts about that. Sweet-tempered Lady Josephine likely would never even notice if some of the excess was put into storage. Then Laura had to remind herself that organizing the household wasn't really her concern. It wouldn't do to become attached to her employer, either, since her stay here was temporary.

Befuddlement on her heavily wrinkled face, Lady

Josephine stopped at the base of the stairs. "Now, where did I say I was going? It has quite escaped my mind."

"Outside," Laura said. "Since it's such a pleasant day, you expressed a desire to sit in the garden."

"Ah yes, the garden." Lady Josephine began hobbling down the corridor that led to the rear of the house. "I do like the sunshine, always have. Too many girls these days look as pale as ghosts." She flashed a smile at Laura who walked alongside her. "Not you, though. You've a healthy glow to your cheeks. Are you married, dear?"

"No, my lady."

"Ah, more's the pity. A sweet girl like you should have a husband and lots of children." Lady Josephine sighed wistfully. "Would that I might have borne a child for my darling Charles. 'Tis my only regret in life, though he always said he didn't mind. Then he would declare that so long as we were together, he had everything he'd ever wanted."

Laura's heart melted. "He must have been a wonderful man."

"Indeed, he was the kindest, most considerate of husbands. Oh, but you would never have guessed so when first we met. Such a dashing fellow he was back then, and a shameless flirt, the darling of all the ladies. I was the only one who would not put up with his nonsense, so of course he could not allow *that*. Have I ever told you the lengths he went to win my affections?"

Although she'd heard the story several times, Laura pretended ignorance. "Pray tell me."

"One day he saw me in Hyde Park, fretting over a kitten that was stranded in the high branches of an oak. The poor thing was mewling most pitifully. Well,

Charles climbed up that tree and rescued the little mite, tucking it inside his coat to keep it safe. But on the way down, the kitten clawed him and escaped down the tree trunk. Charles was so startled, he fell straight into a patch of shrubbery. Oh! I had a time scolding him. He might have broken his neck, I said."

Laura held open the back door. From the lockbox of memory came the image of Alex standing upright on the back of a horse, riding around the stable yard, showing off with his arms outstretched like a carnival performer. A barking dog had startled the horse, Alex had tumbled off, and upon discerning he was unhurt, Laura had blistered him with rebukes. "One can scarcely blame you for being distressed, my lady."

Her gnarled fingers wrapped around the cane, Lady Josephine shuffled down the three broad steps into the garden. "Oh, but I was not distressed for long! In the midst of my tirade, Charles pulled me down onto him, tickling me until I couldn't help but laugh merrily. The scoundrel kissed me, too, so that I forgot aught else but him." She was smiling, lost in the mists of time. "'Twas always like that with dear Charles. If ever we quarreled, I could never stay angry at him."

As Laura assisted the elderly woman in navigating the uneven flagstones of the path, she didn't want to reflect that Alex had dispelled her anger with a kiss, too . . . their first of many kisses. Instead, she marveled at the clarity of Lady Josephine's recollections of the distant past. It seemed that only present-day events eluded her memory.

With a grateful sigh, the dowager settled her bulk onto a straight-backed wooden bench beneath a rose arbor. "You're a dear to spend your morning with me," she said. "There must be some way for me to repay your kindness."

Laura propped the cane against the arbor, brushed a few pink petals off the seat, and sat down beside her. "It's my pleasure to be here, truly it is."

Lady Josephine went on as if she hadn't spoken. "Why, I've the very idea! I shall play matchmaker for you. I am not so ancient as to be unaware of the many eligible young gentlemen in society. My nephew perhaps." That vague look entered her faded blue eyes. "At least I don't *believe* he is married . . ."

The prospect alarmed Laura. The last state of affairs she needed was to have attention drawn to herself. "My lady, you mustn't even *think* to do such a thing. It would be futile, anyway, for I am entirely without fortune to recommend me."

"Bah, a man of wealth has no need of a marriage portion. He can be caught by a pretty face and a pleasing disposition, as Charles was with me."

"Perhaps so, but I've really no need for a husband."

"No need? Good gracious, child, the union between a man and his wife is the happiest state imaginable." Teasingly, Lady Josephine shook a pudgy finger at Laura. "Mind you ignore those ladies who whisper that what happens in the marriage bed is distasteful. Quite the contrary, it is glorious! Why, I shall never forget my wedding night—"

"I'm sure it was lovely," Laura said hastily, before the dowager could spill all the intimate details. "Didn't you mention that you'd traveled to Italy for your honeymoon? Did you go to Venice?"

"Oh, yes, indeed! What an enchanting city with all the canals, the churches, the palazzos. And my word, we tramped over so many quaint little bridges that Charles and I both wore out several pairs of shoes."

Having been successfully distracted, Lady Josephine continued to chatter for a while about the long-ago trip. Then, as was her custom in late morning, her eyelids drooped and her chin fell to her ample bosom. Soon she was fast asleep and snoring softly.

Plucking a wilted rose from the trellis, Laura idly brushed her fingers over the velvety pink petals. She acknowledged a wistful ache inside herself. Where would she herself be now if the jewel theft hadn't altered her life forever? Would she have wed Alex? Their whirlwind romance *had* seemed headed for the altar . . .

Her lips compressed, she tossed the dead rose into the bushes. He had not been the man she'd believed him to be. Thank goodness she'd learned of his cruel nature before being bound to him by holy vows. She had purged him from her mind long ago, and the memories had crept back only because she'd had the ill luck to spy him on Regent Street.

Though perhaps, in a peculiar way, he'd done her a favor this time. By hiding in the coach, she'd met Lady Milford and secured this position. The series of providential events gratified Laura, for it seemed as if the fates were finally smiling upon her mission. Very soon, she would put into motion her plan to find out who had committed the robbery. Only then could she solve the mystery of her father's death.

Unable to sit still any longer, she rose from the bench and took a stroll around the garden. Though somewhat neglected, it was a pleasant little retreat with ivy growing on the stone walls and pathways that meandered in between beds of overgrown herbs and flowering plants. In one corner, a pear tree had dropped a shower of white blossoms over a tangle of shrubbery. A wooden gate in the back led to the stables, where an old groom tended a pair of carriage horses kept for Lady Josephine's barouchet.

Here and there, pansies lifted their yellow and purple faces to the sunshine. Laura did the same, enjoying the warmth of the spring day. How marvelous it felt to be out in the fresh air. Of late, she'd been cooped up inside too much, kept busy caring for Lady Josephine and stitching a new wardrobe for herself.

Lady Milford had been kind enough to arrange for a modest clothing allowance to be advanced from Laura's wages, which had enabled her to visit the drapers. There, she had purchased materials to sew three daytime dresses and also a bolt of dark brown muslin sober enough for mourning yet suitable for an evening gown.

A few days ago, she had discovered a pile of unanswered invitations stuffed into a drawer of Lady Josephine's writing desk. Many of them had been outdated, but others were new, and Laura had drafted several acceptance notes for her ladyship's signature.

Tomorrow evening she would finally have the chance to accompany Lady Josephine to a ball. Knowing the aristocracy overlooked servants as if they were invisible, Laura hoped to have the freedom to listen in on conversations. Her first order of business would be to determine the whereabouts of several people who might have had a role in the disappearance of the Blue Moon diamond.

Laura had thought long and hard about two in particular. The need to uncover the truth burned in her. Since nothing could be done at the moment, however, she must keep herself occupied or go mad from impatience.

A clump of rhododendron bushes screened a small shed that was tucked against the wall. The door creaked open under a tug of her hand. Inside the dim interior, she found a rusty trowel and a pair of gardening gloves on a cobwebbed shelf. There was also a floppy straw hat, which she donned over her lace spinster's cap, tying the ribbons under her chin.

Armed for gardening, she knelt down to tidy the flower beds. The spectacles kept slipping down her nose, so she stuck them into the pocket of her apron for the time being. As always, working with the soil had a calming influence on her. She pulled weeds and scraped away layers of dead leaves, gradually making her way down the length of the back fence. Every now and then, she glanced up to make certain that Lady Josephine still snoozed comfortably on the bench.

A thick mass of lily-of-the-valley covered one area, and she parted the glossy dark green leaves to find multiple stalks of tiny white bells. She would have to bring a sketch pad out here and see if that delicate beauty could be captured by paper and pen. Perhaps somewhere in the cluttered house, there might even be a set of watercolor paints.

Humming as she worked, Laura felt happier than she had in weeks. The rich fragrance of the earth pleased her senses. A bee buzzed to a lone red tulip in a patch of straggly daffodils. The clip-clopping of a horse's hooves came from the mews on the other side of the fence, along with the voices of servants from the stables. She paid only fleeting heed to the intrusions on her little slice of heaven.

Beneath the pear tree, much to her delight, Laura discovered a hidden clump of late-blooming violets. Weeding the small purple flowers reminded her of Violet Angleton, who had liked to wear posies of her namesake flower. Ten years ago, as debutantes in their first season, they'd become fast friends, sharing the same sense of the absurd for the odd characters in society. Violet had been the one person to whom Laura had confided all of her hopes and dreams.

Then Laura had had to flee England without saying good-bye. There had been no communication between them ever since.

Would they meet again in the coming weeks? Did Laura dare to reveal her true identity to Violet? She wanted to think she could trust an old friend, but what if Violet believed the accusations against Papa? Laura couldn't risk compromising her investigation . . .

The tread of quick, heavy footsteps reached the periphery of her awareness. In the next moment the back gate swung open and a man entered the garden.

Kneeling in the shade of the pear tree, Laura turned her head to see past the wide brim of her hat. If he was a deliveryman, he ought to have knocked rather than barge into her ladyship's private sanctuary.

Then she realized her mistake. The newcomer was a gentleman, tall and broad-shouldered, clad in a claret-wine coat over tan breeches and knee-high black boots. A slight breeze ruffled his thick, cocoa-brown hair. One glimpse of his profile had her reeling in disbelief.

No. *No!* Alex couldn't be here. It was impossible.

She blinked hard. Too much sun must have addled her senses. Surely this fellow merely resembled him . . .

He didn't glance back to the corner where she crouched, half hidden behind the overgrown shrubbery. Instead, he headed down the flagstone path to the arbor where Lady Josephine dozed peacefully.

Laura tensed, ready to leap up if he meant to do a harm to the elderly woman. But he merely sat down beside her, took her hand in his, and patted the back.

Lady Josephine awoke and blinked her eyes. For a moment she appeared disoriented. Then a smile beamed across her lined features. "Alexander! Is it really you?"

He kissed her cheek. "Good morning, Aunt Josie. Forgive me for not visiting the past few days. I had to ride to Hampshire to settle a matter with my estate agent."

"I do hope it wasn't anything serious."

"Only a tedious problem with the drainage system. When the flood last year altered the course of the river, I ought to have had the dairy barns moved. But the project is under way now, and better late than never, I suppose."

"Oh!" Lady Josephine said. "Well, my dear boy, I'm glad you're back, safe and sound. By the by, did you see Mrs. Broomfield, the cook? I have been wondering if her sons are married yet."

Stunned, Laura only half listened to their conversation as they went on to chat about people from the estate whose names she didn't recognize. *Aunt Josie* . . . Alex must be the nephew that Lady Josephine had mentioned.

Laura had only a vague recollection of him making reference to a favorite aunt. Of course, at the time she had been caught up in the whirl of her first season, the parties and the flirtations, the excitement of being pursued by so many gentlemen, including society's most eligible bachelor, the dashing young Earl of Copley. Their romance had been swift and intense over the course of a mere few weeks, and there had not been occasion to meet his elder sister or any other family members . . .

Oh, dear God in heaven. Alex was *here*—and he wasn't a figment of her imagination. How was it even possible that she'd have the horrid luck to encounter him twice in one week?

The answer caused a sickening lurch in her stomach. Her first sighting of him on Regent Street had been a ghastly coincidence, but such was not the case today. Lady Milford had *known* that he and Laura had once been an item. Which meant her ladyship must have placed Laura in this house on purpose, hoping that she would run into him.

Why? To rekindle a romance? That made no sense, since Lady Milford also knew that Laura was the one who'd scarred him. Perhaps she'd wanted to give Alex the opportunity to confront Laura, to question her about the theft.

Whatever the reason, it boded disaster.

Realizing she had a death grip on the trowel, Laura ever so quietly placed the implement on the ground. Then she eased off the gardening gloves, groped in her pocket for the spectacles, and slipped them back onto her nose.

Maybe by some miracle Alex wouldn't recognize her. He'd always been a flirt and a rogue, and after ten years and untold numbers of ladies parading in and out of his life, perhaps he'd forgotten all about Miss Laura Falkner.

The girl who had bloodied his face with a penknife.

Her teeth worried her lower lip. The odds were not in her favor. As the daughter of a supposed thief, she would be an unfit companion to his aunt. All of her grand plans would be ruined, for how else could she gain entry to the exalted ranks of the ton?

Worse, what if Alex hauled her off to Bow Street Station to face charges of being her father's accomplice?

She glowered at him over the rims of the spectacles. Maybe he would depart as swiftly as he'd arrived. Maybe she would be spared a confrontation. Maybe he would never even notice her here . . .

All of a sudden, Laura realized they were discussing *her*.

"Upon my return home," Alex told his aunt, "I found a rather odd note from Lady Milford, saying that she'd engaged a companion for you. While I realize Lady Milford is an old acquaintance of yours, I can't imagine why she would have taken such a step without first seeking my approval—or even providing me with this woman's name. Tell me, who *is* your companion?"

"Companion?" Lady Josephine frowned a moment; then her lips curved in a comprehending smile. "Oh, you must mean Laura, my houseguest. Such a sweet, lovely girl. You'll like her very much, I'm sure."

Laura cringed. Of all times for her ladyship to remember the correct name.

"Laura?" Alex repeated rather sharply, his head tilted as he frowned at his aunt. "Laura who? What is her surname?"

Lady Josephine slowly shook her head. "I . . . I cannot recall. Upon my soul, I don't know *how* I could have forgotten something so simple."

"Never mind," he said, briefly placing his hand on her shoulder. "I'll find out for myself. Now, why has she left you out here alone? Do you know where she is at the moment?"

"I seem to recall that she sat here talking to me for a time . . . but then I must have dozed off."

Laura didn't dare hide any longer. As much as she dreaded this interview, it was better to face the inevitable than to let herself be caught cowering in the bushes.

Rising to her feet, she straightened her skirts and cleared her throat. "I'm here, my lady," she said in a subdued tone that hopefully disguised her voice. "I was pulling weeds and thought it best not to interrupt your conversation."

Her chin lowered, Laura adopted the meek stance of a servant. She prayed that the wide brim of the hat along with the spectacles would suffice to camouflage her features.

Was Alex staring at her? She couldn't tell. The round glasses had transformed him into a blurred dark form, fuzzy at the edges, his features indistinct.

"So there you are!" Lady Josephine said with a cheery laugh. "Do come and join us, my dear girl. I should like you to meet my nephew."

Laura edged down the path toward the house. "Thank you, but I wouldn't dream of intruding—"

"Come here," Alex stated. "At once."

Chapter 6

His terse words conveyed the force of command. Laura had no choice but to obey the edict. Her heart thudding, she started toward the rose arbor, her steps slow from both reluctance and the distorting effect of the spectacles. She dared not look over the tops of them for fear he might remember her blue eyes—eyes he had once ardently professed to admire.

At her approach, Alex rose from the bench. *The earl*, she corrected herself. He was the Earl of Copley. She must cease thinking of him with any familiarity. He was a stranger to her now; in truth, she had never really known him at all.

Yet his arrogant presence made the very air come alive. It was as if he were larger than life, demanding her attention in utter disregard for her will. Her skin prickled from an intense awareness of his tall, well-muscled form, and the unwanted reaction irked her. This man had used his physical power to subdue Papa. If she hadn't stopped the earl by slashing open his cheek, he would have hauled her father off to prison to be sentenced to death.

"Laura, this is my nephew, the Earl of Copley," Lady Josephine said in a sprightly tone. "Alexander, my houseguest, Laura . . . Forgive me, what did you say was your full name, my dear?"

Laura sank into a deep curtsy. He didn't deserve obeisance, but at least it afforded her the chance to hide her face. "Laura Brown."

"Brown," he repeated in a faintly ironic tone. "A common name, to be sure."

"If you say so, my lord."

His fingers clamped around her upper arm, causing Laura to draw a sharp breath. For an instant she feared he had recognized her and intended retaliation for striking him. But he merely assisted her to her feet before withdrawing his hand.

"I've never heard of any Browns among the gentry," he said. "From where does your family hail?"

"Northumberland," she lied, hoping the distance would thwart any investigation he might be contemplating. "The Browns are landowners there, though inconsequential by comparison with an exalted family such as yours."

"Tell me, what are your qualifications for this position?"

Avoiding eye contact, she kept her head tilted down in a modest pose. "I'm well versed in all the requisite skills of a lady, from deportment to dancing, playing the pianoforte to managing a—"

"My aunt requires specialized care. Not someone who is distracted by frivolous pastimes."

Laura bristled at his interruption. What had happened to the charming man he'd once been? It only proved that his amiability had all been a facade. "If you'll permit me to finish, my lord. In addition to managing a *household*, I've ample experience in caring for an aging member of my own family."

It was only a small fib. He needn't know that her father had been in the peak of health before his fateful trip to England.

"Laura has been a perfect delight," his aunt said from her seat on the bench. "Truly, Alexander, you will see that once you become better acquainted with her."

"Thank you, Aunt Josie. However, I'd be remiss in my duties if I allowed just anyone to live in your house." On that rude remark, he addressed Laura again. "Who was your previous employer?"

"I've only the one reference from Lady Milford."

"To my knowledge, Lady Milford has never engaged a companion."

Laura knew she was on treacherous ground. His questions were too pointed, his tone too mocking. "She's a family friend. It was very kind of her to help me since I've spent a good deal of my life abroad."

"Abroad? Where?"

Laura decided to keep as close to the truth as possible. "Portugal. My father had business interests there."

"What manner of business?"

"Trade," she said, being deliberately vague. "He seldom spoke of such matters at home. He believed commerce to be a man's domain."

The earl took a step closer. "And where, pray tell, is your father now?"

His frigid tone sent prickles over her skin. Risking a peek over the spectacles, Laura took her first clear look at his face. The concentrated force of those dark eyes probed into her. Where once he had smiled warmly at her, now his lips were thinned and hostile. The grim set of his mouth confirmed her fears.

The Earl of Copley knew precisely who she was. Her masquerade had not fooled him one whit.

As if to dispel the slightest lingering doubt, he fingered the diagonal scar that bisected his left cheek. Laura gazed in morbid fascination at the results of her handiwork. The long, thin line had spoiled his once-boyish good looks. No longer was he the carefree charmer she had been foolish enough to love. Maturity had hardened his features, his taut expression making it clear that he was not a man to be crossed.

In a flicker of memory, she saw him staggering backward from the strike of the penknife, his hand to his face, red blood dripping from between his fingers.

Laura banished a faintly queasy feeling. She hadn't suffered any regret over maiming him back then, and she wouldn't do so now, either. The attack had gained her enough time to rush her father out of the study. She had slammed the door shut and turned the key in the lock to imprison Alex.

He must have been livid. No man liked being outwitted by a woman, least of all an arrogant lord like him.

Lady Josephine's raspy voice broke the spell. "Alexander, for shame. You mustn't quiz the poor girl with questions of a personal nature."

The old woman sat on the bench, gazing up at the two of them with a vaguely perplexed expression.

His harsh countenance softened somewhat as he turned to his aunt. "I doubt Miss Brown is so easily offended. Someone who's traveled all the way to Portugal must be made of sterner stuff than that."

Lady Josephine gave a vigorous nod. "She's a fine, upstanding girl. And exceedingly pretty, too, don't you agree?"

The earl shifted his cool gaze back to Laura. "It's

difficult to tell with that unsightly hat. One would think she's trying to hide something."

In a quick move, he untied the ribbon beneath her chin and snatched off the floppy straw bonnet. Laura lifted her hands to stop him. But he'd already sent the hat sailing over the garden wall and into the mews.

Furious, she readjusted the lace spinster's cap and checked her prim bun for any dislodged pins. "That was hardly necessary, my lord," she said, managing a stiff smile for Lady Josephine's benefit. "I would have removed it myself had I been allowed the chance."

"Then I'll permit *you* to dispense with the spectacles."

Her mutinous gaze bored into his. "But I need them."

"Do you really, dear?" Lady Josephine asked hesitantly. "I don't wish to gainsay you, but I *have* noticed that you look over the tops of them more often than not. And they conceal your pretty blue eyes."

Laura glanced down at the old woman's guileless face. "I'm not quite used to them yet, that's all."

Lord Copley cocked a dark eyebrow. "Stubbornness is not a commendable trait in a companion. I trust you *will* do as you're told."

Everything in her rebelled against obeying him. Yet she didn't wish to give him an easy excuse to dismiss her from his aunt's employ. Removing the glasses, she tucked them into a pocket of her apron. "There, I hope you're satisfied, my lord."

"Far from it," he muttered under his breath.

Their gazes locked for a moment, and Laura sensed a seething anger behind his hard mask. It was only to be expected, she told herself. Every time he looked in a mirror, he saw what she'd done to him—and he remembered how she had outfoxed him.

He surely would want revenge.

Well, so did she—though *her* retribution would be exacted upon the villain who had incriminated her father. She must be very careful lest the earl overturn those plans. Like it or not, she would have to swallow her resentment and placate him in the hope of saving her position here.

He returned his attention to his aunt. "I would like to complete my interview with Miss Brown in private. If you don't mind, we'll excuse ourselves for a few minutes."

"Of course! Pray take as long as you like." Lady Josephine wagged her finger at him. "Only remember, you mustn't bully Laura. I won't have you frightening her away from here."

"I'll keep that in mind."

Chapter 7

Alex hoped the cagey answer would satisfy his aunt. He didn't want to make a promise to her that he might not be able to honor. The truth was, he had not yet determined how to proceed.

Laura—in his aunt's garden! Despite the droopy hat and the rimless spectacles, he had recognized her at once. The sight of her walking toward him had knocked him utterly off kilter. He'd long ago made peace with the belief that he'd never see her again.

But here she stood, as headstrong and as beautiful as ever.

What was her purpose in returning to London? Why had she sought employment with his aunt of all people? Did she hope to erase the past and finagle her way back into his good graces?

Heat seared him, but logic swiftly put a damper on it. If that was her reason, then why had she gone to great lengths to conceal her identity? Why did she act as if he was the last man on earth she'd wanted to encounter?

And where was her father?

Damn, he needed answers from her. At once.

Taking leave of his aunt, Alex noticed that Laura already had marched halfway down the path to the house. Her dark gray gown was high-necked, long-sleeved, and devoid of adornment. No longer the fashionable debutante, she wore the white apron of a servant. Yet the drab costume could not conceal the slimness of her waist or the alluring sway of her hips. Nor could the spinster's cap hide the glory of her tawny-gold hair. In truth, the plain garb merely served as a blank canvas for her rare beauty.

Head held high, she stepped into the house; he only just caught the door in time before it slammed in his face. Her displeasure could not have been clearer—and it grated on him. Though ten years had passed, she apparently still held *him* to blame for the fact that she'd been forced to flee England. *Him*, and not the father who had committed the most sensational robbery of the century.

A crime that had yet to be resolved.

Alex squinted as his eyes adjusted to the dimness inside the house. Halfway down the corridor, Laura had stopped to converse with Mrs. Samson, a gaunt-faced woman with a ring of keys dangling from the waist of her dark gown.

". . . shouldn't leave her ladyship unattended," the housekeeper was scolding. "You'll find we don't tolerate such lax behavior in this household!"

Laura held herself rigidly. "I am perfectly aware of my duties—"

"Is there some difficulty?" Alex interrupted. "I requested a private interview with Miss Brown."

"Your lordship!" A toadying smile banishing her sour expression, Mrs. Samson bobbed a curtsy. "Forgive me, I wasn't informed of your arrival."

"Send a maid outside to wait with my aunt."

"Yes, my lord. At once."

As the housekeeper scurried to do his bidding, Laura didn't appear to appreciate his intercession. She barely glanced at him before leading the way into the back office that had once been his uncle's domain.

The wall shelves held a few account books along with an array of snuffboxes, horse and dog figurines, and other useless novelties. The clutter exasperated Alex, but his aunt became misty-eyed when asked to part with anything that had belonged to Uncle Charles. Years ago, Alex had given up on the task.

He closed the door as Laura headed to the single window and threw open the tall wooden shutters. Sunlight flooded a pair of leather chairs and the large oak desk. Atop a blotter sat a collection of ink pots, pens, and other writing paraphernalia.

He suspected her choice of venue was purposeful. It conveyed the message that she considered him unworthy of being received in the formal drawing room. He would allow her this one small victory. There were more important battles yet to be won.

Facing him, she crossed her arms, but the action only served to draw his attention to her shapely bosom. He tried not to stare. Laura Falkner still took his breath away—even more so now that she was a mature woman. Despite the passage of time, she had retained her feminine figure, her flawless skin, her natural sensuality. And no one else of his acquaintance had eyes that deep ocean blue. It might be a poetic cliché, but a man truly could drown in those big eyes.

Curiosity twisted his gut. She could not have been without admirers all these years. What other men had she known? Had she given herself to any of them? It seemed impossible that such an extraordinary woman could have reached the age of eight-and-twenty with her virginity intact.

"Is Brown your married name?" he asked.

She frowned. "No. It was merely one that Papa and I adopted. Even though we were living abroad, we feared someone might come looking for us."

"You must have stayed out of public view, then."

"We did what was necessary," she said dismissively. "Now, you'll be wondering why I'm here in this house. Pray be assured it is only to earn my living. I would never have taken this post had I known Lady Josephine was your aunt."

Alex didn't want Laura to change the subject. He craved to learn every detail about what she'd been doing in the decade since she had sliced open his cheek with a penknife. But her personal life was not the line of questioning that he needed to pursue.

Settling onto the edge of the desk, he said, "Lady Milford arranged for you to be employed here. It all makes sense now."

"Sense?"

"Over the past year, she's gained something of a reputation as a matchmaker. She must have recalled the ill-fated romance between us and decided to meddle."

Her lips pursed, Laura walked back and forth. "Your aunt, too, seems to have taken a wild notion that we'll suit. Clearly neither of them has the slightest inkling of how very much we detest each other!"

He fixed her with a hard stare. Her vehemence spoke volumes. Nothing remained of the naive debutante with the sparkling smile, the adoring girl who'd melted in his arms. Whatever fledgling love Laura had once felt for him had been destroyed on the day he'd found the proof of her father's crime.

If only he hadn't discovered those stolen earrings, he wouldn't have felt honor-bound to apprehend Martin Falkner. And the trust in her eyes would not have turned to hatred.

But the past could not be changed.

"Aunt Josie and Lady Milford are old women with nothing better to do than to play matchmaker," he said. "However, I cannot profess to being entirely displeased that you've returned."

Laura's eyes widened; then she gave him a guarded look. "I hope you don't mean to expose my identity to . . . to anyone."

Did she fear he would turn her over to the police?

Alex gave a cool smile intended to keep her as off balance as he'd felt in the garden. "That remains to be seen. Though I'll wager Lady Milford has no idea that her little scheme will serve an entirely different purpose than she intended."

"Different?"

"Come now, you must know that we've certain matters to settle . . . given how abruptly we parted ten years ago."

A militant sparkle entered her eyes. "If you intend to take retaliation for that"—she pointed to his scar—"then you are *not* a gentleman."

Rubbing the long ridge with his fingertip, Alex wondered what she'd say if he told her there was no need for reprisal. The score between them was settled already—because he had wronged her, too. He had deceived Laura all those years ago. Initially at least, his courtship of her had been calculated. He had sought her out on purpose in order to investigate her father.

Not that he intended to tell her so now. It would only lead to questions that he was not at liberty to answer.

"All I wish from you is the truth," he said. "First and foremost, where is your father?"

Her cheeks paled. She averted her face, glancing down at her clasped hands. "He's . . . dead."

Alex could deduce nothing from her bowed head. Jumping up from the desk, he caught her chin in his fingers and forced her to look at him. "You protected him once and you could be protecting him again. So tell me, why should I believe you?"

"He's lying in a pauper's grave at St. Giles cemetery," she said, her voice low and strained. "He was buried there several weeks ago. You may view the gravestone for yourself—look for Martin Brown. He couldn't even be laid to rest under his real name."

Tears glistened in her eyes as she wrenched out of his grasp and walked to the window to gaze outside. He didn't think she was playacting. Laura had always been one to freely express her deepest feelings—that was part of what had intrigued him about her long ago. Unlike himself, she wore her emotions on her sleeve.

Besides, he had to believe her since she'd given him the means to check her claim. Martin Falkner was dead. That left his daughter as the only link to the missing diamond necklace.

Alex walked closer to put himself into her line of vision. The glint of a tear track on her cheek stirred in him the unsettling need to comfort her. But she wouldn't welcome his embrace. Especially once she realized he intended to probe further into the matter of the robbery.

"Please accept my condolences," he murmured. "Nevertheless, I do need answers. The Blue Moon diamond has never been found—and I must know what happened to it. Was it sold? Or did your father come back to England to retrieve the necklace from wherever he'd hidden it?"

Laura spun toward him. Her fingers clutched at the windowsill, the knuckles turning white. "No! Absolutely not. I told you long ago that my father was *not* the thief. He was made a scapegoat by someone else."

"Then explain why he returned here."

"I . . . don't know for certain. He left Portugal without telling me. I can only presume he intended to confront whomever he thought had framed him for the deed."

Her voice rang with fervor. It seemed Laura really *did* believe her father was innocent of the crime.

That fact put Alex in an uncomfortable situation. It meant she knew nothing of Martin Falkner's private past. The man had had secrets that he must not have seen fit to confess to his daughter. Secrets that gave him ample cause to steal the priceless jewels from the Duchess of Knowles. Secrets that Alex had no intention of divulging.

The devil of it was, he couldn't reveal the truth even if he was inclined to do so. When he'd been charged with the task of finding the stolen pieces, he had sworn a vow of silence.

"And just who might that be?" he asked for the sake of argument. "Did he ever name the person he'd suspected?"

"I'm afraid not." Laura lowered her lashes slightly. "However, I've a theory of my own. It's the only one that makes sense to me."

"Go on."

"Perhaps, my lord, it was *you* who placed Her Grace's gems in my father's desk."

If she had drawn a pistol, she could not have startled him more. "What! That is preposterous."

"Is it?" She gave him a look of reckless disdain. "*You* were the one to discover the earrings, were you not? Perhaps you thought to avoid a marriage to someone beneath you in rank. Perhaps you wanted my father imprisoned so that I would be ruined by association. Then you could offer me the role of mistress without suffering the encumbrance of a ring upon your finger."

His jaw tightened. He would never forget the awful jolt he'd felt on opening the desk drawer to see the cold glint of the diamonds. Despite his prior knowledge of Martin Falkner's secret life, Alex had not wanted to believe the man capable of such a deed, for Laura's sake. But duty had compelled him to accept the truth and see justice done.

Now she was so far off the mark that he felt insulted, his honor sullied. Maybe that was her intention.

Stepping closer, he caught her face in his hands and let his thumb graze her soft lips. "If I'd wanted to make you my mistress, Laura, I'd have needed no subterfuge. I'd have taken you to my bed—and you'd have come willingly."

A faint flush stole over her skin. Time seemed to stop as they stared at each other. With every breath he inhaled her scent of sunshine and flowers. How tempting was the thought of seducing her—if only it wouldn't lend credence to her wrongheaded opinion of him.

He traced the bow shape of her mouth, and she gave a little shiver of pleasure. "See?" he murmured. "You haven't forgotten how it was between us."

Laura turned her head to avoid his caress. "What I

haven't forgotten is your disdain for propriety. You never did behave as a gentleman."

She stopped, apparently thinking better of mentioning their stolen embraces in darkened gardens, in closed carriages, and one memorable interlude in a closet in the midst of a party. But Alex needed no reminder. Every stroke, every kiss, every sigh, was branded into his memory. Despite his purpose back then, he'd fallen hard for her. What had begun as a calculated courtship had swiftly become genuine.

So genuine that he could feel it still burning inside himself.

He let his breath feather her cheek. "What we once shared was only the first course. A mere taste of the feast that I could have given you—and could still give you if only you would allow it."

Her lips parted slightly, and the sight tempted him sorely. He wanted what he'd been forced to deny himself, the chance to clasp that curvaceous body to his, to stir her to passion, to revel in her surrender. Ever so slightly, he moved closer, determined to claim that soft, sinful mouth of hers . . .

Laura twisted free. She flew to the desk and snatched up a penknife, pointing the blade at him. "Stop! Or you'll have a matching scar on your other cheek."

Alex held up his open palms to show that he meant her no harm. God! He didn't trust her with that weapon. Not after the way she'd slashed him the last time they'd met.

Yet he was more irked with himself than with her. If he'd been thinking with his brain, he'd have removed all sharp objects upon entering the office. Hell, he would never have attempted seduction in the first place. Laura was no longer the adoring debutante.

She held a deep-seated grudge against him, and perhaps that was for the best. He needed no distractions from the task of determining what her father had done with the Blue Moon diamond.

He strolled to the door, leaned a shoulder against the frame, and crossed his arms. "A simple *no* would have sufficed," he said. "I haven't yet sunk to such depths as to force a woman."

"I won't be your light skirt. Not now or ever."

"A wise decision. An affair undoubtedly would be discomfiting for my aunt."

Laura eyed him mistrustfully as she slipped the penknife into the pocket of her apron. "I hope that means you won't send me away," she said. "Lady Josephine needs my companionship. She enjoys being with people. Yet apparently she never calls on anyone or goes anywhere—nor has anyone visited her in the time I've been here."

"What? She's always had many friends."

"One has to pay calls in order for them to be returned." Laura took a determined step toward him. "It's apparent to me that she's become too forgetful to organize her own schedule. Did you know that she had a desk drawer stuffed full of unanswered invitations?"

Alex shook his head. He tried to think back on the last time he'd seen his aunt out in society—had it really been several years? Of late, his life had fallen into a pattern: playing cards at his club, taking his seat in Parliament, supervising his various estates. He still visited select friends when in town, but he'd grown bored with the superficiality of the ton. Each year the new crop of debutantes seemed more naive and giggly than the last, so that he had taken to avoiding most social events altogether.

Some weeks ago, while at the races, he'd run into Lady Milford. She had expressed concern about his aunt, and he had agreed that a companion might be needed. Then he had engaged in a round of betting and had promptly forgotten about it.

"I suppose it's my fault," he now admitted ruefully. "I seldom attend balls and parties. I didn't realize I'd been neglecting Aunt Josie."

"You have an elder sister, don't you?" Laura asked. "Why hasn't *she* seen to your aunt's needs?"

"Cynthia is wed to the assistant governor-general of India. She's been living in Calcutta these past twelve years." Not to mention, he'd never been close to his only sibling, since she was six years his senior. He'd still been in short pants when she'd gone off to finishing school.

"I see," Laura said, her gaze intent on him. "Then you must allow *me* to arrange Lady Josephine's calendar. I'll make certain that she renews old friendships and attends events where she might relish a good gossip with other ladies her age. You do wish for her to be happy, don't you, my lord?"

"Of course."

Even as guilt yanked a swift response out of Alex, he recognized that he was being maneuvered. Gut instinct told him that Laura had something up her sleeve. She seemed far too eager to venture out into society—as if for a purpose of her own.

Why?

Ten years ago, her lively wit and vivid beauty had made her the center of attention. Now her drab appearance would only fool those who hadn't known her very well. She had to realize that if anyone recognized her, she would be expelled in disgrace. So what would induce her to risk such humiliation? If she merely needed income, a governess post in the country would have been a safer choice; no one there need ever guess her true identity.

It made no sense to Alex. Maybe she was a better actress than he'd imagined. Maybe he was mistaken to think she didn't know where the Blue Moon diamond was hidden . . .

"I'll allow you to stay on a trial basis," he said.

Laura released a breath. "Thank you," she said rather stiffly. "I'll give you no cause to regret it. I'll take excellent care of Lady Josephine, you'll see."

The hint of relief on her face only intrigued him further. Alex opened the door, then turned back as if in afterthought. "By the way, my aunt's jewels are secured in a lockbox at Barclay's Bank. As my uncle's executor, I'm the only one with a key."

Laura gazed blankly for a moment. Then she clenched her fists at her sides and took a step toward him. "Are you suggesting that I came here to *filch* her ladyship's valuables?"

Alex allowed a sardonic half smile, one that had been known to make lesser mortals quail. "I only thought you should know in case Aunt Josie wishes to wear a certain piece."

Laura gave him a withering look. "Then tell me, does she own a fine emerald necklace? Something that will complement a green-and-white gown? If you feel it is *safe*, do send the jewels here on the morrow so that her ladyship might wear them to Lord Scarborough's ball."

With that, she flounced past Alex, giving him another alluring whiff of her feminine scent. She offered no curtsy or nod of farewell, only continued on as if he were a footman that she'd already forgotten.

He watched from the doorway as she marched

down the wood-paneled corridor. Her shoes kicked up her back hem, affording him a glimpse of slim ankles clad in white stockings and clunky dark shoes. He hadn't actually expected her motive to be robbery, but he'd wanted to assess her reaction just to make certain.

It was clear that she had been greatly insulted by his insinuation.

Alex combed his fingers through his hair. There was something he was missing. If she sincerely believed in her father's innocence, why would she be so eager to associate with the highbrow people who had condemned Martin Falkner—and herself by association?

The answer came to him in a flash. *Of course.* Laura hoped to clear her father's name. She must be planning to find the phantom thief. It was exactly the sort of wildly imprudent scheme that she would devise.

Alex scowled at the spot where she'd disappeared. He could only imagine the uproar if she were to make false accusations toward any member of the ton. It would spark a fiery scandal—and to no purpose since the real thief, her father, was no longer alive.

Laura, however, might just land *herself* in big trouble.

Chapter 8

The following evening, Laura surveyed her reflection in the long pier glass of her dressing room. The light of a sputtering candle revealed an unremarkable woman in a high-necked gown of dark, coffee-colored muslin. Her tawny-blond hair was concealed by a puritanical white lace cap with side lappets that brushed her shoulders.

Spinsterish, she concluded in satisfaction, picking up the spectacles and donning them to complete the disguise. Among the brilliant butterflies at Lord Scarborough's ball, she would be a dull brown moth.

She had striven purposefully to create the dowdy persona. Which was why it made no sense at all for her to walk across the small dressing room to a cupboard and draw forth one of the fancy slippers that had been a gift from Lady Milford.

Laura glided her fingertips over the lining of garnet-dyed satin. The splendor of the crystal beadwork fed her beauty-starved soul. It transported her back to a time when she had owned an extensive wardrobe with gowns and accessories for every occasion. A time when she had been oblivious to all but the pleasures of privilege and wealth. A time when she had been pursued by many suitors, though only one had made her heart race.

That had been before Alexander Ross, the Earl of Copley, had proven himself to be a beast.

Laura clutched the slipper to her bosom. The audacity of the man to imply that she could not be trusted with his aunt's gems! He'd meant it, too. He had *not* sent a courier today with the jewels she had requested, which only verified his low opinion of her character.

Then why had he allowed her to remain in his aunt's house? Only one reason seemed plausible: he preyed upon servant women. He viewed Laura as a ripe plum for his plucking.

He had demonstrated his intentions by gliding his thumb over her lips and murmuring an intimate proposal. *What we once shared was only the first course. A mere taste of the feast that I could have given you—and could still give you.*

At the time, she had not been able to stop an involuntary shiver. The allure of his presence had startled her with its intensity. Despite all that had happened, his magnetism still affected her. Even now, the memory of his touch made her feel flushed and unsettled.

Her spontaneous reaction defied all good sense. It would be madness to let down her guard around such a scoundrel. Long ago, she had been naive enough to fall under his spell. But now she was wiser, having witnessed the heartless way he'd treated Papa.

Alex could go to the devil for all she cared.

The earl, Laura corrected herself for the umpteenth time. It was only force of habit that kept her thinking of him in a familiar fashion. She needed to be careful not to voice his first name aloud in company.

That shouldn't be a problem since he seldom attended society events. His presence would only have to be endured when he came here to visit his aunt. Laura had no intention of letting him catch her alone again. He'd soon realize the futility of trying to seduce her.

She gazed down at the slippers, conscious of a strange compulsion to slide them onto her feet. How foolish of her to wish she was still that frivolous young girl. Finding Papa's murderer was the only thing that mattered now. And since she wouldn't be dancing at tonight's ball, she needn't exchange her plain leather shoes for these fine beaded slippers.

With firm resolve, she replaced Lady Milford's gift in the cupboard. Then she extinguished the candle, picked up a black knitted shawl, and headed through the gloomy guest bedchamber to the door. Out in the corridor, an assortment of age-darkened landscapes decorated the walls. The only light came from a flickering oil lamp on a side table.

Peering over the tops of her spectacles, she went the few steps along a faded floral carpet runner to Lady Josephine's quarters. There she paused, somewhat alarmed to find the door partway open.

Had her ladyship become confused and left her chambers? Had she forgotten Laura's instructions not to navigate the stairs unaided? Or had a maid merely forgotten to shut the door?

Laura rapped twice on the panel to announce herself before stepping inside the bedchamber. Shadows cast by a branch of candles wavered over the cavernous ceiling with its frescoes of cherubs frolicking among the clouds. The heavenly theme continued in the gilt-and-white furniture, the gold brocade hangings on the windows and the four-poster bed, and the carved alabaster mantel where a fire danced softly.

The room might have been a private paradise if not for the excessive bric-a-brac. Every nook and cranny had been filled with displays of ivory painted fans, music boxes, and cloisonné vases on pedestals. On all available surfaces rested a vast collection of ceramic figurines from shepherdesses to goddesses, cavalrymen to Greek heroes, all gifts from Lady Josephine's beloved late husband.

An array of clocks ticked in discordant rhythm, ormolu on the mantel, delicate porcelain on the writing desk, French gilt on the bedside table. They showed the time to be more or less half past eight, depending upon which one Laura consulted.

In the far corner of the chamber, a yellow rectangle of light spilled from the dressing room doorway. She took it as an encouraging sign that Lady Josephine was still here, after all.

Lowering her chin to peer over the spectacles, Laura picked a path through a maze of footstools and ottomans. No one on the staff except for her seemed concerned that their aging mistress might trip and break a bone. She itched to rescind Mrs. Samson's order to keep everything in precisely the same place. Perhaps she ought to ask her ladyship's permission in the presence of the housekeeper. Yes, that might work, for Lady Josephine was always agreeable to suggestions . . .

Laura had almost reached the dressing room when the glow of light suddenly dimmed. Glancing up, she spied a man blocking the open doorway. A tall, broad-shouldered gentleman in dark evening clothes and snow-white cravat.

Alex.

Her heart catapulted into her throat. His presence in her ladyship's bedchamber caught Laura so much by surprise that she stopped in mid-step, one foot forward.

"*You?*" she sputtered, then realized how imprudent it would be to let rudeness give him cause to dismiss her. She managed a token curtsy. "Forgive me, my lord. I didn't expect to find you here."

"Ah, Miss *Brown.* I came to deliver my aunt's emeralds. The ones you ordered yesterday."

The murmur of voices came from inside the dressing room, Lady Josephine's along with that of her maid. Out here, the clocks ticked into the silence as Laura strove to hide her bitterness that he didn't trust *her* with the jewels. "I'm sure she appreciates the gesture, my lord. On your way out, you may wish to instruct the butler to lock up the jewelry upon her ladyship's return tonight. I wouldn't want to see thieves make off with her valuables."

So much for meekness. But Laura just couldn't help herself.

One corner of his mouth quirked, though whether in displeasure or humor, she couldn't tell. "An excellent suggestion," he said. "Especially since those ridiculous eyeglasses would blind you to a robber creeping right past you in the corridor."

"I can manage perfectly well, thank you. If you'll excuse me now, I'll check on her ladyship. She may need my assistance."

Laura stepped forward, and so did he. With her gaze on his blurry figure, she nearly stumbled over a footstool. He caught her elbow and held her upright. "Steady there."

She found herself hemmed in by chairs and tables with the earl blocking her path. A deep awareness of him flowed through her body. Never in her life had she been in a bedchamber with Alex. It brought to mind unbidden, unsuitable, *unwelcome* thoughts.

"Pray move aside," she said stiffly. "Your aunt

may be ready to depart, and I don't wish to keep her waiting."

"You've a few minutes yet. The maid is still doing her hair."

He didn't budge, so Laura tilted up her chin to aim a stern look at him. The glasses distorted her vision and no doubt spoiled the effect. She scooted them down to the very tip of her nose, only to realize that Alex was ogling her quite outrageously. His gaze roamed from the top of her prim white cap down over her dark frock and shawl, lingering a long moment on her bosom before returning to her face.

A faint smile touched his mouth. "My governess taught me that a gentleman always offers a compliment to a lady. Since I cannot profess to admire such an unattractive gown, may I say that you have very pretty eyes." He snatched off the spectacles and tucked them inside his coat. "At least now that I can see them."

Laura's immediate impulse was to plunge her hand inside his coat and retrieve her property. But there were some boundaries she didn't dare cross. "Give those back to me at once!"

"In due time. Do you really think you'll fool people with your disguise?"

"Yes! Not all men stare at women the way you do. Now, haven't you a gambling club to visit or a debutante to ravish?"

He chuckled, the gruff sound causing a bothersome stir in the pit of her stomach. "I didn't come here just for my aunt," he said. "I brought something for you, too."

"For *me*?"

Intensely curious in spite of herself, Laura watched as he reached into an inner pocket of his coat—the opposite side from where he'd stashed her precious eyeglasses. He drew forth an oblong box made of black enamel and decorated with colorful inlaid flowers.

It looked suspiciously like . . . a jewel box.

The earl held it out to her. When she didn't touch it, he grasped her frozen hand and placed the box in her palm. "Open it," he ordered.

Her fingers closed reflexively around the hard edges. The smooth surface felt warm from being tucked against his chest. She didn't look down at the box, though; she couldn't take her eyes from his face. With his dark brown hair tumbled onto his brow and the candlelight bathing his scarred cheek, he resembled a fallen archangel.

No, he was a mere mortal, and a wicked one at that. He had the *droit du seigneur* arrogance of a feudal lord. An earl didn't give expensive presents to a servant without having a nefarious purpose in mind. He was plying her with trinkets for one reason—to coax her into his bed.

Laura tried to shove the box back at him, but he refused to take it. "All I want from you is my spectacles," she said tightly.

"You'll have them. After you open that."

"Is that a promise?"

He placed his palm over his heart. "On my honor as a gentleman."

Laura wanted to retort that attempting to buy the favors of his aunt's hired companion branded him a rogue. But he soon would realize his mistake. No gift of jewelry, regardless how spectacular, could ever tempt her to surrender her virtue to him.

She undid the little latch and slowly opened the box. For a moment she could only stare down at the object that lay nestled against the lining of pale blue velvet. A pair of gold-rimmed spectacles.

Laura glanced up at him in confusion. "What—? Why would you give *this* to me?"

"Allow me to demonstrate."

He plucked the spectacles from the case and stepped closer to fit them on her nose, carefully sliding the stems inside her spinster's cap and behind her ears. The brush of his fingers sent tingles over her skin, and the heady masculine scent of his cologne distracted her.

At least until she realized something.

Gazing through the eyeglasses, she could discern every minute detail of his face, from the faint shadow on his jaw to the long thread of his scar to the amber flecks in his brown eyes. "I can see perfectly!"

"Of course," he said with a smirk of satisfaction. "They're fashioned of plain glass. Much more convenient than your old ones, don't you agree?"

"But . . . where did you find them? I searched up and down The Strand, but no one sells spectacles without magnification. What purpose would they serve?" She paused, then added, "Except for disguise, of course. But apparently there isn't a very large market for that."

"There should be. I plan to put them on my daughters someday to discourage the swains."

Laura stared at him. His statement caused an earthquake inside her. "You have daughters? From . . . a mistress?"

He cocked an amused eyebrow. Then he bent down to look straight at her as he adjusted the glasses slightly. "No need to get your maidenly feathers in a ruffle, Miss Brown. I was speaking in mere supposition."

"Oh." Laura found herself transfixed by the notion of him with a family. Was he seeking a wife this season? Was that why he'd made such a statement? Having turned thirty-one the previous February, perhaps he was considering the need to beget an heir. He still had a glint in his eyes, so she added, "I'm not in a *ruffle* over anything, by the by. Your private sins are of no concern to me."

"It's been my experience that women who declare a lack of interest in my activities are usually ones who are the *most* interested."

"Clearly you've involved yourself with deceitful women, then. Now, you never told me where you found these spectacles."

"I had them made especially for you."

An unwelcome thought occurred to Laura. Considering that the rims were gold and the special order had been filled within a day's time, Alex must have gone to considerable expense on her behalf. "How much did the pair cost? You may deduct the amount from my wages."

He waved a dismissive hand. "It was a paltry sum."

"I'm afraid I can't accept them. I won't take a gift from you."

Reaching up, Laura started to remove the spectacles, but he caught her wrist and stopped her. "You can and you will," he stated. "Consider it a gift to my aunt."

"Your aunt?"

"She'll be caught up in the scandal if anyone recognizes you. It would be extremely upsetting to her." Still grasping Laura's wrist, Alex pulled her over to a gilt-framed mirror on the wall. He brought her to stand in front of him, and their closeness felt shockingly like an embrace. "See? The disguise works much better now that you aren't constantly peering over the rims."

Laura gazed at her reflection. Or rather, *their* reflection—the spinster and the rogue. In the candlelit bedchamber, Alex loomed behind her like a dark angel of temptation. The fluttering of her heart set off a pulse beat deep within her womb. She was conscious of the heat of his body against her back, the weight of his hands resting on her shoulders, the knowledge that she had only to turn in his arms and he would fulfill her most forbidden desires.

She stepped toward the mirror on the pretext of adjusting the spectacles. "I can manage with the old ones."

"And trip down the stairs or fall over a footstool while you're escorting my aunt? No. It's a small price for me to pay to save her from injury."

She hoped he felt a true duty to his aunt. Better that than having a secret scheme to make Laura feel beholden to him. But she'd be lying to herself if she didn't admit her pleasure in keeping the eyeglasses. They were crucial to her masquerade. "All right, then, I suppose it's reasonable to accept them."

"Excellent. And just in time—here's Aunt Josie now."

Leading the way, Alex navigated the maze of furniture to the dressing room doorway, where Lady Josephine was walking out with the use of her cane. The green brocade gown with its trimming of lace suited her round form and merry nature. Her gray hair had been beautifully styled and adorned with a bird-of-paradise flower. Beneath the multiple folds of her throat gleamed a magnificent emerald-and-diamond necklace with matching gemstones at her ears.

Laura smiled warmly at her. "You look quite festive, my lady. We shall have a grand time tonight."

A faintly puzzled look came over Lady Josephine's face. "Why have you not dressed for the ball, Lenora?"

"Laura," Alex corrected smoothly, offering his arm to the old woman. "She's a bluestocking, that's why. It's a well-known fact that such females lack any interest in fashion. But no matter, being seen in my company ought to lend her at least the veneer of style."

Laura had been frowning at his assessment of her when his last sentence left her aghast. "You're going with us?" she asked. "But you don't attend balls. You told me so yourself just yesterday."

"Then it's time for me to mend my wicked ways. I've neglected my dear aunt for long enough."

He patted Lady Josephine's arm, and she beamed up at him while Laura watched in dismay. He had another objective in mind—she knew he did, because a man of his sinful tastes didn't tarry with dowagers and spinsters. Perhaps, Laura thought bitterly, he didn't trust her not to plunder the house of their host.

She intended to sleuth for information, to eavesdrop on conversations and ascertain the location of certain people from her past. But how was she to succeed if Alex watched her all evening?

"I've ordered the barouchet," she said in desperation. "There's only room for two to sit comfortably."

"Oh, but I'm certain we can all squeeze in together!" Lady Josephine said. "Don't you agree, Alexander?"

His sardonic stare bored into Laura. "There's nothing I would relish more."

Chapter 9

Laura had not expected to take such pleasure in the ball. She sat in a chair behind Lady Josephine and a group of matriarchs who were chatting about the plans for young Queen Victoria's coronation at the end of June. Alex had left his aunt in this spot some time ago. The old ladies had fawned over him, while affording Laura only a cursory greeting. She was, after all, a nobody unworthy of their attention.

The arrangement suited her perfectly. Free to observe the swarms of guests, she marveled at the sheer number of them. Having lived so many years isolated in the mountains, she had forgotten just how crowded a London ball could be.

Or how exciting.

The pomp and splendor of it all engulfed her senses. Towering columns stretched up the pale green walls of the vast ballroom. A trio of massive chandeliers spilled golden candlelight over the ladies in their stylish gowns, the gentlemen in finely tailored suits. At one end of the long chamber, a wall of French doors had been opened to the gardens. At the other end, an orchestra played for a multitude of dancers who whirled gracefully over the polished parquet floor.

Laura hoped no one noticed that she tapped her shoe in time to the music. She couldn't help herself; she hadn't heard such lovely melodies in ten years. The very air hummed as the guests who were not dancing gathered in clusters to laugh and gossip. She caught snatches of conversation, none of which had any bearing on her investigation.

No matter. The mystery wouldn't be solved in one evening. It would take numerous forays into society to gather all the facts. For the moment, she could indulge in the luxury of being among the upper crust again.

Her good humor abruptly evaporated as she spied a familiar tall form among the dancers. Alex. She peered through the spectacles at his partner, a petite brunette in a virginal white gown with puffy, elbow-length sleeves. Aware that her lips had tightened, Laura forced her expression to relax. It was of no concern to her if the earl was seeking a bride among this year's array of debutantes.

In truth, she had every reason to be glad. A courtship would occupy his attention so that he wouldn't keep a close watch on Laura's actions. If he saw her leave this spot—as she fully intended to do soon—he might accuse her of prowling for valuables to rob.

Sitting across from him in the small barouchet had been bad enough. He'd taken every opportunity to annoy her by brushing his knees against hers, making a sly remark, or giving her that ironic stare she found so maddening. But once they'd arrived here, Alex had transformed into a lordly stranger. He had escorted his aunt into the party, leaving Laura to trail behind as the lowly companion. He'd ignored her except to offer a dismissive introduction in the receiving line. Consequently, their host and hostess hadn't cast a second glance at the meek, bespectacled Miss Brown.

Alex claimed to be concealing her identity for Lady Josephine's sake, although Laura suspected his real reason was to keep her close for the purpose of seduction. Little did he know, he was aiding her quest to find whoever had stolen the Blue Moon diamond necklace. And when she succeeded, she would take great pleasure in exposing the villain to all of society— Alex, in particular.

How she would relish seeing him humbled. He'd be forced to admit his mistake in accusing Papa of the crime. Had Alex trusted in Papa's innocence, they wouldn't have had to flee England—and Papa might still be alive.

A lump caught in her throat. At one time, he had been a well-liked member of the ton, having many friendships among the gentlemen. He'd been popular with the ladies, too, always gallant even to the shyest wallflower. But whenever Laura had encouraged him to marry again, he'd declared that his heart belonged to her dear mother, who had died shortly after Laura's birth. He had been such a warm, kind, affable man that she could not conceive of how anyone could have sought his ruin.

Let alone his murder.

Yet someone had done so. Someone that her father had come back to England to confront. And Laura had two key possibilities, if only she could locate them in this crush of guests.

The enormity of the undertaking daunted her. Many years had passed, appearances had altered, hairstyles had changed. Besides, she had been in society for a scant six weeks when she and Papa had left

England. There hadn't been time for her to learn the names of everyone outside her close circle of friends and admirers.

Scanning the crowd, she spied several former swains, including a dapper man with flaxen hair. What was his name? Something hyphenated . . . Mr. Rupert Stanhope-Jones. She remembered him because he'd always sent her small, exquisite, expensive gifts—unlike Alex who was more apt to give her a bouquet of daisies plucked at random during a stroll in Hyde Park. At times, Alex also had surprised her with practical presents like a new set of drawing pencils when she'd worn her favorite ones down to nubs.

Or a pair of spectacles.

Frowning, Laura shifted position on the straight-backed chair. She had no interest in Alex. Since Lady Josephine and her friends had spent the past hour alternately discussing the coronation and trading stories about their youth, Laura had learned nothing of value. It was time to take a promenade to see who else might be here.

As she leaned forward to ask permission to be excused, an older gentleman strolled toward her employer and bowed. "Lady Josephine, what a pleasure to see you here."

That square-jawed, ruddy face beneath a thatch of silver hair looked vaguely familiar to Laura. She tried to dredge a name out of her memory, but came up blank. So, apparently, did Lady Josephine.

"A pleasure indeed, er . . . sir."

"Lord Oliver," he said, gallantly kissing the back of her hand. "Perhaps you've forgotten me. I was a friend of your husband's."

Lord Oliver also had been acquainted with Laura's father. She remembered them playing cards together at parties. In the same moment that recognition struck, Lord Oliver shifted his steel-gray eyes to her. A slight frown furrowed his brow, as if he was trying to identify her.

Laura averted her face and rose from the chair, hoping that she hadn't betrayed herself. Though she didn't have permission to go, she left anyway, making her way through the masses of people. Only when she was a safe distance away did she dare to glance back.

Lord Oliver stood conversing with Lady Josephine. Thank heavens he wasn't staring after Laura. That had been a very close call.

Releasing a breath, Laura decided to keep to the outskirts of the throng. She had let down her guard for a moment, and that mustn't happen again. If she kept her head bowed, people would know by her plain attire that she was no one of consequence, and then she could discreetly survey the company. Here and there, she spied familiar faces, though none were the ones she sought.

Where had Alex gone? She wanted to know only in order to avoid him. Since the orchestra had stopped for an interlude, he wasn't on the dance floor. Perhaps he'd never intended to watch her. Perhaps he'd come here tonight to pursue his own entertainment—or to seek a bride.

Then, as she neared the great arched doorway, she spotted him. Half a head taller than the other gentlemen nearby, he stood by a grouping of ferns in the far corner of the ballroom. He was engaged in conversation with a slim lady whose back was turned to Laura.

Diamonds glinted in the woman's elegant auburn coiffure. A pale blue satin ribbon cinched the waist of her marine-blue gown, and the fullness of the skirt enhanced her slenderness. Tilting her head coquettishly, she placed a gloved hand on his lapel and laughed at something he said.

That one gesture stabbed Laura's heart with recognition. A visceral disgust twisted inside her, an echo of the past. His companion was Lady Evelyn, daughter of the Marquess of Haversham.

A decade ago, she had been Laura's nemesis. From the moment Alex had shown a preference for Laura, Evelyn had made it her mission to win him for herself. She had flirted with him, coerced him into fetching her drinks, and tried to lure him away when he was dancing with Laura.

Lady Evelyn had learned her predatory nature at her father's knee. Lord Haversham was one of the few in the ton who'd treated Papa with icy disdain. Their feud dated back to their youth when they had been rivals for the affections of Laura's mother. Papa had won the girl—and Lord Haversham had never forgiven him.

He was the man whom Laura suspected of having framed her father—very likely with Lady Evelyn's help.

Laura had good reason to believe that, because on the day prior to Papa being accused of theft, Evelyn had come to their town house on a pretext. It had been somewhat early for morning calls from the ton. Laura had still been upstairs dressing—unwittingly giving Evelyn sufficient time to plant the jewels in Papa's desk. There had been no legitimate reason for her visit other than to gloat over a promise she'd finagled from Alex to take her for a carriage ride.

Now it appeared Evelyn was still pursuing him. Had she never married? Or perhaps she *was* married and fidelity mattered little to her. Laura resolved to keep her ears open for gossip. Any bit of information, no matter how small, might be used to formulate a plan to see justice done.

An elderly couple bumped her arm, murmured an apology, and continued on their way. Realizing she'd stopped in the flow of traffic, Laura cast one last burning look at Alex and Evelyn. Whatever it was they were discussing, he clearly found the woman enthralling. How could he be so brainless as to associate with that hussy? It only went to prove that he lacked even a shred of moral decency.

Suddenly he lifted his eyes and stared straight through the crowd at Laura. An involuntary flush suffused her body in heat.

She spun on her heel, hurried out of the ballroom, and entered a large reception hall with potted palm trees that towered up to the night-darkened glass roof. Many guests were milling here in between dance sets, and Laura made haste to lose herself among them. A furtive glance back at the arched doorway assured her that Alex hadn't followed.

She calmed the frantic rhythm of her heartbeat. The previous day, in a fit of pique, she'd very nearly blurted out to him her mission to find the real thief. Thank heavens she'd had the sense to guard that secret. Otherwise, he might have let something slip to Lady Evelyn.

Now that Laura knew Alex kept company with the vile woman, she would have to be doubly on her guard around him. The last thing she needed was for him to alert one of her chief suspects.

Slipping past clusters of guests, she peeked into the busy card room where gentlemen and ladies sat in groups of four at small tables. Did Lord Haversham play whist or vingt-et-un? Laura didn't know. During her debut season, she'd been too caught up in the excitement of her own youthful pursuits to pay much heed to the older generation.

The library held a number of gentlemen who had gathered to smoke. Although a haze in the air obscured her view somewhat, Laura didn't see Haversham's snobbish features as she strolled past. Perhaps that was just as well. If they were to come face-to-face, she would be hard-pressed to hold her tongue. Until she had all the facts in hand and could prove her case against him, it would be wise to remain incognito.

Her search took her by a dining room where a long buffet table was being prepared for a midnight supper. A black-suited butler directed an army of footmen on where to place the platters of food.

Laura continued down the wide passageway lined with gilt-framed paintings. She had suspected for a long time that Haversham, with Lady Evelyn as his accomplice, must have stolen the Blue Moon diamond necklace and put the blame on her father. Papa had never wanted to discuss the matter. It hadn't been in his gentle nature to seek revenge.

Yet he must have returned to England to confront his old rival. He had done it for *her* sake.

A yoke of guilt weighed on Laura. When he'd brought that London newspaper back to their cottage in Portugal, and she had discovered the little article commemorating the ten-year anniversary of the theft, she had carelessly expressed anger at the injustice that had driven them into exile. It was a quarrel they'd had on and off over the years. This time, Papa's delight at giving her news from England had vanished into melancholy. Though she'd been quick to reassure him, the damage had been done. The next day, he had kissed her good-bye without telling her his true destination.

It was the last time she'd seen him alive.

Laura drew a shuddery breath. Blaming herself wouldn't bring him back. But she *could* make certain that justice was done on his behalf. Perhaps someone had seen Papa enter Lord Haversham's house in Berkeley Square. Had he threatened to expose the marquess for his villainy? Had Haversham then cold-bloodedly arranged for Papa's murder to keep the truth from coming out?

Pondering how to find answers, she turned a corner and spied several guests. In the forefront strolled a couple, cooing and chatting, with eyes only for each other. They were too young for Laura to have known. As they passed her by, she saw another pair talking at the end of the passageway. Both were of her father's generation.

Laura's steps faltered to a stop. She stared at the man's narrow, foxlike features, the balding head with its monkish fringe of brown hair.

Lord Haversham!

His companion was a rather stout, middle-aged woman in a gold-and-crimson gown with massive rubies at her throat and ears. Several large rings sparkled on her fingers. She held her chin at a haughty angle, and the most memorable feature of her otherwise ordinary face was a sharp nose like the beak of a hawk.

The Duchess of Knowles. She was the rightful owner of the Blue Moon diamond.

Chapter 10

Alex managed to extricate himself from Evelyn's clutches on a vague promise to dance with her later. Relieved at his escape, he strode through the crowd and headed for the grand arched doorway.

Evelyn might be outwardly attractive, but the eyelash-batting and veiled hints revealed her to be just another predatory widow. She had prowled while her husband had still been alive, too. No surprise there, for the ancient Duke of Cliffington had been a doddering bridegroom at their nuptials. It was a wonder he'd survived the ceremony—let alone the wedding night.

Alex would have paid handsomely for a ringside seat to that event. Or not. He wouldn't be surprised if Evelyn had slipped laudanum into the old fool's nighttime tisane and then bedded the footman instead. That was the only way she could have conceived a son and heir before Cliffington had expired a few months later. Since shortly after the child's birth a few years ago, she had taken a succession of lovers from among the gentry and, it was rumored, the serving class.

From time to time, she'd tried to lure Alex into her web. But he had no taste for Evelyn's brand of poison.

He preferred a woman with principles. A woman who spoke her mind and didn't pander to him. A woman whose pride made her balk at accepting even a simple gift of eyeglasses.

Ever since Laura Falkner had walked back into his life the previous day, he had thought of little else but her. There was something about her that had always fascinated him, a vivacity of spirit that the drab disguise could not mask. He found her every bit as appealing now as she'd been ten years ago—perhaps more so.

Alex nodded to an acquaintance without stopping to chat. A few minutes ago, he'd spotted Laura in that unsightly puritan's cap. Their gazes had met across the crowded room, and the jolt to his senses had banished his boredom. Then she'd left the ballroom and vanished into the throngs of guests.

Where the devil had she been heading? Could it have something to do with her foolish plan to clear Martin Falkner's name?

Alex hoped not. She played a futile and dangerous game. If she started poking into people's lives, asking too many questions, someone would guess her true identity. The ton would not look favorably on the daughter of a thief in its midst. At best, she'd be banished from society, unable to fulfill her duties to his aunt. At worst, she'd face questioning as an accomplice to burglary.

Something else troubled Alex, as well. Laura might dig up secrets that were best left buried. There was one secret in particular that he'd sworn an oath to protect.

Heading out into the main reception area, he continued walking while he scanned the throngs. His height gave him the advantage of looking over the multitude, though it did him little good, for Laura was nowhere to be seen.

People spoke to him, ladies smiled and curtsied, gentlemen slapped him on the back. Alex evaded all conversation with a cool nod and a few dismissive words. At least until a dainty woman in magenta silk stepped into his path.

Lady Milford smiled warmly up at him and extended her gloved hand. "Lord Copley, what a delight it is to see you and your aunt here tonight."

Hiding his impatience, Alex bowed over her fingers. He knew precisely why she'd stopped him. She was curious about the results of her matchmaking scheme. "I fear you've caught me in something of a hurry, my lady. Perhaps we can speak later—in private."

"Pish-posh. This is a party, not a derby race. You must allow me a moment to inquire if Lady Josephine likes the new companion that I found for her."

"Yes," he bit out. "Though it would have been wise of you to have consulted me first."

Lady Milford raised an eyebrow. "I trust you've shown kindness to the poor girl. She's been forced to endure much that is not her fault."

"I've permitted Laura to stay so long as she remains anonymous." As soon as the words were out, Alex regretted using her first name. He hadn't meant to give anything away to Lady Milford, whose half smile reflected a shrewd interest. He leveled a hard stare at her. "Pray do not expect anything more. I'm simply not interested."

Lady Milford nodded toward a corridor across the room. "In case you change your mind, she went that way a few moments ago."

* * *

As Laura froze with her gaze on the couple at the end of the passageway, Lord Haversham bowed to the Duchess of Knowles, then walked away and disappeared around the corner. Alone, Her Grace started down the corridor.

Laura panicked at the woman's approach. She spied an open doorway and veered through it.

Finding herself in an antechamber, she made haste for another door. She pulled it open and paused in dismay. The large room held a veritable crush of ladies. The chatter of their voices and the scent of perfume filled the air. A bevy of women vied for a position at the mirrors. Another stood still while a kneeling maid repaired a rip in the hem of her ball gown. There was a long line waiting to use the chamber pots, which were located behind a discreet curtained area.

Laura decided against taking refuge in the room, for it would be too risky to venture into close quarters with so many women. Here in the antechamber, only a few ladies sat fanning themselves and gossiping. Aside from an initial cursory glance, they paid no heed to Laura.

She sat on a gilt chair and bent down as if to examine her shoe. Her gaze slid to the outer door where a slice of the corridor was visible.

How silly to suffer an attack of nerves, she scolded herself. The duchess likely wouldn't recognize Laura even without the glasses and the prim garb. They'd been introduced only briefly long ago, when Her Grace had acknowledged Laura's curtsy with a regal nod before strolling away. There had never been any occasion for them to converse further. The woman was a snob who associated only with the bluest of bluebloods.

Lord Haversham, for one.

How had the marquess managed to steal the priceless

necklace and earrings from Her Grace? According to newspaper reports at the time, the jewels had been taken from her bedchamber. Which meant Haversham had gained access to her private quarters. Was it possible that he and the duchess were more than acquaintances?

Had they been lovers?

Laura found the scandalous notion quite plausible. The marquess was exactly the sort of cad who would think nothing of betraying his mousy, browbeaten wife.

A movement out in the corridor caught her attention. The duchess was walking past the antechamber. Abruptly, the woman stopped so that the back of her opulent gown remained visible in the doorway.

Then Laura realized why. A deep, distinctive male voice drifted into the antechamber. The duchess had paused to chat with . . . *Alex*?

Laura sat paralyzed. She couldn't see him; he must be standing just out of sight. But there was no mistaking that smooth, urbane tone. He must have come in search of her after all. Pretending to check her shoe, she strained to hear the conversation.

"It's been far too long since you've deigned to attend a society event," the duchess was scolding him. "All the young ladies have been distressed by your absence."

"How kind of Your Grace to think me so much admired. Yet they seem to have managed quite nicely without me."

"Bah. You're well heeled, handsome, titled . . . and you've a duty to take a wife. I trust you're here tonight to examine the prospects."

He chuckled, the low sound causing tension in Laura's bosom. Intensely curious, she found herself leaning toward the door to hear his answer. "You should be pleased, then, that I've danced with a number of debutantes," he said. "Beyond that, I shall keep my own counsel."

"Humph. Tight-lipped, are you? As your godmother, I've every right to declare that it's high time you settled down and filled your nursery. Now pray lend me your arm and escort me back to the ballroom. And don't give me that ironic stare. If you've an assignation with some tart upstairs, you shall not keep it. I won't have you frightening away the young virgins with your rakish behavior . . ."

Laura abandoned the phony examination of her foot, sat up straight on the chair, and swiveled toward the corridor—just in time to see Her Grace's skirts disappear from the doorway.

Godmother?

Alex had never mentioned that the Duchess of Knowles was his *godmother*. Why had he withheld such a vital connection?

Ten years ago, he'd courted Laura with singular determination, taking her on outings, for drives in the park, to the museums and the circus and the Tower. A fortnight had passed between the theft of the Blue Moon diamond necklace and the fateful moment when her father had been caught with the matching diamond earrings. Surely in all that time, when the spectacular robbery had been the topic on everyone's lips, Alex should have at least *mentioned* his link to the victim of the crime!

How very peculiar that he had not.

Two hours later, Laura helped Lady Josephine hobble toward the waiting barouchet. A long line of coaches and carriages snaked around the darkened square, their lamps glowing like stars. The lilt of music still drifted from inside the mansion. Now that the buffet supper was over, many of the older guests had begun to depart, leaving the younger set to dance away the night.

Laura had had no opportunity to question Alex, not even the one time when he'd come to check on his aunt. Perhaps it was just as well, she thought. As keenly as she wanted answers from him, there had been too many listening ears in the packed ballroom.

She had last glimpsed him leading Lady Evelyn toward the dance floor. The sight had fortified Laura's decision to depart without informing him. Their conversation could wait until the next time he visited his aunt.

With her assistance, Lady Josephine settled her large bulk in the barouchet as the coachman on his high seat held the pair of horses. The old woman heaved a sigh of weary contentment. "I seem to recall that someone else came with us. Who could it be, do you suppose?"

"No one of consequence, my lady." Laura placed her foot on the iron step and clutched her hem so she wouldn't trip while climbing into the open carriage with its half hood. "It'll be quite cozy with just the two of us—oh!"

A pair of male hands caught her waist from behind. Her heart leaped in recognition as the masculine scent of dark spice invaded the cool night air. "So, Cinderella is fleeing the ball," Alex murmured into her ear, his warm breath stirring the nape of her neck.

Laura steeled herself against a delicious shiver. "Lady Josephine is fatigued and wished to retire."

"Then by all means, let us depart."

His grasp firm, he gave her a boost into the barouchet. Much to her dismay, a flush of attraction suffused every inch of her body. It had to be a remnant of youthful folly when she had been susceptible to his charm—because a man of his fickle nature certainly didn't appeal to her now that she was older and wiser.

Hastily drawing away, she sat down beside Lady Josephine. The interior was tight, and Alex's knees bumped hers as he took the fold-down seat that faced the two women.

Lady Josephine peered through the darkness at him. A smile bloomed on her round face. "Alexander! Oh, I remember now. *You* escorted us here!"

"Yes, although Miss Brown apparently forgot that fact when she called for the carriage."

His lighthearted mockery irked Laura. "You appeared to be enjoying the dancing," she said as the barouchet began its gently rocking ride over the cobblestone street. "I assumed you'd have your pick of ladies willing to take you home."

"How gratifying that you would notice. Were you watching me all evening and wishing *you* were on the dance floor with me?"

"You flatter yourself. I can think of nothing that would interest me less."

Lady Josephine glanced quizzically from one to the other as if she sensed the undercurrents but was too exhausted to decipher their meaning. Smothering a yawn, she said, "Did you not dance at all, Laura? I'm sure Alexander would have been happy to squire you."

"Indeed so," he agreed. "The ballroom would have been abuzz with speculation over the identity of the mysterious creature in my arms. If we'd played matters right and piqued everyone's interest, we could have made dowdiness all the rage. By next week, I vow all the young ladies would be in spectacles and prudish gowns!"

The picture he painted was so ridiculous that the knot of resentment inside her loosened. "How absurd," Laura said, subduing the tickle of a smile by glancing out at the passing scene of darkened row houses. "Not even *you* could accomplish such a feat."

"Mind what you say. I've been known to accept a dare on far less provocation than that."

"No doubt you have. Idle wagers are the province of jaded gentlemen with too much time on their hands."

"I do find challenges irresistible—especially when they involve a beautiful woman." He leaned forward, his smile glinting through the darkness. "I recall once, a long time ago, a young lady offered me a kiss if only I'd stand up on the back of a horse and ride around the stable yard like a circus performer."

Despite the nip of the evening air, Laura felt a sting of warmth in her cheeks. His voice had a caressing intimacy that she feared would betray their past relationship to his aunt. But when she looked over, Lady Josephine's chin had fallen to her massive bosom and her eyes were closed. Lulled by the swaying of the vehicle and the lateness of the hour, the old woman had dozed off.

Laura's gaze returned to Alex. So he hadn't forgotten that incident. At the time, she'd never expected him to actually remove his shoes, leap onto an unsaddled horse, and rise to a standing position. Nor had she been prepared when a dog had run out to startle the horse.

Conscious now of the coachman sitting on his high perch just behind the earl, she used an oblique jab. "Did you tumble to the ground, my lord? That would have been your just deserts."

"Oh, I had my dessert, all right. When I collected the kiss that was owed to me."

Laura vividly recalled that kiss—her first kiss. She remembered how she'd rushed to him, fearing he was hurt, how he had pulled her down on top of him and held her to the hard muscles of his body. And she remembered how his lips had grazed hers, softly at first and then with increasing fervor . . .

An echo of desire ached in her innermost depths. She willed it away at once. Alex had always been a master at turning every phrase, every comment into an enticing innuendo. Such banter may have fooled her as a naive girl, but no longer. Now she knew it was merely a mask designed to hide his unprincipled character.

"I can only imagine all your exploits," Laura said coolly. "They must number in the hundreds. But I suppose a titled gentleman can get away with virtually anything. Especially when he counts the Duchess of Knowles as his godmother."

She knew her jab had hit home because he offered no quick rejoinder. The clopping of the horses' hooves and the jingling of the harness filled the night air. With his back to the headlamps, his face lay in shadow. But Laura sensed the force of his stare boring into her.

He rose abruptly from his seat and thrust himself in between her and the wall of the carriage. He attempted to sit down, though there was no room for him.

Laura put her hands to his chest to stop him. It was as effective as pushing against a brick wall. Her heart fluttered with alarm and something else, something she didn't care to examine.

"Stop!" she hissed. "Go away—"

He pressed his finger to her lips and nodded toward the stout coachman whose back was to them. Although the man was preoccupied with guiding the horses down the gloomy streets of Mayfair, he might overhear snatches of their conversation in the open carriage if they weren't careful.

"Slide over," Alex said, his voice a mere breath of sound. "Please, Laura. It's the only way for us to talk freely."

Her choice was either to obey him or to raise a fuss that could prove embarrassing. After a moment's indecision, she shifted herself as close as possible to Lady Josephine, who snored softly in slumber.

Laura envied that oblivion. Yet she did have a few choice words she wanted to say to him. Perhaps now was as good a time as any.

Alex angled himself sideways to fit into the cramped space while resting one arm along the back of the seat. Laura could scarcely catch her breath with him so close. His nearness made the carriage seem even smaller, and their proximity felt scandalously like an embrace. To make matters worse, the jolting motion of the vehicle caused them to keep bumping against each other no matter how far she tried to pull back.

Bending his head, he murmured in her ear, "You were eavesdropping in the ladies' retiring room."

She bristled at the accusation in his tone—as if *she* were the one at fault. "Yes," she whispered, tilting up her chin to look at him through the clear spectacles. "You can imagine my surprise at finding out the connection. You never told me of it. I deserve to know why."

"I didn't deem it important."

"*Not important?*" Laura struggled to keep her voice low. "Your *godmother* was the victim of a famous robbery. People talked about the crime for *weeks*."

He glanced away for a moment before returning

his gaze to her. "My relationship to her was common knowledge. Perhaps it never occurred to me that you were unaware of it."

"*Perhaps?*" She pounced on the word. It gave her the distinct impression that he was being evasive. At least now she understood why he'd recognized the earrings that had been planted in her father's desk. He'd seen his godmother wearing them. "Pray forgive me for being skeptical, my lord. There has to be another reason why you never mentioned it. Maybe I was right to suggest that *you* set up my father."

He gave a sharp shake of his head. "Nonsense."

"Is it? As her godson, you had access to the duchess's home and to her jewels. If you'd had Papa arrested, I'd have been ruined by association and left without protection. Then you could have taken advantage of me."

She didn't really believe that theory—she was too certain the thief had been Lord Haversham in collusion with his daughter, Lady Evelyn. Yet Laura sensed there was something Alex wasn't telling her. Some key piece of the puzzle that she was missing. And she hoped to goad him into revealing it.

The glow of a streetlamp cast the angles of his face into sharp relief. The scar slanting down one cheek gave him an aura of danger as he brought his face closer to hers. "You desire the truth, then?"

His warm breath tickled her cheek. The length of his leg lay against hers, and the hard wall of his chest pressed into her arm. The contact made it difficult for her to stay focused on the conversation. "Yes, tell me."

"As you wish." His fingertip followed the curve of her lower lip, igniting sparks of pleasure in its wake. In a husky murmur, he said, "Everyone else may have been talking about the robbery. But all *I* could think about was you, Laura. Only you. Nothing else mattered to me."

On that wildly romantic declaration, his mouth sought hers. Laura was too stunned to form a coherent thought. He cupped her neck with one hand, his thumb caressing her jaw as he attempted to coax her reluctant mouth into surrender. A beguiling desire lapped at her resistance and her lips softened ever so slightly. Sweet heaven, she had forgotten how tempting Alex could be, how very much she'd always craved his kisses . . .

No. He was a deceitful scoundrel. He had destroyed her father's life—and hers.

Averting her face, Laura thrust her hands against his chest. "Stop!" she hissed. "Don't try to cozen me. I'm no longer a naive girl straight out of the schoolroom."

"Quite so." His thumb stroked a mesmerizing pattern on the side of her neck. "You're a woman now—a very beautiful woman."

Her heart quivered. How, in the face of all she knew about him, could she still be susceptible to his flattery?

She gave voice to her grievances against him. "You said that *I* was all that mattered to you back then. Yet you didn't listen when I begged you not to take my father away. You didn't care if you hurt me. And you refused to trust me when I vouched for Papa's character."

Alex's fingers stilled on her shoulder. In the faint light, he appeared troubled, his lips thinned. "My purpose was never to hurt you, Laura. If you believe nothing else, believe that."

The strangest thing was, she *did* believe him—to a

degree. He hadn't set out purposefully to ruin her life. She had been nothing more than an idle flirtation to him. And the game had ended abruptly when he'd found those stolen earrings in her father's desk.

The carriage jolted over a bump. The vehicle had turned a corner, and the coachman was steering the horses toward the curbstone in front of Lady Josephine's town house.

The sight acted as a dash of ice water. Laura pushed Alex away, but he needed no prodding. In a blink he'd slipped across the barouchet to resume his own seat as she scooted back over to her side.

Just in time, for Lady Josephine awakened, blinking and yawning. "Where are we?" she asked in befuddlement.

"You're home again," Alex said smoothly as if he hadn't been locked in a scandalous embrace only a moment ago. "How wise of you to have dozed away such a dreary drive. Not so Miss Brown, who was forced to suffer my vexing company."

Laura frowned through the darkness at him. How confident he was, how secure in his lordly superiority. He didn't care that anyone could have witnessed their intimate tête-à-tête. But she did. The half hood of the carriage had afforded them little privacy. Her only consolation was the lateness of the hour and emptiness of the streets.

Now Alex sat watching her, seeming entirely too pleased with himself. It was clear now, more than ever, that he wanted to seduce her. And Laura wondered if, in that brief moment of weakness when she'd kissed him back, she had foolishly given him cause to believe his mission might succeed.

Chapter 11

"Laura? Laura, can it really be you?"

Laura had been examining a length of sky-blue ribbon near the window of the milliner's shop when the female voice yanked her attention to the door. A young matron had just walked in. Pleasantly plump, the woman had freckled skin and russet hair beneath a straw bonnet. She was also noticeably pregnant. Her gloved hands rested on the gentle swelling beneath the yellow sprigged gown and the leaf-green shawl.

But it was her face that made Laura's breath catch. How well she knew those warm brown eyes and that sweet smile. Violet Angleton!

Her old friend approached with hesitant steps as if doubting her own judgment. Her brows were drawn together in a faint, questioning frown.

Laura stood rooted to the spot. Should she pretend to be a stranger? In the gold-rimmed spectacles, plain black bonnet, and dowdy dark gown, she no longer resembled the fashionable debutante of her youth. It was not yet too late to escape detection. How easy it would be to feign ignorance and slip out the door.

But she couldn't abandon her mistress. At the other end of the shop, Lady Josephine was trying on an ostrich-feathered hat in front of a mirror with the assistance of the stout proprietor. Neither woman had noticed Laura's dilemma.

Thankfully, they were the only other two people present in this small establishment off Bond Street. Had it been a larger, more crowded place, Laura might have drawn the attention of watching eyes and listening ears.

As Violet ventured closer, she said in wonderment, "It *is* you, isn't it? Oh, Laura, don't you recognize me?"

That pleading tone melted Laura's heart. It had been ten years since she'd allowed herself any close friendships. A yearning for companionship overshadowed the risks involved in abandoning the masquerade.

She closed the distance between them and caught hold of Violet's hands. Keeping her voice low, she said, "Of *course* I remember you, Violet. How could I ever forget such a dear friend as you?"

Violet's face lit up with delight. She threw her arms around Laura's neck. "I *knew* it was you when I walked past with Frederick just now. Even with those spectacles, I knew. Oh, where have you been? I've missed you so much! I was terribly worried when you disappeared."

As Laura returned the hug, joy uplifted her spirits. It was like greeting a long-lost sister. Not until this moment had she felt a true sense of homecoming. Seeing Alex again had awakened only distressful memories and tangled emotions, whereas Violet transported her back to the happiest of times.

Then Laura felt a distinct kick against her midsection. Startled, she drew back and glanced down at

Violet's thickened abdomen. "It seems you have quite a lot to tell me, too."

"This is my third," Violet said, proudly caressing her belly. "I've two sons already and I'm hoping for a daughter this time. So is Frederick—did I tell you I'm Mrs. Blankenship now?"

"You married Frederick Blankenship?" The slightly horrified question popped out of Laura before she could stop it.

Violet laughed merrily. "I know we always poked fun at his stodgy manners and dull conversation," she said. "How silly we were back then. I can assure you, he is the very best of husbands. And he does love me dearly, as much as I love him."

Even as Laura smiled with pleasure at her friend's marital bliss, her gaze strayed toward the bay window with its display of feathered and beribboned bonnets. She had an uneasy sense of being exposed in this spot. "Is he waiting outside, then?"

"No, he went into the tailor's next door. That should keep him busy for a while."

"Did you tell him you saw me just now?" Laura murmured. "Did you mention me by name?"

Frowning in puzzlement, Violet shook her head. "I wasn't sure it was really you and besides, he was prattling on about the new cravats he intended to order . . ." She slid her arm through Laura's and lowered her voice to a conspiratorial whisper. "What's the matter? Are you in hiding? Because of what happened?"

Laura nodded. "And I must beg you to be silent on the matter, if you will."

"Oh, most certainly! Goodness, you look so different with those spectacles. I very nearly didn't recognize you. Is it part of your disguise?"

"Yes. Come, and I'll tell you all about it." Laura

pulled her friend over to a display of hat trimmings in the back corner of the shop. "We must pretend to be browsing lest we draw undue attention."

"A wise notion," Violet said, seizing upon a cluster of *papier-mâché* cherries and lifting them up to the natural light of the window. Her gaze cut over to Laura. "Now, I am dying to know everything. Pray tell me where you've been all this time."

Twirling a peacock feather between her fingers, Laura related an abbreviated version of how she and Papa had been living in Portugal, and that she'd moved back to London upon his death. She decided to keep mum about her quest to find out if he'd been murdered. No one must be privy to that secret but herself. "Since my reputation is in tatters, I'm going by the name of Laura Brown. I recently took employment as a companion."

She nodded toward Lady Josephine, who was still absorbed in choosing among an array of hats being presented by the fawning proprietress.

Violet's eyes widened. "But . . . that's Lady Josephine!" she hissed. "Lord Copley's *aunt*."

"Unfortunately so, though I didn't realize it when I accepted the position," Laura murmured. "You'll be relieved to hear that I've already encountered his lordship and he's agreeable to letting me stay on . . . at least for a time."

Would he change his mind when she refused to become his mistress? Remembering their close encounter in the carriage the previous evening, Laura felt a shiver deep inside herself. She was playing a dangerous game. He would be furious to learn that she was at his aunt's house under false pretenses.

A smile spread across Violet's face. "I *knew* he still carried a torch for you. I knew it!"

"Carried a torch? Nothing could be farther from the truth. Why would you even entertain such a mad notion?"

"When you fled England," Violet confided in a whisper, "the earl stopped attending most balls and parties. People said it was due to his scarred face, but *I* always believed that his heart had been broken."

Laura was speechless. She hadn't known that his scorn for society events had begun with her departure. But it was a far leap to assume that he'd been pining for her. More likely, he'd turned to gaming at his club or cavorting with a string of mistresses.

"He doesn't *have* a heart," she stated. "Have you so quickly forgotten that he's the one who forced Papa and I to flee? He tried to tie Papa's hands behind his back. He was intending to take Papa to jail."

"Oh, Laura, that was *such* a tragedy. I could scarcely believe it when I heard the news." Violet dropped the bunch of fake cherries to give Laura's hand a squeeze. "I don't mean to defend the earl at your expense, truly I don't, but . . . what else was he to do when he came upon the stolen earrings? He could hardly have ignored what your father had done."

Laura withdrew her hand. It was difficult enough to know that Papa's name had been slandered by all of society; even more painful to hear it from a friend. Did no one but her believe in his integrity?

She looked Violet square in the eye. "Papa was a fine, upstanding gentleman, not a criminal. How the duchess's property came to be in his desk, I can't imagine. But he had no reason to turn to thievery—no reason at all."

"What about his many debts? He must have been worried about paying them off . . . oh! Did you not know?"

Shocked, Laura slowly shook her head. "I never heard of any debts. He had an inheritance, and income from his investments . . . he wasn't a gambler, nor was he extravagant. We lived quite frugally."

Except for her debut. He'd had to bear the expense of purchasing an entire new wardrobe for her, along with hosting a lavish party to launch her into society. He also would have wanted to provide her with a generous marriage portion in the event of her betrothal.

But even if he'd accrued liabilities, that did *not* mean he'd stolen the Blue Moon diamond. His character had been exemplary, and she would never believe otherwise.

"I don't know all the particulars, so perhaps I'm mistaken," Violet hastened to say. "I *am* certain, however, that about a year after you and your father disappeared, all of his possessions were sold at auction to settle the debts. I wanted to go, to see if I might acquire some memento for you in case you returned someday, but Frederick wouldn't allow it. He said that auctions are no place for a lady, especially since I was expecting our first child and . . . oh, Laura, I should have insisted. Then you wouldn't have lost *everything*."

She looked so woebegone that Laura summoned a bracing smile. "Never mind, they were only things. It's all in the past now. And since Papa is no longer here, I may never know the whole truth."

Violet picked up a length of lace and combed it through her fingers. "If I could, I'd wave a magic wand and restore your reputation. It isn't right that you should be forced into employment."

"I'm no different from any other lady who must earn a living. It's a blessing to have found a position with a kind mistress." Hoping to gain some information,

Laura decided to steer the conversation in a more useful direction. "Besides, I've the opportunity to go about town a bit with Lady Josephine. Last evening, we attended Lord Scarborough's ball. Were you there?"

"No, it would be most indelicate in my present condition . . ." A light entered Violet's eyes, and she tossed aside the lace. "So *that's* why Lord Copley went to the ball. The news was in *The Tattler* this morning along with speculation that he's in the market for a bride. But I'll venture he was there because he knew that *you* would be present."

Laura gave a firm shake of her head. Violet must still be a starry-eyed romantic, the same as she herself had been at one time. "I assure you, the earl utterly ignored me. He spent an inordinate amount of time with Lady Evelyn, though. They made quite the cozy couple."

"She's the dowager Duchess of Cliffington—did you know? And as rich as Croesus, too. Now that she bears the title of Her Grace, she believes she's too high and mighty for the rest of us!"

It didn't surprise Laura to learn that Evelyn had married well. Or that having been widowed, she'd set her sights back on Alex. "Her father, Lord Haversham, was at the ball, too. I spied him with the Duchess of Knowles."

Violet gasped, catching hold of Laura's arm. "Oh, my gracious. Did she see you?"

"No, but I did wonder at the nature of Haversham's friendship with the duchess. They were standing close together, and I thought you might have heard gossip that they're . . . more than mere acquaintances."

But Violet wasn't listening. She had glanced at the bow window, where a youngish man in a top hat and brown coat was trudging past. "Oh, no! There's Frederick now. I must go quickly, else he'll see you and ask awkward questions. Perhaps I can find an excuse to visit soon so that we might talk further. In the meanwhile, pray do give Lord Copley a chance to redeem himself. I always envied you for the way he looked at you. Good-bye!"

Violet offered a quick hug of farewell and scurried out the door. The overhead bell tinkled, and then she was gone.

Walking slowly across the shop to rejoin Lady Josephine, Laura brooded over her friend's parting words. Give Alex a chance to redeem himself? Because of the way he'd once looked at her?

Never.

Yet she acknowledged the seductive pull of memory. Deep down, she *did* crave the pleasure of his touch. The interlude in the barouchet the previous evening had awakened her to that undeniable truth. Nonetheless, it would be wildly imprudent to succumb to the man who had been instrumental in the downfall of both her and her father.

Better she should use Alex for her own purposes.

"Well, now, this is a rare event," Roger Burrell said. A toothy grin on his florid face, he started to rise as Alex stepped into the parlor.

"Pray don't leave your chair," Alex said with a languid wave of his hand. "Far be it from me to disturb a man at his leisure."

"Come and join me, then." Roger plopped back down and propped his booted feet on a side table, ignoring the ottoman only inches away. The action was indicative of the man himself, an untidy bachelor tending toward corpulence, the buttons of his waistcoat straining at his mid-section. A pall of smoke hung in the air from the cigar that dangled from his fingers. It brought to mind the many times he and Alex had puffed on stolen cheroots behind the dormitory at Eton. "Haven't seen you in a month of Sundays," Roger went on. "Care for a smoke?"

He pushed a wooden humidor toward Alex, who selected a cigar and brought it to his nose to inhale the fragrance of fine tobacco.

"I daresay it hasn't been as long as that," he said, bending down to light the tip at the flame of a candle. "We met at Newmarket only a fortnight ago."

Roger loosed a bark of laughter that startled the spaniel lying on a cushion by the fireplace. Her soulful eyes flicked back and forth between her master and the four half-grown pups gamboling on the hearth rug. "So we did, by gad. How could I forget? I lost a bundle on the favorite in that last race—while you raked in a fortune."

"It's your own fault for not realizing that Tempest was slightly off the pace."

"Off the pace, bah, 'twas your blasted Copley luck, that's what. Though I still can't believe you'd risk such a vast wager on a horse named Long Shot."

Alex avoided the maze of puppies as he proceeded to a wing chair and sat down. "Not luck at all," he said coolly, taking a draw and blowing out a smoke ring. "I merely make a habit of observing the horses in the parade ring."

"Don't we all, by Jove? Yet no one else but you thought the damn bay could place, let alone win. You've the Midas touch, that's what."

Alex gave a self-deprecating chuckle as his thoughts flitted to Laura. If only a touch could erase her enmity toward him. Thus far, except for a brief moment in the carriage the other night, he'd been soundly rebuffed.

It would take patience to convince her that he was not the evil brute she believed him to be. Patience—and a plan, which was why he'd come here.

"I've made my share of blunders," he said. "A man can only calculate the odds, act accordingly, and hope for the best."

For a few minutes they discussed the merits of various racehorses, then Roger said in jest, "Speaking of thoroughbreds, Lord Copulate, are you still bedding that French opera singer? What was her name?"

"Bianca, and she was Italian. No, we parted ways some months ago."

"You cast her off? With that hourglass shape! That bosom!"

"That temper," Alex countered, reaching down to scoop up a puppy that was trying to latch its teeth onto the tassel of his boot. He scratched the floppy ears, but instead of growing calmer, the bundle of fur batted at his gold watch fob. "Bianca took umbrage at my refusal to shower her with carriages and jewels. Having perfume jars and dirty crockery lobbed at oneself from upper windows can grow tiresome."

Roger burst out laughing. "The price of pleasure, I suppose."

"You may take her with my blessing, provided she hasn't been deported for bad manners."

"Oh, not I! Too much bother. I prefer 'em tamed to the saddle. In and out with no irksome drama."

Alex set down the puppy and picked up another that was not so feisty. This one melted happily at his petting, so he let it settle into his lap. "Perhaps you should marry a shy little wallflower, then."

"What—me?" The cigar stub in Roger's fingers held a column of ash, which he flicked into an empty glass, narrowly avoiding a stain on the Turkish carpet.

"Enjoying my bachelorhood too much. No nagging wife to make me dress for dinner or drag me off to the shops." He paused to cast a baleful eye at Alex. "What brings this up? I heard you were at Scarborough's ball the other night, eyeing the flock of nymphs. You're not considering the leg shackle yourself, are you?"

Alex allowed a slight, mocking smile. It wouldn't do for anyone to guess just how much his aunt's new companion occupied his mind. For years he had believed himself recovered from losing Laura. But that illusion had ended upon seeing her in his aunt's garden. Now he was determined to have her in his bed no matter what the cost. "Not quite yet. Though I *will* have to wed eventually."

"Damn bother, being a peer," Roger said with a pitying shake of his head. "Well, better you than me, old chap. Now what brings you to my humble abode this night? Some devilish scheme on the brain, eh? I recognize that look on your face."

"Not quite devilish." Stroking the puppy's silken coat, Alex gave his friend a keen stare. "However, I do have a favor to ask of you."

Chapter 12

Laura slid the tufted footstool underneath Lady Josephine's high bed, pleased to see that it fit perfectly, along with several others. As she twitched the gold-and-blue coverlet back in place, Mrs. Samson came bustling into the bedchamber with an armload of linen towels. The housekeeper paused to take in the scene.

On this gloomy day, with rain pattering on the windows, Lady Josephine reclined on a chaise, leafing through a book of nature drawings. The vast bedchamber with its celestial ceiling had an airier appearance now. A wide swath of floral carpet was visible, for Laura had spent the afternoon rearranging and storing several small pieces of furniture.

Mrs. Samson hastened forward. A sour expression pinched her lips. "What mischief is this, Miss Brown?"

"I'm making space for her ladyship to walk freely," Laura said, meeting the woman's snapping dark eyes with a calm stare. "It should be easier for her to maneuver with the cane now."

Mrs. Samson set down the linens on a chair and stooped to look under the bed. "What are all those items doing there? You can't be moving things around willy-nilly." Bypassing Laura, she addressed Lady Josephine. "My lady, do you not wish for the master's footstool to be kept by the hearth where it's always been?"

"Why, certainly. It should be ready for dear Charles when he comes home . . ." Lady Josephine stopped in sad confusion. "But he's gone, isn't he?"

Laura went to kneel beside the chaise, rubbing the back of Lady Josephine's age-spotted hand. Some days were worse than others, and ever since awakening that morning, her ladyship had been in a state of fuzzy bewilderment. For that reason, Laura had instructed the footman to turn away all callers, and she'd canceled plans for her and Lady Josephine to attend a musicale that evening.

"Yes, your husband is indeed gone," Laura affirmed gently. "But I can assure you, he would not wish for you to trip and fall. The footstool can be fetched quickly if ever it's needed."

Lady Josephine gave her a smile. "You're such a sweet girl . . . what did you say your name was, my dear? Norah?"

"Laura, my lady. Now, would you like for me to pour you another cup of tea?"

"That would be most kind."

Mrs. Samson harrumphed, grabbed the stack of linens, and, after giving Laura a glare, vanished into the dressing room for a moment. She was gone out the door again before Laura had finished filling the teacup and placing it on the table beside the chaise.

Laura had decided not to be bothered by the woman's enmity. From gossip below stairs, she had learned that the housekeeper had never married, her title of missus having been conferred in honor of her status in the household hierarchy. Mrs. Samson had ruled the staff here for the past five-and-twenty years, so perhaps she needed time to adjust to having her authority challenged. How lonely it must be to have no family, no one to love.

Then Laura was struck by the similarity to her own situation. For ten years, she and Papa had lived quietly with only minimal contact with other people. They'd dared not make friendships for fear of someone discovering Papa's true identity. Now, at age twenty-eight, she was firmly on the shelf without any prospects.

Would she end up alone and bitter like Mrs. Samson?

Laura refused to let melancholy take root in her. There would be ample time to decide her future once she'd solved the mystery of Papa's death. Her low spirits were merely an effect of the rainy, overcast day. That, and her frustration at being unable to do any sleuthing while her mistress was indisposed.

Lady Josephine had dozed off on the chaise. Laura carefully removed the heavy book from the old woman's lap without disturbing her. Wanting to stay busy, she began sorting through the glut of knickknacks on the shelves and tables, the highboy and the writing desk, even the windowsills. Surely some of the items could be put away without being missed.

Picking up a small statue of a fat cherub, she had a sudden memory of a tiny foot kicking her belly when Violet had hugged her close. How strange and wonderful it must be to carry a baby inside one's body. Would she ever know that experience? Of course, first she would have to acquire a husband . . .

Without warning, her thoughts strayed to Alex. At one time, she had waited with breathless anticipation for his proposal of marriage. He had given her every reason to believe her affection for him was reciprocated. She'd been naive not to see through the veneer of his charm. Nevertheless, she felt a nostalgic ache for that blissful, idyllic time of innocence.

I always envied you for the way he looked at you.

Violet didn't understand that all Alex had ever felt for Laura was a shallow physical attraction. There had been no true love in his heart. His devotion to her had not been strong enough to induce him to listen to her pleas to spare Papa. Nor had it been enough for him to trust in her judgment of her own father.

Alex had shown no mercy. He had treated Papa like a common criminal. He had revealed his true loyalty by siding with his godmother, the Duchess of Knowles, over Laura.

Had he known about Papa's debts? Was Violet even correct about the state of Papa's finances? Or was it just a rumor bandied about by a society determined to condemn him?

A sudden rapping on the door startled her. Afraid that Lady Josephine would be disturbed, Laura set down the cherub statue and made haste to answer the summons. She opened the door, expecting to see the footman with the late-afternoon post on a silver salver.

Instead, her heart took a mad leap.

As if conjured by her thoughts, Alex loomed on the threshold. He looked breathtakingly handsome in a cobalt-blue coat tailored to fit his broad shoulders and a pair of tight fawn breeches. The long scar on his cheek lent him an aura of piratical wickedness that Laura found perversely appealing. Even his scent was tempting, with a hint of deep spice that made her want to tuck her face into the crook of his neck—never mind that she disliked him immensely.

His perfect grooming made her conscious of her

own drab attire: the mousy gray frock, spinster's cap, and round spectacles. She might as well be a peahen beside a dazzling peacock.

What was he doing upstairs without being announced?

"May I come in?" he asked, craning his neck to peer past her. "I'd like to visit my aunt."

Laura held the door partly shut. "Lady Josephine is resting at the moment," she murmured. "The footman ought to have told you that she isn't receiving visitors this afternoon."

He frowned. "Is she ill?"

"She's been somewhat confused today, that's all. Perhaps you should return on the morrow."

"No, that'll be too late. I came to bid her a happy birthday."

"Birthday?"

Alex took advantage of Laura's surprise to nudge open the door. As he brushed past her, she was too stunned to stop him. Today was Lady Josephine's birthday? Laura wished that she'd known, for she would have arranged some special treat for her mistress.

Then she noticed two things in quick succession. Alex was toting a large, lidded basket at his side. Second, peculiar scratching and whining sounds emanated from inside the container.

He leaned over the chaise and gently shook Lady Josephine's shoulder. "Aunt Josie? Do wake up, darling."

The old woman stirred, blinking her bleary eyes at him. "Who . . . ? Oh! You're . . ."

"Alexander." He bent down to kiss her wrinkled cheek. "Your favorite nephew."

Looking confused, she reached up and traced his scar. "My dear boy, what happened to your face?"

His gaze briefly cut over to Laura as he replied, "I was bested in an altercation a long time ago. It doesn't matter anymore." He stepped back, a faint smile crooking one corner of his lips. "Now, it's your birthday and I've brought you a surprise. Would you care to see it?"

Laura stared dubiously at him. What did he mean, the scar didn't matter anymore? The offhand comment left her wary and wondering. Was he trying to convey the message that he didn't resent her for it? That he was willing to let bygones be bygones?

Well, he could keep his magnanimity. She didn't want his pardon for something he'd well deserved.

A smile wreathed Lady Josephine's round face. She wriggled up straight on the chaise. "My birthday? Oh, my. Are you quite certain?"

"Indeed I am. I could never let such an important day pass by without a proper celebration. Allow me to present you with your gift."

He placed the basket on the floor, knelt on one knee, and undid the strip of leather binding that held it closed. Curious, Laura went to stand beside the chaise. She had to admit that it was decent of him to have remembered the occasion.

The binding fell away and Alex removed the lid. Instantly, two tiny paws appeared on the edge of the basket and a small black-and-tan head with long black ears popped out. The spaniel surveyed them all with alert dark eyes and then attempted to climb out of the basket, only to fall back in a heap and try valiantly again.

Charmed in spite of herself, Laura laughed at the sight. "Oh! Do help the poor creature."

Alex reached inside and scooped up the half-grown dog, and it regarded him with adoring eyes, wriggling in an attempt to lick his hands. "Behave yourself now," he admonished the animal. "I won't tolerate any misconduct."

The pup cocked its head as if listening, then calmed down.

He gently deposited the dog in his aunt's lap. "There you are, Aunt Josie. He's already house-trained. I recall when I was growing up, you always kept a lapdog, so I had a hunch you might like him. But if you don't . . ."

"Oh, I do, indeed!" Lady Josephine cried in delight. She gathered up the puppy and cradled it on the shelf of her large bosom. "What a dear, precious little darling you are."

Tail wagging furiously, the dog lapped her ladyship's chin. Then it wriggled into the crook of Lady Josephine's neck for cooing and stroking.

Laura couldn't resist patting that silken little body. She glanced at Alex. "It appears he'll be quite pampered in this household. Where did you find such a pretty pup?"

"An old friend had a spaniel with a litter, and he was good enough to let me have first pick. I chose the most docile of the four." Alex paused, his brown eyes keen on her. "I trust you won't mind the extra work that might be involved."

Laura flushed under his scrutiny. Perhaps it was the fact that he was still kneeling as if in supplication, but he actually seemed concerned for her opinion. "I don't mind in the least. You've made Lady Josephine happy, and for that I must thank you . . . from the bottom of my heart."

"Only the bottom?" he murmured with a faint smile. "Well, that's something, anyway."

Laura flushed, ignoring the fluttery sensation that stirred to life inside her. She turned her attention to the puppy, which clearly had shifted its loyalty from Alex to Lady Josephine. The pair looked to have formed a mutual adoration society.

"I daresay you should choose a name, my lady," she said. "He does have beautiful markings, but Spot is far too common for such a handsome animal. Perhaps something royal . . . like Prince."

"Or godly like Adonis," Alex offered. "What do you think, Aunt Josie? Have you any ideas for a name?"

The old woman gave him a bemused look before returning her attention to the fawning dog. She cuddled it close, kissed its black nose, and then pronounced, "Charles."

Laura and Alex exchanged a startled glance.

"Perhaps Charlie might be better," Laura said tactfully. "Just so you don't mix him up with your husband's name."

"Charlie." Lady Josephine cuddled the puppy close. "Yes, I like that. My sweet baby Charlie."

The little animal wagged his tail in approval.

"Well, that settles the matter," Alex said, rising to his feet. "I've brought a lead if Miss Brown will be agreeable to taking Charlie out for a walk on occasion."

"I'd be happy to do so," she said.

Laura tried not to show just how much the prospect thrilled her. With Mrs. Samson always watching, it had proven nearly impossible to venture out alone. Perhaps now Laura might have the chance to go out and do some sleuthing in the neighborhood.

She noticed Alex gazing at her. His speculative stare made her uneasy, so she headed across the bedchamber to rearrange the artifacts on a shelf. It was silly to imagine that he could peer into her mind. He could have no inkling of her plan to find proof of who had really stolen the Blue Moon diamond.

And to determine if that same villain had murdered her father.

The dull pain of loss assailed her as it did on occasion. She still found it difficult to believe Papa was gone. When this was all over, she would plant lilies on his grave site and scrape together the funds to purchase a suitable headstone. She daren't risk returning there now in case that dreadful constable might be keeping an eye out for her . . .

All of a sudden a prickling at the back of her neck alerted her that Alex was standing at her shoulder. His footsteps on the carpet had been silent. Gripping the ceramic figurine of a shepherdess, she turned to look at him. "Was there something else, Lord Copley?"

"I merely had a question. If you promise not to hurl that at me."

"What?" She put down the statuette. "Don't be absurd."

He rubbed his forefinger along his scar. "You can't blame a man for being careful."

Laura pretended not to notice the teasing glint in his eyes—or the warmth it provoked inside herself. Instead, she wondered if the scar was a nuisance when he shaved. As a little girl, she'd been fascinated by the sight of her father gliding the razor through the lathered soap on his face. But she shouldn't be thinking of Alex stripped to the waist with a towel slung over his bare shoulder. "What did you want to know?"

"Am I correct in presuming you're the one who cleared the floor in here?" he asked.

"Yes. With your permission, I'd like to put some of these smaller objects into storage, too."

"It's my aunt's permission you'll need, not mine."

"Nevertheless, I'm asking *you*." Laura gave him a challenging stare. "I wouldn't wish to be accused of stealing them."

With a wry chuckle, Alex glanced back over his shoulder at Lady Josephine, who was too enamored with the puppy to heed their quiet conversation. "Rest assured, I'll not complain if some of these things go missing. But how will you manage it? Aunt Josie is very attached to all the clutter. Most are gifts from my late uncle."

"She won't miss a few items here and there. If she does, I'll bring that piece back. But if I remove things gradually, she isn't likely to even notice."

His gaze lingered a moment on her lips. "A brilliant strategy, Miss Brown. I should have thought of it myself. You're taking excellent care of my aunt, and for that I'm in your debt."

Strolling away, he moved a chair closer to the chaise and sat down to chat with his aunt. The exchange left a glow of pleasure inside Laura. But she had been the recipient of his easy charm too many times to be fooled by him again. It was important to remember that she had every reason to despise the Earl of Copley.

Thankfully, his visit would be ending soon. Lady Josephine liked to eat dinner unfashionably early, and a scoundrel like him surely had more exciting plans for the evening than tarrying with his dotty old aunt.

Chapter 13

"I hope you don't mind that I've invited myself to dinner," Alex said as he settled Lady Josephine at the head of the long table. "On such an important occasion, it would be a pity for you to dine with only a paid companion for company."

Lady Josephine smiled up at him. "You're always welcome here, my dear boy."

As Laura seated herself at her ladyship's right hand, she felt compelled to respond to his jibe. "It must be quite lowering for an earl to share a table with the hired help. I'd be happy to take a tray in my room if you prefer, my lord."

"Stay right where you are, Miss Brown. We need at least three people to properly call this a party." His dark eyes gleaming in the candlelight, Alex sat down in the opposite chair and turned to his aunt. "Since this is a birthday dinner, don't you think Miss Brown ought to put her spectacles aside? They make her appear far too solemn."

"Oh!" Lady Josephine said, peering at Laura. "Why, I do believe you're right. She has such lovely blue eyes."

"Simply gorgeous," he agreed. "Go on, Miss Brown, take off the eyeglasses."

As one footman poured a burgundy wine and another ladled out bowls of beef consommé, she bristled at Alex's high-handed manipulation of her. But Lady Josephine's jovial features warned Laura not to make a fuss and spoil the celebration. She removed the spectacles and placed them near the saltcellar in the center of the table.

"There," she said. "Is that better?"

But her mistress wasn't listening. A look of dismay crossed the old woman's face, and she glanced around the dining chamber in alarm. "Oh, dear, where is Charles?"

Alex placed his hand over hers, his skin tanned against the pristine white of the table linens. "I'm afraid Uncle Charles isn't with us anymore."

The old woman shook her head. "No, I mean my *little* Charles, my baby."

"Charlie," Laura clarified. "Never fear, he's in the kitchen, gnawing on a bone that Cook found for him."

"And enjoying a very fine dinner of scraps," Alex added. "The way the servants were fawning over him, I suspect he'll grow fat very quickly."

Her fretfulness fading, Lady Josephine chortled. "Fat and jolly just like his new mama." She picked up her soup spoon. "Did I ever tell you about the sweet little pup that Charles and I brought back from our honeymoon? Such a skinny mongrel she was at first, and quite mischievous, too. Why, she stole the breakfast sausage right off my plate on our terrace in Rome. It took quite a bit of coaxing for Charles to convince her to eat out of his hand . . ."

As she rambled on during the soup course, Laura sipped the delicious burgundy and marveled at the clarity of Lady Josephine's memories of the distant past. Her mind seemed perfectly normal whenever she was reminiscing. It was only current events that confused her.

The elderly woman continued to chatter about several other pets she'd owned. Having never been blessed with children, apparently she and her beloved Charles had lavished all their love on a menagerie of dogs. Laura had heard some of the stories already, so surely Alex must have, too, though he never gave any sign of it. He listened attentively and offered a comment every now and then. By asking questions, he encouraged his aunt to do most of the talking.

At least until she brought up an anecdote from his past.

"You loved to play with my dogs, remember? I always thought it a pity that you weren't permitted any pets."

"Not permitted?" Laura said with a surprised glance at Alex.

He shrugged. "I went off to boarding school at age eight. When would I have had time for a dog?"

"But you *did* want one." Her smile faltering, Lady Josephine held her silver fork without touching the poached fish on her plate. She looked at Laura. "My brother-in-law—Alexander's father—despised animals and forbade any in his house. Oh, it was such a dreadful mistake for Blanche to bring that dear little spaniel home—"

"I fear we may be boring Miss Brown with all these stories about people she never knew," Alex broke in. "Perhaps we should allow *her* a chance to speak. She could tell us about her time in Portugal."

The candlelight revealed a trace of tension in his jaw. Curious as to why he seemed anxious to distract

Lady Josephine, Laura said, "I'd much rather hear about *you*, Lord Copley. My lady, do continue with your account. Who is Blanche?"

"Why, my younger sister. She was Alexander's mother, Lady Copley. Such a flighty, whimsical creature my sister was, quite the opposite of her stern husband! She was prone to acting on impulse without a care for the consequences. It was quite shocking the way the two of them would scream at each other! I daresay poor Alexander witnessed far too many quarrels in his time."

Laura looked to him for confirmation, but he merely frowned into his wineglass, his fingers twirling the stem. "Did I hear you mention a spaniel, my lady? Was it a dog like Charlie?"

"Indeed so! You see, Blanche gave a puppy to Alexander for his seventh birthday. When his father found out, there was a fearful row and he . . . he kicked the puppy down the stairs and broke its hind leg." Lady Josephine's eyes grew watery. "Alexander tried to stop him, but his father struck him, too. I found the child cowering on the landing, trying to protect his little dog from my shouting brother-in-law." She sniffled, dabbing at her eyes with a corner of her linen serviette.

The savory fish turned to ash in Laura's mouth, and she had to take a drink of wine in order to swallow. "I'm so sorry," she told Alex. "I never knew about this."

He flashed that ironic smile she'd seen him employ to dampen talk on a topic not to his liking. "It was a long time ago. I scarcely remember the incident."

Was that true? Or did he just prefer not to speak of something that had caused him such pain?

Laura had never realized it before, but he had a

skill for directing the flow of conversation away from himself. Ten years ago, he'd dazzled her with his witty banter. She had been naive enough to believe they were close companions without any secrets between them. But now she could see he'd revealed only the most superficial generalities about his past.

Perhaps that was why his betrayal had come as such a shock. She had never truly *known* him.

Laura told herself to drop the subject. Yet she wanted to hear the rest. It wouldn't come from Alex, so she addressed Lady Josephine. "You said you found your nephew guarding the injured puppy. What happened then?"

"I did what I could to help, of course. Blanche was screaming like a banshee, so I sent Alexander up to the nursery with his governess. Then I took the dog home and nursed him back to health. His name was . . . was . . . oh, dear, I've quite forgotten." Her lower lip wobbling, Lady Josephine looked at Alex in supplication.

"Buttons, if I'm not mistaken." His expression cool, he regarded his aunt. "Pray don't fret anymore. All's well that ends well. Because of you, I was able to visit him here from time to time."

"That was a dreadful thing for you to witness, my lord," Laura said in an attempt to elicit a reaction from him.

"We've all had experiences we'd as soon forget. I'm sure even you have, Miss Brown."

For once, she felt no offense at his mocking jab. Her heart ached for the mistreated boy that he had once been. With two such imprudent parents, he must have had a difficult childhood. Could that be the source of the aloofness she often glimpsed behind his illustrious charm?

It didn't matter, Laura told herself. *He* didn't matter. The moment she proved who had really stolen the Blue Moon diamond, she would be gone from this house. Gone from his life forever.

"There'll be no more gloomy tales tonight," Alex said firmly, motioning to a footman to replenish their wine. He lifted his glass in a salute to Lady Josephine. "I'd like to propose a toast to my favorite aunt. May she enjoy many more birthdays to come."

Lady Josephine perked up at once, all trace of sadness vanishing from her heavily wrinkled face. Alex asked her to name the favorite gifts she'd received from his uncle Charles, and she launched into a litany of her most beloved knickknacks. Laura listened closely so that she wouldn't put anything into storage that was a favorite of her ladyship.

Alex seemed determined to keep the conversation light, making droll remarks designed to elicit laughter from his aunt. Initially, Laura had hoped to slip in a few casual questions about certain members of society, but now she thought better of it. It wouldn't do to take the risk of upsetting Lady Josephine again on her birthday.

Laura gave herself up to enjoying the company and the superlative feast. For many years she had eaten only plain country fare prepared by her own limited culinary skills. Tonight, Cook had outdone herself, perhaps to impress the earl. There were several more courses, a lamb cutlet with tiny peas and pearl onions, along with thinly sliced golden potatoes, and finally a gooseberry tart piled high with fluffy whipped cream. The wine flowed freely and a footman kept their glasses filled, including a sparkling white to accompany the dessert.

By the end of the meal, Lady Josephine's eyes were

drooping. She required both her cane and her nephew's assistance in order to hobble to the arched doorway. There she paused, clinging to Alex's arm. "I must fetch my baby from the kitchen," she said plaintively. "He shouldn't be all alone tonight without his mama."

"John will bring him to you," he said with a nod to one of the footmen, who set off at a trot down the corridor that led to the cellar workrooms. Then Alex escorted his aunt to the staircase.

Following them, Laura gripped the mahogany banister with one hand and her skirt with the other. Her head swam a little from the uncustomary amount of wine, and she had to concentrate to keep from tripping on the hem of her gown. It was difficult, for her gaze kept straying to Alex just a few steps ahead of her.

How she longed to comb her fingers through the dark brown hair that curled slightly over the back of his collar. She remembered the feel of it, thick and silken, just as she remembered the solidity of his body held against hers. She furtively admired the breadth of his shoulders, and the play of muscles beneath his formfitting trousers. Whatever his character faults— and she couldn't quite recall them in her woozy state—his physique was sheer perfection. Her fingers itched for a sketchpad and pencil to capture all that masculine splendor on paper.

It would be even more inspiring to draw him naked.

The scandalous notion weakened her knees so that she nearly stumbled on the top step. Grabbing hold of the newel post, Laura scolded herself. How shocking that her mind would stray to such an indecent reflection about a man whose very nature she abhorred.

Yet did she truly abhor him? No, not completely. He had been very kind and generous to his aunt today.

With Lady Josephine leaning on his arm, Alex led the way down the lamp-lit corridor. He kept his pace slow to accommodate the old woman's unsteady gait. Laura felt certain that he loved his aunt—and yes, that was something in his favor.

Within moments of their arrival at her bedchamber, the footman arrived carrying the spaniel, followed by a maid to help her ladyship prepare for bed. A joyous reunion ensued between mistress and puppy, and it was hard to tell which of the two was more ecstatic. Then Alex kissed his aunt's cheek, promising to stop by again soon to check on the dog.

He afforded Laura only a nod and a brief stare before striding out of the bedchamber.

While Lady Josephine carried the puppy into the dressing room, Laura frowned at the open door where Alex had vanished. Was he heading off for a night of carousing? The evening was still young. The several discordantly ticking clocks showed the time to be barely half past nine.

She felt unaccountably deflated. It felt too early to retire for the night. The balls and parties would be just now beginning. She'd half expected Alex to seize this opportunity to bewitch her as he had in the carriage a few nights ago.

If truth be told, she'd *wanted* him to do so. Not for the purposes of romance, of course, but because questions swirled in her head, questions that needed answering.

Well! Let him go, then. She wouldn't give him the satisfaction of chasing after him like a desperate debutante.

Laura snatched up a folded blanket from the chest at the foot of the bed. As she leaned down to prepare a place for the dog to sleep inside the carrier basket, she automatically lifted a hand to her face, for her spectacles often slipped down her nose whenever she bent over.

But they weren't there. Oh, drat. She had forgotten them on the dining table.

Then it occurred to her that she now had the perfect excuse to go back downstairs. If she happened to encounter Alex on his way out, so much the better.

Without further ado, Laura darted out into the corridor and quickly descended the stairs. She could hear voices somewhere far below—or perhaps it was just the pulse beat in her ears. The dining chamber was located on the first floor with the reception rooms. The candles in the wall sconces already had been blown out by the servants, leaving the central hall cloaked in eerie shadows.

Since the spectacles weren't her primary purpose, she didn't turn toward the dining chamber. A soft yellow glow emanated from inside, along with the clink of cutlery and china. The two footmen must be clearing the table; theirs would be the voices she'd heard.

Laura flew to the balcony overlooking the front entrance. Her fingers curling around the carved mahogany rail, she peered down into the gloomy darkness of the lower hall.

Her eyes widened on a murky figure standing directly beneath her. Even as the name *Alex* formed on her tongue, she blinked in unhappy comprehension. It was only the suit of armor on display.

Her heart sank. He was gone. She'd missed him, after all.

How foolish to feel so disappointed. She had wanted to talk to him in private. Not to invite his kisses, though. No. She'd wanted to milk him for information. To solve the wretched mystery of her father's death.

With a sigh, Laura resigned herself to going back upstairs for a solitary evening of reading by candle-light. Her interrogation of him would have to wait for another time. She turned around—then stopped dead in her tracks.

The tall black shape of a man loomed directly behind her. She gasped. In the next instant, the shadowy features of his face registered on her beleaguered brain. "Alex!"

Chapter 14

Laura looked adorably flustered in the pale light that spilled from the dining room. One hand had flown to her bosom in a classic pose of surprise. Her wide eyes shone like pieces of the evening sky.

Alex wondered if she even realized that she'd spoken his first name. Ten years had passed since he'd last heard those beautiful lips utter it. Ten years of wondering where she had gone. Though he had managed to put her out of his mind, there had been occasions when something had sparked a memory. A glimpse of tawny-gold hair. A lady's merry laugh. A drab servant in his aunt's garden.

That last time hadn't been a figment of his imagination. Fate—with the help of Lady Milford—had given him a second chance. Now he had only to find a way to keep Laura.

In a deliberately seductive undertone, he said, "Looking for me?"

"No! I . . . merely forgot my spectacles. On the table."

"But you didn't go into the dining chamber. You

went straight to the railing and looked down into the entrance hall."

She elevated her chin. "I thought I heard someone talking as I came downstairs. I wondered who it was."

"I see."

But he didn't see. Had she come in search of him or not? Alex wanted to think she had. Hell, he wanted to believe that she intended to lure him into one of these darkened rooms, strip off that prim high-necked gown, and invite him to have his way with her.

He'd have better luck wagering that the Blue Moon diamond would drop from the sky.

Laura Falkner was like a skittish mare, and it would take patience and persuasion to tame her. His attempt to kiss her in the carriage had met with only fleeting success. Then she had rebuffed him in no uncertain terms.

You didn't listen when I begged you not to take my father away. You didn't care if you hurt me. And you refused to trust me when I vouched for Papa's character.

She'd had a decade to nurse those grievances. He wouldn't overcome them in one night. He would wear her down by inches, slowly reignite her passion until it burned away her resistance.

"There's something we should—" he began.

"I've a matter to discuss—" she said.

They both stopped abruptly to stare at each other. He waved his hand in concession. "Ladies first."

She parted her lips, then pinched them closed as if reconsidering her words. Adopting a formal tone, she said, "Since you're still here, my lord, I'd like to speak with you on a private matter. If you aren't in a rush to depart, that is."

"Not at all. I'll fetch a candle. We can talk in the drawing room."

A genuine grin sprang to his lips as he made haste into the dining chamber. One footman still lingered there, removing the linens from the long table. "You may go now," Alex told him. "I'll extinguish the candles and let myself out."

The white-wigged servant bowed. "Yes, my lord."

Alex seized the heavy silver candelabrum with its three guttering tapers. A droplet of hot wax fell onto the back of his hand but he paid no heed. He half feared Laura would be gone when he came back out. But she was still in the staircase hall, her arms crossed beneath her bosom, walking back and forth as if lost in thought.

He noted a slight wobble to her steps as she turned around. She had drunk quite a lot of wine tonight. If she was a trifle tipsy, then so much the better. He had no qualms about exploiting such a breach in her defenses. It would take every ounce of his persuasive powers to overcome her scruples against him.

Alex led the way into the darkened drawing room, wending a path through the maze of furniture. Whatever weighed on her mind must be important, because she seemed to have forgotten about the spectacles. They were tucked in an inside pocket of his coat, where they'd stay for the moment. When he'd noticed upstairs that she was missing the eyeglasses, he'd come down to fetch them as an excuse to win her favor.

Circumstances had worked out even better than he'd hoped. There was nothing like an intimate tête-à-tête to appeal to a woman's heart.

With that purpose in mind, he proceeded to a corner where they wouldn't be readily visible from the open doorway. Moving aside several figurines, he made room for the candelabrum on a piecrust table. Then he caught Laura's arm and guided her to a diminutive, gold-striped chaise with just enough room for two. "Shall we sit?"

She took a step toward it, gave him a sharp glance, and seated herself in the gilt chair positioned perpendicular to the chaise. He almost smiled. She was no fool, his Laura.

A sense of possessiveness firmed his resolve. Yes, she *was* his, though she did not yet accept that. They belonged to each other. And this time, he had no intention of letting her go.

He settled back on the chaise to watch her. In the golden glow of the candles, she sat with her spine erect and her hands folded in her lap. How prim she looked in the lace cap and high-necked gray gown. No longer the carefree debutante she had once been, Laura had locked her passionate spirit behind a spinsterish facade. But he knew it was there, just waiting to be freed.

She regarded him coolly. "You must be curious as to why I asked you for an audience."

"If I've committed some offense today, pray forgive me. It was not intentional."

"Offense?" A frown flitted across her smooth brow. "No, you were most kind. You made Lady Josephine very happy."

"That was my intention." *And to please you, too.*

"Well, the puppy did make her birthday very special. I'm only sorry I didn't give her a gift myself."

"Praise God you did not. My aunt already has enough trinkets to fill every house in Mayfair."

Laura laughed, and he basked in the sound. Maybe this wouldn't be so difficult, after all. But her amusement lasted only the briefest of moments. Then she lowered her lashes slightly, her eyes taking on a secretive aspect.

"Well," she said in a detached tone, "it's late and I don't wish to keep you too long, my lord. I hope you'll be good enough to provide me with some information. I recently heard a rumor that my father left considerable debts. Is that true?"

The blunt question caught him off guard. "Who told you that? I doubt my aunt knew anything of it."

"My source doesn't matter. Just do me the honor of providing an honest answer."

Alex ran his fingers through his hair. The firm expression on her delicate features demanded candor on a topic guaranteed to doom any hope of romance this evening. Blast Martin Falkner for never informing her of the dire state of his finances. "All right, then, yes. If you must know, he did have debts."

"How much?"

"Several thousand pounds."

Those expressive blue eyes widened. "Did you know this when you found the stolen earrings in his desk?"

"I'd heard something about it, though I wasn't aware of the precise amount until later."

The Duchess of Knowles had told him that, along with additional information that Laura would never learn if Alex had any say in the matter. Those other damning facts had been relayed to him in confidence. He could speak of the debts, but not the rest; he was honor-bound to obey the vow of silence he'd made to his godmother.

"There was an auction," Laura said, her gaze intent on him. "All of our belongings were sold, Papa's library of books, the sterling silver, the carriage and horses, the furniture"—her voice caught—"and even my mother's jewelry, I'm sure."

Alex didn't like to see the hint of distress in her expression. Once, long ago, Laura had spoken wistfully of the mother she'd never known. "I'm afraid everything was sold," he confirmed.

"Then surely there was more than enough to pay off the debts?"

"Correct. You've no worries in that respect."

She released a shaky sigh and briefly closed her eyes. Then she studied him again. "Were there any funds left over that I could claim—somehow?"

Wishing he could evade the question, Alex glanced away at the shadowy room with its black lumps of furniture. He would sooner cut out his tongue than cause her more pain. But better she hear the news from him than some malicious scandalmonger.

He leaned forward, wishing he dared to take her into his arms to soften the blow. Gentling his tone, he said, "Laura, you should know that your father was tried and convicted in absentia by a judge and jury. Any remaining proceeds from the auction were given to the Duchess of Knowles in compensation for her loss of the Blue Moon diamond."

Her knuckles turning white, Laura gripped the arms of her chair. "What? As if that rich old biddy needs a ha'penny of Papa's money! Just how much is that wretched diamond worth, anyway?"

"It was assessed at thirty thousand pounds."

"Thirty thousand!" Laura gave a bitter, disbelieving laugh. "I can only imagine if Her Grace knew I was back here in London, she'd have me tossed into debtors' prison until I paid off the rest!"

Alex covered her slim hand with his. Her fingers trembled slightly—or perhaps they merely convulsed around the chair arm. "No one will demand anything of you, Laura. I promise you that. You cannot be held responsible for your father's crime."

The very moment he uttered the words, Alex knew it was the wrong thing to say. He should have been more circumspect. She had a daughter's steadfast belief in her father's impeccable character.

Unlike Alex, she hadn't grown up with the constant reminder that one's parents could be flawed beyond redemption.

She flung away his hand and surged to her feet, pacing to the perimeter of the candlelight and then whirling back to confront him. "My father is innocent. But I don't suppose that matters to those who are determined to condemn him."

Alex stood up, too, prompted as much by gentlemanly manners as the need to assuage her anger. And to convince her to face the truth.

Stepping closer, he placed his hands on her shoulders and used his thumbs to tip up her chin. "You knew him far better than I," he conceded. "Yet the threat of ruin can tempt a man to do acts that go against his moral fiber. And you can't deny that the earrings *were* in his desk."

She gazed at him with haunted eyes. "But *not* the diamond necklace. The police surely must have looked for it before our house was sold. They never found it."

Unbeknownst to her, Alex had searched alongside the police. He had spent the better part of a week going over the town house with a fine-tooth comb, looking for a secret hiding place. He had knocked on every inch of paneling, checked every stone and floorboard for any sign of looseness. He had scoured each room from the attics down to the cellar. Then he had covered the grounds, as well, the gardens and the stable. He had been desperate to find the Blue Moon diamond so that he could prove beyond a shadow of a doubt that he had not been wrong in his accusation. That he had not ruined Laura's life on a false assumption.

"You're right," he said heavily, "the diamond wasn't found. Not in the house nor in any bank deposit vault in London. It was presumed that your father had taken it with him."

Laura twisted away from him. "Well, he didn't. And now the trail is cold because no one bothered to check out other possibilities. It's too late to trace the person who put those earrings in Papa's desk."

"Is it, Laura? Or do you intend to find the perpetrator yourself?"

The slight widening of her eyes proved his surmise to be correct. "I can't imagine what you mean."

"I believe you can." Alex deemed it time he confronted her on the issue of her sleuthing. "You took this position with my aunt so that you could go into society and investigate on your own. I only wonder why you didn't come back to London sooner. Perhaps your father forbade you to do so."

She crossed her arms. "You can't prove anything of the sort."

Frustrated, Alex pushed back his coat and placed his hands on his hips. He wanted to strangle her—or kiss her until she forgot all about her foolish plan. "You're playing a dangerous game," he warned. "You can't be poking into the lives of the nobility, making accusations of prominent members of the ton. You'll lose your post here, and then where will you be?"

"So you would dismiss me from Lady Josephine's service. Why does that not surprise me?"

He scowled. "Don't twist my meaning. I won't let my aunt be dragged into a scandal."

"There is no scandal—nor will there be."

"You can't be certain of that. Now, who is it that you suspect of this deed?"

When she stubbornly pressed her lips shut, a plan sprang full-blown into his mind. A plan that would allow him to shield her—and his aunt—from harm. A plan so brilliant, he wondered that he hadn't thought of it before.

He went directly to Laura, gripping her hand with both of his so that she couldn't retreat from him again. "I can help you. I have all the connections that you lack. In your present station, you can't call on people or ask them questions. But I can. I'll find out whatever it is you wish to know."

"You? That's like asking the fox to guard the henhouse."

"At least you're no longer denying your real purpose here."

A flush of high color sprang into her cheeks. For a moment she looked charmingly befuddled. Then she tossed up her chin in defiance. "All right, so why would I trust *you* to help me? You, who tried to arrest my father. You, who told me little to nothing about your past."

"*My* past? What the devil does that have to do with anything?"

She gave him a sly look from beneath her lashes. "For one, you never told me the Duchess of Knowles was your godmother. She must have a close connection to your family. Tell me, is she a blood relation?"

"No. She was a friend of my father's. They grew up in the same household."

Laura raised a quizzical eyebrow. "But you just said they weren't related."

"She'd been orphaned and my grandfather was her

appointed guardian." Alex had no intention of discussing the duchess any further. It was too risky a topic if Laura were to probe deeply. "But all that is immaterial. What matters is the name of whomever it is you suspect."

Laura eyed him warily. Then she gave a shake of her head that stirred a few wisps of golden hair around her face. "I daren't say. You might warn that person— or persons. The nobility protects its own."

"Nonsense. If someone other than your father stole the Blue Moon diamond, I'd suffer no qualms over tracking down the villain, no matter how high his rank." He drew her hand to his lips and pressed his lips to the smooth back. The faint scent of flowers stirred his blood like an aphrodisiac. "I promise you that, Laura. I don't know how much clearer I can be."

Alex meant every word, although he remained certain the culprit was Martin Falkner. But maybe she needed to go through this exercise to set her mind at ease on the matter. Maybe convincing her that she was chasing a ghost was the only way she could ever trust him again.

Laura drew a deep breath that lifted her bosom. Releasing a sigh, she gazed warily at him, their hands still joined. Those expressive blue eyes were a window to her soul, though he couldn't read her thoughts as readily as he once could. She had an intriguing sense of mystery about her now. He burned to uncover all her secrets, from the taste of her lush mouth to the feminine curves beneath the concealment of her gown.

With any other woman, he would have already asserted his desires. Yet with Laura he felt as hesitant as a callow youth. One precipitous move and he might wreck this fragile peace between them . . .

Quite shockingly, she lifted up on tiptoe, placed her hands on his shoulders, and held her face close to his. Her nearness affected him in a visceral rush of lust. Her parted lips hovered half an inch from his mouth, so close he could feel the warmth of her breath. She murmured, "I shouldn't trust you, Alex . . . truly I shouldn't."

"Truly, you *should*."

He needed no further enticement to join their mouths in a deep kiss. A tidal wave of desire inundated him. At last he had Laura in his arms again, exactly where she belonged. Hot blood pumped through his veins and pooled in his loins. No other woman had ever become an obsession to him as she was. He thought of her constantly, day and night. Yet he was conscious now of the need to woo her.

As fiercely as he wanted to explore the uncharted territory of her body, he would not—could not—debase her with the full force of his passion. With great effort, he focused on pleasing her with his hands and mouth. He cupped her face, letting his fingers thread into her hair as he used the kiss to cajole and caress. Whenever Laura thought about him in the days to come, he wanted her to ache with longing. He wanted her to pine for his touch. Then perhaps she finally would regard him again with the same loving adoration she had once lavished upon him.

She ended the kiss, though her eyes were slumberous and her body soft against his. "This doesn't mean anything, you know."

In the grip of a fever, Alex was charmed by her need to dupe herself. He ran his fingertip over her moist lips. "It's merely the wine we drank at dinner."

"Yes," she murmured. "The wine."

Laura let him nuzzle her face for a few moments

longer, tilting her head like a kitten indicating where she wished to be petted. Then as abruptly as she'd entered his arms, she retreated a few steps. Despite the faint flush in her cheeks and the redness of her lips, she appeared otherwise composed.

"You will give me a few days to consider," she said.

Alex gawked at her. His passion-soaked brain refused to comprehend her meaning. Had he asked her to—? No, he couldn't have. He would have remembered *that*. "Consider?"

"Whether or not I shall allow you to help me find who stole the diamond. You may call on me in two days' time."

"I'll see you tomorrow," he commanded.

"No. I insist upon having time to think." Her mouth curved in a slight smile as if she found his impatience amusing. Amusing! "Good night, my lord."

Turning, she walked out of the drawing room, leaving him alone in the circle of candlelight. Alone with his unquenched lust. Alone without any certainly about her intentions.

Alex scowled at the darkened doorway. He should be delighted that Laura had initiated that kiss. She had come willingly into his arms at last. Yet she also had ended the kiss on her own terms. And he had the irksome suspicion that somehow, she had gained the better of him.

Chapter 15

On such a fine springtime afternoon, Mayfair teemed with pedestrians out for a stroll in the sunshine. A few fleecy clouds grazed in the blue meadow of the sky. During the night, a rainstorm had blown away the stench of coal smoke and left in its wake the scent of blooming flowers and fresh greenery.

His long ears flapping, Charlie trotted happily along the foot pavement with Laura. The young spaniel paused now and then to sniff a bush or to lift his leg on a lamppost. He was remarkably well mannered, never barking at other dogs or trying to chase after carriages in the street. At the slightest infraction, he responded obediently to a firm word and a tug on his lead, so Laura felt confident that he would not draw undue attention to her.

She had taken care to dress the part of the paid companion in a drab gray gown devoid of any trimmings. Keeping her chin down in a modest pose, she avoided the gaze of any passersby. Her features, she hoped, were obscured by a combination of the wide-brimmed bonnet and the round spectacles.

Laura had been worried that morning when the eyeglasses were nowhere to be found. She hadn't wanted to venture outside without the disguise. Then a footman had delivered them to her along with a sealed note. The bold black script of the message was burned into her memory.

> *I look forward with great anticipation to our next meeting. May I propose we drink more wine? I remain,*
> *Yours, Alex*

An unseemly elation suffused Laura, making her heart flutter despite the cudgel of common sense. *May I propose we drink more wine?* It was the height of foolishness to dwell on the teasing hint that they indulge their desire for each other. Perhaps it also had been the height of foolishness for her to kiss Alex in the first place.

In the bright light of day, she couldn't escape the truth. The mad attraction to him that she had felt as a debutante had survived disillusionment and ten years' separation. She had been certain of her scorn for him . . . until his kindness to Lady Josephine on her birthday had tempted Laura to look more charitably upon his character.

The disturbing glimpse into his unhappy childhood had further eroded her resentment of him. Try as she might, she couldn't keep from picturing him as a mistreated little boy who had suffered the cruelty of his own father.

Then later, when they had been alone in the drawing room, Alex had been candid in their discussion of the missing necklace. Instead of shielding her as many gentlemen would have done, he had spoken frankly. He had even offered to help Laura in her investigation.

She intended to accept his aid. That was why she had kissed him, to ensure that he truly would dedicate himself to her quest. She had put him off for two days solely as a means to make him cool his heels in the hope of heightening his determination to please her.

His standing in society would give him a greater chance of success, she knew, although there were drawbacks. For one, Alex had seemed reluctant to discuss his godmother, the Duchess of Knowles. He might not be willing to reveal whether she had had an affair with Lord Haversham. For another, Alex still believed Papa to be the true culprit. Worst of all, there was a distinct possibility that the earl was merely humoring her in an effort to make her his mistress.

Pursing her lips, Laura spotted Berkeley Square just ahead with its lush greenery and numerous plane trees. It had been a pleasant stroll from the town house where she'd left Lady Josephine napping on the chaise. Laura paused at the corner to let a carriage rattle past, and Charlie strained at the leash, clearly eager at the prospect of another long route to explore with all its myriad new smells.

They proceeded at a brisk pace across the street. Instead of going to the gardens, where fashionable people promenaded along the paths, Laura headed on a circuit of the residences surrounding the square. She studied the row of elegant buildings, occupied by many of London's finest families. Multiple chimneys topped the tall, four-story homes. Here at the ground level, most of the windows had lace under-curtains that blocked the interior rooms from view. Checking the polished brass numbers over the doors, Laura ascertained that the domicile of interest to her lay at the far end of the broad road.

She passed other people on the street, a postman in his cap and red coat, a governess shooing a little boy and girl toward the park, two elderly gentlemen ambling along in deep conversation. Laura avoided looking directly at any of them. Yet despite the gravity of her purpose, she found an irrepressible smile softening her mouth.

It had to be the fine weather that caused the buoyancy of her mood. The breeze tugged at the brim of her bonnet, birds twittered and swooped in the trees, and the sunshine bathed her in warmth. In Portugal, she had been accustomed to spending much time outdoors in the garden, and she'd missed that. As much as she liked Lady Josephine, it was a relief to escape the confinement of her cluttered house. Most of all, Laura finally could take action in her quest to investigate Lord Haversham and his snooty daughter Evelyn.

Alex didn't know it, but he had provided this opportunity when he had given Charlie to Lady Josephine. Now Laura had a ready excuse to take frequent walks through Mayfair.

Her thoughts lingered on Alex. Perhaps she should admit that their kiss also played a part in her high spirits. It was gratifying to recall how discombobulated he'd looked afterward, and to realize that she could stir such passion in him. For all his cool, urbane air, the almighty Earl of Copley had been deeply affected by their embrace.

But she must *not* allow him to kiss her again. No. It would be dangerous to encourage him. Her present situation was entirely different than it had been ten years ago as a lady of privilege. Now her father had been convicted—albeit unfairly—of thievery. With her reputation ruined, she could only ever be Alex's mistress. A man of his stature would never make an honorable offer to a fallen woman.

Nor did she want one from him. For as long as she lived, Laura would never forget the sight of him tying Papa's hands behind his back with the intention of taking him to the magistrate at Bow Street Station. Had she not struck out at Alex with the penknife, Papa would have been locked in Newgate Prison to await sentencing to death.

Laura took a deep breath to clear her mind of those disturbing memories. Nearing her destination, she needed to observe without distraction. The last house on the corner was the address the footman had provided her. She had never visited Lord Haversham's home because of his feud with Papa.

Unlike the other row houses with their brick facades, this one was built of gray stone. Triangular pilasters topped the tall windows on the first floor where the reception rooms were located. A decorative iron railing ran along the front of the property, with a narrow strip of well-tended red tulips on either side of the short front walk.

Had Papa come here on his return to London? She desperately needed to find out.

A smart yellow phaeton, of the type driven by dashing young gentlemen, was parked along the curbstone with a groom holding the horses. The Marquess of Haversham must be entertaining a caller.

How Laura wished that she dared to walk up the three granite steps to the portico and knock on the brass-trimmed door. She could only imagine his lordship's reaction at recognizing the daughter of his nemesis standing in his entrance hall. Would he turn pale with shock?

Would he wonder if she'd guessed that he'd arranged for Papa's murder?

Tugging lightly on the leash, she slowed Charlie's pace to match her own. She pretended to be admiring the frontage but could see no sign of life inside the forbidding stone residence. Unfortunately, it was too soon to let Lord Haversham learn of her presence in London. First, certain facts must be ascertained.

Her hope had been to catch a maidservant polishing the brass or a footman collecting the post from the box. Then Laura would have reached into her pocket for the sketch she'd drawn of Papa's face. She could have asked if by chance he had visited here some six weeks ago.

Disappointment filled her as she strolled past the entrance and headed for the corner. Perhaps if she returned early in the morning, she might meet with more success. Most servants did their cleaning before the family was awake. If she walked Charlie past here twice a day at varying times, eventually someone would be outside . . .

From behind her came the click of a door opening and the sound of voices, then the trill of ladylike laughter. Laura glanced over her shoulder and spied a liveried footman holding open the front door as a woman emerged from the house. Lady Evelyn!

Or rather, Her Grace, the Duchess of Cliffington. Violet had said that Evelyn was now a rich widow.

Laura quickly veered course to an iron bench by the street and sat down. Charlie cocked his head at her in a puzzled glance. She bent down to scratch his floppy ears. "We're only stopping to rest for a moment, darling. We'll be on our way again soon."

Pretending to be absorbed in petting the dog, Laura

watched the porch from beneath the rim of her bonnet. Evelyn wore an exquisite emerald-green gown with a daffodil sash that nipped her slender waist. A straw bonnet sat cunningly atop her stylish auburn hair and framed her delicate features. With her milky pale skin and fine figure, she looked more like a debutante than a widow of eight-and-twenty.

A gentleman appeared directly behind her in the doorway. He stepped into the sunshine and clapped a tall black hat onto his flaxen hair. In his silver-gray pin-striped coat, burgundy waistcoat, and starched white cravat, he had a dapper air that struck a chord of recognition in Laura.

Mr. Rupert Stanhope-Jones. She remembered seeing him in the crowd at Lord Scarborough's ball. Long ago, he had been among Laura's circle of admirers. In fact, he'd been one of several ardent gentlemen who had proposed marriage to her. But now it appeared he had transferred his affections to the merry widow.

How interesting, for Evelyn had been playing up to Alex, too. Was she merely a flirt, as she'd once been, or did she now take lovers to her bed?

Laura clenched her teeth. She didn't care what Evelyn did—even with Alex. All that mattered was proving Evelyn had aided Lord Haversham by planting the stolen earrings in Papa's desk.

Carrying a decorative gold-topped cane, Mr. Stanhope-Jones offered his arm to Evelyn and escorted her down the steps toward the waiting phaeton. Laura didn't want to be caught staring, so she took Charlie up into her lap and cuddled him while she strained to eavesdrop. Much to her frustration, however, a carriage rattled down the street and she caught only snatches of their conversation.

". . . the perfect day for a drive in the park," Evelyn said. "I wonder if . . ."

". . . your beauty will outshine them all . . ."

A warble of laughter drifted on the breeze. ". . . such a flirt, Rupert . . . I daresay . . . why, look! Have you ever seen such a sweet little darling?"

Laura continued to fuss over the spaniel ensconced in her lap. Delighted with the attention, the pup licked her chin while wagging its tail.

All of a sudden she noticed the tap of approaching footsteps. From the corner of her eye, she spied an emerald-green skirt sweeping toward her across the paving stones. Evelyn.

A horrifying realization struck Laura too late. The *sweet little darling* Evelyn had referenced was none other than Charlie.

A white-wigged footman led the way through the arched doorway, announced the arrival of the Earl of Copley, and then departed on silent feet. Alex stepped into an airy morning room bedecked in subtle shades of rose and yellow. The decor was as elegant and feminine as the woman seated in a gilt chair by the window. Seeing him, she closed her book and placed it on a nearby table.

He went straight to her and bowed over her slim, outstretched hand. "Lady Milford. It's good of you to receive me on such short notice."

"Short notice? Why, shame on you for giving me no notice at all. You may count yourself lucky to find me at home on such a fine afternoon." The scolding was a tease, for her smile warmly welcomed him. "I regret to say, I am engaged in half an hour for a carriage ride in the park with Lord Melbourne."

That she was a confidante of the prime minister spoke well of her sense of discretion. "I shan't keep you long. I merely need a second opinion on a private matter."

"How intriguing. Do pour yourself a brandy and sit down."

He went to the set of crystal decanters on a side table, the contents glowing golden-brown in the sunlight. "I should rather call it more mystifying than intriguing," he said, removing the stopper and pouring a neat measure into a glass. "You're the only person in whom I dare confide."

A vision in lavender silk, she eyed him closely as he seated himself in a nearby chair. "Ah. I would surmise, then, that this visit has to do with Lady Josephine's new companion?"

"Quite. We are the only two in London who know Miss Falkner's true identity."

Alex took a swallow, though with his wits in such a flux, the superlative quality of the liquor was wasted on him. He had lain awake late into the night, staring into the darkness and trying to deduce the workings of Laura's mind. At one time he had known her every thought. She'd worn her emotions on her sleeve for all the world to see.

But Laura no longer regarded him with starry-eyed adoration. She kept him at arm's length—except when it suited her. She had invited his kiss the previous evening, only to end their embrace far too precipitously. More than anything, her poise irked him. She had been too much in control of herself—while he had been mad with passion. Now he resented being ordered to wait two days while she decided whether or not to accept his offer of help.

What the devil was there for her to ponder? She knew that he had the advantage of her in society. Whether she liked it or not, that was reality.

He realized that Lady Milford was politely waiting for him to continue. "I'm in something of a quandary," he said. "Miss Falkner is adamant that her father did not steal the Blue Moon diamond. She believes that someone else in society framed him for the deed. And I fear the little fool is determined to apprehend the culprit herself."

Lady Milford raised a dainty eyebrow. "Indeed? I wondered if she might have a hidden reason for wanting a position. Now, just to clarify, you aren't simply speculating. Did she tell you this herself?"

"Yes. She admitted it to me yesterday evening—after she'd consumed several glasses of wine." When that eyebrow arched higher and a shrewd light came into those violet eyes, he quickly clarified, "It was my aunt's birthday."

"I see. And did Miss Falkner reveal the name of the person she suspects?"

"No. That's the devil of it. She refused to breathe a word." Alex scowled at the liquid in the bottom of his glass before fixing his gaze on Lady Milford again. "I was hoping that with all your knowledge of society, you might help me determine the answer."

A cool contemplation entered her exquisitely beautiful features. Her hair was rich and dark in the sunshine, and not for the first time he wondered just how old Lady Milford was. She had to be of his parents' generation, and yet she seemed ageless.

"First I must ask you a question that has been troubling me," she said. "Is there even the slightest chance that Miss Falkner may be correct about her father's innocence?"

The question struck Alex like a deep blow. He had asked it of himself all those years past. And he had done everything in his power to ascertain the truth. "No," he said curtly. "None whatsoever."

Lady Milford gave a nod. "Well, then. Let me see. I scarcely knew Martin Falkner, though he seemed to be a gentleman of upright character. Like everyone else, I was shocked to learn of his thievery." She paused. "Tell me, has Miss Falkner been making inquiries about anyone in particular?"

"Only my godmother . . . Good God, you don't suppose she's formed some wild notion that Her Grace planted the diamond earrings herself?" Alex paused, wondering if Lady Milford even knew that the Duchess of Knowles had a reason to want to ruin Martin Falkner. "Never mind, that's absurd. There would be no purpose to it."

"Unless Her Grace had noticed your interest in Miss Falkner and wanted to nip it in the bud before an engagement could be announced."

Far from it. The duchess herself had dispatched him to court Laura as a means of secretly investigating her father. But no one knew that—least of all Laura.

Alex shook his head. "The duchess would have had to pretend the Blue Moon had been stolen. It would mean she could never wear it again—and merely to stop an engagement? My godmother is fond of me, but not to that degree!"

Lady Milford gave him an astute stare. "I am only trying to put myself in Miss Falkner's frame of mind. To her, that may be a viable possibility. Do you know if the duchess ever expressed her disapproval of the match directly to Miss Falkner?"

"No. Laura—Miss Falkner—would have told me of it." Anxious to leave the topic of his godmother,

Alex said, "I've been pondering a more likely possibility. Martin Falkner had had an old quarrel with Haversham. Do you know the source of it?"

A pensive look came over her face. "There was a scandal some thirty years ago. They nearly came to blows over a woman, Miss Falkner's mother, Aileen, if I remember correctly." Glancing into the sunlit garden, Lady Milford tapped her chin. "She was a great beauty, connected to Irish nobility. When Mr. Falkner won her heart, Haversham shunned them both. Of course it was all for naught since Aileen died shortly after giving birth to Laura. Such a tragic tale."

A long time ago, Alex recalled, Laura had spoken wistfully of the mother she had never known. "Martin Falkner must have told his daughter about the feud, perhaps many times while she was growing up. She would have acquired his dislike of Haversham."

"And be quick to blame him for planting the earrings." Lady Milford pursed her lips. "I certainly can see where the ancient feud might have led her astray. However . . ."

"Yes?"

"Miss Falkner might be more inclined to suspect Haversham's daughter of planning the hoax. They were, after all, rivals for *your* affections."

"Evelyn?" Alex gave a burst of sardonic laughter. "She can be a cunning creature, but I doubt she was *that* much in love with me to set up so elaborate a scheme."

Lady Milford's lips curved in a slight smile. "You underestimate your appeal to the ladies, Lord Copley."

He shook his head in abject denial. "Laura is a sensible woman. She's bound to see that Evelyn wouldn't have had the opportunity to commit a jewel heist, even if she'd been so inclined. Was she to have crept into the duchess's house in the dark of night like a footpad? How ridiculous!"

"Miss Falkner will surmise that Haversham helped his daughter. And Miss Falkner will be trying to determine if *he* had access to Her Grace's bedchamber."

Alex's amusement vanished in a flash. "I hardly think—"

"I'm aware that very few know of Her Grace's occasional affairs," Lady Milford broke in. "She has been exceptionally discreet. That is why Miss Falkner will land herself in quite a lot of trouble if she pursues this course."

Alex drained the last of his brandy. "Precisely," he said grimly. "Yet short of dogging her every step, how am I to stop her?"

"You must find a way. Society will flay her alive if you fail." Lady Milford gave him a keen look. "And you must ensure that Laura Falkner does not suffer any longer for the sins of her father."

As Evelyn came closer, Laura froze with her hands around Charlie's warm, furry form. Now what? She considered jumping up from the bench and making a mad dash down the street. But running away would only draw undue attention to herself. No servant would behave in so peculiar a fashion.

Better she should brazen it out. Play the timid, paid companion afraid to speak to her betters.

Evelyn stopped in front of her. "Do pardon me, miss," she said in a haughty tone. "I couldn't help noticing your spaniel. He's quite the handsome fellow. How old is he?"

Laura kept her chin tilted down, whispering, "I-I don't know, m'lady."

"Speak up," Evelyn commanded. "It is exceedingly annoying when servants mumble."

Her gaze fixed on Charlie, Laura raised her voice ever so slightly. "I wasn't told his age, m'lady."

"Who is his owner, then? I should like to speak to your employer and find out if there's another in the litter that I might acquire for myself."

Laura sat mutely. Good heavens! She didn't dare give out Lady Josephine's name. The last thing she needed was for Evelyn to call at the house and catch a better look at Laura without the concealment of the wide-brimmed bonnet.

Mr. Stanhope-Jones took his place beside Evelyn. Laura could see the tips of his polished black shoes beneath the perfect crease of his trouser cuffs. His well-manicured fingers leaned on the gold-topped cane. "There, there, Duchess, don't badger the poor girl. It's clear she's frightened to death to speak to someone of the Quality."

"But I want a dog exactly like this one." Evelyn bent down and stretched out a kid-gloved hand to Charlie. Her petulant tone switching to baby-talk, she murmured, "Ooh, look at the precious little puppy. Do you have a brother or sister who needs a mama?"

Charlie, the traitor, wagged his tail and panted for attention.

Laura had to get rid of the woman. Her head bowed as if she were terrified, she said in a quavering tone, "I-I fear he was the last of his litter, m'lady. My-my mistress said there were no more."

"No more!" Evelyn said in a huff as she straightened up. "That won't do. That won't do at all!"

"I might ask Roger Burrell," Mr. Stanhope-Jones said rather languidly. "His spaniel bitch always has pups."

"No!" Evelyn tapped the toe of her little green slipper on the pavement. "They won't be as pretty as this one. Look at that dear little face. Rupert, have you a gold sovereign?"

"Why, whatever for, darling?"

"Just hand it over, if you will."

Mr. Stanhope-Jones reached into his pocket and gave the coin to Evelyn. She promptly waved it in front of Laura. "Here, take this. Tell your mistress the dog has run off. She can get herself another—and you can turn a neat profit."

A chuckle rumbled from Mr. Stanhope-Jones. "Really, Evelyn. Bribing the girl is a bit over the top, don't you think?"

Evelyn ignored him. "Go on, miss, take the coin. You can buy yourself a much prettier bonnet and no one will be the wiser."

Laura had had quite enough of the woman's scheming. What a coldhearted conniver to suggest such a scam!

She set Charlie on the ground. Her chin tucked to her chest, she rose from the bench, her fingers tight around the leash. It took every ounce of her willpower to pretend meekness. "I'm sorry. I-I just couldn't. Pray excuse me . . ."

She set off at a swift pace toward the corner. Charlie trotted alongside her, seeming to have caught her sense of urgency. How she would have loved to give Evelyn a severe dressing-down about stealing someone's pet and tempting a poor servant into thievery. It just went to prove the woman's lack of scruples.

Someone caught her arm and swung her back around before she could duck her head. "You drive a hard bargain, miss—"

Holding two sovereigns in her outstretched hand,

Evelyn stopped in mid-sentence. Her brow furrowed as she stared straight at Laura's face.

Laura wrenched herself free and averted her head. "No, thank you, m'lady. I daren't take your money."

Her heart pounding, she hastened with Charlie around the corner. Had Evelyn recognized her? Surely not. She might puzzle over a fleeting resemblance. But she wasn't likely to connect a drab, bespectacled mouse with the vibrant debutante who had once been her rival for Alex's affections.

Nevertheless, Laura obeyed an impulse to cut through the mews behind the row of town houses rather than stay on the main road. Here trees cast parasols of shade over the brick walls of backyard gardens, and the odor of horses tinged the air. Suddenly the rattle of carriage wheels came from the street behind her. Just in time she pulled Charlie into the alcove of a stable door.

Mr. Stanhope-Jones drove the yellow phaeton at a fast clip past the mews. Beside him, Evelyn sat on the edge of the seat and pointed at something—or someone—ahead of them on the street. Neither of the two spied Laura.

Heaven help her, Laura thought. She would have to take a circuitous way home. Because she couldn't shake the horrible, sinking fear that they were looking for her.

Chapter 16

"Dog hair everywhere," Mrs. Samson grumbled as she swooped into the kitchen, her shoes tapping on the stone floor. "I found a clump on the drawing room rug just now. There'll be trouble aplenty when I find that lazy Fanny!" The housekeeper glowered at Laura, who was collecting a pair of teacups and saucers from the tall oak shelves of the sideboard. "What are *you* doing down here?"

"Lady Josephine decided she wanted blackberry jam with her crumpets, and since the footman had already gone, I—"

"Jam and crumpets! That is far too common." Mrs. Samson gave a sharp shake of her head. "It won't do. It won't do at all. Not for the visitors waiting in the drawing room."

"Visitors?"

"We are greatly honored to serve two of society's most exalted members. Cook, we'll need a plate of watercress sandwiches at once. Betty, fetch the plum cake." The housekeeper clapped her hands, and the stout cook made haste to the larder, followed by a

mob-capped maid who had been peeling carrots at
the long table. "Mind that it's sliced daintily for our
lady guest. It isn't every day that this house entertains
a duchess!"

The saucer slipped from Laura's fingers and clat-
tered to the silver tray. Which duchess? Evelyn?

No, that couldn't be. Lord Haversham's snobbish
daughter would have no reason to call on a doddering
old lady. Even if she'd recognized Laura on the street
the previous day, Evelyn couldn't possibly have traced
her here to this house. Laura had watched carefully
all the way home and had not seen the yellow phaeton
again.

"Have a care!" Mrs. Samson snapped. "That is her
ladyship's finest Staffordshire. If you break anything,
it shall come out of your wages."

"Forgive me," Laura murmured.

She busied herself with collecting the silver tea-
spoons from a drawer. All the while, her thoughts
raced. Today was the day she had told Alex to call,
she realized. *Of course.* It wasn't Evelyn at all. Alex
must have come with his godmother, the Duchess of
Knowles. As a family friend, she would be acquainted
with Lady Josephine.

But that realization didn't alleviate Laura's tension.
Why would Alex bring the duchess here when he
knew she might recognize Laura?

The last time she had seen him, on the night of the
birthday dinner, he had guessed that she was seeking
the culprit who had stolen the Blue Moon diamond.
He'd been skeptical since he firmly believed Papa was
guilty. He had offered to assist her, but she had put
him off with a calculated kiss. She had told him to
wait two days in the hope of honing his desire for her
and, thus, his willingness to help.

But perhaps her plan had gone awry. Perhaps instead of pining, Alex had decided to stop her, once and for all, from dragging the scandal back out into the open. What better way than to expose her ruse to the Duchess of Knowles?

A chill swept over Laura, followed by a flush of anger. She had to thwart him. If she stayed out of sight down here . . .

"Miss Brown!" With a thump, Mrs. Samson set the mahogany tea caddy onto the worktable. "This is no time for woolgathering!"

Laura turned to look at the hatchet-faced woman. "Sorry?"

"You have not been listening to me," the housekeeper said in a disgruntled tone. "You're wanted upstairs at once."

"Upstairs!"

"Yes, upstairs, in the drawing room. Where else should you be but at Lady Josephine's side, lending her your assistance as you're paid to do? Now, hurry along with you and don't dawdle!"

Laura had to bite her lip to keep from snapping back at the officious woman. Everything in her resisted obeying. But she didn't dare give herself away, not until she knew exactly what it was that Alex had planned. Mindful of her place, she headed out the door and up two flights of steep, narrow stairs.

She emerged though the servants' door concealed in the paneling of the passageway. A short distance away, voices emanated from inside the drawing room. There was a man's deep muffled tone, followed by Lady Josephine's delighted laugh. A dog yapped; Charlie must be over-excited by the visitors.

Laura paused to adjust her spectacles. She didn't have to go in. She could run upstairs and conveniently vanish until they were gone. Yet wouldn't that be merely postponing the inevitable? Alex was an earl. He would have his way eventually no matter what her wishes.

Feeling trapped, she smoothed her hands down the dreary gray of her gown. How she yearned to be wearing an exquisite rose silk with her hair arranged in stylish curls instead of being covered by the ugly lace cap. Well, she would cloak herself in pride rather than cower in front of the haughty Duchess of Knowles. As for Alex, he could go to the devil!

Girded for battle, Laura stepped into the drawing room. The crimson draperies had been drawn back to let in the afternoon light. This chamber was as cluttered as the rest of the house, with an abundance of porcelain figurines crowding the tables and shelves. Several groupings of chairs and chaises scattered the room, and in front of the marble fireplace, three people sat in a cozy circle.

Laura faltered to a stop just inside the doorway. A knot twisted her stomach and she blinked, unable to believe her eyes. The visitors weren't Alex and his godmother. It was Evelyn and Mr. Stanhope-Jones, after all.

How had they had found her?

Along with Lady Josephine, they were gazing down at the hearth rug, apparently absorbed in watching some antic of Charlie's. In a panic, Laura decided to withdraw from the room before anyone noticed her.

But she'd retreated only a step when Evelyn looked up, straight at Laura. Beneath the stylish straw bonnet, those topaz eyes had a catlike glitter in her refined face. "Ah, there she is. The mysterious companion we met yesterday in front of my father's house."

Evelyn knew. The glee in her expression confirmed

that she had recognized Laura. Mr. Stanhope-Jones also was watching Laura closely, his manner alert, his blue eyes focused on her.

"Do come and join us, Laura," Lady Josephine called, her wrinkled face wreathed in a smile as she beckoned in excitement. "You'll never guess who's come to call!"

Laura conquered the craven impulse to run. It was no use hiding herself anymore. They had seen through her disguise. Gathering the shreds of her courage, she lifted her chin and walked toward the group. She would have to determine if any part of her plans could be salvaged from this disaster.

Besides, she had a duty to shield Lady Josephine from distress. Better that Laura should be here to answer their questions than allow them to badger the old woman.

With that in mind, Laura played the part of the servant and curtsied to both guests. Then she seated herself beside her mistress on the chaise. "Will you introduce your guests, my lady?"

A blank look crossed Lady Josephine's face. "Oh! Er . . . the duchess, I believe . . ."

Evelyn gave the elderly woman a slightly contemptuous glance before returning her gaze to Laura. "I am the Duchess of Cliffington. This is Mr. Stanhope-Jones. And you would be . . . ?"

"Miss Brown."

"Ah, Miss Brown," Mr. Stanhope-Jones said. He raised a gold-rimmed monocle to one eye and studied her closely. "Miss *Laura* Brown. Not a very common first name. In truth, I've only ever met one other Laura in my life."

Laura kept silent. Were they expecting her to confess to them? She wouldn't do it. Shifting her gaze back to Evelyn, she imagined the woman maliciously placing those earrings in Papa's desk. Evelyn must have celebrated when Laura and her father had been forced to flee England.

Lady Josephine tugged on Laura's arm. "My dear, you haven't even seen! Dear little Charlie has a playmate today."

Only then did Laura realize that not one, but *two* puppies gamboled on the hearth rug, growling and play-fighting. She had been so intent on her own dilemma that their frolicking had utterly escaped her notice.

Despite the dire circumstances, she managed a brief smile for Lady Josephine's sake. "How wonderful. They're both spaniels, I see. And about the same age."

Evelyn scooped up the smaller of the two puppies and cradled it in the lap of her blue brocade gown. "Fancy that. Rupert found little Daisy for me. He knew of a man whose spaniel had a litter."

"Roger Burrell is known for breeding King Charles spaniels," Mr. Stanhope-Jones said. "We paid him a call directly after we saw you on the street, Miss *Brown*."

His slight emphasis on her false name didn't escape Laura's notice. Although his manner was otherwise courteous, his keen stare had not abated. He had once courted her, so perhaps he was merely curious to see the reduction in her circumstances. "I'm pleased you were successful in your quest to acquire a puppy," she said with feigned politeness. "I do hope he cost more than a gold sovereign."

He chuckled. "Cost is no object to Her Grace when she has her mind set on something. And by an amazing coincidence, Burrell said that Lord Copley had been there only a few days ago to acquire a puppy."

"I visited Alex yesterday evening," Evelyn added with an arch smile. "He told me that he'd given the dog to his aunt. Wasn't it good of him to share that news? Now we can let brother and sister play together."

She bent down, giving everyone a view of her fine bosom as she released the wriggly puppy back onto the hearth rug to rejoin Charlie.

It had been far too easy for them to trace her, Laura reflected bitterly. They had come here today to confirm her identity. Oh, why had Alex abetted Evelyn? Had he done so unwittingly?

Laura wanted to believe that it had been inadvertent. Then she scolded herself for being naive. It was far more plausible that in the two days since she'd confessed her plan to him, Alex had decided to stop her from stirring up trouble. Perhaps he had seized upon this opportunity to leak the scandalous news to society about her presence in London. Evelyn was merely his convenient pawn.

Laura had long known that the nobility had a loyalty to its own kind. Her present predicament only served as a reminder that she must never place her trust in the Earl of Copley.

A footman wheeled in the tea tray. Laura caught a glimpse of Mrs. Samson hovering out in the corridor. The housekeeper would be horrified to know that if it weren't for Lady Josephine cooing over the puppies, Laura would have found some way to eject the visitors. Instead, she was forced to pour the tea, since Lady Josephine was too unsteady to perform the role of hostess.

Laura passed steaming cups to Evelyn and to Mr. Stanhope-Jones, who were chatting politely with Lady Josephine about the dogs. She dutifully served plum cake and dainty sandwiches. But as she resumed her seat, Mr. Stanhope-Jones fixed his gaze on her again.

"You must forgive us for our interest in you, Miss Brown," he said, stirring in a lump of sugar with a dainty silver spoon. "It is only that you bear an uncanny resemblance to a young lady we once knew."

"A Miss Falkner," Evelyn said with cunning delight. "Alas, she was caught up in a horrid scandal involving thievery. She and her father vanished into thin air some ten years ago. I've long wondered what could have happened to the poor girl."

The two visitors exchanged a secretive glance.

"Perhaps her father returned to London recently," Laura said, gazing at Evelyn. "Perhaps he hoped to clear his name of these false charges by exposing the true thief."

Evelyn's eyes widened. For just a moment she appeared taken aback, and she set down her cup so swiftly that it rattled in the saucer. "You cannot mean to suggest that . . . he's right here in town. Why, the man is a menace to decent folk!"

Laura tried to determine if Evelyn really didn't know about Papa coming to London——or if she was just a good actress. It was entirely possible she knew nothing of his visit. Lord Haversham may have kept quiet about it in order to protect his daughter.

"I'm not suggesting anything of the sort," Laura said, taking a sip of her tea. "Were we not merely speaking in conjectures?"

"Do not play coy with me! Martin Falkner is a dangerous criminal who belongs behind bars!"

Mr. Stanhope-Jones cleared his throat. "Now, now. I'm sure Miss Brown didn't mean to frighten you, Duchess."

"How do you know that, Rupert?" Evelyn said,

giving Laura a chary look. "I'm of a mind to notify the police posthaste!"

That caught Lady Josephine's perplexed attention. "The police? Why, upon my soul, what's happened?"

Laura placed a soothing hand on her mistress's plump arm. "It's nothing, my lady. Just a lot of silly gossip and speculation. Look, Charlie and Daisy are lying on the rug, quite worn out from all their play. Shall I pour them a saucer of cream?"

"Oh, thank you, my dear! With a bit of tea, as well. All of my dogs have liked a spot of tea."

Evelyn snatched up her puppy as if fearing Laura might poison it. "None for Daisy. I'm afraid this visit must come to an end."

The pair stood up, and Mr. Stanhope-Jones made a courtly bow to Lady Josephine. "It has been a pleasure, dear lady. Perhaps we shall see you—and Miss Brown—at Lord Witherspoon's ball tonight."

He glanced at Laura, who managed a polite smile. He and Evelyn must be looking forward to exposing her true identity. They would lose no time spreading venomous gossip about how the infamous Laura Falkner had entered London society. She could do nothing to stop them.

Nothing at all.

Nor did she dare to hope that Alex might come to her aid. If—*when*—the news traveled through the ton, he would take steps to protect his aunt and his godmother from the scandal.

Laura was entirely on her own.

Chapter 17

The whispers became noticeable as Laura and Lady Josephine slowly made their way through the crowded ballroom. At least it seemed that way to Laura's heightened sensibilities.

This being one of the premier balls of the season, a veritable crush of guests filled the large chamber with its vaulted ceiling and cream-painted walls. In a gallery overlooking the long room, the musicians tuned their instruments in preparation for the dancing. Hundreds of blazing candles in the chandeliers made the air warm and stifling.

Or perhaps, Laura thought, it was her overwrought emotions that made the atmosphere seem oppressive. She imagined every eye trained on her, every murmur directed at her. Nevertheless, she had chosen to come here tonight.

Shortly after Evelyn and Mr. Stanhope-Jones had left Lady Josephine's house that afternoon, Alex had come to call. But Laura had refused to see him. She'd pleaded a headache and remained in her bedchamber. From her window, she'd watched until he had mounted his chestnut gelding and ridden away. Then she had ordered the carriage for half an hour early in case he intended to return to escort his aunt to Lord Witherspoon's ball.

Laura hadn't wanted Alex to forbid her from attending the ball with them. Tonight might be her last opportunity to gather information.

Yet as Lady Josephine hobbled slowly with her cane, Laura half wished it had been possible for him to accompany them on this interminable walk to the corner where the matrons were gathered. The earl wouldn't allow any dishonor to befall his aunt. He would freeze any offenders with his cool, satirical stare.

Laura held her chin high, offering a brief nod or a slight smile now and then as a guest met her eye. Ladies whispered behind their fans. Gentlemen talked among themselves, staring at her longer than was polite. Some turned away in a direct cut. Others spared her not even a glance. Perhaps not everyone had heard yet. It would take time for the tittle-tattle to make the rounds of hundreds of people.

Tonight, she had worn the garnet slippers that Lady Milford had given to her. It might be wishful thinking, but the fine shoes seemed to bolster her courage. With each step, the crystal beads sparkled beneath the hem of the coffee-colored muslin gown. That was the only change Laura had made to her appearance. After giving the matter much thought, she had decided to continue wearing the spectacles and the lace spinster's cap with its long lappets, in order to appear humble and unpretentious. She was, after all, merely a paid companion.

A silver-haired, ruddy-faced gentleman stepped into their path. He was the same man who'd approached

Lady Josephine once before, and the sight of him jolted Laura. Long ago, Lord Oliver had been friends with her father. They'd often played cards together at parties.

"Lady Josephine, you are a vision of loveliness to-night."

The old woman's face broke into a smile beneath the yellow silk turban that complemented her blue silk gown with its yellow ribbons. "Why, how kind of you to say so. Have we met . . . ?"

He gave her hand a courtly kiss. "Lord Oliver, ma'am. I was acquainted with your late husband, Charles. He would have wanted me to ensure that you did not involve yourself in scandal."

Lord Oliver's judgmental gaze cut over to Laura, and she felt a flush rise to her cheeks. Lowering her eyes, she stood rigidly at her ladyship's side. Since it was not her place to intrude on the conversation, she said nothing. But inside she burned from humiliation.

"Scandal?" Lady Josephine said with a jolly laugh. "I fear I'm far too old to be involved in anything more scandalous than falling asleep over my tea."

"I'm pleased to hear it, my lady. If ever you should need assistance, pray do not hesitate to send for me."

As Lady Josephine smiled and strolled on, Lord Oliver startled Laura by catching hold of her forearm to detain her. In a reproachful undertone, he said, "So I wasn't wrong to think I'd recognized you at Scarborough's ball. You're Martin's daughter."

"Yes. You and Papa used to enjoy a game of whist now and then."

"Alas, I was sadly mistaken about his character." Lord Oliver's steel-gray eyes bored into her. "Be forewarned, Miss Falkner, don't think to take advantage of her ladyship's good nature. Henceforth, I'll be watching you."

Laura pulled away and hurried after Lady Josephine. Lord Oliver's icy manner echoed the cold looks she intercepted from others in the crowd. *Henceforth, I'll be watching you.*

That frosty statement sent a shiver down her spine. Never had she felt so alone—or so thankful that her ladyship was oblivious to it all. But oh, how she yearned for anonymity again. It had been far simpler to be ignored as an inferior. Yet she must endure the scowls and jabs if ever she hoped to prove that Papa had been falsely accused.

For that reason, she kept an eye out for Lord Haversham's balding pate and his thin, snobbish features. She didn't see him, though she did spy Evelyn surrounded by a multitude of cronies. No doubt the duchess was gleefully relating her own cleverness in discovering exactly how the notorious Miss Falkner had stolen into their exalted midst.

Laura and Lady Josephine reached the area where the matrons sat in a gaggle in front of a backdrop of lush green ferns. It was clear that Laura was the topic of their gossip tonight. They slid looks at her, fans waving furiously as they whispered among themselves.

A middle-aged lady with sausage curls and a face like a bulldog's left her chair in the center of the group. Mrs. Dorcas Grayling came straight to Lady Josephine. "I've been saving this seat for you, my dear. You'll be quite comfortable here among your friends."

"Thank you . . . but I don't wish to take *your* chair."

"I insist, Josephine. Allow me to help you."

As Mrs. Grayling reached for her ladyship's arm, Laura stepped aside, a blush on her cheeks. Of course, these woman would close ranks around Lady Josephine. None of the others would meet her gaze straight-on, although there were plenty of sidelong glances. Laura stood by a potted palm, feeling pinned in place by their sly, censorious gawking.

Having settled Lady Josephine, Mrs. Grayling bustled back to Laura. In a chilly whisper, she said, "We shall see to her ladyship tonight. It would please us if you would find somewhere else to sit."

So she was to be shunned by the matriarchs of society. In spite of her resolve to remain calm, Laura felt the sting of mortified anger. She compressed her lips to keep from denouncing their rudeness. Uttering an invective would only give them another reason to despise her.

She brushed past Mrs. Grayling and went to her mistress. "My lady, I should like to take a stroll around the ballroom. Can you manage without me for a time?"

The old woman's trusting eyes glowed at her. "Of course, my dear. I shall enjoy a nice chat with my friends."

No doubt they would attempt to poison her mind, Laura thought bitterly. She couldn't bear it if Lady Josephine turned against her, too.

Deliberately looking at each unfriendly face in turn, Laura said, "Lady Josephine is in delicate health. I would ask that all of you take especial care to refrain from upsetting her."

Several of the ladies had the good grace to look ashamed. Perhaps they, at least, would show kindness and stop the others from gossiping.

"Aren't you sweet to fuss over me?" Lady Josephine said, patting Laura's hand. "Now, do run along, my dear. I know how you young folk like to dance at these parties."

A lump in her throat, Laura did go, although she wouldn't be dancing. Who would dare to ask her and invite reproach from the other guests? Certainly none of *these* gentlemen. They were either too namby-pamby or too insufferable—like Lord Oliver and his rude warning to her.

Yet her gaze stole longingly to the other end of the long chamber. The orchestra had begun to play a waltz, and through the shifting of the crowd she could see the couples whirling around in vivid splendor. How delightful it would be to dance in these fine slippers, to see if she still remembered the steps. If Alex were here . . .

No, he would not dance with her, either. He was far more likely to escort her to the door. Now that her secret was out, he would seek to guard his aunt from gossip. From the start, he'd warned Laura that she could keep her post only on a trial basis. It was useless to hope he would allow her to stay on any longer as his aunt's companion.

Was he here tonight? Had he gone to Lady Josephine's house only to find them already gone? Or had he assumed they would not be attending since Laura had pretended to be indisposed?

She kept an eye peeled for him while walking along the fringes of the multitude. Unwilling to invite any more nasty remarks, she spoke to no one. Yet the whispering and the stares continued. Clearly her disguise had lost its usefulness. Now the drab masquerade only served to accentuate the difference between herself and the other ladies in their stylish gowns.

Seized by a reckless whim, Laura left the ballroom

and headed down the nearest passageway. She turned a corner and discovered a back staircase on a quiet corridor. Since this was not the grand stairs in the entrance hall, there was no one around to see her.

Grasping the iron balustrade, she ran lightly up the steps and found herself in an opulent corridor that must lead to the bedchambers. At intervals along the walls, there were lighted lamps on tables for the use of family members or guests.

She picked up a lamp, knocked on the first door to her right, and when no one answered, boldly entered the room. The flicker of the flame within the glass chimney illuminated a four-poster bed with a white coverlet and perfectly plumped pillows. Various other chairs and tables graced the spacious chamber.

Venturing into the dressing room, she noted the dearth of personal items. The shelves and cupboards were empty. If this was an unused guest chamber, then so much the better. No one would ever know if she spent a few minutes here.

Laura placed the lamp on the dressing table and sat down on the stool. It was time to remove her disguise.

The round spectacles she tucked into her small, netted reticule. Next, she stripped off the ugly spinster's cap, then the wide lace fichu that was tucked into her bodice. Now, at least, the neckline of her gown revealed a hint of bosom.

Drawing out the pins from her tight bun, she let the tawny-gold waves spill to her waist. Laura used her fingers as a comb, twisting up her locks and trying different styles before using the pins to secure her hair in place. It took several attempts before she achieved the perfect look. Gazing into the oval mirror of the dressing table, she appeared soft and feminine, utterly unlike the prudish paid companion.

Laura arose to inspect herself in front of the long pier glass. The dark, long-sleeved gown was still quite modest, so she twirled around. As the hem flared, the exquisite beaded shoes sparkled in the lamplight and made her smile. Lord help her, she hadn't realized how the somber disguise had weighted down her spirits. She felt lighter and younger now, a true lady ready to face down the withering stares.

More than that, she was ready to proceed with her plan. It was time to see if Lord Haversham was in attendance.

A few minutes later, Laura strolled through the cavernous reception hall. The lilt of music emanated from the ballroom next door, but she didn't turn in that direction. Rather, she made her way through the crowd with her chin held high and pretended she was young Queen Victoria taking no notice of her subjects.

Much to her relief, she didn't attract nearly as much attention now. People must be looking for the dowdy companion in the eyeglasses and spinster's cap. A few guests still stared and whispered, but Laura simply ignored them. If this was to be her last foray into society, then she must make the most of it. For Papa's sake.

She glanced in the card room, where several foursomes played at small tables, but Evelyn's father wasn't among them. There were any number of amusements for those who didn't care to dance, and Laura decided to inspect all the other possibilities first before she attempted to find the marquess in the packed ballroom.

As she started down the corridor, someone called out, "Miss Falkner?"

Laura turned and then instantly regretted it. Mr. Rupert Stanhope-Jones hastened toward her, his keen blue eyes studying her transformation. He looked debonair as always in a burgundy pin-striped coat over black breeches, a diamond stickpin winking in his snow-white cravat. With his flaxen hair and patrician features, he embodied the consummate English gentleman.

Laura, however, would have preferred a sewer rat over him.

"You," she said coldly. "You would dare to approach me?"

He took hold of her arm and steered her into a private alcove. "I've no right to beg your forgiveness," he said in a humble tone. "But I shall do so, anyway. When Evelyn recognized you on the street, I should have discouraged her from tracking you down. But she would not allow the matter to rest."

Laura wasn't fooled. She remembered how quickly his yellow phaeton had come in search of her. And how avidly he had watched her at tea. "I'm sure you enjoyed helping Evelyn spread the gossip. Thanks to the both of you, I shall no doubt lose my position."

He lowered his chin in a pose of abject shame. "That was never my intention, Miss Falkner. I have always been an admirer of yours. Have you forgotten how devoted I once was to you?"

He'd been one of several gentlemen who'd sought Laura's hand in marriage all those years ago. "That life is long behind me. And it seems this one is, too. Good evening, sir."

As she turned to depart, he stepped into her path. "Wait. If you are to be sacked, where will you go? How will you live?"

Laura frowned, wishing she knew. She had limited funds, and no one would hire her now without references. Not that she intended to tell this man. "Your interest in my welfare is touching," she said. "However, I cannot see where it is any concern of yours."

"Please, you must allow an old friend to help you," he said urgently. "It is a way for me to make reparations." He caught hold of her wrist, his gaze moving admiringly over her. "You are so very beautiful. I could be of great assistance if only you will allow me."

A cold knot formed in the pit of her stomach. She tugged at his grip, but his fingers were like iron around her wrist. "Release me at once, or I shall scream."

"My dearest Laura, do listen. I can give you everything you could ever want—a house, a carriage, jewels. I would ask so little of you in return. Only that you share yourself with me from time to time—"

She brought the heel of her dancing slipper down hard onto his instep. He uttered a strangled exclamation of pain, and his fingers loosened. Pulling free, Laura hurried back out into the corridor.

Her heart was pounding madly. Walking away at a fast pace, she had to force herself not to run lest attention be drawn to herself. Oh, dear God. The vile proposal made her ill. She had expected such an offer from Alex, but not from other gentlemen, too. Was that to be her fate? Was every man at this party either a critic like Lord Oliver or a lecher wondering if she would warm his bed in exchange for a few trinkets?

Tears burned in her eyes, but she furiously blinked them away. If Alex were here, he, too, would make his move on her. After all, she was no longer suitable to be his aunt's companion. She would be turned out of the house lest the taint of her ruination bring dishonor upon Lady Josephine. As a penniless pariah, Laura would be left without recourse. Hadn't that been Alex's diabolical plan all along?

Pain and anger warred within her. How she despised him. If only there was a way to bring about *his* downfall, she would do so without a qualm . . .

Directly in front of her, a gentleman emerged from the doorway of the library. Balding with a fringe of graying brown hair, he was garbed in black evening clothes and had a familiar haughty tilt to his chin.

The sight of him drove all other consideration from her mind. "Lord Haversham!"

He turned, his narrow features reflecting a cool disdain. His gray eyes revealed not a hint of recognition. Thankfully, his daughter wasn't beside him to whisper Laura's name in his ear. "Yes?" he asked.

Laura curtsied. Her mouth felt dry, her pulses racing at the prospect of finally questioning the villain who had arranged for Papa's arrest and possible murder. Though the circumstances weren't ideal, she would have no better chance than this. "I wondered if I might have a word with you in private, my lord. If it isn't too inconvenient."

"Now? Who are you?"

"The daughter of an old acquaintance." Laura didn't want to reveal any more. Not yet. Pasting on a demure smile in hopes of softening his sour expression, she added, "Please, it would be a great kindness if only you would walk with me . . ."

Another man stepped out of the library. In the space of a blink, his cool dark gaze scanned Laura up and down, paralyzing her tongue.

"I'm afraid that's impossible," Alex told her. "Haversham is on his way out. He's going to his club." To the marquess, he added, "There, I'm claiming this lovely young lady for myself. Unless you'd rather we fight for her fair hand with pistols at dawn?"

Haversham gave a rusty chuckle. "I'm too old for

such tomfoolery, Copley. I'd sooner enjoy a few rounds of hazard and a bottle of port, far away from this crush. Good evening."

With a curt nod, the marquess strode down the corridor leading to the entrance hall. Aghast, Laura found her voice. "Wait—!"

Alex deftly caught her arm and guided her in the opposite direction, his hand at the base of her spine. "Where the devil have you been?" he muttered. "I've been searching everywhere."

"You had no right to interfere in my conversation." Laura glanced over her shoulder, but the marquess had vanished into the crowd. She turned her gaze back to Alex, who looked infuriatingly handsome from the broad shoulders in a midnight-blue coat to the white cravat at his throat. In an irate whisper, she repeated, "No right at all!"

"I've every right to stop my aunt's companion from creating a scene in the midst of a ball." His gaze pierced Laura as he drew her farther away from the prying eyes of the other guests. "I know about his feud with your father. I won't have you accusing Haversham of theft and trickery without a shred of proof."

"I might have learned the proof if you hadn't interrupted!"

"Oh? I suppose you thought you could simply ask him if he'd stolen the diamond and he'd confess on the spot."

"No! I had a plan. But thanks to you, it's *ruined*."

Crossing her arms, Laura scowled at him. Actually, she didn't have a clear idea of what she might have found out. Perhaps a guilty look when she asked Haversham if Martin Falkner had come to call recently. A slip of the tongue might have revealed much. But now she wouldn't have that chance.

Then it occurred to her to wonder how Alex had determined that her target was Haversham. The earl must have been poking into her father's past in the two days since last they'd met, perhaps trying to disprove her theory. It was yet another black mark on his character.

Alex's gaze flicked to her bosom, skimmed over her restyled hair, and then returned to her face. "Well. You're lucky Haversham didn't recognize you. Evelyn probably told him you were a drab with spectacles and a spinster's bonnet."

"I went upstairs just now and removed the disguise. It served no purpose anymore, as I'm sure you've heard."

"Indeed. From at least ten different people as I walked through the ballroom." He paused, a smoldering heat in his eyes as he regarded her. "This *does* alter your situation, you know."

Laura was aware of his palm burning into the base of her spine. His touch felt stirringly intimate—as he surely meant it to be. If things had turned out differently ten years ago, Alex might have asked her to be his wife. Now she was only suited to be his light skirt.

How strange to think that her life had been the reverse of Cinderella's. She had been a princess first before falling from grace. And her Prince Charming had proven himself to be an incorrigible beast.

"Of course I realize that things have changed," she said stiffly. "I shall be packing my valise in the morning. Until then, however, I am still employed, and if you'll excuse me, I must go check on Lady Josephine."

He shook his head. "First, you and I need to talk."

"Not now. People are watching." A half-formed plan sprang to her mind. It was mad, it was reckless, but it also was preferable to being forced to parry another wicked proposition—this time from a man she had once loved with all her youthful heart. "What time is it?"

Frowning, he consulted his pocket watch. "Eleven. It would be wise if we collected my aunt and left here directly after the supper. There are matters to be settled between us."

Matters! He wanted to lay his claim on her person in the most shameful way possible. Let him think he had her won!

Laura curved her lips into a sensuous smile. "Why wait until we leave, my lord? If you'll go to the end of this corridor, you'll see a back staircase. At the top, there's an empty bedchamber on the right. I'll meet you there in an hour's time."

His eyes darkened, his gaze searching her face. Heat radiated from his body as he bent his lips to her ear. "Laura," he said in a caressing murmur. "This is hardly the place for an assignation."

An illicit tryst had been his first thought, just as she had known it would be. A wild fury gripped her heart. At least he had dispelled any doubts lingering in her. His colossal conceit needed to be taken down a notch or two.

Gazing up at him through the screen of her lashes, she lightly ran her fingertips over the back of his hand. "Just be there," she murmured. "At the stroke of midnight."

Chapter 18

The rest of it proved simple to arrange. After parting from Alex, Laura went in search of paper and pen. She found those items in a quiet morning room off a deserted passageway. There, by the glow of a candle, she sat down at a small desk to compose a note. The message took her a few tries before it was perfect; then she sanded and folded the paper and sealed it with a bit of red wax. Tucking it into her sleeve and out of sight, she returned to the ballroom.

People didn't seem to notice her so readily now that the cap and spectacles were gone. Laura was able to slip through the maze of guests without attracting undue attention. She spied Evelyn chatting with a group of gentlemen. From her animated expression, it was clear the duchess was enjoying her popularity as the herald of salacious gossip.

She, too, deserved to be knocked off her pedestal.

Laura stopped a harried footman carrying a tray of champagne glasses. She handed him the note. "Pray give this to the Duchess of Cliffington. She's the auburn-haired lady in the green gown over there."

From a grouping of ferns, Laura watched as the footman delivered the missive and then proceeded on his rounds. The duchess stepped to the side and opened the paper to peruse it. When she returned to the group, the secretive smile on her lips told Laura the dupe had been a success.

Now, if only the final piece could be arranged, her hasty, improbable plan might just succeed.

Laura approached the group of matrons where Lady Josephine was sitting. Thankfully, her ladyship's wrinkled features held a cheery smile. These busybodies must have heeded Laura's warning.

Hovering at the edge of the group, she gave a little wave to catch the attention of the bulldog-faced woman. Mrs. Dorcas Grayling scanned her without recognition; then her eyes widened and she rose from her chair in a hurry.

"My word, you have tarted up your appearance already," Mrs. Grayling said disapprovingly. "Have you no shame?"

Laura strove for a woebegone expression. "Please, ma'am, I am not feeling quite well. I only wanted her ladyship to know where to find me. I shall be lying down for a short while. If I'm needed, pray send someone to take the back staircase to the first bedchamber on the right."

"I hardly think you should trouble Lady Josephine if you're indisposed."

"Well, at least assure her not to worry, then. A certain gentleman has very kindly promised to stay with me . . . in case I am in want of anything."

The woman's face turned apoplectic. "A gentleman—? In the bedchamber with *you*—? Who—?"

Pretending not to hear, Laura set off through the crowd. Mrs. Grayling would not be able to resist confiding this latest outrage to the other matrons. They would stew over it for a little while. Then Laura hoped—though she couldn't be certain—that a bevy of them would take it upon themselves to go upstairs and expose the disgraceful conduct of the notorious Miss Falkner.

Instead of her, though, they would find Alex and Evelyn.

Laura wouldn't let herself feel any qualms. Yes, her plan might be spiteful, but at least those two might think twice next time before taking advantage of someone who lacked their standing in society.

Out in the reception hall, she spied a casement clock that marked a quarter hour before midnight. There should be just enough time for her to find a hidden spot from which to observe the results of her handiwork.

She kept a sharp eye out to make certain that no one was watching her too closely. Only then did she hasten up the back staircase. In the upper corridor, the glass-globed lamps still burned on tables here and there, and the faraway music of the orchestra drifted from the ballroom.

Otherwise, the place was silent, deserted.

Instead of turning to the right, Laura went to the door on her left. It was not completely closed, so she rapped lightly. When no one answered, she slipped into a gloomy bedroom. Elongated shadows flickered on the high ceiling from the coals that glowed on the hearth. There was enough just illumination for her to see the black outline of a four-poster bed and other furnishings. The banked fire indicated that this room was in use, but the occupant wasn't likely to come upstairs during the ball.

Ever so quietly, she closed the door while leaving it open just a crack. Peering through the slit into the corridor, Laura satisfied herself of the view. The opposite door could be seen easily and now she need only await the arrival of her quarry.

A pair of hands circled her waist from behind.

Her heart jolted against her ribs. Gasping, she lashed out at her captor, bumping against the muscled body of a man. She struggled without success to dislodge his firm grip. The alluring scent of dark spice washed over her even as she parted her lips to cry out for help.

His hand clapped over her mouth. "Calm down, Laura. It's only me."

That deep voice dispelled her panic and she went limp in his arms, breathing hard against his fingers.

"Do you promise not to scream?" he asked.

As she gave a jerky nod, he removed his hand and swiveled her around to face him. She found herself facing his tall dark shadow in the gloom. Her fingers convulsed around his upper arms. "Alex!" she gasped. "For mercy's sake, you frightened me half to death!"

"Sorry. I thought you were expecting me."

"Yes!" Quickly she amended, "But not here. I told you to meet me in the bedchamber across the corridor."

"I'm well aware of that. And I suspected you had some scheme in the works. What did you write in that note to Evelyn?"

A quiver ran through Laura. Blast him, he must have been watching her. How had she not noticed? She thrust up her chin. "I don't know what you mean."

He chuckled softly. "Jade. You most certainly do."

He went still, his fingers still loosely holding her by the waist. All of a sudden he let go and paced to the door to peer out. A thin wash of lamplight from the corridor illuminated the hard angles of his face. The scar made him appear to be a pirate embarked upon a wicked mission.

Laura crossed her arms. "I've changed my mind," she said stiffly. "I don't wish to talk to you anymore—"

"Shh. Someone is coming up the stairs."

Struck silent, she joined him and looked out. Just in time to see Evelyn approach the opposite door and then disappear inside the bedchamber.

Alex closed the door. "I begin to see," he murmured. "Such a diabolical mind you have, Miss Falkner. Instead of your beauteous self, I was to find the gossipy duchess awaiting me. No doubt you had some plan for us to be discovered together, hmm?"

She said nothing. The acid of resentment burned her throat. Why did Alex always have to ruin everything?

He took a step closer. "Now tell me, what exactly did you write to convince Evelyn to come up here?"

Laura couldn't bide her tongue a moment longer. "I imitated your penmanship and said that you were impressed by her cleverness in exposing Miss Falkner. And that you wished to celebrate by having your own private supper dance with her in that bedchamber at midnight."

He laughed aloud. "If only you knew Evelyn, you'd realize just how ingenious that is. She's been trying to seduce me for ten years."

Laura stared at him through the darkness. "You can't mean that you and she have never . . ." Feeling the rise of a blush, she stopped. It was just too scandalous to speak aloud—especially since she had absolutely no interest in his intimate affairs. None whatsoever.

While she was distracted, Alex pulled her into his arms. "I can assure you, I've never made love to Evelyn. So there's no need for you to be jealous."

"Jealous!" A plethora of emotions churned inside her, the chief of which was fury at him for assuming she still viewed Evelyn as a rival for his affections. With a shove to his chest, Laura thrust him away. "Is that what you think this is about? Jealousy? After you *told* Evelyn that I was in disguise—and where she could find me?"

He took her hands in his. "Laura, listen to me," he said, his voice turning serious. "When she came to call yesterday with her new puppy and wanted our dogs to play together, I had to tell her that Charlie had been a gift to my aunt. I swear it never occurred to me that she'd seen you on the street with him. I was only trying to get rid of the woman. I never imagined she'd visit Aunt Josie for the purpose of exposing you to society."

His words held the ring of truth, but Laura didn't want to be pacified. "Well! You still can't mind very much that the truth has come out. Now that I'm known to be a ruined woman, you're intending to make vile advances toward me—just like Mr. Stanhope-Jones!"

"*What?*" Alex tightened his hands around hers. "What did that miscreant say to you?"

"Nothing worse than what *you've* been planning to say." She tried to pull her hands free, but the endeavor was futile. Maybe it didn't matter, anyway, because she preferred to tell him off straight to his face—if only she could see him through the gloom. "That's why I wanted you to be caught with Evelyn. I wanted the both of you to know exactly what it feels like to be involved in a horrid scandal. To know that everyone is staring at you. Judging you. Scorning you."

Much to her chagrin, her voice caught on the last

two words and spoiled the effect of her righteous tirade.

At once, Alex enclosed her in the circle of his arms. He molded her to his solid body while his lips nuzzled her hair. "Darling, has it been so dreadful for you tonight? Never mind, I know it has been, and I should have been here to offer you my protection. If it hadn't been for my stupid pride . . ."

"Stupid pride, yes. That's the perfect description of you. I would also add depraved and arrogant, as well!"

He had the audacity to laugh softly, his breath stirring her hair. "Let me finish, minx. When you refused to see me this afternoon, I assumed you'd decided against allowing me into your confidence. It was a blow, I'll admit, and I left in a fit of anger, vowing never to darken your doorstep again."

"Didn't Lady Josephine tell you that Evelyn had come to call?"

He shook his head. "You know the state of my aunt's memory. She never mentioned a word. I wouldn't have known, either, except that my valet heard through the servants' grapevine what had happened and told me this evening. I made haste back to my aunt's house, but the two of you had already left for the ball." His fingers gently rubbed the nape of her neck, sending warm shivers down her back. "I came here as swiftly as I could. Alas, the damage had already been done. And I was beginning to panic because I didn't see you anywhere. I was afraid you might have run off."

Panic? Over her? Laura intended to scoff, but his deep, mesmerizing voice had a softening effect on her anger. So did his soothing touch. She wanted desperately to believe that Alex truly cared for her, that she was not just another warm female body for him to conquer.

Foolish though it might be, she laid her head on his shoulder. His coat felt smooth against her cheek, and his familiar scent both comforted and thrilled her. "You must have arrived while I was upstairs here removing my disguise."

"And was that when you concocted your devious scheme, hmm?" His hands drifted downward to massage the tension from her back. "The one that I have so cleverly foiled?"

She tilted her chin to scowl at him through the darkness. "Stupid prideful man," she said without rancor.

"Prideful, yes. After all, I did end up with the right woman."

He brought his mouth down on hers, lightly at first, then with an escalating ardor that Laura felt powerless to resist. Rising on tiptoes, she fully participated, parting her lips to welcome the intimacy of his tongue. It was a fierce, intense, exhilarating kiss and she wrapped her arms around his neck, the better to savor the compelling sensations that swept through every inch of her.

The right woman . . . did he truly regard her that way, or was he just employing his famous charm? She yearned to believe he had suffered from their abrupt separation ten years ago as much as she had. Alex had been very attentive during their whirlwind courtship, though he had never declared his love in so many words. She'd thought that the many stolen kisses they'd shared had conveyed the depth of his devotion to her.

But those memories paled in comparison with the womanly passion he aroused in her now. Laura could not recall ever feeling such a fire in her body. It consumed her, weakened her, frightened her.

In an attempt to recover her equilibrium, she drew back slightly. "I won't be your mistress, Alex."

He gave a soft laugh as his thumb traced her damp lips. "Have I asked you to be? Of course not. My stupid pride could never bear the rejection."

"Stop teasing. I'm quite serious. I won't be seduced by you."

"Not ever?" Holding her close with one arm, he moved his other hand downward over the curve of her breasts. "What a pity. For I should very much like to caress you without the restriction of gown and corset."

She caught her breath as he cupped her fullness, his fingertip deftly stroking the tip. Never before had he touched her with such boldness; all of their youthful kisses had been quite chaste. Shuddering with desire, Laura told herself to stop him, but couldn't find the words. And he was far from finished. Much to her shock, he slid his hand between her legs as far as her gown would allow. He bent his head closer and murmured huskily, "I'd like to see you entirely unclothed, Laura. So that I might learn every inch of your lovely body."

"Alex . . . you shouldn't *say* such things . . ."

But even as she spoke, Laura negated her own words by lifting her mouth for his kiss. All of her awareness was focused lower, where he continued to stroke her in lazy circles through the layers of cloth. The forbidden pleasure of it caused a mindless rush of heat. His arm gripped her waist, holding her upright, or her legs might have melted. The insistent beating of her blood proved far more enticing than any prudish objections. The darkness of the room seemed to enhance the pleasurable sensations, and her need for him pulsed like a persistent pounding . . .

He abruptly removed his hand. Laura moaned, beset

by a vague sense of being robbed of something enticing just beyond her reach. In the next instant, it struck
her that the pounding was actually someone rapping
on the door.

Even as that comprehension flooded her, the door
was flung open and she squinted against the brightness of lamplight. Several people crowded the corridor, though she could not discern their faces.

A collective gasp came from the onlookers. One
figure advanced ahead of the others into the bedchamber. The lamp she held up illuminated her bulldog features, and the sight was a dash of ice water to
Laura's overheated senses. Mrs. Dorcas Grayling.

Laura bit back a groan. Dear God in heaven. Her
scheme had gone awry in the worst possible manner.
She had been caught with Alex.

"What is the meaning of this?" Mrs. Grayling
snapped. "Lord Copley, how could you allow yourself
to be duped by such a female? As for you, you little
hussy"—her gaze had shifted on Laura—"you shall
be banished from decent society at once!"

Alex still held Laura in his arms. Bending down,
he whispered in her ear, "Go along with whatever I
say. Trust me in this."

Trust him? How could she?

But she had no other choice. The Earl of Copley
had far greater influence than a disgraced companion.
These ladies would disdain any word out of her
mouth. There was nothing to be said anyway, Laura
thought bleakly. She had been caught in a compromising situation, and no adroit explanation could ever
excuse her behavior—even if she could think of one.

Alex caught her hand and drew her toward the
goggle-eyed women. One of them, Laura realized with
a jolt, was Evelyn. It was small consolation that the

duchess looked exceedingly peeved, her lips pruned and her brow wrinkled in an unattractive frown.

"Ladies, I'm very pleased to see each and every one of you." With a charming smile, Alex surveyed the small gathering. "You could not have arrived at a better time."

"I beg your pardon?" Mrs. Grayling said huffily.

Laura was just as confused. Whatever ploy he was about, it would be useless. These women already had made up their minds. Now she longed only to duck her head, walk out of the room, and escape this ordeal. But Alex kept a firm grasp on her fingers.

"Indeed you *should* beg our pardon," he chided in a teasing manner. "You've interrupted a tender moment, as I'm sure you'll realize when I share the news."

Evelyn pushed her way to the front. "News? What news? What are you doing in here with that . . . that coquette? You sent me a note . . ." She fell silent, apparently realizing it wouldn't be wise to mention that *she* had come up here to meet him.

His smile took on an ironic sharpness. "Since you ask, Duchess, I shall allow *you* to be the first to congratulate us. I'm happy to announce that Miss Laura Falkner has just accepted my offer of marriage. She is to be my bride."

Chapter 19

Amid the clamor of gasps and exclamations from the ladies, Laura stood motionless. Her mind was blank, her body numb. She felt Alex's arm drawing her close to his side in the manner of an adoring fiancé. He pressed a kiss to her brow and embellished his tall tale by telling the ladies that Laura had made him the happiest man alive.

Agree with whatever I say. Trust me in this.

Woodenly, Laura smiled and murmured thank you when several of the women offered their tentative congratulations. Evelyn was the only one who refused to do so, and flounced away down the stairs.

Alex proceeded to declare that such fine, upstanding, fair-minded ladies couldn't possibly hold his innocent bride-to-be to blame for the long-ago actions of her father, now, could they? He said they would soon realize that Laura would make him the perfect wife, and that as Lady Copley, she would be sure to invite them all to the first party they gave as newlyweds.

Listening to his spiel, Laura felt certain that this had to be a twisted trick he was playing. At any moment he would laugh and say, *What, did you really believe I would marry her? Of course it's merely a hoax!*

But he didn't. He asked the ladies if they would hold their tongues for the moment so that his aunt would not learn the news from anyone else but him. Then he enlisted their aid as chaperones while he finished discussing the wedding arrangements with his affianced bride.

"I admit that it was most improper for Miss Falkner and I to be alone in a bedchamber," he said to them. "Perhaps we might leave the door ajar and let you ladies keep an eye on us while we talk?"

That was too enticing a prospect for these avid gossipmongers to refuse. He hunted down several straight-backed chairs and placed them in the corridor just outside the open door.

Having finally mastered her shock, Laura took a lamp and marched to the far end of the bedchamber, where a chaise sat in front of the blue-draped windows. She set the lamp down on a table, perched on the edge of the seat cushion, and stiffly clenched her fingers together in her lap while she waited for Alex.

With the impatient strides of a prospective bridegroom, he advanced through the bedchamber and then settled down right beside her. He caught hold of her hand and brought it to his lips. In a loud, booming voice, he declared, "Laura, my darling. How I have longed for this moment."

The ladies in their chairs outside the door twittered like starving hens that had been tossed a handful of grain. Apparently his wooing of their good opinion had met with some success, and they had decided that the infamous Miss Falkner was not nearly so wicked now that she was betrothed to one of the Quality.

Laura was hard-pressed to contain the surfeit of

emotions swirling inside herself. The only one that made any sense to her was a furious disbelief. In an undertone, she hissed, "Enough with this charade. What purpose can it serve?"

"Charade?" He brought his face close to hers, lowering his voice to a mere thread of sound. "The only charade was in my saying that you'd already accepted me. So perhaps I should begin anew."

His gaze held hers so that she could not look away. The lamplight picked out flecks of gold in his dark brown eyes. When he gazed so intently at her, she could scarcely string two thoughts together. "Begin what anew?"

"My proposal of marriage. This is hardly the way I intended to ask you, with an audience watching, but . . . Laura, will you do me the great honor of becoming my wife?"

A tremor of longing threatened the wall around her heart. Despising herself for it, she closed her eyes and glanced away. "Don't say that," she uttered in a fiercely sibilant whisper. "You know you don't mean it."

His warm palm cupped her cheek as he turned her face back toward him. "Look at me," he commanded. "We don't want them to think we're already quarreling."

Laura opened her eyes and feigned a smile for the benefit of their chaperones. The women were practically falling through the doorway in an effort to hear this whispered conversation. "But we *are* quarreling," she said under her breath. "Because you *know* you really only want me as your mistress."

He chuckled. "I never said that. *You* said that. *I* intended all along to marry you."

"All along?"

This time his gaze shifted away, though only for a

moment. "For ten years, I convinced myself that I'd forgotten you. But when you reappeared in my aunt's garden, I quickly realized that my passion for you had never died."

"Passion! There, you see what I mean?"

He brushed a chaste kiss to her cheek, and his action caused an excited buzzing from the doorway. With his lips close to her ear, he murmured, "Passion isn't only the province of illicit affairs, my darling. I'm inclined to think it must be an extremely valuable quality in a marriage, too."

Desire smoldered in the hidden places where he had touched her only minutes ago when they'd been alone. The notion of giving him free rein to explore her in their marriage bed stole her breath away. Was she actually thinking of accepting him?

Heaven help her, she had every reason to despise the man. "You tried to arrest my father. You didn't believe me when I said he was innocent—you still don't. How am I ever to forget that?"

His eyes turned to dark mirrors that reflected the lamplight. "May I remind you, I've promised to help ease your mind on that matter. If, however, you refuse me, my aid will be withdrawn. And without my protection, no one in society will answer your questions."

"That's bribery!"

"I prefer that you view it as an enticement." The hint of a smile crooking one corner of his mouth, he lifted her hand to his lips again. "It's only one of many enticements that I can offer you."

Her pulse leaped as she gazed at his strong features beneath cocoa-brown hair, the dark brows over piercing eyes, the square jaw and the faintly ironic smile that so often displayed cynicism. She would be a fool not to acknowledge that *he* was doing *her* a great honor. Especially given the fact that she had caused that scar across his cheek, even though he had deserved it. A man of his rank and standing in society could have any eligible woman he wanted.

Nevertheless, he had chosen her. The realization made Laura aware of a deep hunger inside her, as if her body and soul had been denied sustenance these past ten years.

Oh, it was no use denying it. She desired him, too, with an intensity unsuited to a well-bred lady. Yet he had spoken only of lust. He had said nothing of love. "What will *you* gain from this . . . arrangement?"

"It's high time I took a wife and produced an heir. I believe we both will find the begetting of a child to be a most pleasurable experience."

He held her hand, his thumb slowly rubbing her palm. His caress stoked the heat inside her. She *did* want children, very much so, and with startling clarity, Laura could imagine no other man but Alex as their father. To have a family with him . . . the notion made her heart ache. Yet how could she speak her vows to a man who felt only a shallow desire for her? A man whom she did not fully trust?

She had no other real choice. To refuse him meant to give up all hope of bringing her father's murderer to justice. It also would mean giving up Alex, who still owned her heart after all these years. But what would happen if their passion burned out someday? She would find herself trapped in a cold marriage.

"So you wish a son from me, nothing more?" she asked.

"Two sons. An heir and a spare, as the saying goes."

"I might bear girls."

"With a mother like you, we will have beautiful daughters. As for the boys, we can always keep trying."

His fingers crept up to her wrist, and one delved beneath her long sleeve to stroke her skin. To the chaperones, it would appear an innocuous touch, though it sent delicious shivers through her body. "I anticipate spending many long, enjoyable nights in bed with you, Laura."

A ripple of warmth caused a tightening in her bosom that traveled down to her very womb. The pleasure of it threatened to distract her from all other considerations. Alex knew full well his effect on her; Laura could tell by the hint of self-satisfaction in his face. She also sensed a certain aloofness in him and remembered how quickly he had reminded her she'd be cast out of society without his protection.

Yes, it was clear he felt nothing deeper for her than bodily passion.

She couldn't fault him for that, for she burned, too. Perhaps this yearning for his love was nothing more than a fleeting naive dream, anyway. Better to face the fact that his infatuation wouldn't last forever. Without love to provide a solid foundation for their marriage, disillusionment eventually would set in. Alex might very well become a tyrant subjecting her to his acerbic remarks and his lordly whims.

Laura drew her hand away and laced her fingers in her lap. "We will sign a legal agreement," she said coolly. "After I bear you two sons, you will grant me the freedom to live as I wish."

The cocky look vanished from his face. "To take lovers? No!"

At last she had provoked a strong emotion in him. Perversely pleased by his disagreeable expression, Laura bent forward to whisper, "Not quite so loud, my lord. Remember, we have an audience."

He lowered his voice to a fierce growl. "Then explain yourself."

"It's quite simple. I want a house deeded to me along with a generous allowance. The children and I will live there if I so desire it."

"For what purpose, by God? I possess three estates along with the London town house. You may have your pick of them."

"I will own a house in my name alone," she stated firmly. "You will purchase it upon the birth of our second son. We will sign a document to that effect before any vows are spoken. That is my condition for wedding you."

His eyes narrowed and his fingers flexed on his knees. Glancing away, he blew out a breath as if struggling to contain himself. He turned his angry gaze back to glare at her. Through clenched teeth, he said, "If ever I discover you with another man, Laura, I will divorce you. That is *my* condition."

Under any other circumstances, Laura would have been goaded to strike back with a retort of her own. But now she found herself oddly exhilarated by his reaction. Alex appeared more livid than she'd ever seen him. She had certainly touched a nerve. Was it just an innate male possessiveness? Or might it indicate a deep river of emotion in him, feelings that he did not wish her to see?

She cupped his face in her hands and stroked the tense line of his jaw. His skin felt warm and deliciously rough to her fingertips. "I accept your offer, my lord. Now, for the benefit of our watchers, do kiss me to seal our pact."

Closing her eyes, she brushed her lips over his. For an instant he didn't respond. Then she was richly rewarded when he groaned deep in his chest and yanked her close, his mouth crushing hers in a kiss meant to dominate. She returned it with her own fierceness as a means of showing him that she would be his equal partner and no less. Passion leaped between them, and the joining of their mouths subtly shifted from heated battle to pure bliss.

They broke apart only when a noise of coughing and throat-clearing penetrated the sensual stupor. As one, they both turned their heads to look at the chaperones.

Mrs. Grayling had risen from her chair. Shaking her finger at them, she stood glowering in the doorway. "That is enough mischief! Quite enough, indeed!"

Alex appeared disgruntled by the interruption, and to forestall him from making a caustic comment that he might later regret, Laura stood up and offered him her hand. "Shall we return to the ball, my lord? I do believe it's time we conveyed our news to your aunt."

"I had the loveliest dream last night," Lady Josephine confided, leaning on her cane and on Laura's arm as they proceeded slowly through the bedchamber the following morning. "You won't believe it when I tell you! I dreamed that you and Alexander became betrothed. And then you waltzed together, just the two of you, while all of society watched!"

Laura smiled. The shock in the ballroom had been palpable, she recalled. That was the real reason why no one had joined them on the dance floor. Whether she'd snared an earl or not, she was still the notorious Miss Falkner in their eyes.

Nevertheless, a thrill leaped to life inside her. She tamped it down, unwilling to become starry-eyed over a marriage that was more a business arrangement than a love match. "You'll be pleased to hear it wasn't a dream at all, my lady. You're remembering matters exactly as they happened."

"Truly?" As Laura helped her onto the chaise, the old woman beamed up at her. "Why, that means you are to be my . . . my . . ."

"Your niece-in-law. Soon I shall be calling you Aunt Josie as your nephew does. Unless you prefer to be Aunt Josephine?"

"Either will do. Oh, my dear girl, I could not be happier!" Lady Josephine opened her arms, and Laura let herself be enveloped by that cushiony form and rosewater scent. Tears prickled behind her eyes. It had been a long time since she'd basked in the love of family. Yes, she'd had her dear Papa, but she'd never known her mother, who had died when Laura was just a baby.

Charlie jumped up onto the chaise, wagging his tail and nosing his way into the cuddle. Laura drew back with a laugh. "It appears I have a rival for your affections, my lady."

"Oh, there's plenty to go around," Lady Josephine said, settling the puppy into her lap. "Dear little Charlie. Don't you know you'll always be Mama's sweet little boy?"

The spaniel lapped her plump fingers with his pink tongue and appeared to grin up at her.

A knock sounded on the door, and before Laura could answer, Mrs. Samson swept into the bedchamber. On seeing Laura, the housekeeper stopped short and thinned her lips. "Miss . . . Falkner. I have been looking for you. You must come downstairs at once."

The woman's insolent manner made it clear that she had not yet accustomed herself to the change in Laura's status. It had to be difficult for her to see an underling transformed into the fiancée of the mistress's nephew and the future Lady Copley.

Although Laura felt a modicum of sympathy for

the housekeeper, Mrs. Samson could not be allowed to continue her impertinence. But she didn't want to engage in a tiff in front of Lady Josephine. After seeing the old woman was comfortably settled, Laura took her leave and walked out into the corridor.

Mrs. Samson marched to the staircase, where she stopped and whirled around, her bony fingers grasping the newel post. "I would be remiss not to express my objection to your use of a false name, Miss Falkner. You have played all of us in this household for fools. And I see that you have left off your spectacles and your spinster's cap today now that you have snagged your quarry!"

Laura didn't bother to challenge the nonsensical accusation of donning a drab disguise in order to ensnare society's biggest catch. "My quarry, as you so ungraciously put it, is the Earl of Copley. I very much doubt he would appreciate hearing himself described in such a disrespectful manner."

Mrs. Samson had the good grace to lower her eyes—though only for a moment. "Nevertheless, you have deceived us all. Of course one would expect no less from the daughter of a common thief!"

Any trace of compassion in Laura vanished in a twinkling. "That is quite enough, Mrs. Samson. Henceforth, you will behave as befitting your station—and mine. You will show me proper deference. And you will politely *ask* me to accompany you downstairs rather than order me."

"But you must go down. A visitor awaits you in the drawing room." A faint smirk touched the housekeeper's hatchet face. "It is Her Grace, the Duchess of Knowles."

Chapter 20

Laura paused in front of an oval mirror in the corridor and tucked a few stray strands back into her chignon. From the conversation she'd overheard at Lord Scarborough's ball, the Duchess of Knowles took a keen interest in her godson's private affairs. She was, after all, a close family friend who had grown up in the same household as Alex's father. It was only natural that she'd wish to meet the woman Alex had chosen as his bride.

Pasting on a resolute smile, Laura stepped into the drawing room. Morning sunlight streamed through the tall windows and bathed the spacious room with its clutter of knickknacks. The hour was too early for visitors, but of course this particular caller wouldn't wish to have witnesses to whatever she intended to say.

The duchess sat in a chair by the cold fireplace. An olive-green brocade gown encasing her stout form, she appeared as haughty as a queen on her throne. The crimped brim of her bonnet framed features that were unremarkable except for a pointed nose rather like the beak of a hawk. Jeweled rings glinted on the clawlike fingers that gripped the gilt arms of the chair.

She did not return Laura's smile.

Gliding forward, Laura suffered no illusions that this interview would be pleasant. The duchess had *not* come to offer felicitations. However, for the sake of family peace, Laura would do her best to be civil.

She sank into a deep curtsy. "Good morning, Your Grace. Perhaps you won't remember, but we met briefly ten years ago."

"I do indeed remember," the duchess said, critically eyeing her up and down. "You were a flibbertigibbet with your eye on my godson even back then."

Laura sat down in a chair opposite the woman. Keeping her expression diligently agreeable, she folded her fingers in her lap. "I should rather say that *he* had his eye on *me*. As for now, he pursued me from the moment he learned that I'd returned to London."

"You took this post in Josephine's house on purpose. So that you could work your wiles on him."

Laura didn't bother to explain that it had been Lady Milford who had conspired to throw her into Alex's path. It wouldn't do any good. "Until yesterday, I was disguised in spectacles and drab gowns like this one," she said with a wave at her brown bombazine dress with its long sleeves and modest bosom. "Hardly the garb of a *femme fatale*."

The duchess's beaky nostrils flared. "Do not play me for a fool, Miss Falkner. As this is a grave situation, I will speak plainly. You are a most improper wife for the Earl of Copley. I will not allow you to drag my godson down into the gutter with you. I insist that you cry off this reckless engagement at once!"

Laura kept her gaze steady. "No. I will not."

"No?" The Duchess of Knowles leaned forward, her bejeweled fingers glinting in the sunlight. "Your father was convicted of stealing the Blue Moon diamond from me. If you refuse to do as I say, I will have you arrested as his accomplice."

The threat made Laura quail inside. Although Alex had assured her that she could not be prosecuted, she remembered the constable in the cemetery and how avidly he had given chase through the slums. If the police believed that she knew what had happened to the legendary diamond, and if the duchess applied her influence, a magistrate surely could be persuaded to lock up Laura in prison.

But there was one point that Her Grace had failed to take into account.

"Lord Copley will fight on my behalf," Laura said. "Are you prepared for him to become your adversary? Will you estrange yourself from your godson and willfully create a feud?"

"Don't be impertinent. It is *you* who have put him in a difficult position. You, with your tarnished reputation. You will always be known as the daughter of a common thief."

Laura stifled an ironic laugh. Mrs. Samson had uttered nearly those same words to her. It was not quite eleven o'clock and already Laura had been snubbed by a housekeeper and a duchess.

"I see you find my concerns amusing," Her Grace said with a sniff. "Tell me, to whom did Martin Falkner sell the Blue Moon? I demand to know at once!"

"My father did *not* steal your wretched diamond. I don't care that the matching earrings were found in his desk. Someone else put them there—to implicate him."

"What a cockamamie tale! If you believe that, you are harebrained as well a fortune-hunting hussy."

Laura had suffered enough insults. Abandoning civility, she seized this chance to root out the truth. "My father did have one enemy. A man who is known to you. Tell me, Your Grace, did you perchance allow Lord Haversham access to your bedchamber ten years ago?"

Those pale blue eyes widened, enough for Laura to see a flash of something secretive. But it vanished so swiftly that she couldn't be certain what it meant.

A thunderous expression twisting her face, the duchess shot to her feet. "I will not remain here to be affronted by the likes of you. Is it not enough that your father stole my most valuable jewel? Must you rob my godson of his future happiness, as well?"

Laura stood up, too. She refused to be any less than eye-to-eye with this snooty, hateful peeress. "Alex's future is not yours to decide. If he chooses to squander it on me, then I won't stop him—nor will you!"

"Well! This conversation has come to an end. Summon your footman to show me out."

"Better yet, I will show you out myself. With great pleasure!"

In high dudgeon, Laura marched out of the drawing room, through the reception hall, and down the staircase. Irate footsteps tapped in her wake. She sailed right past the astonished footman and threw open the front door. Proceeding outside, she held the door while Her Grace's imposing figure emerged from the house.

The duchess aimed an icy glare at Laura. With a final "Harrumph," the middle-aged woman stalked to a waiting black coach, where a crimson-liveried footman hastened to assist her in entering it.

As the coachman drove off, another vehicle drew up in front of the town house. It was not one Laura recognized, and belatedly she realized that her fit of anger had left her exposed. Though it was somewhat early, the gossips must be anxious to gawk at the up-start Miss Falkner who had finagled an offer from one of society's biggest catches. Her being out here only gave them an excuse to stop and talk, thus gain-ing an advantage over the other tattle-mongers.

But when the door opened, Laura saw that the young woman who emerged from the carriage had a familiar cheerful face beneath her straw bonnet. A sunny yel-low gown draped her noticeably pregnant form.

Laura flew down the steps. "Violet!"

The two friends hugged, and Violet's warm brown eyes were like saucers in her freckled face. "I came as soon as I read the news in *The Tattler*. But . . . was that the Duchess of Knowles in the coach that just now left here?"

"Yes, and I'm afraid I let my temper gain the better of me."

"Oh! What did that harridan say to you? I can only imagine she must object to your brilliant match."

"Quite." Glad for the loyal support of a friend, Laura slipped her arm through Violet's. "Come inside and I'll tell you all about it."

They went into the house, heading upstairs to the morning room where they could talk without inter-ruption. Going to a chaise by the open window over-looking the garden, they settled down for a chat.

"I've been dying to come and visit you for *days*," Violet declared. "But little Michael was fretful with a fever, and I couldn't leave the poor dear without his mama. And look at all that I've missed in the in-terim! Lord Copley has made you an offer and you have accepted him. Oh, I *knew* he was madly in love with you!"

"I'll allow, you did advise me to give him a chance to redeem himself," Laura hedged, without explaining all the particulars of the betrothal. Somehow, she felt reluctant to reveal that the bargain they'd struck had little to do with love.

Alex wanted an heir. Laura wanted to vindicate her father. And the bond holding them together was passion. A fiery, powerful, seductive passion. She would never admit it aloud, but the anticipation of their wedding night smoldered like an ever-present flame inside her.

"I could not be happier for you," Violet said, her face alight with a smile. "Have you set a wedding date yet?"

"Yes, in three days' time—"

"*What?*" Her gaze dropped to Laura's midsection. "You aren't . . . are you?"

Laura laughed. "No, I am not with child! For pity's sake, I only returned to London a fortnight ago."

"Then the earl must be *very* eager if you're to wed by special license! Oh, isn't it *so* romantic!"

Laura felt a deep wistful ache that she quickly denied. "Rather, it's quite sensible. If we wait until the end of the Season, our wedding will be overshadowed by the queen's coronation. I much prefer to have a small, quiet ceremony at home, anyway. You know that my father died less than two months ago."

Violet reached out to give Laura's hand a sympathetic squeeze. "I'm so sorry, of *course* you're right. It's just that holding your nuptials so swiftly puts you in quite a bind. How will you arrange your trousseau in time? We must make haste to the shops at once!"

Laura shook her head. "I haven't the funds for extravagances. I'd planned to go out this afternoon while her ladyship is napping and purchase the materials for my wedding gown."

"Only *one* new gown? And sewn by yourself?" Resting her hands on the gentle mound of her belly, Violet gave her an incredulous look. "Laura, you *know* you can't go about society in anything but the finest fashions. You'll need *piles* of new gowns. You're to be Lady Copley, after all, and you must look your best to counter any naysayers. And don't fret over the expense. The earl is an exceedingly rich man."

"That isn't why I'm marrying him," Laura said stiffly.

"Of course not, it's a love match. But you mustn't let your pride get in the way of practicality. Only consider, you may buy whatever you please, for the bills won't arrive until after your vows are spoken!"

The notion of presuming upon Alex's wealth disturbed Laura. On the first day he had spied her in the garden, he had insinuated that she might be a jewel thief like her father. She didn't want to mention that, but perhaps she owed her friend some sort of explanation. "Violet, I must confess . . . it isn't a love match, not precisely. Perhaps that's why I feel so reluctant to lay claim to his funds."

Violet tilted her head in surprise. "Not a love match? But I'm sure it must be—"

"Good morning, ladies." With ghastly timing, Alex walked through the doorway without an announcement by the footman to give them warning. "I do hope I'm not interrupting a private conversation."

Laura's heart catapulted into her throat. Her fiancé strolled toward them, appearing every inch the fashionable man-about-town in a russet coat tailored to fit his broad shoulders and fawn breeches that hugged his long muscular legs. He looked so perfect that she could only stare, rapt at the notion that he would soon be her husband. Then, as he drew closer, she noted the distinct gleam in his dark eyes.

Had he overheard their conversation?

Leaning down, he pressed a lingering kiss to Laura's cheek. In a voice fraught with exaggerated tenderness, he murmured, "How beautiful you look today . . . my love."

Yes, he *had* overheard. And just as he undoubtedly intended, Violet observed them with wide-eyed interest. She gave Laura a smirk that said *See, I told you he's madly in love.*

A hot blush stained Laura's cheeks. She fought it unsuccessfully, knowing it would only confirm Violet's stalwart belief in his romantic attachment.

Before Laura could collect her thoughts and make a cogent reply, he turned to her friend. "Mrs. Blankenship, is it not?"

Violet smiled prettily and offered him her hand. "Yes, my lord. You have an excellent memory for names."

"I never forget a pretty face. Alas, you're already taken, so I've had to settle for Laura as my bride." As Violet giggled, he brought up a chair and sat directly in front of Laura, leaning forward to take her hand and lace their fingers together. "Not that I mind, of course," he added, gazing deeply into her eyes. "Laura is everything I've ever desired in a wife."

He was quite the charmer today, she thought giddily. A pity it was all playacting for Violet's benefit. And what had happened to the river of powerful emotions she'd glimpsed in him the previous evening? Had she imagined it? No, he kept his deepest feelings hidden, and she felt a maddening zeal to uncover all his secrets.

But now was not the time.

"Unfortunately," Laura said, withdrawing her hand from his, "I'm *not* everything your godmother wants in your wife. The duchess came by this morning to tell me so."

His affable look vanished and he frowned slightly. "No wonder she wasn't at home when I called on her a short time ago."

"Yes, you just missed her here." Although still miffed by the woman's high-handed insults, Laura regretted that the incident would create a rift. Causing trouble in his family was hardly an advantageous way to start their marriage. "Please be assured that I tried my best to be civil. But she made it extremely difficult and, well, she left in rather a huff."

"Never mind the duchess," Alex said. "I'll have a word with her."

"It'll take more than a word, I'm afraid."

"That bad?" A dry smile touched one corner of his mouth. "We'll see. Now, it appears you're in need of a new wardrobe. I should like to see you in something a bit less . . . spinsterish." He gazed askance at her dowdy dress, his eyes lingering on her bosom, before he looked at Violet. "Wouldn't you agree, Mrs. Blankenship?"

"Oh, most assuredly! Why, I was telling Laura that very thing before you arrived, my lord, that she and I should go to the shops at once."

"Excellent. Then I can depend on you to see that she spares no expense in her purchases?"

"Absolutely. I shall dedicate myself to the task!"

Their conspiracy against her exasperated Laura,

and she lifted her chin. "Are you sure, Alex? Being the daughter of a thief, I wouldn't want you to think me mercenary."

He cocked a too-innocent eyebrow. "Have I ever said that? If so, I must apologize wholeheartedly."

Violet looked a trifle puzzled as she glanced from one to the other. "Oh, just accept the gift, Laura. When your husband-to-be offers to refurbish your wardrobe, why, it's best to simply thank him!"

Laura laughed. "You're connivers, the both of you. All right then, thank you, Alex, for your generosity. But I can't depart just now. Lady Josephine is expecting me to spend the day with her."

"You must invite her to come with us," Violet declared. "It shall be great fun!"

"Then it's settled," Alex said, taking Laura's hand in his. "I've only one condition to place on your purchases."

He idly swept his thumb across her palm, the caress stoking the banked fire inside her and making it difficult for her to think. A bit breathlessly, she said, "Do tell."

Alex bent his head closer as if to confide a secret, though he spoke in a whisper loud enough to deepen her blush. "Mind that you choose something special for our wedding night."

"She *must* know what happened to the Blue Moon," the duchess insisted. "She's playing you for a fool."

His jaw tight, Alex leaned against the marble mantelpiece in a pose of unconcern. But his temper seethed as he watched his godmother walk back and forth, her olive-green skirt swishing against the crimson rug. He had come here to her house in Grosvenor

Square with the intention of smoothing her ruffled feathers. Instead, it had proven to be a struggle to maintain his characteristic coolness.

"Laura knows nothing about the diamond," he stated. "I thought she might at first, but I quickly realized my mistake. She has a steadfast belief in her father's innocence."

The duchess stopped to stare at Alex. "She asked me today if I'd ever had an affair with Haversham. Have you given her any reason to suspect what really happened back then?"

Good God. Laura would never forgive him if she knew. Ten years ago, he had lied to her. He had courted her purposefully in order to investigate her father—only to fall hard for her.

"Absolutely not. I gave you my word on that." He took a step toward his godmother. "But pray be forewarned, she hopes to clear her father's name. It's entirely possible that she could unearth the truth on her own."

"Then you must discourage her!"

"I've done so. However, Laura is a very determined woman."

"She's an ambitious woman, that's what. Even if she knows what Martin Falkner did with the diamond, she'll still try to clear her own name of the scandal. You should consider that!"

Alex took her hands in his. "I assure you, Your Grace, she has absolutely no knowledge of the whereabouts of the Blue Moon. I would stake my life on it."

"No, you'll squander your life on an adventuress. You should have heard how disrespectfully the chit addressed me today." Pulling her hands free, the duchess paced away from him, then spun back around.

"Who are her family? Nobodies, all of them. Irish through her mother, and a father who is a convicted jewel thief."

"According to Debrett's, Martin Falkner had a distinguished lineage. However, I seem to recall that one of *your* grandfathers made his fortune as a wool merchant." When Her Grace's face flushed a livid red, Alex strove to master his own anger at her denigration of Laura. "I mean no insult, Your Grace. My point is merely that one cannot help one's forebears. Laura is her own person. You cannot hold her to blame for the actions of her father."

"Like father, like daughter. She wants your wealth and all the benefits of your title. She will bleed you dry."

Little did his godmother know, she'd touched a nerve. Ever since the previous evening, his mind had dwelled obsessively on the legal agreement that Laura had demanded of him. A house of her own once she'd borne him an heir and a spare. The independence to leave him if she so wished. Her insistence gnawed at his gut. If fate gave them two sons in quick succession, she could be gone from his life in the same number of years.

By God! Did she really think he'd let her go?

Would she really *want* to go? That was the crux of the matter. He hungered to resurrect in her the love that he had crushed ten years ago. If he couldn't do so, he knew only one way to bind her to him: by making her burn with passion.

Realizing the duchess was expecting a response, he forced a slight smile. "Pray show a little confidence in my ability to manage my own finances—and my own wife."

"Stronger men than you have been taken in by the wiles of a fortune hunter."

"Nonsense. There *are* no stronger men than me."

"This is no time for arrogant jests." Her fingers curling into fists at her sides, the duchess continued to pace as if lost in her own private world. "Only look at how your father's marriage turned out. He, too, had his head turned by a pretty face. Blanche brought out the worst in him with her silly, madcap ways. He should have married someone more suited to his sober disposition."

An entrenched aversion crept over Alex. He had grown up with loud, prolonged quarrels, his father shouting and his mother screaming. They'd *both* been to blame, Alex knew. But he saw no purpose in correcting his godmother's misapprehension. "Laura is nothing like my mother," he said. "We are perfectly well suited."

The duchess shook her head. "She's a selfish upstart who will cause you no end of trouble. Your father would have forbidden this hasty, ill-advised marriage."

Women are vain, selfish creatures who will stab a man in the heart. How many times had his father told him that? Too often, Alex had been thrust into the role of his father's confidant after his mother had run off weeping to her bedchamber. Would he and Laura end up like that, at each other's throats?

He buried the thought. It would *not* prevent him from marrying her. She was a fever in his blood.

"My father would have no say in my marriage even if he were still alive," he said. "I shall be wedding Laura in three days' time at Copley House. I would consider it an honor if you would set aside your objections and attend."

"No. I will not be a party to this farce. I will never receive that schemer, do you hear me? Nor will anyone else of the ton invite her into their homes."

Her face held a haughty stubbornness that infuriated him. The Duchess of Knowles had been a fixture in his life since childhood, and he had a fondness for her. But no more. He was done with anyone who would malign his bride.

He took a step closer. "If you mean to spread poisonous gossip or speak ill of Laura in any way, I will consider my vow to you nullified. Is that understood?"

"Impertinent boy! You would break your word as a gentleman? Is that what this creature has done? Destroyed your sense of honor?"

His godmother didn't know it, but he would never reveal her secret. Because then Laura would realize exactly how he'd used her.

Alex gave a curt bow. "I wouldn't advise you to test me on the matter. Good afternoon."

As he strode out the door, the duchess called after him, "You'll rue your actions someday. You'll wish you'd listened to me!"

Alex clenched his jaw. He kept walking through the grand hall, down the marble stairs, and to the front door. He did not look back.

Chapter 21

"Oh, I do love weddings," Lady Josephine said as the coach rolled though the busy streets of Mayfair. Then her bright smile faded and a hint of befuddlement clouded her blue eyes. "You *did* say you were marrying Alexander today, didn't you?"

"Yes, my lady. Most assuredly."

Laura hid a bone-deep quiver behind a pleasant smile. Her palms felt damp inside her kidskin gloves. Sitting across from her ladyship in the luxurious black coach that Alex had sent to fetch them, she ought to feel like a princess—or at least a countess-to-be. Instead she had the anxious sense of being caught up in another masquerade.

She wore a dove-gray gown of the finest silk, the subdued color in deference to her mourning, with garnet ribbons threaded at her waist and through the short sleeves. The beaded garnet slippers from Lady Milford peeked from beneath her hem. With the help of one of the housemaids, Laura had done up her tawny-blond hair in soft curls adorned with a cluster of deep pink rosebuds that she'd clipped dewy fresh from the garden that morning.

Her transformation, when she'd surveyed herself in the pier glass of her dressing room, had been remarkable. The dowdy spinster had been vanquished in favor of an elegant lady of the ton. Oddly, it had been the improvement in her appearance that had sparked this attack of doubts. She looked like the naive girl whose world had been shattered by the man she'd loved and trusted. And now she was about to give herself into his keeping again.

Forever.

Misgivings churned inside her. Was she taking the right step in wedding Alex? They'd signed the prenuptial agreement the previous day in his solicitor's office. Alex had been coolly charming, his manner seductively witty, and she'd felt a fervent desire to be his wife.

But today it was as if she'd awakened from a lovely dream to bitter reality. It could be a terrible mistake to marry the man who had once broken her heart. Perhaps it was not yet too late to turn back . . .

The coach drew to a halt in front of Copley House. A footman opened the door and let down the step. Her movements wooden, Laura accepted his aid in climbing out of the coach. While the servant lent his hand to Lady Josephine, Laura glanced up at Alex's home.

Situated across from Hyde Park, the imposing residence had a grand facade of pale stone with a columned portico over the double front doors. It rose a full four stories and was crowned by many chimneys. The tall windows of the first floor showed azure blue draperies drawn back by gold cord. She had never been inside his house, but one of those chambers must be the drawing room where the wedding ceremony would be conducted.

A lurch assailed Laura's stomach. Within the hour, she would be mistress of this house. She would have the right to direct the servants, to redecorate the rooms, to plan parties and entertain guests. She would be wife to a wealthy, handsome earl who would elevate her to an exalted place in society.

It was every lady's dream. So why did she feel the urge to turn and flee?

Lady Josephine clutched Laura's arm and aimed a guileless smile at her. "Come, my dear, we mustn't be late."

Laura placed her hand over the old woman's. Curiously, the warmth of those knobby fingers gave her the strength to mount the three shallow steps to the porch, where another footman opened the door. They passed over the threshold into a grand entrance hall with a divided staircase, each side curving upward to the first floor.

Compared with Lady Josephine's cluttered house, this one had a minimum of furnishings, each piece clearly chosen for its superb quality. A gilded chair had been placed on either side of the doorway. In the center of the cream marble floor, the alabaster statue of a winged goddess in Grecian robes stood on a pedestal. The pastel green walls displayed a series of splendid landscape paintings that she would have been interested to inspect under normal circumstances.

The surroundings were so lovely, so vast, and so *rich*, Laura felt her qualms intensify. Her breath came faster under the force of an incipient panic. Did she really belong here? Or back in her comfortable little cottage in Portugal?

The patter of footsteps drew her gaze to one of the ground-floor doorways. Her freckled face wreathed in a smile, Violet came hurrying forward. A leaf-green gown draped her pregnant form, and she had arranged her hair in a pretty cascade of russet curls.

Her brown eyes sparkled with excitement. "Laura, you look absolutely *gorgeous*! I've been waiting for you to arrive. Come with me, we haven't much time."

"But . . . Lady Josephine . . ."

"The footman will assist her upstairs."

The strapping servant was already offering his arm for the old woman to hold, and with her customary good humor Lady Josephine hobbled with him to the grand staircase.

Laura let herself be tugged into a library decorated in masculine tones of coffee and cream with leather chairs and numerous bookshelves. Spying an oversized volume on a table, she distractedly opened it, her attention caught by the colored illustrations of exotic flora. If only she could curl up in a chair and lose herself in these lovely drawings . . .

"Whatever are you doing?" Violet chided, reaching out to shut the book. "You can't be reading now. This is your wedding day!"

"I know . . . I only . . ." Tears burned her eyes, and she lifted her hand to her mouth while gazing beseechingly at her friend. "Oh, Violet, I don't know if I can go through with this. Truly I don't."

A commiserating look softened Violet's expression, and she threw her arms around Laura. "Oh, my dearest, I felt the same way the morning of my own wedding. As if I were about to swoon from sheer fright. But you'll feel *so* much better once you go upstairs and speak your vows to the earl, I promise you will!"

As if to add an exclamation point, a tiny foot kicked Laura. She stepped back in surprise.

Violet lovingly stroked her belly. "See? Penelope is ordering you to cheer up, too."

Laura managed a wobbly smile. "Penelope may well be a boy. And please do explain how I am to cheer up. I'm about to wed the man who once attempted to arrest my father."

Perhaps that appalling fact lay at the heart of her dilemma. She had despised Alex for so many years. He still believed her father was guilty of theft. How could she even *think* of binding her life to him forever? It seemed unforgivably traitorous to Papa's memory.

"Your father would have wanted you to be happy," Violet declared. "And the earl *will* make you happy. I know he will."

Laura felt a curl of longing in the midst of her doubts. But what would happen if—*when*—she proved that Lord Haversham was the true culprit? Would Alex be willing to dredge up the old scandal and send a fellow nobleman to prison? "I wish I could be certain of that."

"He spared no expense in buying you a trousseau. He could scarcely wait a moment to be married to you. And look, there's also his wedding gift." Violet held forth a small box in her hand. "He asked me to give this to you. That's why I was waiting downstairs here for your arrival."

Laura took the oblong container. It was a jeweler's case made of rich brown leather with silver trim.

She bit her lip. The last time Alex had given her such a box, it had contained a pair of gold-rimmed spectacles. But today it surely would be jewels, something magnificent and costly as befitting the bride of an earl.

A lump formed in her throat. Didn't he *know*? All she really wanted from him was love—along with his trust that she was a better judge of her own father's character.

"Do open it," Violet urged. "I've been dying to see what's inside. Do you suppose it's the Copley diamonds? Mama told me just yesterday that the earl's mother used to wear them everywhere, even when she went out for a drive on Rotten Row."

Intrigued by the prospect of viewing a Copley family heirloom, Laura slowly lifted the lid. But it wasn't the cold sparkle of diamonds that met her eye. Inside, a simple string of pearls glowed against a nest of crimson velvet.

Her breath caught. In the throes of astonishment, she stared down at the pearls. "It can't be," she murmured.

"Can't be what?" Violet asked, peering over her shoulder.

Laura didn't answer. In haste, she plucked out the necklace, abandoned the box on the table, and hurried to the window to examine the clasp in the sunlight. Her heart throbbed in heavy strokes. There, engraved in tiny letters, were the initials AF.

Aileen Falkner, who had died shortly after Laura's birth.

She blinked to clear the happy tears that misted her eyes. As she cradled the string in her hands, the pearls felt warm and alive. Seeing Violet staring at her strangely, she laughed in delight. "These are my mother's pearls. They were a gift to her from my father on their wedding day. I wore them at my come-out ball. How did Alex remember? How did he *find* them—?"

"Why, he must have bought them at the auction all those years ago," Violet said in wonderment. "Oh, my stars! I've never heard of *anything* so romantic. That *proves* he was pining for you back then. He was hoping he'd see you again so that he could return the necklace into your keeping."

Was that true? Laura found it difficult to imagine Alex *pining*. He had a sophisticated wit that belied any hidden, mawkish emotions. Yet she could think of no other explanation for his actions. And she felt suddenly keen to see him.

She placed the strand around her neck. "Please, will you fasten the clasp for me?"

Violet obliged, then steered her to a mirror on the wall. "How absolutely perfect! I daresay, the earl will be bowled over to see what a beautiful bride you are."

Laura had to agree that the necklace enhanced the delicate dove gray of her gown. But more than that, she loved the way the pearls lay heavy and warm against her skin, providing a connection to the mother she had never known. Had Mama felt this surfeit of emotions on her wedding day, too? This aching desire for happiness?

Laura drew a deep breath. "I'm ready now. Shall we go?"

Together she and Violet mounted the marble staircase to the first floor, where a forest-green carpet cushioned their footsteps. This reception hall was even grander than the entry, with an enormous crystal chandelier suspended from a domed ceiling painted with mythological scenes. As they neared an arched doorway, Violet stopped at a gilt table against the wall and handed Laura a nosegay of pink roses.

She kissed Laura's cheek, then whispered, "When

you hear the music, come inside. And never fear, the earl is madly in love with you. I *know* he is."

If only Laura could believe that. But she *wanted* to think so. She wanted it with a desperation that overcame her uncertainties.

With a twitch of her pale green skirts, Violet disappeared through the doorway. Laura waited on pins and needles for what seemed like an hour, though by the ticking casement clock, only a minute or two had passed. Then, hearing the harmony of harp and violin, she walked to the doorway of a magnificent drawing room.

The decor had a tasteful simplicity with gold and blue appointments, Laura noted in somewhat of a daze. A quartet of musicians occupied the far corner. In the center of the long room, the wedding guests filled three rows of chairs in front of a mantelpiece of cream marble.

As one, the company turned to look at her. An excited buzz of whispers ensued, and she spied Violet's husband Frederick, Lady Josephine, Lady Milford, and several other people she didn't recognize.

The Duchess of Knowles had refused an invitation. In a clipped tone, Alex had said that his godmother had washed her hands of them. Laura couldn't be sorry. At least she wouldn't have to suffer glares on her wedding day.

Then she forgot all else as her gaze settled on the tall man standing by the fireplace, his head cocked to listen as the black-robed minister spoke a few words to him.

Alexander Ross, the Earl of Copley, looked positively alluring in a charcoal-gray formal coat with long tails, a pewter waistcoat, and black trousers. The perfect white cravat complemented his dark hand-

someness. He was the epitome of the proud nobleman, and the scar on his cheek added the merest hint
of a dangerous rogue.

Straightening, he looked across the room at her.
His stern gaze caressed her from head to toe. As his
eyes met hers, a faint smile crooked his lips. Warmth
lurked there in place of his customary sardonic disdain. A warmth that stirred a tremor of hope in her
heart.

From the back row, a stoop-shouldered gentleman
with thinning brown hair came scurrying to her side.
He must be Alex's cousin and heir, Mr. Lewis Ross,
who was to escort her in lieu of her father. With a
solemn nod, Mr. Ross offered his arm, and they proceeded up the aisle between the chairs.

At last she reached Alex. They stood side by side
facing the minister, who opened his prayer book and
began, "Dearly beloved, we are gathered together
here . . ."

The ceremony passed in a blur for Laura. She tried
to heed the words, yet all the while she was conscious
of Alex's tall, masculine form beside her. In a fog of
wonderment, she reflected that only a few weeks ago,
she had come to London in disguise for fear of encountering him. And now here they stood in his
house, each in turn speaking "I will" in response to
the cleric.

They turned to face each other. Alex took her right
hand in his, his grip firm. Watching her with an un-
wavering stare, he solemnly recited his vow: "I, Alexander, take thee, Laura, to be my wedded wife, to have
and to hold from this day forward, for better for worse,
for richer for poorer, in sickness and in health, to love
and to cherish, till death us do part, according to God's
holy ordinance; and thereto I plight thee my troth."

His face was grave, though his eyes conveyed the heat of passion. Was it only bodily desire he felt for her—or did his emotions run deeper?

Laura repeated her own pledge to him, feeling every word resonate in her heart. She wanted to believe that he meant his, too. If he did not, then by the heavens, she would *make* him love and cherish her.

Somehow.

At last she removed her glove, and he slid a gold ring onto her finger. Then he bent to brush a lingering kiss across her lips. Her hands rested lightly on his lapels, and her heart felt in danger of beating out of her breast. They drew apart, and the final blessings were pronounced by the cleric before he presented them to the gathering as Lord and Lady Copley.

Alex glanced down at her, and their gazes held for a brief eloquent moment before he turned away to greet their guests. His expression held warmth as well as something oddly like . . . satisfaction. But Laura had no time to ponder. The string quartet resumed playing, and everyone crowded forward to express their congratulations. She found herself enveloped in hugs by the ladies and pecked on the cheek by the gentlemen. Alex kept his hand at the small of her back, his face relaxed and smiling.

After a time, they signed the register that the cleric had brought; then Alex directed the milling throng to proceed into the dining chamber for the wedding luncheon—without the bride and groom. "It's customary to introduce the new countess to the household staff directly after the ceremony," he said. "My wife and I will join all of you shortly."

My wife.

A shiver of bliss coursed through Laura. She slipped her hand into his, and as they walked out the door and left the guests behind, he looked down at her with a hint of dry humor. "You were late, Countess. I was beginning to wonder if you'd absconded with the pearls."

"The pearls!" Her fingers flew to them, caressing their smooth roundness. "Oh, Alex. I can't begin to tell you how much they mean to me. Did you buy them at the auction when my father's possessions were sold?"

"Yes. I have a fond memory of you wearing that necklace on one occasion in particular. It was at a party and we'd gone into an antechamber for a bit of privacy from the crowds. But there were voices approaching, so—"

"So you dragged me into a linen closet to escape them. And we were trapped there in the dark for half an hour while people talked right outside the door."

"We passed the time rather agreeably, wouldn't you say? I've never enjoyed kissing a girl quite so much. Though we didn't do a fraction of what I was craving to do." He lowered his voice to a husky murmur. "But now, my lady, proprieties need no longer constrain us. We may indulge ourselves as we wish."

His words ignited a burn deep inside Laura. By the faintly smug quality to his smile, she knew the reaction was exactly what he'd intended her to have. So she stood on tiptoe and whispered in his ear, "What a pity we have guests, then. Else we might have indulged ourselves right now."

His eyes darkened, and his expression took on a look of intense frustration. "I'll send them all home."

"Absolutely not," she scolded with a smile. "I won't start our marriage with such scandalous behavior. We will have our wedding celebration first."

As they walked downstairs, Laura reflected that he

had not acquired the pearls out of love for her. The necklace had reminded him of a passionate encounter, that was all. But she wouldn't let herself dwell on that disappointment. From the start, Alex had been frank about his desire for her. He had not misled her. She had only her own foolish heart to blame. Nevertheless, she intended to garner as much happiness as possible from this marriage.

Some twenty servants lined up in the entrance hall, from the lowliest scullery maid to the upper staff. Alex introduced them one by one, and Laura concentrated on committing the names to memory. The butler was a distinguished man named Hodge, while the housekeeper was Mrs. Mayhew, a plump, smiling, grandmotherly type who was quite the opposite of the spiteful Mrs. Samson. A sober, middle-aged woman named Winifred had been hired to act as Laura's personal maid.

Having grown up without a mother, Laura had learned from a young age the responsibilities of running a household. She found herself slipping easily into the role as if the intervening ten years had never happened, and she made arrangements to meet with Mrs. Mayhew in the morning to discuss the menus and other pertinent issues, including the procuring of a new companion for Lady Josephine.

"I intend to conduct the interviews myself," Laura told Alex as they went back upstairs to rejoin their guests. "In the rush of making our own plans, I fear that I've left your aunt in the lurch."

"Aunt Josie will be fine. She has a staff to watch over her until other arrangements can be made."

"Perhaps we should have moved her here to live with us."

"She wouldn't be happy without all her clutter. You

know that." Reaching the top of the stairs, he drew her close and kissed her brow. "Now, I forbid any more fretting. You're to enjoy our wedding day—and look forward to the night to come."

His smile held a banked desire that filled her with a buoyant sense of expectation. Going into the dining chamber, they took their places at opposite ends of a long table. Laughter and chatter filled the bright sunny room. The champagne flowed freely, while a team of footmen delivered an endless array of superb dishes, and Laura made a valiant effort to sample every one of them.

Violet sat to her right, with her husband beside her, and Laura was pleased to see that the dull and proper Frederick Blankenship adored his wife. It was evident in the way he smiled at her, the attentiveness with which he watched over Violet, worrying that she might overtire herself. They shared a cozy familiarity that Laura envied. Oh, that her own marriage might hold such mutual affection in the years to come . . .

At Laura's other hand sat Lady Milford, resplendent in a soft plum silk that intensified the amethyst hue of her eyes. "Well, Laura," she murmured in a moment of relative privacy, "things have turned out rather well, wouldn't you say?"

"Something tells me you planned it that way," Laura said, laughing as she took a sip of champagne.

Lady Milford smiled rather cryptically. "It wasn't entirely me, I'm sure. By the by, I'm pleased to see that today you're wearing the slippers I gave to you."

"Yes, I also wore them on the night Alex asked me to marry him."

"Then one might say they have brought you good fortune."

Gazing into the woman's serenely ageless face,

Laura felt the inexplicable compulsion to reply, "Perhaps I should return them to you. I've so many new shoes that I won't need yours anymore."

"An excellent decision, my dear. I'll collect the pair from you soon." Lady Milford's enigmatic smile deepened. "One never knows when there might be another deserving young lady in want of good luck."

Chapter 22

Laura sat propped against a nest of feather pillows in the four-poster bed with its hangings of seafoam-green silk. A low fire burned on the hearth. On either side of the alabaster mantelpiece, a silver branch of candles cast a soft glow over the spacious chamber with its luxurious furnishings.

She had readied herself in record time. Preparing for bed had been effortless with someone there to untie the corset strings, to fold the petticoats and stockings, to fetch warm water for washing, to braid her hair. Winifred had been respectful and efficient, and so deferential that it had made Laura very aware of the elevation in her status.

At any other time, she would have attempted to befriend the woman. Kindness fostered loyalty in a servant, she knew. But tonight her thoughts had been too distracted for conversation. She'd swiftly donned her filmy nightdress and dismissed the maid.

Anticipation nibbled at her composure. The mattress was cushiony, the linens soft. But she felt no inclination to relax and close her eyes. Instead, her gaze strayed to the connecting door in the corner. That had to be the entry to the earl's suite of rooms.

Where *was* Alex? When they'd parted more than half an hour ago, he had been heading down to the library with his cousin Lewis to lend the man a book on his way out.

Were they still there talking?

With a sigh, Laura unbraided her long hair, deciding to leave it loose. If only *she* had thought to fetch a book, it would have kept her mind occupied. But she could hardly wander downstairs now in her night-clothes. And there was nothing whatsoever to be read in this pristine room.

That would have to change in the future—though making such a resolve didn't help her in the present.

Seeking a distraction, she inspected the white coverlet with its elaborate pattern of embroidered pink roses and green leaves. Had the previous countess done the needlework? Lady Josephine had described Alex's mother, Blanche, as flighty and whimsical. Would Blanche have bent over a tambour frame for hours on end? Laura knew too little about the woman to be certain.

But she didn't intend for such tame pursuits to be *her* fate. She liked to be active, to stay busy and involved, not to be left to sit . . . and wait.

Temporarily abandoning her plan to be ensconced in bed when Alex arrived, Laura threw back the covers. The carpet felt plush against her bare feet as she padded to a bank of pale green draperies. Parting them, she peeked out an open window that overlooked the darkened garden at the back of the house. The cobalt blue of twilight lingered on the horizon, and pinpricks of light shone in neighboring residences.

At this very moment, members of the ton would be

dressing for balls and parties, which often didn't begin until ten o'clock. How novel to think that while the nobility danced the night away—and gossiped about the scandalous marriage of the Earl of Copley to the notorious Miss Falkner—she and Alex would be lying in each other's arms, engaged in unknown intimacies.

Her thoughts dwelled on the consummation. She had a general notion of what went on between husband and wife, though not the specifics, and she craved to learn all of it. Curiosity caused a quickening of her blood, stirring an impatience that she found difficult to assuage.

Where is my husband?

Laura paced to a dainty writing desk beside the fireplace and seated herself on a straight-backed chair. The cherrywood surface gleamed in the candlelight. If she could locate the proper supplies, she might pass the time by sketching.

Opening the single drawer, Laura felt like a thief rifling through someone else's possessions. She had to remind herself that every item in this chamber now belonged to her—even though her sense of decorum hadn't quite accepted the reality of that yet.

Inside the shallow drawer lay a tidy stack of notepaper embossed with the Copley crest. She also discovered sealing wax, a silver ink pot, and an assortment of quill pens. Not seeing a pencil, she slipped her hand into the very back of the drawer in case one might have rolled out of sight.

Instead of a cylindrical writing implement, however, her fingers encountered a small, oval object. She brought it out, tilted the flat surface to the candlelight, and saw to her surprise that it was a miniature. The protective glass had been shattered, with several cracks directly over the diminutive painting.

Despite the fractures, she could discern the image of an older gentleman with dour features, a strong jaw, and dark eyes and hair. He bore an uncanny resemblance to Alex.

Was this the old earl, Alex's late father? Surely it had to be.

But why was the glass broken? Had his mother dropped the miniature, then slipped it into the drawer to be repaired later? Or had she smashed it in a rage and hidden the damage from sight?

Lady Josephine had said that his parents had often fought. *It was quite shocking the way the two of them would scream at each other! I daresay poor Alexander witnessed far too many quarrels in his time . . .*

A door clicked open at the other end of the bedchamber. Startled, Laura guiltily dropped the miniature back in its place, shut the drawer, and turned on the chair to peer over her shoulder.

Alex strolled into the bedchamber.

With a wild leap, her heart set off racing. He had changed out of his wedding clothes into a loose linen shirt over a pair of breeches. His feet were bare, and she had the sudden fantasy of him climbing the rigging of a pirate ship with a knife clenched in his teeth.

He came halfway into the room and stopped, his gaze intent on her. "Pray forgive the delay," he said in his usual tone of dry wit. "I had trouble pushing Lewis out the door. Once my cousin starts jabbering about military history, it's nearly impossible to . . ."

His words petered out as Laura stood up from the chair and took a few steps toward him. His gaze dropped to her nightdress. She wore nothing underneath it. And she realized belatedly that the backlight of the fire through the gossamer fabric must be giving him a spectacular view of her curves.

A blush seared her from head to toe. If only she'd waited in bed like a good wife. With the covers drawn to her chin. Then again, she *liked* the entranced look on his face. She liked it enormously.

Those thoughts flitted through her mind in swift succession. Since Alex appeared too transfixed to move, Laura felt a compulsion to be bold. And why not? They were husband and wife now.

She walked forward with a deliberate sway to her hips. "Military history, you say? Do you truly find that more interesting than your bride?"

"No! I only thought you needed time . . . to do whatever women need to do."

Reaching him, she flattened her palms on the wall of his chest. The heat of his skin penetrated the thin fabric of his shirt. In a soft, throaty voice, she said, "What I need, Alex, is *you*. Only you. And I don't like to be kept waiting."

To her delight, she found herself instantly caught up in his arms, clasped in a hard embrace, his mouth crushing hers. He kissed her with a ferocity that left no doubt as to his desire for her. She returned his passion with her own wholehearted participation. All the while, his hands traversed up and down her body, cupping her bottom and holding her so close that she could not fail to notice the hardness at his loins. Obeying instinct, she tilted her hips, the better to satisfy her illicit interest.

A groan emanated from deep in his throat. Alex drew back slightly, his breathing rough as he nuzzled her hair. Against her breasts, she felt the heavy pounding of his heartbeat. "Enough," he muttered. "There's no need to rush. We have all night."

With that, he caught her up into his arms and she clung to him, inhaling the allure of his spicy scent.

He carried her to an overstuffed chair by the hearth, where he sat down and settled her in his lap.

Laura melted into the solid crook of his arm. She loved being cuddled against his muscled body, yet his action surprised her. "Not . . . the bed?"

"In a little while," he said, pressing a kiss to her brow. "I've waited too long to hold you like this. I won't allow matters to be concluded too swiftly."

"But if we desire each other . . ."

"Then we should take our time to hone our pleasure. Trust me, Laura. I know exactly what you want."

For once, his arrogant manner didn't irk her. She *did* trust him—in this at least—and she craved to go wherever he led her. Catching hold of his hand, she pressed a kiss in his palm. "Then pray do not delay."

Alex chuckled. "As you wish, my lady."

He brushed his lips over hers in teasing kisses that made her become as pliant as clay, ready to be molded by his expert mouth and hands. The heat in his dark eyes sent shivers over her skin. Plucking open the row of dainty pearl buttons down the front of her bodice, he reached inside to weigh the globe of one breast in the palm of his hand. The lazy stroking of his thumb over the tip sent ribbons of pleasure unfurling downward to her inmost depths.

A sigh eased from her lips. "Oh, Alex, that *is* what I want."

He merely smiled, then lowered his head to take her into his mouth. As she gasped in appreciative surprise, he suckled her, unleashing a chaos of new sensations. He turned his attention to her other breast, and Laura could only look down in a blissful bemusement at his head, bent over her open bodice while he feasted on her bare bosom. In all her secret fantasies of lovemaking, never had she expected him to do such divine things with his tongue and mouth.

Her fingers threaded into the thick silk of his hair to encourage him. How strange to think that only a fortnight ago, she had despised this man with all her heart and soul. She had relegated their youthful romance to the ash heap of history. Yet now she was his wife and she desired him with a desperation that could only be termed unladylike.

At last he brought up his head to hers again, awarding her another deep kiss that ended with a gentle nip of his teeth on her lower lip. When he tugged at the hem of her nightdress, she mindlessly lifted herself to let him pull the garment up to her waist, leaving her privates hidden beneath a pool of draping. Her breathing had become quick and shallow. The smoothness of his breeches beneath her bare legs felt wickedly wonderful. So did the movement of his hand as it slipped up her thigh and delved beneath the fabric to idly caress her hip.

A faint smile quirked his lips. "Might I say, Countess, the gown is perfect. The sight of you standing there stunned me . . . I'm *still* stunned by your beauty."

It had taken a good deal of convincing by Violet to talk Laura into the purchase. But now that she could see the admiration on his face, she understood the genius of wearing such a revealing garment. It gave a wife power over her husband.

Laura caressed his cheek. "I'd hoped it would please you. Though I feared it might be *too* risqué."

"You can never be too risqué—so long as you're with *me*." He paused, his brooding gaze flicking down to her bared breasts. "And let it be known, I intend to make certain that you never desire any other man."

His possessiveness both thrilled and intrigued her.

He must still be irked over that legal agreement she had made him sign. Didn't he realize that she had only been trying to protect herself in case *he* lost interest in *her*?

Then all rational thought fled her mind as he shifted his hand to the apex of her thighs and began to caress her there. His finger glided into the dampness of her most secret folds, rubbing lightly and igniting a deep pulse beat that spread fire through her insides. Dizzy with the onrush of desire, Laura clutched at his arms for support. "Oh, heavens . . . what are you . . . ?"

He nuzzled her neck. "Shh, my darling. Just let yourself enjoy it."

Alex continued his slow exploration, and she melted into him, giving herself up to the tempting sensations he provoked in her. It truly *was* the most enticing turmoil she had ever experienced. As her passion mounted, she arched against his hand in an attempt to find surcease from the maddening rise of excitement. Time ceased to exist, and a craving built in her for something she couldn't name. She moaned, her hips moving, seeking, as he plied her with ever-deepening strokes. At last his finger slipped inside her in a shockingly intimate caress, and she tumbled into waves of the most powerful pleasure of her life.

Lying against him in the aftermath, limp and blissful, Laura felt herself lifted in his arms as he carried her to the bed. The coolness of the sheets against her back restored a modicum of awareness to her, though she could only smile at him in an incoherent daze.

Alex stood beside the bed and stripped off his linen shirt. In the candlelight, he had the perfect physique of a deity, his shoulders broad, his chest lightly dusted with black hair, his waist firm and narrow. The rippling muscles across his abdomen fascinated her, as did the flat nipples that resembled ancient bronze coins.

Rolling onto her side, Laura propped herself up on her elbow and watched him unbutton his breeches. "You are truly magnificent," she murmured, voicing the first lucid thought that entered her mind. "I would very much like to sketch you . . ."

The words died in her throat as he peeled down his trousers and kicked them aside. He wore nothing beneath, and the sight of his jutting member rendered her speechless. She knew the male anatomy from her study of Greek and Roman statuary in books. But those elegant illustrations had not prepared her for the fullness of him.

A smirk on his lips, Alex stood there in all his naked glory. Then he strutted the few steps toward her and sat on the edge of the bed, the mattress dipping beneath his weight. He leaned down to brush a kiss over her mouth. "Magnificent, hmm?"

A blush burned her, even as she stole another glance below his waist. The sight robbed her of breath. "And shameless."

"So you will be, too, I hope. Now sit up a moment. Risqué as it is, that gown has outlasted its purpose."

An ingrained modesty made Laura hesitate to divest herself of the scant covering. But hadn't she already abandoned all propriety by allowing him to stroke her between her legs? And she did so want to find out what other delights he had in store for her.

She scooted into a sitting position and tugged the garment over her head. The action mussed her loose hair so that several tawny gold strands curled around her bare bosom. It gratified her to see that Alex's smirk had vanished. He sat watching her with a fierce intensity, as she had watched him. His lashes were slightly lowered, his eyes nearly black with concentration.

On a whim, Laura combed her fingers through her long locks as if to straighten them. She continued playing with her hair, letting it fall over her shoulders and down onto her breasts like an ever-stirring curtain. Each rippling movement revealed a tantalizing glimpse of the peaks that so engaged his interest.

This went on for several minutes until Alex frowned, lifting his gaze to her face as if it had just dawned on him that her actions were purposeful. Then an appreciative grin tipped one corner of his mouth.

He caught her by the shoulders and pressed her back against the pillows, bringing his body down over hers. "Wicked little jade. Where did you learn that move?"

Despite his smile, a possessive note tinged his voice again. Laura didn't want him to think even for a second that she'd ever done this with any other man. What was it that had made him so suspicious of women? The answer was something she yearned to find out, though now was not the time.

She tenderly touched his jaw. "You inspire me, my lord. I want to make you as happy as you've made me."

He released a long breath, and in his eyes she glimpsed something rich and deep before he lowered his mouth to hers. "Laura," he whispered against her lips. "Just being here with you makes me happy."

He kissed her with a fierceness that she met with her own unleashed desires. She loved the heaviness of his body on hers, the caress of his hands, the groans she elicited in him by her own explorations. Already, the drumbeat of passion throbbed again in her inmost depths, and now that Laura knew the ecstasy that awaited her, she opened her legs in wanton invitation.

With all her heart, she wanted to experience that joy again, this time with Alex.

"Please . . . ," she whispered, impatient for him to get on with matters. "Oh, please . . ."

"*Yes.*"

On that guttural word, he lifted himself slightly and she felt the probing pressure of his entry. She experienced a moment of burning discomfort and gave an involuntary wince as he filled her completely. He went still, breathing hard, his entire body taut as he threaded his fingers into her hair.

His eyes searched hers. "Am I hurting you?" he asked hoarsely.

"No! No, not at all." Laura cupped his face in her hands as the joining of their bodies made her heart overflow. "Oh, Alex, I . . ." *I love you.* Just in time, she stopped herself. She couldn't love him, she mustn't, not when they had agreed on a marriage of mutual convenience. "I've wanted you for so long."

"We belong together." His tone fierce, he moved deep inside her. "Like this. Forever."

His arms quivered as if he were exerting great effort to control his passions. But she didn't want restraint. She craved the wild, uninhibited indulgence of their desires. Her head tilted back on the pillows and she arched her hips, the better to feel him inside of her.

Muttering her name, he buried his face in her throat. Carnal pleasure built in her with every plunge of his hips. As her need mounted to a fever pitch, she writhed like a creature of pure sensuality. They found the same rhythm, striving together, kissing and caressing until even those actions seemed superfluous to the demands of their loins. The world narrowed to the fevered beating of her blood, the seductive friction of his thrusts, and at last the shattering euphoria of release. Before the heavenly waves had ebbed, Alex uttered a primal groan, his body convulsing, then settling heavily over hers.

They lay entwined in perfect peace as their breathing eased and their hearts slowed. She was well and truly his wife now, Laura thought in drowsy contentment. There was no going back. For better or for worse, her life was intrinsically bound to his.

Alex came to an awareness that he must be crushing Laura, though she uttered no complaint. He shifted onto his side and drew her close with his hand resting on the charming curve of her bare bottom. She slipped an indolent arm around his waist. Her eyes were slumberous, her hair in a glorious golden tangle. She was the very essence of a well-satisfied woman.

"Mmm," she murmured, nestling her cheek onto his shoulder.

A rush of tenderness left him shaken. Disavowing the mawkish sentiment, Alex placed his chin on top of her head and gazed into the shadowy corners of the bedchamber. Laura was everything he had ever imagined—and more. A man couldn't hope for a more sultry, captivating wife to warm his bed. She had been incredibly responsive and eager. Yet his mind dwelled on one moment in particular.

Alex, I . . . I've wanted you for so long.

Was that what she'd initially meant to say? Or had she almost spilled out her love for him? There had been a distinct pause, as if she'd reconsidered her words and caught herself in time.

No. He mustn't delude himself just because he craved to secure her undying devotion. Of course she'd spoken in fits and starts. It was only natural that her thoughts had been disjointed at that time. He had just entered her body and initiated her into joys of lovemaking.

A vast sense of satisfaction crowded out all else. She belonged to him now. He intended to keep her so happy in bed that she would forget about that document she'd required him to sign. A house of her own after giving him two sons— as if he would ever allow her to leave him!

His arms tightened possessively, and she tilted a dreamy smile up at him. He had a keen awareness of her sleek body pressed to him, the soft breasts, the slim hips, the long legs. A pity it was too soon to make love to her again. She had wrung him dry for the moment.

He feathered his lips over hers. "I must confess to being extremely pleased that no other man has laid claim to you these past ten years."

"Oh, a few tried, but I was quick to discourage their interest." Her warm smile softened to a more pensive look. "My father and I kept to ourselves by necessity, you know. We lived in a small cottage in the mountains. We didn't dare encourage any friendships for fear that someone might ask too many questions."

Alex had a sudden stark picture of her life, cut off from all society. He pressed a remorseful kiss to her brow. "Forgive me, darling. I didn't mean to stir unhappy memories for you."

"Oh, but I wasn't *unhappy*. It's perfectly beautiful there. I'd like to show it to you someday." A sparkle lit up her gorgeous blue eyes, and she touched his cheek. "Do you suppose we might go to Portugal for our wedding trip? Not now, but perhaps later in the summer?"

That syrupy softness took up residence in his chest again. He would go to the ends of the earth if it made her happy. "We can depart next week if you like. As soon as arrangements can be made."

"No, not yet." Her expression sobering, she gave a firm shake of her head. "First, I must speak to Lord Haversham. Pray remember, I am determined to clear Papa's name."

Alex fought to keep his face neutral. He disliked seeing Laura so caught up in chasing shadows. "Leave the matter to me. I'll see what I can find out."

"But I want to question Haversham myself. I owe it to Papa's memory." A haunted sadness stole over her delicate features. "Alex, there's something I haven't ever mentioned to you. I believe . . . I *fear* that my father may have been murdered."

Had she poked him with a pin, she could not have startled him more. "*What?*"

"It's true," she murmured, a catch in her voice. "I should have told you the circumstances of his death. It happened here in London, shortly after his arrival."

Deeply disturbed by her words, Alex sat up against the pillows, bringing Laura with him and tucking her within the circle of his arms. He gently pushed a strand of hair off her cheek. "I want to hear everything, Laura. Don't leave anything out."

She explained about receiving the express letter from the London police, that Martin Falkner had been found beaten insensible in an alley near Covent Garden, and how she had rushed to England to nurse him, only to discover that he'd already expired from his wounds.

"The police said . . . . that he'd been set upon by

footpads. But it *can't* be merely a coincidence, since he'd come to confront Haversham. It just can't be."

Alex had a disquieting thought. What if Martin had returned to London to fetch the Blue Moon diamond from a secret hiding place? What if he'd been observed by thieves and then attacked?

He kept that suspicion to himself. Laura believed staunchly in her father's innocence. She was certain that she'd hit upon the true culprit in Haversham. But she wasn't privy to all the facts about what had happened back then. Nor was Alex at liberty to tell her.

As much as the secret burdened him, however, he abhorred the notion of Laura ever finding out the truth. She would never forgive him.

Grasping her shoulders, he said, "Listen to me, Laura. I've known Haversham most of my life. He may be a dour man, but he's no murderer."

Her teeth worried her lower lip. "Perhaps he hired a ruffian to do the deed. If the marquess believed that his crime was about to be exposed, he might very well have taken drastic action to stop Papa."

Alex refrained from pointing out the flaw in her reasoning. She had assumed Haversham to be the guilty party solely on the basis of a long-ago feud. She didn't have a scrap of proof. Yet Alex knew he wouldn't easily talk her out of her suspicions—and he didn't wish to spoil their wedding night.

"Allow me time to consider the matter, will you? We'll speak of it on the morrow when I can think more clearly." Drawing her close, he rubbed a soothing pattern over the silky-smooth skin of her back. "For now, I confess to being a trifle . . . distracted."

He meant only to tease her out of the doldrums, to

make her smile again. But when she tilted back her head, all trace of anxiety had vanished from her face, and she regarded him with a provocative flutter of her lashes. "I can't imagine what you mean, my lord."

That sultry look stirred his blood. "Then allow me to show you."

Their lips met in a deep, open-mouthed kiss that went on forever. He had never cared much to dally over kisses—except with Laura. And now that their initial madness had been sated, they could enjoy each other in a more leisurely fashion. While his body recouped its vigor, he could take his time dawdling over the delights of her breasts and hips, showing her how to bask in the pleasures of unhurried lovemaking.

But Laura threw his plans into disarray when she slipped a hand between his thighs to glide her fingers over his shaft. His stamina surged back in full, hot-blooded arousal. He sucked in a breath and released it in an attempt to control himself. "*Laura . . .*"

She flashed him a too-innocent smile. "Am I being too forward?"

"Am *I*?" he countered, reaching down to stroke her moist heat.

Moaning his name, she parted her legs to encourage his ministrations. The outside world fell away as they lost themselves to the pleasures of the flesh. Alex was driven by a fierce desire to imprint himself on her, body and soul. No other woman had ever roused such depths of raw feelings in him as Laura did.

In the aftermath, while she slept in his arms and the candles guttered out, he gazed into the gloom of the bedchamber and thought about the violent circumstances of her father's death. He couldn't shake the nagging sense that he was missing something vital, something to do with the disappearance of the Blue

Moon diamond. The news had cast a disturbing new light on his long-held convictions about the robbery.

Was it even possible she was right? That someone else really *had* committed the crime? If there was the slightest chance of that, he would move heaven and earth to help her uncover the truth.

Chapter 23

As the casement clock in the reception hall struck eleven the following morning, Laura started down the grand staircase. She wore one of her new gowns, a cobalt-blue watered silk with matching ribbons on her straw bonnet. How strange it felt to be dressed so stylishly, and to be mistress of this elegant house. She had spent over an hour touring the residence with Mrs. Mayhew and had come away satisfied with the housekeeper's superior management skills.

In the entrance hall below, sunshine streamed through the long windows on either side of the doors, lending an airy brightness to the pale green walls and cream marble floor. The life-sized alabaster statue of a winged goddess glowed on its pedestal in the center of the room. The rural landscapes on the walls appeared to have been painted by notable artists, although Laura had not yet had time for a closer inspection.

A mere two months ago, she had been living in a cozy cottage in the mountains of Portugal, spending her days weeding in the garden, cooking the meals, sweeping and tidying the rooms. Now she had a gardener, a French chef, and a host of upper and lower servants to do her bidding. A tug on the bell rope would bring a footman or a maid within moments. Already she had been the recipient of more bows and curtsies than she had known in the last ten years combined.

It was all so overwhelming—and a bit smothering, if truth be told. If only Alex were here, perhaps she might have felt more at ease.

Laura had awakened to an empty bed. He must have left her chamber around dawn, shortly after they had made love again to the sleepy twittering of birds out in the garden. Then she had dozed for a time, coming awake to full sunlight and Winifred directing a line of maidservants carrying cans of steaming hot water to fill the brass tub in the dressing room. While bathing, Laura had learned from her maid that the earl had departed the house for parts unknown.

She had tried not to feel disappointed. It was only that her heart felt as tender as the rest of her body, which ached a little from the uncustomary activities of the night. She'd known not to expect a romantic honeymoon with an adoring husband always at her side. Alex wanted an heir. Theirs was a marriage of mutual convenience based on lust, not love.

Yet he had been so affectionate in bed that she had allowed herself to hope his feelings for her might run deeper than the physical. She had let herself imagine that his wedding gift of her mother's pearls really *could* mean more than a mere token of a passionate encounter long ago. But he had spoken no words of love. And he had not even left her a note this morning.

Where had he gone?

Myriad possibilities flitted through her mind. Aristocratic husbands and wives often went their separate ways during the day. A gentleman might take a ride in the park, visit his tailor, or go to his club to read the newspapers and to discuss politics. However, Laura couldn't help but wonder if his disappearance had something to do with her revealing the circumstances of Papa's death. It vexed her to think that Alex might have gone to see Lord Haversham without her.

She wanted to be there to observe the marquess's face as he answered their questions. What if Alex didn't probe deeply enough into the matter? He still believed her father to be the thief. Laura didn't want this opportunity to be squandered.

For that reason, she intended to call on Lord Haversham herself.

Reaching the bottom of the stairs, she headed across the pale marble floor of the entrance hall. A white-wigged footman in blue livery stood on duty. At her approach, he reached a gloved hand to open the front door.

"My lady, might I have a word?" The deferential male voice came from behind her along with the echoing tap of footsteps.

She turned to see the butler approaching from a long corridor. A dignified man in a black suit, he had age-lined features and thinning gray hair. At the moment, his brows were drawn in faint worry.

Laura smiled. "Good morning, Hodge."

He bowed. "My lady, I do beg your pardon. But I wasn't told you would require the carriage. Shall I have it brought 'round at once?"

"That won't be necessary. I'm going for a walk."

"But his lordship expressly bade that you not venture out alone. Might I call a footman or a maid to accompany you?"

Why would Alex issue such an order? Was he merely looking out for her comfort? Or did he think solitary strolls inappropriate to her newly exalted position?

She wouldn't be coddled. "No, thank you. When the earl returns, pray tell him that I've gone to visit his aunt."

It wasn't precisely a lie. She *did* intend to visit Lady Josephine, but not until making a stop at Lord Haversham's house.

The footman opened the door, and Laura escaped out onto the portico where she paused to absorb the surroundings. Copley House faced Hyde Park, and a good deal of traffic moved up and down the busy thoroughfare. Cabs and drays jockeyed for position with fine carriages and coaches. A stout gentleman on horseback was likely heading into the park to exercise his mount on the long dirt road known as Rotten Row, which later in the afternoon would be crammed with aristocratic vehicles.

The fine June morning already had attracted a fair number of people into the vast park. She could see them through the iron fence strolling among the leafy green trees, nannies with their young charges, groups of ladies, and courting couples. On the street side of the fence, pedestrians streamed back and forth along the foot pavement, tradesmen and workmen, housewives carrying parcels or shopping baskets.

Laura was about to step down from the portico when she noticed a man lounging against a lamppost directly across the broad avenue. An odd familiarity about his stocky form caught her attention. Her skin prickled with uneasiness. She shaded her eyes to discern his features. Although his cap was pulled down low on his forehead, she could see that he had muttonchop whiskers and the bulky build of a pugilist.

He appeared to be staring straight back at her.

Recognition jarred Laura. He bore an uncanny resemblance to the police officer who had escorted her to Papa's grave site, then chased her through the slums.

Her heart banged against her ribs. Alarmed, she didn't stop to think. She spun around and pushed open the heavy door to return to the safety of Copley House.

Hodge and the footman were speaking in the entrance hall. Both servants turned startled faces toward her, the footman springing forward to help her with the door.

The butler hastened to her with a solicitous expression on his aging features. "My lady? Is aught amiss?"

Realizing how unorthodox her action must appear, Laura feigned a smile. "Of course not. It's . . . warmer outside than I'd realized. I do believe I *shall* take the carriage, after all."

"Excellent. I'll order it at once."

As the butler started toward the back of the house, Laura veered straight into the library. It took all of her self-control to walk with measured, ladylike steps so she didn't appear unhinged.

Had Constable Pangborn heard that Martin Falkner's daughter had married the Earl of Copley? Had the man stationed himself across the street to spy on Laura in the hope of catching her alone? Perhaps he believed she could lead him to the Blue Moon diamond. He might be hoping to collect a substantial monetary award for its recovery.

Shaken to the core, Laura took little notice of the pleasant chocolate-and-cream decor of the library, the comfortable groupings of chairs, and the tall bookshelves along the walls. Going to one of the windows that overlooked the street, she peered outside, being careful to stand back from the glass so she couldn't be visible to him.

No one stood by the lamppost. She hastily scanned the throngs of people hurrying in both directions, looking for a brawny man in a flat cap. But he was nowhere to be seen.

Constable Pangborn had vanished.

By the time the carriage had gone the short distance to Berkeley Square, Laura had convinced herself that she was mistaken. The man she'd spotted must have been only a common laborer stopping to rest for a moment. That burly build and whiskered face could belong to a thousand workers in London.

Perhaps her error was only natural considering that she'd just told Alex about her father's possible murder. Although she hadn't mentioned it to Alex, the incident at the cemetery with Constable Pangborn had been in her thoughts. But her fears today surely were groundless, based on nothing more than a passing similarity.

Better she should turn her mind to Lord Haversham. She must not be rattled during the impending interview of him.

The carriage stopped and a footman opened the door. After bidding the coachman to wait, Laura headed toward the gray stone residence with the iron railing across the lower front. How different her situation was compared with just a week ago when she had walked Charlie past this house. Her new status as countess allowed her the right to approach Haversham without fear of overstepping her position.

She reminded herself of the questions that needed answering. Questions that Alex wouldn't think to ask since he didn't know the history of the feud.

Had he even come here this morning? She soon would find out.

Her gloved fingers curling around the brass knocker, she collected her nerve and rapped hard. The hollow echo resounded inside the house. In a moment the door opened to a hound-faced butler with drooping jowls who looked at her inquiringly.

"Good morning," she said. "I'm here to see Lord Haversham."

"I am afraid the marquess is not at home. If you would care to leave your card . . ."

Laura owned no calling cards as yet. Not that she would have offered one, anyway. Better his lordship not learn her name until they were face-to-face or he might refuse to receive her. "He won't know me by my married name," she hedged. "I'm the daughter of an old acquaintance of his. Pray tell, when will he return?"

"Possibly by the end of next week."

"Next week!" Laura's heart dropped in dismay. "Why, where has he gone?"

The butler frowned as if he found her question presumptuous. "To Lincolnshire, ma'am. You may return here on Saturday next."

He started to close the door, but Laura put her hand out to stop him. "Please, might I come in for just a moment?"

His lips pursed, but no well-bred servant would dare to refuse the request of a lady. The man stepped aside to allow her to enter.

She found herself in a dim-lit, echoing hall with a black-and-white-checkerboard floor and a broad staircase. Several doors stood open along the corridor to reveal a library on one side and an antechamber for visitors on the other.

A pang squeezed her breast. Had Papa waited there all those weeks ago? Had he stood in that very room and planned what to say to Lord Haversham? Had their quarrel been overheard by any of the servants?

The butler cleared his throat.

Recalling her purpose, Laura opened her beaded reticule and drew out a paper, which she unfolded and handed to him. "If you wouldn't mind," she said, "I should like to know if this man has ever called on his lordship."

He barely glanced at the meticulously detailed sketch she had drawn of her father's face. "I fear I cannot recall every person who has ever come to this establishment."

"It would have been about six to eight weeks ago," she persisted. "Please, it's very important that I know."

The butler looked again and then shook his head. "I've never seen the fellow."

"Would there have been a footman on duty? Might I also show him this sketch? I'd be very grateful for any help you can give me."

"I'm afraid you'll have to save your questions for his lordship's return, ma'am. Now, if that is all . . ."

Frustrated, Laura stood her ground. She didn't want to leave knowing no more than she had upon her arrival. Someone in this household *had* to have let Papa in to see the marquess. "Surely it won't take but a moment to—"

"Whatever is going on out here?" A slender lady in a pale yellow gown stepped into the open doorway halfway down the passageway. "Corwyn, do tell her that my father is away."

Laura stiffened. The gloominess of the hall and her elegant new attire must have concealed her identity from Evelyn. Having little wish to tangle with the woman, Laura considered escaping out the door with no one the wiser. But this opportunity must not be squandered.

She quickly folded the drawing and slipped it back into her reticule. Then she stepped around the butler and glided forward, her chin held high as befitting a countess. "Good morning, Evelyn. What a pleasure to see you."

Those topaz eyes widened. The flash of recognition there held a resentful awareness of Laura's newly elevated stature. Gossip about the Earl of Copley's reckless betrothal and marriage must have lit the ton on fire these past few days.

Evelyn pruned her lips. "Laura Falkner. How dare you set foot in this house."

"You surely know that as of yesterday, I am Lady Copley," Laura said coolly. "I would appreciate a moment of your time—in private."

Evelyn's delicate features twisted before she mastered herself. She glanced at the butler, who hovered nearby like an attack dog prepared to strike. "You may go, Corwyn. I'll see her here."

With that, the duchess turned on her heel with a flick of her stylish skirts and marched back through the doorway. Laura followed, finding herself in a study designed for a man. Burgundy draperies hung at the windows, and a pair of comfortable chairs were positioned by a fireplace. Instead of sitting there, however, Evelyn went to the mahogany desk that dominated the room and took a seat behind it.

Laura lowered herself to one of the straight-backed chairs facing the desk. The cushion was so hard and uncomfortable, she could only think it had been designed for recalcitrant employees who had been called onto the carpet by the master.

She folded her hands in her lap. "I confess to being

surprised to find you here, Evelyn. Do you live with your father, then? One would assume the Duchess of Cliffington would have her own place of residence."

An indignant flush touched Evelyn's fair skin. "Being shunned from society for so long, you wouldn't be familiar with the best homes in Mayfair. I live with my young son, the duke, at Cliffington House in Hanover Square. My father merely asked me to come and write regrets to some invitations."

A stack of note cards lay on the desk, along with a quill pen that looked as if it had been flung down in haste. Laura pondered the sight. Was she wrong to think it odd that his departure from London coincided with her identity being exposed to society? "Was he called out of town unexpectedly, then?"

"My grandmama is ill—not that it is any concern of yours." Evelyn sent a hard stare across the desk. "Why did you come here? What business can *you* possibly have with my father?"

Laura knew that whatever she said would be relayed to the marquess. She needed to throw out bait that would lure him back to London—even if she had to make it up on the spot. "As you may recall, he once knew my father. I thought the marquess might be interested to hear the contents of a letter I found among my father's effects."

Evelyn gave a disbelieving laugh. "Why would he care about any correspondence from a common thief?"

"He will," Laura fibbed, "because there is information about him in the letter."

There, let Haversham wonder if Papa had recorded all the dirty details of Haversham's involvement in the jewel theft. Haversham would then be anxious to seek out Laura and discover exactly how much she knew.

"How absurd of you to imply that *my* father had any connection whatsoever to yours," Evelyn snapped. "There's gossip that Martin Falkner is dead—and good riddance, I say. Though it's a pity he did not rot in prison for his crime!"

Laura's muscles went rigid. Never in her life had she been so tempted to scratch out someone's eyes. Holding tightly to her composure, she rose to her feet. "Things are not always as they seem," she said tightly. "I believe the marquess knows that."

Evelyn surged up from her chair to fix Laura with a glower. "What is *that* supposed to mean? I vow, you're as deceptive as your sire. Why Copley would have debased himself by marrying you, I cannot begin to imagine!"

Perception struck Laura. She had been so caught up in defending her father that she hadn't stopped to consider the true source of Evelyn's venom. The woman was furious, nay, *jealous* about the marriage. She had looked pea green with envy on the night Alex had announced his engagement to Laura, too. He'd said that Evelyn had been chasing after him for years.

Had she truly hoped to win Alex for herself? Apparently so.

At least now Laura could be assured that Alex hadn't come here this morning—because Evelyn surely would have crowed about it.

Her tension lifting, Laura allowed a slight smile. "I wouldn't expect you to understand his devotion to me. Good day, Duchess."

Chapter 24

Upon reaching Lady Josephine's house some minutes later, Laura discovered a state of affairs that overshadowed Evelyn's malice and Lord Haversham's duplicity. Alex's aunt was missing.

The footman had admitted Laura, and she had gone directly upstairs to the old woman's suite of rooms. Not finding anyone there, she'd peeked into the other upstairs chambers and did the same on the other floors. She even glanced out a back window into the garden, but the bench beneath the rose arbor was deserted. Neither the footman at the front door nor a maid dusting the clutter in the drawing room had seen their mistress in the past hour.

Descending the narrow steps to the cellar, Laura spotted the black-clad figure of the housekeeper ahead in the corridor, walking toward the laundry room. "Mrs. Samson!"

Pivoting, the hatchet-faced woman stared blankly as if wondering why a fine lady in dark blue silk should have invaded the domain of the servants. Then her eyes widened and she bobbed a curtsy. "Lady . . . Copley."

Laura ignored the woman's obvious discomfiture at the change in their relationship. "Has Lady Josephine gone out in the barouchet?"

"Gone out? Why, no. I left her sitting in the garden not half an hour ago."

"She isn't there. Nor can I find her anywhere in the house."

"You must be mistaken!"

"Am I? Then do help me locate her at once."

Laura ran back up the steep wooden steps, emerged into a gloomy passageway, and made haste to the rear of the house. Maybe she had overlooked the woman in the garden. There was a stone bench against the house that was difficult to see from the window. Perhaps when she'd glanced out, she had missed Lady Josephine sitting there.

Pushing open the back door, Laura stepped out on the loggia. In this shaded area, the air was cool and fragrant with the scent of roses. But when she glanced over to her left, this bench was empty, too.

Where was Lady Josephine?

The housekeeper hurried outside, the ring of keys jingling at her waist. Clutching her white apron with knobby fingers, she scanned the small garden. "Her ladyship was dozing under the rose arbor where she always sits, I swear it. Her little dog was lying right at her feet. I can't imagine where she would have gone."

Laura bit her tongue to keep from snapping that a maid should have been out here with the befuddled old woman. "She can't have ventured very far in half an hour. I want you to check the house from top to bottom. Send the footman outside to look up and down the street. I'll see if perhaps she wandered out the back gate into the mews."

To Mrs. Samson's credit, she didn't argue. She merely nodded and vanished inside the house.

Laura made haste down the winding flagstone path. Unmerited or not, a sense of guilt weighed heavily on her. If only she'd come straight here, rather than stopping at Lord Haversham's house, this might not have happened. She had been so caught up in her own matters that she'd neglected Lady Josephine. Despite the elevation of her position, Laura felt more responsible than ever for watching over Alex's aunt until another companion could be hired. She *knew* how confused the woman could be at times.

The back gate opened with a creaking of the hinges. Laura stepped into the mews, a rectangular yard that was permeated by the odors of hay and horses. Wide enough to permit the passage of a coach, it was connected to a long alley that led to the side street. She had hoped to find a groom or a coachman who might have seen her ladyship, but the doors to the nearest carriage houses were all closed.

She proceeded along the dirt alley. A glance downward revealed circular impressions at regular intervals in the hard-packed earth. Had they been left by the tip of Lady Josephine's cane? Spying a small paw print here and there encouraged Laura to believe that the woman *had* passed this way with Charlie on his leash.

Why? What could have induced her to leave the garden?

Emerging from the alley onto the cobbled street, Laura looked up and down the short block. Only a few people were out on this side road. There was a nursemaid briskly pushing a perambulator, a middle-aged gentleman stepping down from a carriage, a laborer trudging along with a burlap sack slung over his back.

Lady Josephine was nowhere in sight, though at least she would be moving slowly.

Which way would she have headed?

Laura hoped not toward Piccadilly with all its traffic. The other direction led to quieter streets and squares that surely would be more appealing to her ladyship. Unless, of course, she became lost, and then heaven only knew where she might roam.

Laura would never forgive herself if Lady Josephine came to harm.

Clutching her silk skirts, she rushed along the foot pavement. A torrent of dire scenarios inundated her mind. What if the elderly woman stepped into the street in front of a fast-moving carriage? What if she was set upon by footpads in an alley? What if Charlie's leather lead caused her to trip and fall? She could be lying with a broken bone somewhere, too bewildered to tell any rescuer where she lived.

Reaching the corner, Laura stopped again to survey the street in all directions. It was busier here, with many pedestrians and carriages. Perhaps one of the walkers had seen her ladyship. Or someone in the rows of elegant brick town houses might have been looking outside. But if she started knocking on doors, precious minutes would be wasted. Minutes in which all manner of calamities could befall the old woman.

Then her eyes widened on a stooped, round figure in a burnt orange gown at the far end of the block. The woman was shuffling along with a cane, a small spaniel at her side.

Awash in a sea of relief, Laura flew toward Lady Josephine. Since a number of people strolled along the street, she didn't realize until she was almost there that a dapper gentleman kept pace with Lady Josephine. He, too, had a young spaniel on a lead.

In a fleeting glance, Laura took in his bottle-green coat and tan pantaloons, the flaxen hair beneath a tall brown hat. She acknowledged him with a surprised nod. "Mr. Stanhope-Jones."

Then she caught Alex's aunt in a quick hug, glancing over the woman for assurance that she was unharmed. "My lady! I've found you at last. We didn't know where you'd vanished."

"Why, hullo, Norah," her ladyship said with a wobbly smile. She clung to Laura's hand. "You ran away. Charlie and I have been searching for you."

Laura's heart squeezed. Lady Josephine must be having one of her bad days, so Laura didn't bother to correct the mistaken name. "You should have waited for me in the garden," she said gently. "You know you oughtn't go out the gate without telling anyone."

"But I *did* tell someone. This kind young man here—"

"I was out walking when I noticed Lady Josephine wandering along the street," Mr. Stanhope-Jones broke in. "It was fortuitous indeed that I visited her only last week and could show her the way home."

That had been the day when he and Evelyn had come to see Lady Josephine with the express purpose of exposing Laura's true identity.

"Look, he has Charlie's sister." A delighted smile lit up Lady Josephine's wrinkled features. "Aren't they the most darling little pair?"

The two puppies were rolling on the ground and nipping playfully at each other, their tails wagging.

Glad to see Lady Josephine happy again, Laura took hold of Charlie's lead. If the canine antics became livelier, the old woman might lose her balance and stumble into the nearby traffic, where carriage wheels rattled and horse hooves clopped incessantly.

Laura turned her attention to Mr. Rupert Stanhope-Jones. Now that she had weathered the emotional storm of anxiety and worry, she found it somewhat peculiar that he would be out walking a dog. He seemed too vain to bother with a task that could be left to servants.

"Isn't that Daisy?" she asked warily. "Evelyn's puppy?"

"Indeed," he admitted. "You see, yesterday there was a bit of an altercation at Cliffington House. Apparently, the young duke pulled Daisy's tail, and the little vixen bit him. Evelyn was so furious that I offered to take the dog off her hands for a day or two."

Laura had always thought Mr. Stanhope-Jones a rather shallow, self-absorbed man. She was still miffed by his insulting offer to her on the night of the ball. But perhaps she should make an effort to forgive him, for he'd shown generosity to Alex's aunt.

She managed a genuine smile at him. "That's very kind of you. And I do owe you a debt of gratitude for assisting Lady Josephine."

Warmth entered his blue eyes. Stepping closer, he reached for her hand, bringing it to his lips and kissing the back. "I am your devoted servant, Laura. If ever you should need me—"

"Now, here's a pleasant sight," Alex drawled from behind her. "You must be congratulating my wife on our recent nuptials."

Laura gasped. Pulling her hand free, she spun around to see her husband's tall figure on his chestnut gelding. A heart-swelling elation filled her at the sight of his muscled shoulders clad in a claret coat, his long legs in buckskins with knee-high black boots. He wore no hat and the breeze played with the chocolate strands of his hair, letting one fall across his brow.

That mocking quality tilted one corner of his mouth. It lent him an arrogant look quite the opposite of the affectionate man who had held her in his arms and made sweet love to her for half the night.

"Alex!" she blurted out. "Why are *you* here?"

He dismounted, sauntering forward with the reins in his hand. He went to kiss Lady Josephine on the cheek before answering Laura. "I came looking for my aunt. It was quite a surprise a few minutes ago to find the entire household in an uproar."

"She wandered out the garden gate, that's all. As you can see, she's perfectly fine. Mr. Stanhope-Jones happened upon her and was bringing her home."

"Was he? How uncommonly decent of him."

The men eyed each other like two stiff-backed dogs with one bone. Laura didn't care to be that bone.

"It's time for Lady Josephine to return home," she said, slipping her arm through the old woman's. "Good day, Mr. Stanhope-Jones, and thank you again."

She started down the street and around the corner, for the route would take them back faster than returning all the way back through the mews. In a moment she noticed Alex walking alongside them in the street, leading his mount. Where had he been? She wanted to confess how awful she'd felt upon encountering his aunt.

You ran away. Charlie and I have been searching for you.

Those plaintive words haunted Laura. But she said nothing to Alex, for Lady Josephine was chattering about how nice it was for Charlie to have a little friend in the neighborhood, and giggling at the way the spaniel's ears flopped as he trotted along.

The going was slow with Lady Josephine leaning on her cane and Laura's arm, but eventually they

arrived at the town house. After tying his mount at
the iron railing, Alex helped his aunt inside. There
was a great outcry as all the servants came running,
including Mrs. Samson.

The housekeeper wore a hangdog look of remorse.
"I'm terribly sorry, your lordship. I don't know how
this could have happened."

"I'll want a word with you later," he said in a
clipped tone.

He took his aunt upstairs, where she sank onto her
chaise, her plump face flushed from exertion and the
warmth of the day. Laura snapped open a fan and
waved it at her ladyship, while Alex knelt on one knee
to remove his aunt's shoes. Charlie plopped onto the
floor, alert and happy, his pink tongue lolling. Within
moments a maid came hurrying in with iced lemon-
ade, which Lady Josephine accepted with a grateful
smile.

Once she had been settled, Alex excused himself.
"I'll be back shortly," he said.

Laura followed him out into the passage. "Where
are you going?"

He turned to her, his expression inscrutable. "To
have a locksmith install a padlock on the garden gate.
How is your progress in finding another companion?"

"Mrs. Mayhew has asked the agency to send some
candidates in the morning."

"Excellent. This cannot be allowed to happen
again."

Laura had a suspicion that his lordly manner
masked deeper feelings. She stepped closer, reaching
out to touch his sleeve. "Shall we bring Lady Josephine home with us for the time being? I don't like to
see you so worried."

One dark eyebrow lifted in cool query. "Then why

did you go to Haversham's house against my express wishes?"

Startled by the abrupt question, Laura withdrew her hand. "How did you know—?"

"Hodge overheard you instructing the coachman." Alex regarded her with an expression of stony hauteur. "I thought we'd agreed you were to halt your investigation until I had an opportunity to consider the matter."

She lifted her chin. He'd known from the start that she intended to clear her father's name. "You weren't home this morning, and I was afraid you'd gone there without me. Where were you, anyway?"

"I went to Bow Street Station to review all the particulars of your father's death."

Laura curled her fingers into her palms. Of all the places he could have gone, she had never expected that one. "Did you speak to Constable Pangborn, then?"

"No, I only saw the sergeant in charge of the case. Pangborn is the officer who discovered your father lying in the alley? I read the report that he filed."

Frustration daunted her. She had hoped for confirmation that the officer had *not* been outside Copley House, lounging against a lamppost. Although she'd decided it was a case of mistaken identity, a niggling worry lingered. Should she tell Alex? Or would he think her mad? He already believed her to be imagining guilt in Lord Haversham.

While she was still deciding, Alex went on, "There were no valuables in your father's possession, not so much as tuppence. You won't want to hear it, but that seems to confirm that he was robbed."

"Or it was set up to *appear* as a robbery."

Raking his fingers through his hair, Alex glanced away before meeting her eyes again. "I'll concede to the possibility." He studied her a moment, then stepped closer to place his hands firmly on her shoulders. "Laura, if there is the slightest chance that you're right and someone else *did* steal the diamond, I cannot allow you to endanger yourself with this foolhardy investigation. You're not to question Haversham—or anyone else—unless I'm present."

Laura pursed her lips. Was that why Alex had told the butler that she wasn't to venture out alone? Because he was worried about her?

A part of her balked at agreeing to such a condition. Nevertheless, she felt encouraged by the thought that he finally believed her, if only conditionally. "Will *you* will make the same promise to *me*?" she asked.

His fingers tightened on her shoulders. "Don't be absurd. I'm far more capable of protecting myself."

She didn't want to admit the truth in that. He would only use it to mollycoddle her. "Well, it doesn't matter for the moment, anyway. The marquess is out of town until the end of next week."

"So I heard."

Alex appeared preoccupied, and she suspected that he had stopped by Haversham House after her. What had Evelyn said to him? Had she attempted to make another play for his affections despite his marriage? Laura's insides clenched. But she didn't want to waste another thought on that malicious woman.

In an effort to recapture his attention, she slid her hands over the lapels of his coat. "Alex, you never did answer me. May we bring your aunt home with us for a time? Until another companion is hired?"

His gaze sharpened on her, and a faint smile flirted with the corners of his mouth. His voice falling perceptively lower, he said, "You'd be willing to spoil our honeymoon?"

Just like that, the air became charged with sensual awareness. His heart beat in heavy strokes against her palms. The scent of his masculine cologne stirred her, as did the heat radiated by his muscled body. Her gaze strayed to his mouth, and she remembered all the wickedly wonderful ways he had employed it the previous night.

Even if he never came to love her, she would gladly take the physical closeness that he offered. Raising herself on tiptoes, she murmured, "I do believe we could still find time for our own pleasures, don't you?"

His hands moved down to grip her waist. He drew in a deep breath, his eyes dark and eloquent with desire. Bending his head, he took her lips in a kiss that was cut off too soon when the sound of ascending footsteps came from the stairs.

They broke apart just in time.

Mrs. Samson trudged into view. She stopped short on seeing them. Toting a pitcher of water, she curtsied while eyeing Alex carefully. "Pray pardon me. I came to check on the mistress."

"It would behoove you to do so more often," he said.

Her tall, spare form seemed to wither under his stern gaze. She clutched the blue china pitcher with whitened knuckles. "Yes, my lord. What happened was my fault. Mine entirely, and I . . . I only hope you will grant me the chance to redeem myself."

In spite of their prior animosity, Laura took pity on the woman. The housekeeper had spent twenty-five years of her life under this roof. It would be difficult for her to find another position without a letter of reference.

Laura tucked her hand into the crook of her husband's arm. "I'm sure his lordship would agree that one infraction does not warrant your being discharged from service here."

Alex cast Laura an enigmatic look. She feared he would challenge her statement, but he surprised her. "I'll concede to my bride's generosity," he told the housekeeper. "Nevertheless, I want you to prepare an overnight case for my aunt."

Mrs. Samson appeared torn between gratitude and a new concern that she wasn't to be trusted to watch Lady Josephine. "But . . . where will the mistress be going?"

"To a place where she'll be safe until another companion can be hired. She'll stay at Copley House for a day or two."

Chapter 25

Three days later, Lady Josephine had been settled back in her own house with a brisk, cheerful widow as her companion. Laura had interviewed countless applicants before finding one who satisfied her exacting standards. Mrs. Duncalf had an efficient manner and a warm disposition, which made her perfect for the post. She had immediately established a bond with her ladyship by cooing over Charlie.

When Laura said good-bye after tea, the two women were sitting together in Lady Josephine's bedchamber, alternately trading stories of their youth and laughing at the spaniel's attempts to retrieve a leather ball from beneath a footstool.

Only one moment of confusion ensued. As Laura rose to go, Lady Josephine clutched at her hand. "Oh, my dear, I must warn you. Don't run away as Blanche did."

Laura puzzled over the reference to Lady Josephine's younger sister, Alex's mother. "Run away?"

"She left without telling me or the earl," the old

woman said urgently. "You must never, ever do that or something dreadful will happen."

The earl . . . did she mean Alex's father? She must. At her birthday dinner, Lady Josephine had related the story of how the cruel man had lashed out in anger and broken the leg of Alex's puppy. Had the old earl threatened Blanche? Had she fled because she feared for her life?

Laura burned to know more, but she didn't want to air any family secrets in front of a stranger. Besides, it was Alex's place to tell her about his parents. She mustn't press Lady Josephine for details.

"I won't run away," Laura said, dropping a kiss on that plump, wrinkled cheek. "I promise I won't. I'll be back on the morrow to visit."

Mrs. Duncalf sat watching with wise blue eyes, and she offered a distraction at once. "Look, my lady," she said, pointing down. "Charlie isn't having much luck jumping into your lap."

They all laughed as the puppy made an attempt, then fell back in a heap on the carpet. Clucking sweet nothings, Mrs. Duncalf lifted the small dog and handed him to Lady Josephine, who happily cuddled him to the shelf of her bosom.

Laura took the opportunity to slip unnoticed out the door. She had left a set of detailed instructions on her ladyship's daily routine. The garden gate had been secured with a padlock. A footman was stationed by the front door to prevent another absentminded foray by Lady Josephine into the neighborhood. Finally, Laura felt she could relax again. And in this respite while Lord Haversham was away, it was time to turn her attention to another matter.

Unraveling the mystery of her husband's past.

* * *

That evening, she sat cross-legged in her large, rumpled bed with a drawing pad balanced on her knees. She wore Alex's discarded dressing gown, the bronze cord tied loosely at her waist. Only minutes ago they had been wrapped in each other's arms, awash in mindless pleasure, and the radiant aftereffects lent a fluid ease to the movements of her pencil over the paper.

She was sketching a subject dear to her heart.

A short distance away, her husband lay on his side. Alex had propped himself up on one elbow, the white coverlet draped strategically over his privates. The golden glow from a branch of candles on the bedside table bathed his naked body.

With dark, indolent eyes, he watched her work.

A warm awareness of him nestled low in her belly. He was profoundly beautiful, from his tousled, cocoa-brown hair to his broad chest to his muscled calves. But of course she wouldn't feed his conceit by telling him so. He already had a faint smirk on his lips.

He'd been vastly amused that she wanted to capture his virile form on paper. And he had demanded the promise of payment in the manner of his choosing once she was finished. Although that enticing prospect threatened her concentration, she needed to convince him to speak of serious matters.

"Your aunt was delighted to be home again," she said, the pencil in her fingers flying across the paper. "Of course, it wasn't that she was *unhappy* living here with us, only that she prefers her own familiar surroundings."

"I told you she likes all that clutter. The reminders of my uncle Charles are everywhere." Alex tilted himself forward, straining to see over the edge of the pad. "Aren't you finished yet?"

"In ten minutes? Hardly! Lie still now or you'll spoil the image."

He pulled a disgruntled face as he resumed his pose. "At least I'll have a reward for this degradation of my pride." His gaze dropped to her bosom where, she realized, the dressing gown gaped open to give him a glimpse of her bare breasts. "A long, enjoyable, and gratifying reward."

Laura's insides curled with desire. "So you shall, my lord. Your wish will be my command."

She flashed a brief smile at him while working on the illustration, adding shading to his arms and chest to enhance the contour of his muscles. She always loved seeing an image come to life with the stroke of a pencil or paintbrush. But tonight, her mind dwelled on the matter that had been haunting her since she'd left his aunt's house. "By the by, Lady Josephine said something rather odd to me today. She begged me not run off as Blanche had done."

Had Laura not been watching him closely, she might have missed the almost imperceptible tensing of his jaw. He gave a dismissive chuckle. "She says a lot of odd things lately. Now, I really do think you should let me see that drawing. For all I know, you're depicting me with a forked tail and horns."

He made a grab for the sketch pad, and she scrambled backward to evade his reach. When he wouldn't give up, she rolled off the bed with the notebook clutched behind her back.

"Alex, for pity's sake! I'll show it to you when I'm done and not a moment sooner. You agreed to pose for half an hour. Otherwise, your reward can go to perdition."

His gaze fixed on her breasts again. "You have five more minutes."

"*Twenty*," she corrected with a glance at the or-molu clock that ticked on a wall shelf. "And since you are being unmanageable, I believe you need a prop to hold."

"I'll be pleased to hold *you*." He patted the sheets invitingly. "Why don't you just remove that robe and join me here?"

Laura ached to do so. She also ached to find answers to questions that had been left too long unanswered. Questions that might lead her to a better understanding of him.

"Patience is a virtue," she said tartly.

"Patience is for milksops. And I'm certainly not feeling very virtuous tonight."

"You'll have to be—or you won't have your reward."

Heading barefoot to the writing desk, she set down her pad and pencil, then opened the single drawer and fished around in the back of it. She grasped the oval miniature that she'd discovered on their wedding night. Her fingertip traced the fractures in the glass.

Laura clutched the miniature for a moment before turning toward him. She hesitated at the sight of his cocky smile. A part of her didn't want to spoil his relaxed mood by bringing up the past. But it had to be done or Alex's thoughts and feelings would forever remain a mystery to her.

She walked to the bed. "I'd like you to hold this."

With a wry grin, Alex accepted the miniature. "What am I supposed to do with . . . ?" His words ground to a halt as he glanced down at the small likeness of his father. A scowl wiped away all trace of the contented lover. Sitting up abruptly, he snapped, "What the devil? Where did you find this?"

Laura sat down on the edge of the mattress. "It was

in the back of the desk drawer. I presume your mother placed it there a long time ago."

He held the miniature between his fingers as if it were a piece of excrement. "This bedchamber was supposed to be cleaned from top to bottom. Mrs. Mayhew will hear about this in the morning."

His angry reaction drew her sympathies. Laura yearned to share the burden of his past so that it would not weigh so heavily upon him.

"You will *not* scold the housekeeper. Anyone could have missed something so small." Laura leaned closer to peer at the painting. "That's your father, isn't it? Why not have the glass replaced and put the miniature on display?"

Alex gazed at her with impenetrable eyes. "Fine. I'll take care of it tomorrow."

He turned away, tossing the little oval frame onto the bedside table. The negligence of his action caused the piece to slide off and fall to the carpet, though he made no attempt to retrieve it.

Laura scooped up the miniature and returned it to the desk. She wanted to reproach him for his carelessness. But perhaps the pain of his childhood lay behind the coldness of his manner.

Rejoining him in bed, she grabbed a feather pillow and hugged it to her bosom as she studied his chiseled features. "I suspect you've no intention of repairing the glass," she said. "You'll toss the portrait into the rubbish. The question is . . . why?"

His mouth formed a cool, mocking smile, the one he used to ward off bothersome inquiries. "I've no use for damaged items. Now finish your drawing. I'll want to see it in precisely"—his gaze flicked to the clock—"fifteen minutes."

Laura made no move to fetch her sketchpad and

pencil. "You've a habit of deflecting attention from any questions about your past. Did you realize that? Consequently, I know very little about your youth."

"There's little to tell—"

"Then you may start with why your mother ran away. Or shall I be reduced to seeking a garbled version of events from Lady Josephine?" Seeing his closed expression, Laura softened her tone. "Won't you please tell me, Alex? I'm your wife. I should know about your past."

Grimacing, he sat stiffly against the pillows, crooking up one leg and resting his arm on his knee. He looked distinctly ill at ease, and she knew it had nothing to do with his nakedness. Alex was comfortable in his own skin—but his childhood memories put him on edge.

He glanced away into the shadows of the bedchamber. He rubbed his brow as if searching for an excuse not to talk. Then he scowled at her, took a deep breath, and blew it out in a huff. "If you insist upon knowing, my mother *did* leave my father. It happened when I was thirteen years old. I arrived home on summer holiday from Eton only to discover that she was gone."

"Oh, Alex . . . I'm so sorry. Had your father been cruel to her? Was she fleeing for her life?"

He released a harsh laugh. "For her life? Hardly. She ran off with another man."

Expecting an indictment of the old earl, Laura stared at Alex in shock. "Another man!"

"Yes," he said, his eyes chilly. "My mother had always had affairs for as far back as I can remember. And my father was always threatening to divorce her. But he never did."

He went on in an emotionless voice to describe the

noisy quarrels between his parents, and the picture that emerged sickened Laura. She wanted to comfort him, but he appeared lost in memory and she feared that any interruption might silence him. So she clutched the pillow and just listened as he depicted a fickle mother who would lavish gifts on him and his older sister, then ignore them for months on end while she conducted her illicit dalliances. He also spoke of a harsh father who tried vainly to curb his wife's excesses and stop her endless flirtations.

Laura had been prepared to despise the old earl. It had been a vile act of brutality for him to knock Alex's puppy down the stairs. However, now she could see that *both* parents had been at fault. Blanche had known that her husband didn't like pets yet she had given one to Alex anyway. She had habitually provoked her husband with her own irresponsible behavior.

And Alex had been caught in the middle of it all.

What was it Lady Josephine had said about his parents? *It was quite shocking the way the two of them would scream at each other! I daresay poor Alexander witnessed far too many quarrels in his time . . .*

Laura wanted to weep for the vulnerable boy who had been denied a happy, carefree childhood. At a lull in his narrative, she asked softly, "What happened . . . after your mother ran off?"

He flicked a glance at Laura. "My father went chasing after her and her lover, of course. But he never caught them. They'd had too much of a head start to Dover, where they purchased passage to the Continent." He paused, his face grim. "As fate would have it, the ship went down in a storm. My mother—and her lover—drowned."

Tears sprang to Laura's eyes. Not for his mother,

but for Alex, whose view of marriage had been tainted by the foibles of his parents. Was it any surprise that he would marry for lust instead of love?

His gaze focused beyond her, he went on. "Somehow, my father was able to cover up the scandal. He put forth a story that she'd been traveling to Italy on a holiday. I doubt that anyone in society really believed it, but they went along out of respect for his rank."

"What about her lover?" Laura murmured. "Surely *his* death would have raised eyebrows. For a gentleman and a lady to be on board the same ship—"

"I never said he was a gentleman. He'd been employed at a gaming hell on the fringes of society." His mouth twisted. "Yes, the Countess of Copley threw away her life, her husband, her family, to elope with a common knave."

His bleak, bitter expression tore at her heart. No wonder he'd kept a part of himself distant. The source of his possessiveness of her became clear, too. She could see just how raw a nerve she'd touched by requiring that he purchase a house for her as a condition of bearing his heir. He feared that she, too, would run off and leave him.

Given the circumstance of his mother's abandonment, Laura found it amazing that Alex had signed the legal document at all. Surely his doing so must indicate that he had deep feelings for her . . .

Abandoning the pillow, she scooted across the bed and slid her arms around his neck. "Oh, darling. I wish I could erase all of those memories and replace them with happy ones."

He gripped her waist, his eyes intense on her. Then he shifted his gaze away, as if to maintain an aura of detachment. "It doesn't matter," he said. "It's over with and done."

But it wasn't over, she knew. The past had shaped him, made him guarded and cold whenever anyone attempted to probe too deeply into his emotions. It had given him that ironic outlook with which he viewed the world. And it explained why he found it difficult to trust anyone enough to open his heart.

Laura cupped his cheek, tracing the scar she'd inflicted all those years ago. He hadn't believed her judgment in regard to her own father, either. Because he had never known honor in a parent.

She turned his face back toward her. "Your past will always be a part of you, though you mustn't let it rule you. And may I add that I adore the fine man you've become."

A cool smile lifted one corner of his mouth. He untied the cord of the dressing gown, and his hand delved inside to touch her intimately. "You adore what I do to you."

Laura drew a shaky breath under the onrush of desire. She caught his wrist to halt the delightful caress. "Yes, you're absolutely right. But it's more than that. And pray don't distract me when I'm trying to tell you something important."

His finger performed a lazy swirl that had her gasping. "Nothing could be more important than this."

"One thing is. *Love*." His hand stilled and his dark eyes fixed on her. Now that she had captured his full attention, she leaned closer and murmured against his lips, "I love you, Alex. That's what is truly important. I love you with all my heart and soul."

The aloofness vanished from his eyes. In its place, a deep river of emotion flowed there, stark and needy. She caught only a glimpse of it before he pulled her into his lap and subjected her to a deep, ravenous kiss. He pushed the dressing gown from her shoulders, stroking her silken skin all over as if learning her curves for the first time.

Love, she discovered, enhanced the richness of desire. With caresses and whispered words, she let Alex know just how much he meant to her. Straddling his lap, she took him deeply into her body, gazing into his eyes as she became one flesh with him. The sheer pleasure of moving with him in perfect accord made her moan. Under a flood of irresistible sensations, their passion flourished until it became too much to bear, and they clung to each other during the exhilarating plummet into bliss.

Lying against him afterward, her head tucked in the crook of his shoulder, Laura came to an awareness that Alex had never returned her words of love. How she longed to hear such an ardent declaration from him. And yet . . . she could *feel* his devotion in the tenderness of his touch. At the moment, his fingers reached beneath the curtain of her unbound hair to gently massage the nape of her neck. He pressed a soft kiss to her brow, his breath warm against her skin.

A rush of happiness brought a wistful smile to her lips. If he couldn't avow love for her, then she must be content with him exactly as he was. But perhaps someday he might . . . if only she could convince him to lower the wall around his heart.

Tilting her head to look up at him, she idly traced the hard line of his jaw. "I hope you know you've been terribly unfair to me."

"Have I? How is that?"

"You've collected your reward. Yet I never did finish my sketch of you."

He chuckled deep in his chest. "Just as well, darling. I can't imagine what you were planning to do with it, anyway."

Laura ran an admiring hand over the muscles of his shoulders and down his arm. "Oh, it's merely a preliminary drawing. I thought I might paint a larger version in oils and hang it over the mantel in the drawing room."

He drew back to stare at her. A thunderous frown crossed his features; then the storm cleared as he noticed Laura's impish smile. Grinning, he gave a light slap to her bare bottom. "Wicked jade. You had me fooled there for a moment."

"Well, I ought to do it," she declared, "if only to thumb my nose at those who consider me beyond the pale. After all, I *am* the notorious Laura Falkner."

A sober expression descended over his face, and he caught hold of her shoulders. "You're my countess. By God, society *will* accept you."

The fervency of his avowal thrilled her. But she was pragmatic enough to face reality. The upper crust might invite her into their homes out of respect for his rank. But they would still view her with disdain.

And when she exposed Lord Haversham as the real thief? Laura felt skeptical that revealing the truth about the theft of the Blue Moon diamond would alter their prejudice against her. Some might even blame her for causing the downfall of a venerated member of their ranks.

She stroked his cheek. "It doesn't matter so long as I have you. If a few snooty people refuse to acknowledge me, then so be it."

"But it matters to *me*." A shrewd look entering his eyes, he added, "And it's time that you and I entered the lion's den together."

Chapter 26

Carrying a basket of cut roses, Laura left the garden and went into the coolness of the house. She had spent an enjoyable morning out in the sunshine chatting with the gardener, a leathery old man with an encyclopedic knowledge of rose hybrids. She had clipped a generous sampling of her favorites. As she headed toward the front of the house, her mind was full of poetic names like Damask and Provence and Gallica. She intended to use her fragrant bounty to fill the cloisonné vase beneath the stairs.

The sound of male voices echoed down the long corridor with its arched ceiling. Her heart leaped, and she increased her pace toward the entrance hall, her soft leather slippers tapping on the marble floor. Had Alex returned? The prospect brought a smile to her lips.

He had been assigned an official role in Queen Victoria's coronation ceremony on the morrow. A last-minute meeting at Westminster Abbey had required his presence this morning. It was one of the few times they'd been separated in the three weeks since their wedding.

She hurried in anticipation of his kiss on her cheek, his arm around her waist, the tenderness in his dark brown eyes. Their marriage had been an idyll beyond compare. By day, they'd visited art galleries and museums, shopped on Bond Street and visited the zoo, often taking Lady Josephine with them. By night, they attended the theater, dinner parties, and balls in honor of the upcoming coronation. Though she'd assured him it wasn't necessary, he'd stayed close at her side to guard against anyone who might dare to scorn her.

His campaign to restore Laura's reputation had resulted in considerable success, despite her doubts to the contrary. He also had persuaded Lady Milford to host a small reception to celebrate their nuptials. It had been the most sought-after invitation of the pre-coronation events. Only the cream of society had been present, and the gathering had proven to be a victory against the naysayers. Even Lord Oliver, her father's former friend, had been civil toward Laura, though she had detected a lingering judgmental stiffness in his manner.

All in all, though, the ton had begun to accept her. There had been a significant decline in the derisive looks and sly innuendos. It had made her appreciate the scope of Lady Milford's influence.

Laura could only marvel at the twist of fate that had caused her to hide in her ladyship's coach all those weeks ago. If not for that chance encounter, she would never have had the opportunity to renew her relationship with Alex. She would never have realized that his inability to believe in her father's exemplary character stemmed from Alex's own youth, when he had learned only cynicism and mistrust. Alone and lonely, she would have gone on despising him, never knowing the bliss of being his wife. And she would never have learned the joys of love.

A brief pang touched her heart. Of course, Alex had never spoken of love. He remained as reticent as ever in regard to voicing his innermost feelings. At times, he even reverted to coolness if she probed too deeply into his emotions.

Yet she could see his affection for her in his warm smile, could hear it in his teasing banter. And she could *feel* it in the soul-stirring ecstasy of his love-making. Every night had been paradise, an intense euphoria of physical closeness. Her dearest hope was that eventually, her love for him would heal the wounds of his childhood and grant him the ability to acknowledge that he felt more for her than mere lust.

Laura vowed to see that he did. She intended to love him so much that he would *have* to love her back.

Her footsteps quick and light, she emerged from the corridor into the entrance hall. The basket bumped against her hip as she made her way across the pale marble floor. Hearing voices in the library, she hurried there, only to stop short to avoid a near-collision with the footman as he walked out of the doorway.

She steadied the basket to keep the roses from spilling. "Do pardon me, Gerald. Has the earl returned home, then?"

The young man bowed. "Nay, my lady. Lord Haversham has arrived to see you."

Haversham!

The news pierced her bubble of contentment. On the day Haversham had been due back in London, nearly a fortnight ago, he hadn't returned from the country. Alex had escorted her to the house in Berkeley Square, only to hear from the jowly butler that his lordship had elected to remain in Lincolnshire for another week or two. Since the marquess undoubtedly would be back for the coronation, Alex had promised they would make another attempt this afternoon.

Instead, Haversham had come here.

Her heart beat faster. She had promised Alex not to go alone to visit the marquess. If indeed the man was guilty of killing her father, she would be taking too great a risk. She had agreed only reluctantly to placate her husband.

But surely she was safe here in her own home. There could be no danger in this meeting when a footman was stationed within earshot. Besides, if she waited for Alex's return, this long-anticipated opportunity would be lost.

"Shall I show him upstairs to the drawing room?" the footman asked.

"No, I'll see him here. Pray remain nearby until he departs."

As the servant returned to his station, Laura stepped into the library and partially closed the door, leaving it open a crack in case she needed to call for help. The midday sunshine filtered through the tall windows, illuminating the masculine decor of brown and cream. The scent of leather bindings perfumed the air. She had come to love this spacious room with its shelves of books and the scattering of cushiony chairs. On rare evenings when they had no events to attend, she and Alex would cuddle together on the chaise and read by lamplight.

Those fond memories faded away under the pressing urgency of the moment.

The Marquess of Haversham stood in front of a bookshelf, paging through a thick volume. His back was to her, giving her a rear view of his balding pate with its monkish fringe of graying brown hair. Upon hearing her footsteps, he turned to face her. His narrow, snobbish features wore a look of faint irritation as he scanned her up and down.

He inclined his head. "Lady Copley."

Laura knew she was presentable in dark blue silk, yet his critical stare made her uncomfortable. She set the basket of roses on a table and then dipped a graceful curtsy. "What an unexpected pleasure, my lord. I hope your journey back to London was uneventful."

Clapping the book shut, he replaced it on the shelf. "Never mind my journey. I'd like to know why you keep coming to my house. You're the one who tried to corner me at Witherspoon's ball, too." His lip curled. "Evelyn says you're Martin Falkner's daughter."

"Yes, I am." Laura refused to be intimidated by his abrupt manner. She waved a gracious hand at a pair of chairs by the fireplace. "Would you care to sit, my lord?"

He gave an impatient shake of his head. "I'd as soon you just explain what you mean by telling my daughter this havy-cavy business about my name being mentioned in a letter."

Unwilling to be at a disadvantage, Laura remained standing, too. She wanted to peer straight at his face as he answered her questions. In order to observe every nuance of his expression, she strolled to the window so that he would be gazing into the light.

Lacing her fingers at her waist, she murmured, "I did indeed say there was a letter among my father's effects. I'll tell you about it in a moment. But first, I believe you and my father were once rivals for my mother's affections. Is that true?"

Haversham scowled. "What matter is it? That was thirty years ago!"

"Yet the feud between the two of you lingered for

a long time. I remember you exhibiting a distinct coldness toward Papa at the time of my debut a decade ago."

He raised an eyebrow. "If your delicate sensibilities have been injured, Lady Copley, then pray accept my apologies!"

Was his derisive manner simply a part of his callous nature? Or did it indicate that his deep-seated hatred of Martin Falkner also extended to her?

She gazed steadily at him. "I'm sure you recall the incident that befell my father at that time. A set of earrings belonging to the Duchess of Knowles were found in the desk in his study."

"Indeed." His icy gray eyes looked her up and down. "Though I would hardly say the incident *befell* him. Falkner stole Her Grace's jewels. Pardon my frankness, but it is a travesty of justice that he never went to prison for his crime."

Laura studied his face for any sign that he was playacting. She could see nothing but a cold mask of antipathy. Had Papa confronted this man all those weeks ago? Had Haversham then ordered him killed to prevent him from revealing the truth?

"Perhaps," she said carefully, "my father was innocent of all charges. Perhaps he never stole those jewels."

"Never stole them—? Poppycock. They were found in his possession. Then he viciously attacked Copley and fled the country. That is hardly the act of an innocent man."

She didn't correct his misapprehension as to who had slashed Alex's face. "Papa feared he would be sentenced to death for a crime he hadn't committed."

Haversham gave a decisive shake of his head. "It is

quite obvious that Falkner absconded with the Blue Moon diamond. He no doubt sold it for a king's ransom." Taking a step toward her, he eyed her with lordly distaste. "I understand *you* vanished with him. Perhaps *you* know what happened to the diamond. If you've an ounce of decency, you would tell the duchess so the stone might be recovered!"

Laura's muscles tensed. His insulting verbal attack had to be designed to conceal his own guilt by putting her on the defensive. The zealousness of his tone hinted that he had a personal stake in the case.

"My father did not steal the diamond. I am prepared to swear to that fact in a court of law. When would he have ever had the opportunity, anyway?" She dipped her chin in an attempt to appear less confrontational. The last thing she needed was for him to attack her. "No, I'm thinking the real culprit must have been someone who had direct access to Her Grace's bedchamber, where she kept her jewels."

During this speech, skepticism flitted over his face, followed by a narrowing of his eyes. That secretive, hooded look seemed to indicate he was hiding something. So did his lack of an immediate response. The marquess appeared to be waiting for her to finish.

Driven by the anticipation of discovery, Laura hoped he would believe the deceit she was about to voice. "This brings us to the document that I discovered among my father's effects. Although I called it a letter, it's really more of a diary entry. In it, Papa recorded everything he could remember about the time of the robbery. And that's when I saw your name."

"*My* name? What the devil did that rascal say about me?"

She gave him a guileless look. "He made a very

interesting observation, my lord. Pray pardon me for bringing up something so indiscreet, but Papa wrote . . . that *you* had had an affair with Her Grace."

Haversham stared blankly at Laura.

Then his face twisted. He slammed his fist down on the nearest table, making a dictionary rattle on its stand and causing her to jump. "Good God!" he exploded. "That is a bald-faced lie! I can't imagine why he would write such a falsehood. Especially since . . ." He bit off his words, his gaze piercing her before he spun away to pace the carpet in obvious agitation.

"Especially since . . . what?" Laura prompted.

The marquess turned to face her. But his angry eyes focused beyond her shoulder as if to peer into the past. "I see his diabolical plot now. Falkner was attempting to pin the blame on me. He wanted people to think that *I* had been in the duchess's bedchamber— that *I* stole the Blue Moon and then somehow planted those earrings in his desk. What a colossal deception. I'd never even set foot in his house!"

"Evelyn came to call the day prior to the discovery," Laura murmured. "I was upstairs in my chambers, and she was alone downstairs—"

"Enough! You will *not* sully my daughter's name, too." He shook his forefinger as if Laura were a wicked child. "This is slander. I demand that you burn that paper at once!"

A quiver of unease gripped Laura. Haversham stood between her and the door. He looked so wrathful that she regretted taking this position by the window.

She edged toward the fireplace, where the poker would be a handy weapon if he attempted to do her harm. At the same time, she wouldn't let herself back down now, not when she felt so close to discovering what had really happened.

"I'm truly sorry for upsetting you, my lord," she said with feigned calmness. "But surely you can see why this paper is so important. As I said, my father is innocent. And I feel compelled to pursue this issue in the name of justice for him."

"Justice! I'll give you justice," Haversham thundered with another jab of his finger in her direction. "If you must know, it wasn't me who had the affair with the duchess. It was your father, that's who. *Your father!* It wasn't enough for him to steal Aileen from under my nose, he had to steal the duchess, too."

Laura's jaw dropped. Her father—and the Duchess of Knowles? Her father—and that patronizing, beak-nosed snob?

No. A thousand times, no.

But if it was true . . . and if Alex had known . . . it would explain why he'd begun courting her in earnest directly after the jewel heist . . .

A wave of dizziness struck Laura, making Haversham's image waver and then split in two. Black dots swam before her eyes. Her knees threatened to buckle, and she groped for the back of a chair to steady herself. A small moan escaped her lips.

The marquess was at her side in an instant. When he grasped her arm, she flinched and tried to push him away, but the action only worsened her vertigo.

He urged her forward. "Blast it all, girl, you shouldn't have made me tell you that," he said gruffly. "Now sit down before you swoon."

"Swoon? I've never . . ."

Her legs gave out and Laura collapsed onto the soft cushions of a chair. Leaning forward, she dropped her head into her hands and closed her eyes in an effort to rid herself of the awful whirling faintness. She had to regain her equilibrium. Haversham could strangle her right now and she wouldn't have the strength to ward him off.

Dimly she grew aware from the sound of his re-treating footsteps that he'd left her side. He was at the doorway, calling out to the footman. Male voices echoed in the entrance hall. Laura heard shouting, though she couldn't discern any of the words.

Heavy masculine footsteps hastened toward her. Bracing herself to fight off the marquess, she cracked open her eyelids. To her vast relief, the wooziness had faded completely. Everything appeared normal again, from the tall rows of books to the basket of roses she'd left on a table.

Her gaze focused on the tall man approaching her at a fast clip. She knew his muscular form as well as her own body. "Alex, you're back!"

He tore off his riding gloves and flung them onto a chair. His face grave, he sank onto one knee beside her chair. He caught hold of her hands and gripped them, his dark eyes searching her face. "What happened? Are you ill?"

She struggled to smile. An elusive thought hovered at the edge of her mind, a dreadful suspicion that she didn't want to acknowledge just yet. "It was a slight dizzy spell—perhaps I was out in the sun too long this morning. I'm better now."

Alex didn't look convinced as he studied her face. "I'm taking you upstairs at once. You should be seen by a physician."

He sprang to his feet and made a move to pick her up, but she waved him away. "No, Alex! I'm perfectly fine. Really, I am. I won't go, not when I haven't fin-ished interviewing Lord Haversham."

Glancing past Alex, she saw the marquess standing

just behind her husband. Haversham's bristly brows were drawn together in a scowl and he appeared distinctly uncomfortable, shifting from one foot to the other.

He cleared his throat. "There's nothing more to be said, Lady Copley. In fact, too much has been said already. I'll bid you good day."

As he turned to go, she snapped, "You will wait, sir!"

He turned back, his glower expressing indignation at being addressed in such an impertinent manner. But Laura didn't care about his injured pride. She wanted only to unlock the truth—and he had to be the key.

She returned her anxious gaze to her husband. "Lord Haversham claims that my father . . . had an affair with the Duchess of Knowles. But Papa never breathed a word of that to me. Did the duchess confide in *you*, Alex? Did she ever mention such a relationship?"

Alex stared down at her, his expression austere, his eyes dark mirrors that hid his thoughts. He glanced at Haversham, and Laura had the impression of an intense wordless exchange between the two men.

Only then did Alex speak. "This speculation about my godmother's private life is sordid and unacceptable. Haversham, I'm surprised at your lack of discretion."

"I won't tolerate lies being spread about me," the marquess growled. "As for you, Lady Copley, just ask the duchess if you doubt me—though don't expect her to be very pleased by your questions. She values her privacy even more than her collection of jewels."

"That's enough," Alex snapped. "You'll leave my house at once."

Haversham nodded grimly. "Just do me a favor and destroy that document your wife found. I won't have Martin Falkner defaming me from the grave!"

Turning on his heel, he strode from the library. The rapid click of his footsteps echoed in the entrance hall, followed by the slamming of the front door.

"Document?" Alex turned a quizzical look down at Laura. "What document? What did you find?"

"Nothing. It was a complete fabrication." Collecting her thoughts, she took a deep breath. "I told him that my father had written out an accusation saying that Haversham had had an affair with the duchess, giving him access to her bedchamber where she kept her jewels. I'd hoped to prod him into making a confession. That's when he claimed that it was *Papa* who'd had the affair with her . . ."

Laura's words trailed off as the terrible thought she'd been avoiding sprang into her mind. Suppose . . . just suppose Haversham was telling the truth, that her father really *had* engaged in a liaison with the duchess. Had Alex known about it? Was that why he'd evaded her question a few moments ago?

"You're overwrought, darling," he said, reaching down to brush his hand over her cheek. "You must put this unpleasantness out of your mind. Now, are you able to walk? Perhaps you're light-headed from hunger. I'll order a luncheon tray for you in your bedchamber."

Scarcely heeding his words, Laura noted the guarded shadows in his dark eyes and the hard resolve in his clenched jaw. The secretive quality to his expression indicated something that went beyond mere concern for her health.

She felt suddenly, horribly certain that he *did* know

more than he was letting on. And whatever it was, he had no intention of sharing it with her.

"I won't be coddled, Alex. I'm staying right here." She met his gaze without flinching. "Now, pray close the door. I believe it's high time that you told me the truth."

Chapter 27

For once, Alex didn't want to be alone with his wife. Nor did he wish to have a conversation on anything more serious than the fact that Laura must have skipped breakfast and needed to eat in order to ward off another dizzy spell. Nothing could have alarmed him more than walking into the house to encounter Haversham shouting for the footman to bring smelling salts.

Except this.

A bone-deep dread permeated Alex. No longer did Laura's beautiful face show the softness of love. She had reverted to the coolness and suspicion that he hadn't seen in her since her return to London. It had taken him weeks to win back her trust and to earn her love. Since then, their marriage had been nothing short of perfection. And now Haversham had destroyed everything with one careless statement.

Damn the man, Alex had intended to be present during the interview. He had planned to prevent the exposure of any skeletons from the past. Having found no evidence to support her theory about Martin

Falkner's murder, Alex had hoped to use the opportunity to convince Laura to give up on her quest to clear her father's name.

There was no chance of that now, judging by the determination on her beautiful features. In a matter of moments, she'd guess the rest. And there wasn't anything Alex could do but try to blunt the damage.

Going to the door, he saw the footman hurrying from the back of the house. The servant handed him a small corked bottle of hartshorn. "Shall I send for the physician, my lord?"

Laura would protest. But Alex wouldn't feel at ease until she'd been examined. "Yes, please do."

He closed the door, then set the bottle down in case it was needed. The basket on the table gave off the cloying scent of cut roses. Laura must have been outside in the garden when Haversham had arrived.

If only she'd stayed there.

Steeling himself for the inevitable confrontation, Alex drew a chair close to hers and sat down, reaching out to gather her hands in his. Tawny-gold wisps had escaped her upswept hair to frame her face. She looked delicate as always, her skin translucent, her eyes a deep and somber blue. A rush of tenderness choked him. He wanted to pull her into his lap and kiss her until she forgot all else but the joy they'd found in each other's arms.

"I don't like seeing you so distressed, darling," he began. "It might be better if we—"

She pulled her fingers free. "Do *not* attempt to sway me from my purpose. And you'll be honest with me for once. There'll be no more secrets between us. Do you know if my father had an affair with the Duchess of Knowles?"

Clenching his teeth, he glanced down at the carpet.

Leave it to Laura to be blunt. With effort he forced himself to meet her gaze. "Please try to understand, my godmother is a very private woman. I'm not at liberty to discuss her personal life."

"If *my father* was involved in her personal life, then you most certainly can! Now, answer me. It's a simple *yes or no* question."

"I can't answer you," he growled. "I promised never to speak of this matter. I gave her my word as a gentleman."

Desolation etching her face, Laura slowly shook her head. "Dear God," she whispered, "then it must be true. Otherwise you'd never have made such a vow. Papa *did* have a relationship with her—and you've been hiding it from me all this time."

Unable to bear Laura's censure, Alex shot up from his chair and paced to the fireplace. He propped his elbow on the mantel in a casual stance designed to conceal his inner turmoil. "Believe what you will."

She released her breath in a shaky sigh. After a moment she asked in a low tone, "How long did this affair last?"

He set his jaw. Didn't she understand that a gentleman's word was binding? If he broke it, he had no honor left. And yet . . . this was Laura, his wife, the one woman he couldn't bear to deceive.

She leaned forward, her fingers clenched into fists and her gaze intent on him. "For pity's sake, Alex, tell me! This is my father we're speaking of." When he didn't reply, she rose to her feet and gave him a censorious stare. "If you won't talk, then I'll have to call on Her Grace and ask my questions of her."

As Laura turned to go, Alex sprang forward and caught her arm. Devil take his principles. He was done protecting his godmother's secrets. The sowing of secrets had reaped him only this bitter harvest.

"All right, then," he said roughly. "If you must know, your father *did* have a liaison with the duchess a few weeks before the robbery. To my understanding, the relationship was brief. Your father ended it, and Her Grace remains convinced that his true purpose was to discover the location of the strongbox in her bedchamber."

Laura uttered a small sound of distress. She briefly closed her eyes before looking at him again. "Did you know about this affair ten years ago?"

Alex wanted badly to deny it. But those bleak blue eyes demanded the truth. "Yes," he confessed. "I did."

She stood very still, her arms crossed beneath her bosom as if to protect herself from pain. "I see. And what of the other secret you kept from me?"

His mouth went dry. "What do you mean?"

"Ten years ago, your courtship of me was merely a pretense. The duchess must have recruited you to spy on Papa. You sought me out as a means to investigate him."

Put that way, his actions sounded sordid. But back then, he had been driven by a keen resolve to see justice done. He had felt it his duty to assist the duchess in recovering what had been stolen from her.

No matter whom he deceived in the process.

Desperate to atone for hurting Laura, he laid his hands on her shoulders. "Darling, I admit that it did start out that way. I felt an obligation to help my godmother. But I quickly came to realize how special you were to me, how very much I wanted you in my life. I swear, my attentions toward you were sincere—"

"No! You *tricked* me in order to gain access to my

house." Her manner frosty, Laura wrenched herself away from him and retreated a few steps. "You told me that you were looking for pen and paper in Papa's desk when you stumbled upon the stolen earrings. But that, too, was a lie. You were *deliberately* searching for the Blue Moon diamond. You wanted to prove that Papa was a thief. How triumphant you must have felt when you finally found the evidence to convict him."

Her words sliced like razors into Alex. He *had* been poking through Martin Falkner's desk on a mission. But she was wrong to think he'd felt victorious. Upon discovering the diamond earrings, he had been overcome by dread. Because he'd feared—rightfully so—that it would shatter Laura's regard for him.

Now the revulsion on her face made his chest constrict. He felt wild at the prospect of losing her again. Only last night, she had gazed at him with infinite tenderness in her eyes. She had whispered words of love . . . a love that he craved as much as he needed air to breathe.

He stepped toward her. "Darling, I swear that I never set out to hurt you—"

"No." She cut him off with a slash of her hand. "I've heard enough of your excuses. You've always believed Papa was guilty—you *still* believe it."

Alex hardly knew what to say. He'd pored over the police report. He'd spoken to the sergeant in charge of the case. He'd tracked down several servants formerly employed in the Falkner household and questioned them again, but to no avail.

He spread his hands wide. "For your sake, I'd very much like to think your father is innocent, but then who *is* the culprit? There isn't a shred of evidence that Haversham had anything to do with it."

"The man hated Papa. He has every reason to lie. Can't you see that?"

"The courts will demand proof. Besides, Haversham has never been involved with the duchess. He's never been in her bedchamber."

Laura paced back and forth in front of the chaise. "Then perhaps he bribed Her Grace's maid. Or another servant. Oh, I don't know how he accomplished the robbery! But I *do* know that Evelyn could have helped him. She had the opportunity to place the earrings in Papa's desk on the day before you found them."

"What? You never told me that."

"She came to call on me early, before normal visiting hours. Since I was still dressing upstairs, she had ample time to hide them."

Alex frowned. He had no illusions about Evelyn's character. She could be crafty and grasping—yet such an act sounded too vile even for her. "If you like, I'll speak to her about it."

"Don't bother yourself," Laura said scathingly. "You've never really wanted to help me, anyway. I've been on my own in this investigation ever since Constable Pangborn chased me through the slums."

Nothing could have startled Alex more. "Chased you—? When?"

"Upon my arrival in London, I went to the police to find out what had happened to Papa. The constable escorted me to the cemetery where my father was buried." She rubbed her arms as if from a sudden chill. "He made me uneasy, so I ran from him. That was the same day that I ended up on Regent Street and met Lady Milford."

The news jabbed into Alex. He'd intended to

interview the officer who had found her father lying in an alley near Covent Garden. But on the day he'd gone to the police station, the man had been off duty. Alex hadn't thought it important enough to return.

Yet now he did. "What exactly did he do to make you uneasy?"

"I just had a peculiar feeling that he was aware of my true identity. That he knew my father was not a random victim named Martin Brown. I thought perhaps Pangborn had been bribed by Lord Haversham to watch for my arrival in London. And then . . ."

"Then?"

"A few weeks ago, I thought I saw him standing across the street, watching Copley House. But he vanished, and I presumed it was merely my imagination."

Alex sought a rational explanation. But the constable's behavior alarmed him. "Why did you not tell me this sooner?" he demanded.

Laura gave him a cool stare. "Perhaps because I've never quite believed that you *wanted* to clear Papa's name. I've always wondered if you were merely placating me. And now I'm certain of it." Her voice dropped to a husky murmur. "Besides, how could you possibly have my best interests at heart? You didn't marry me for love. For you, it was only lust."

A knot throttled his throat. He could only stare in silence as she turned and walked out of the library, her slim hips swaying beneath the blue gown. He had feared this day would come. In confessing his unforgivable lie, he had destroyed her trust in him.

Then the memory of her dizzy spell spurred him to the doorway.

Laura was almost to the top of the grand staircase. She looked perfectly well, and he checked the urge to go after her. What could he say to her, anyway? That she was wrong? That he did indeed have deep feelings for her, feelings he'd been too gutless to admit aloud? She'd never believe him now.

Women are vain, selfish creatures who will stab a man in the heart.

No, his father had been wrong—dead wrong. Alex had been the one to stab Laura in the heart. Because of his reticence and his deceit, he had lost her. Likely forever this time.

As she vanished from sight, he took off at a fierce stride toward the back of the house and to the stables. He needed an outlet for his black emotions, or he would go mad. He'd track down that bloody constable. He'd find out why the bastard had chased her. And if the man refused to talk, then by God, Alex would choke the truth out of him.

Laura awakened to the pearly light of dawn and the twittering of birds out in the garden. Clinging to the mists of slumber, she reached out for her husband. But instead of his warm, solid form, her hand met only the cool linens.

She opened her eyes. His side of the bed was empty, the plumped feather pillow showing no sign of having been slept upon. She had a vague recollection of being dreadfully weary and retiring early. Why had Alex never come to her?

Then the events of the previous day washed over her in a sickening wave. Their quarrel over Lord Haversham. The secret that Alex had hidden from her, that Papa had had an affair with the Duchess of Knowles. Even more devastating was the dreadful realization that Alex had used her all those years ago. His wooing of her had been calculated to give him the opportunity to investigate Papa.

No wonder Alex had discouraged her attempts to clear her father's name. He'd known she might uncover his treachery.

On top of that, a very different sort of revelation had shaken her world. Before she'd even had the chance to absorb the pain of her husband's duplicity, the doctor had arrived to examine her. Under his questioning, she'd realized that her courses were a week overdue. The kindly, middle-aged man had assured her that an occasional episode of dizziness was perfectly normal for a woman in her delicate condition.

She was with child.

Lying alone in her bed now, Laura placed her hand over her flat abdomen. A bittersweet happiness brought a tremulous smile to her lips. A baby! It was still too amazing to fathom. She hadn't seen Alex to tell him the news. Would he be thrilled at starting a family with her?

No, she mustn't put a gloss on his actions anymore. He cared only about having an heir. After all, that was why he'd married her.

That—and lust.

She'd been naive to imagine that the tenderness of his lovemaking indicated a deep attachment to her. Alex had never spoken of love. If he was cold-natured enough to charm a young debutante in order to search her father's house, then how could she expect that he had changed now?

A soft tapping sounded on the door of the bedchamber. Surprised to hear Winifred's knock so early, Laura pushed up onto her elbow. The moment she sat upright, a cold clammy sensation enveloped her.

Nausea rushed into her throat. She barely reached the chamber pot in time. As she finished retching, the swift patter of her maid's footsteps approached.

"Oh, my poor lady."

Laura soon found herself helped back into bed, lying back against the pillows with a cool damp cloth pressed to her brow. The awful queasiness had subsided, though she still felt shaky.

"I'll tell the kitchen not to send your usual breakfast," Winifred said as she straightened the bedclothes. "Tea and dry toast will settle your stomach. And never fear, such a reaction is quite ordinary during the first few months, generally upon arising in the morning."

"You know that I'm . . . ?"

Winifred's plain features held a wise smile. "I'm the eldest of twelve, my lady. I often helped my mother in this very situation. Now, do rest while I go see about your tray. And pray don't fret, there will be ample time for you to ready yourself." With a twitch of her gray skirt, the maidservant vanished out the door.

Laura blinked to clear the haze from her thoughts. Ready herself? Where would she be going so early?

In the distance, church bells began to clang, the joyful sound joined by other bells, and she realized with a start that it was Coronation Day. In all the upheaval, she had forgotten. London had been abuzz for the past few weeks with parties and celebrations, the streets crowded as citizens from outlying provinces poured into the city.

Only yesterday the revelry and merrymaking had filled her with excitement. Tonight there would be many balls to attend, with everyone in their jeweled finery. The crowning of nineteen-year-old Queen Victoria was truly the event of a lifetime.

Nevertheless, Laura felt an enormous temptation to burrow into the feather bed and sleep for at least a month. She closed her eyes. The very notion of donning her elaborate court gown was exhausting.

Some minutes later, the click of an opening door invaded her drowsy state. She looked over in bemusement as a grandly costumed gentleman swept into the bedchamber.

It took half a second for her to recognize him. "Alex?"

She lifted her head, but he quickly came to her side and commanded, "Lie back, please. There's no need for you to arise yet."

Swallowing a twinge of nausea, Laura complied without argument. How horrid if she were to be sick all over his coronation robes. She wouldn't tell him so, but he looked glorious in the formal black coat adorned with medals, the white waistcoat and trousers, the spotless kid gloves. From a fastening at his throat fell a full-length crimson mantle lined in white silk with an ermine cape. At his side hung a dress sword in a gold scabbard attached to a crimson sash around his waist.

Gazing up at him, she felt strangely tongue-tied in the face of his lordly splendor. Their quarrel hung between them, too, the hurt of his lies and the awful knowledge that he had courted her for his own clandestine purpose.

"Your maid thought I should look in on you," Alex said. "I understand you're ill this morning."

He was frowning slightly, his expression detached and remote, as if they were strangers instead of husband and wife. Was this to be their life henceforth? This frosty politeness?

Laura wouldn't succumb to the aching sorrow in her chest. She would have to learn to be just as unaffected as he was.

Her fingers gripping the covers, she managed a

wooden smile. "I'm better now. Apparently, it's perfectly natural for a woman in my condition. I haven't told you, Alex, but . . ." The words caught in her throat. An indifferent tone of voice was not the way she'd envisioned relating such momentous news.

"You're to bear my child. I stopped by the physician's office late yesterday and he told me." Alex bent down to brush his gloved fingers over her cheek. "Laura," he said gruffly. "Will you allow me to say how very pleased I am?"

They stared at each other, and the chilly mask slipped from his face. His dark eyes came alive with a powerful intensity. The anger and hurt and bitterness fell away, and in spite of all that had happened, Laura felt the rise of hope that he truly cared for her. She yearned for him to pull her into his arms, to hold her close and whisper loving words. Her foolish heart believed that he wanted to do so.

But how could she trust herself to know his thoughts? Perhaps all he felt was exultation that he'd accomplished the purpose of this marriage. Perhaps he was merely reflecting on the heir she might give him in nine months.

The door opened, and Winifred entered with a silver tray. She stopped on seeing them and bobbed a curtsy. "Do pardon me, my lord. I'll just leave my lady's tea and toast on the table for now."

"You needn't go," Laura said, lifting her head slightly from the pillow. "My husband shall be departing very soon since he's riding in the procession."

"If you're sure you're all right," Alex said.

"I told you, I'm perfectly fine."

At her cool tone, that closed expression came over his face again and he stepped back. It somehow seemed important not to let him view her as an invalid, so Laura sat up in bed. Much to her chagrin, however, the nausea once again rose in her throat.

This time, she managed to control it by taking shallow breaths. But her skin felt clammy and it was impossible to hide her shaky discomfort from him.

Winifred appeared at the bedside with a porcelain cup. "Here, my lady. It's plain tea, nothing that should upset you."

The maid held the cup to Laura's lips. She took a small sip, then another. While the heat of it felt soothing, the tea only marginally improved her stomach. But it was enough so that after a moment she could hold the cup herself. With her cold fingers wrapped around its warmth, she looked up to find Alex watching her with a frown.

"You're going nowhere," he stated. "You're to stay home in bed."

"But I can't possibly! Your aunt is counting on me to take her to the coronation."

The plan had been settled weeks ago. With Alex required to take his place among the peers, Laura was to escort Lady Josephine to Westminster Abbey and sit in the transept with the other ladies. To miss such a momentous event was unthinkable—even in her present state.

Alex appeared unmoved by her plea. "The church will be stifling and extremely crowded. You'd be arriving hours before the ceremony even begins. I'll not have you suffer through such a long service. Aunt Josie, I'm sure, would agree with me."

Laura parted her lips to protest, then thought better of it. Who was she fooling? Nothing sounded less appealing than the notion of being squashed into a pew for hours, unable to breathe from a tightly laced corset, and feeling miserably sick to her stomach.

Yet as Alex turned to go, a sense of desolation settled over her. In spite of their quarrel, she felt a craving for her husband to come to the bed and tenderly kiss her good-bye.

But he didn't. Alex merely gave her a cool nod. Then, in a whirl of rich crimson robes, he vanished through the connecting door.

Chapter 28

Her hands braced on the stone sill, Laura leaned out an open window of a guest bedchamber on the second floor. From this high vantage point, she caught a glimpse of the approaching procession in the distance. Unfortunately, Copley House was not situated directly on the coronation route, and the view also was obstructed by the leafy trees of Hyde Park.

Nevertheless, the far-off roar of the throngs caused a quivering sense of anticipation in her. Only minutes ago, at ten o'clock, the distant crack of gunfire had announced the queen's departure from Kensington Palace. Now the long line of riders and vehicles proceeded slowly in the direction of Pall Mall on the route to Westminster Abbey.

"I do wish you had a better view, my lady," Winifred said from her stance at another window. "It seems such a pity for you to miss everything now that you're much improved!"

After breakfasting on tea and toast, Laura had felt so out of sorts that she'd taken refuge in slumber, only to awaken two hours later refreshed and alert, the nausea completely gone. Her misery forgotten, she had dressed quickly and come to the front of the house, drawn by the palpable excitement of the moment.

"I should much rather count my blessings than complain," Laura said with a smile. "Besides, it would be impossible to squeeze a carriage through the crowds just now. I've never in my life seen so many people."

Vast masses packed the parade route and waited for the state coach that conveyed Queen Victoria. Latecomers darted down the street in front of the house, heading toward the south side of the park. People waved hats and scarves and Union Jacks. Shouts and cheers reverberated through the air.

"Oh, isn't it grand?" Winifred said with a happy sigh. "How lovely it would to see the queen herself, if only we were nearer. I've a sister in service two streets over who will be enjoying a much better view, I'm sure!"

Laura enjoyed the spectacle of her normally reserved maid looking so animated. "Why don't you go there right now, then?" she suggested. "If you hurry, perhaps you'll catch a glimpse of Her Majesty's coach."

"Oh, but I couldn't leave you, my lady."

"Yes, you most certainly can. I'm perfectly well now, and I insist that you go. Now, don't waste time gainsaying me. Just make haste at once!"

Her gray eyes aglow with excitement, Winifred bobbed a curtsy. "Thank you, my lady," she said fervently. "I promise to return within the hour with a full report."

As the servant rushed out of the bedchamber, Laura returned her attention to the approaching parade. Now she could see tiny moving vehicles through the trees and the glint of gilding on the coaches. Alex would be riding down there somewhere in the procession.

Her vibrant spirits dimmed at the memory of their quarrel. Only twenty-four hours ago, she had believed he harbored a tender affection for her. She had been hopeful that in time he would come to love her, if he didn't already. But the discovery of his deception had changed all that. It had awakened her to the cold, hard fact that he had used her in order to entrap her father.

He'd claimed an obligation to help his godmother. But how could he justify deceiving a young girl and breaking her heart? What did that say of his character?

A discreet rapping made her turn around. A footman holding a silver salver stood in the open doorway. "Do pardon me, my lady. A message has arrived for you. I was told that it was urgent."

Puzzled, Laura stepped forward to take the note from the tray. She broke the red wax seal and unfolded the paper to scan the spidery penmanship.

> *My Lady Copley—*
> *I fear to relay the Dreadful News that Lady Josephine has gone missing. I Beg of You to come at once. I know of No One else to whom I might turn.*
> *Respectfully Yrs,*
> *Mrs. Samson*

* * *

Deafening cheers echoed outside Westminster Abbey, while inside, a twittering of excitement buzzed from those lucky enough to have received an invitation to sit in the cathedral. A few moments ago, the firing of the guns had announced the arrival of the procession. The glittering assembly had yet to view their queen in all her raiment, for she had proceeded directly to the robing chamber near the entrance.

There, she would don a long crimson mantle and prepare for her walk up the aisle to the throne.

As Alex went to take his place with the other peers in the transept, his gaze veered to the empty seat among the peeresses where Laura should have been sitting. He wished desperately to be home with her. How was she feeling? Had she overcome her illness? Nothing could have struck him harder than seeing her wan features—and knowing that she despised him too much to allow him to take her into his arms.

Except for one brief moment, when he had spoken of their baby, she had been cold toward him. No love had glowed in her eyes. She hadn't forgiven him for committing the cardinal sin of using her to investigate her father. He couldn't bear it if she never forgave him . . .

"Is it too much to hope that your wife has abandoned you?"

The feminine whisper in his ear startled Alex. Arrayed in an elaborate white satin gown, Evelyn stood close beside him. Diamonds glinted in her auburn hair and at her throat and ears.

"What are doing?" he muttered. "Go back to your seat."

"In a moment." She sidled closer, her bosom artfully brushing his arm. "I heard you came to call yesterday evening. What a pity I was out. Had I been home, I would have been more than happy to receive you."

Alex frowned at her. He'd been so caught up in anxiety about Laura that it took a moment to remember his concentrated efforts the previous day to uncover something—anything—that might exonerate her father. He'd gone to interview Constable Pangborn, only to learn that the officer had resigned abruptly from the police force two days earlier. Alex then had tried Pangborn's rooming house in Lambeth, but the man had absconded without paying his rent.

Pangborn had disappeared without a trace.

The peculiar circumstance had increased Alex's fear and frustration. Unable to shake the uneasy sense that Laura wasn't safe, he had visited Evelyn's house to question her. But Evelyn, apparently, had assumed his call to be evidence of a romantic interest in her.

He should fob her off until a more judicious time, but decided instead to take advantage of the few minutes before the queen made her entrance at the back of the church. With the hum of people talking everywhere, no one should take notice of them.

He bent his head to Evelyn. "You called on Laura the day before she and her father fled the country. I want to know why."

She stared blankly. "I beg your pardon?"

"You heard me. Just answer."

"That was ten years ago. Why do you ask? Don't tell me you believe her vile accusations against my father."

Alex glanced behind him. The Marquess of Haversham stood a short distance away, deep in conversation with the Bishop of Durham.

He returned his attention to Evelyn. "All I want is to clarify a few facts. You must have had a reason to call on Laura that day in advance of normal visiting times. The two of you were hardly the best of friends. Tell me why you went there alone to see her."

A cross look on her face, Evelyn lifted her chin. "I wasn't *alone*. When have *I* ever wanted for male companionship?"

Alex cocked a startled eyebrow. "A man accompanied you? Who?"

When she told him, the name froze his blood. He'd never even considered that knave in conjunction with the robbery. His mind swiftly assembled the pieces of the puzzle. Though he couldn't see the whole picture, Alex knew enough of it to feel an icy certainty. "Odd that Laura never mentioned he was there with you."

"As I recall, he departed before she came downstairs. Oh, what does it matter? It's ancient history!" Leaning into Alex, Evelyn purred, "Now, darling, don't scowl so. Are you jealous because you heard he was to drive me here this morning? Never fear, he begged off at the last minute and now I'm all yours."

It took Laura the better part of an hour to reach Lady Josephine's house. She'd had to cool her heels waiting for the carriage to be brought around. The jam-packed streets had further slowed her progress. She had requested the open barouche in the hopes of spotting Alex's aunt along the way. But the sight of the milling crowds made Laura realize the difficulty of the task. It certainly wouldn't be as easy as the other time when Lady Josephine had left by way of the garden gate—and that had been nerve racking enough.

How *had* the old woman managed to escape this time? The gate was now padlocked, and a footman was stationed at the front door. And why had the new companion not been watching her? Perhaps Mrs. Duncalf had been given leave to view the queen's procession.

The barouche came to a stop at last and the footman let down the step. Laura hurried toward the brick town house. Without pausing to knock, she threw open the front door and stepped into the foyer. The place looked deserted, with nary a soul in sight. There was only the usual clutter of vases and statuary, and the old suit of armor gleaming dully beneath the stairs.

Her footsteps echoed on the marble floor. "Mrs. Samson?"

By way of answer, Laura heard a far-off yapping. The muffled sound seemed to have emanated from upstairs.

Charlie? Did that mean—?

With a hopeful cry, Laura made a dash for the stairs. She hadn't mounted more than two steps, however, when the crowlike figure of the housekeeper flew out of the corridor leading to the rear of the house. "Praise heavens, you've arrived, my lady! But where are you going?"

"I heard Charlie barking upstairs. Did you find Lady Josephine?"

The housekeeper's eyes widened, her knobby fingers gripping her apron as she aimed a frowning glance up the stairs. "No! No, I fear she is still missing. As I wrote in my message, she wandered away a few hours ago. I haven't seen her since, and with all the other servants gone, I've been at my wit's end . . ."

"But she wouldn't have ventured outside without Charlie, I'm sure of it. Are you absolutely certain she hasn't returned? Perhaps she came in the front door while you were downstairs."

Mrs. Samson bit her lip, breathing heavily as if in agitation. "I . . . I don't think so . . ."

A movement behind the housekeeper caught Laura's attention, and a man strolled out of the shadows of the dim passageway. His flaxen hair neatly combed, he wore a finely tailored gray coat over pin-striped gray trousers. "Lady Josephine didn't take the spaniel with her today."

His presence in this house astonished Laura. "Mr.

Stanhope-Jones! Whatever are *you* doing here? And why are you not at Westminster Abbey?"

"I had a change of plans at the last minute, as I was telling Mrs. Samson just a moment ago. You see, something dreadful has happened. By chance, I glanced out my window this morning and witnessed a horrid accident directly in front of my house." His patrician features grave, he added, "I don't wish to alarm you, my dear, but . . . it involved Lady Josephine."

Laura's heart gave a painful jolt. She stepped off the stairs and went straight to him. "Dear God, what is it? What's happened?"

"Oh, it's all my fault," Mrs. Samson cried out, burying her face in her hands. "I shouldn't have given the staff leave to attend the festivities. I thought I could watch her ladyship myself for a few hours. I never imagined she'd steal away while I fetched her breakfast—or that such a dreadful event could befall her."

"*What happened?*" Laura repeated on an edge of panic. "Please, Mr. Stanhope-Jones. I demand that you tell me at once!"

He took her hand and patted it. "Pray don't fret. She'll be fine, I'm quite sure, once she's had time to heal. You see, the dear old lady was knocked down by a pack of wild revelers. Such uncivilized beasts roaming this city today! My manservant was able to carry her into my house, but . . . well . . . it appears she's broken her leg."

"Broken—! Are you quite certain? Could you not transport her back home here?"

"No, my lady, she's in such terrible pain that I thought it unwise to move her until a doctor could be found to administer aid." Mr. Stanhope-Jones caught hold of Laura's arm and steered her down the corridor. "Come along, I'll take you to her straightaway.

We must hurry lest she think she's been abandoned to strangers."

Fraught with anxiety, Laura took a few steps, and then stopped. "My carriage is waiting out front. Shouldn't we go out that way?"

"My coach is parked in the mews. The side street isn't as crowded, and I know a shortcut, anyway. Perhaps Mrs. Samson will be so kind as to inform your servant what's happened."

"I shall, indeed," the housekeeper called after them. "You may depend on me, Lady Copley."

The plan sounded reasonable, yet as Laura allowed herself be tugged down the passage, she glanced back over her shoulder to see Mrs. Samson still standing by the newel post, watching them go. A ray of sunlight illuminated the sneer on her face—though of course that was her permanent sour look. It seemed odd she hadn't made a move to obey the order, but perhaps the woman was still in the grips of shock.

Laura certainly was. Distress flooded her at the thought of Lady Josephine's suffering. As a child, Laura had fractured her arm while climbing a tree, and she knew just how painful a broken bone could be. The befuddled old woman must be even more miserable with no one familiar nearby to reassure her.

As they hurried through the garden, Laura noticed the gate stood ajar. "The padlock is gone!"

"So it is. Mrs. Samson removed it a short time ago. I came around back since the main streets were so congested, and it's indeed a stroke of luck that she heard my frantic knocking."

In the mews, a burly coachman sat hunched over the high seat of a black coach drawn by a team of fine bays. His cap was pulled low, and Laura caught a

glimpse of his muttonchop whiskers. Something familiar about him struck a chord in her. Then the uneasy impression vanished as Mr. Stanhope-Jones
swiftly ushered her into the well-appointed vehicle
with its white satin interior and plush blue squabs. A
gentle sway indicated that the coach had started down
the narrow alley to the side street.

Laura perched on the edge of the seat and peered
out the window. Pedestrians thronged the pavement,
most of them heading in the direction of Westminster.
The muffled blast of distant gunfire brought whoops
and cheers from the passersby. They waved their flags
and shouted huzzahs.

"Ah," Mr. Stanhope-Jones said, cocking his head.
"There's the signal that Her Majesty has arrived at the
Abbey. The ceremony should take nigh on two hours,
don't you think?"

"I suppose so." That reminded Laura of how long it
would be before Alex would return home. She felt a
keen wish for his presence. No matter how hard-
hearted he had been with his own wife, he truly did
love his aunt.

"Then afterward," Mr. Stanhope-Jones went on,
"only imagine the horrid traffic jam with all those
carriages and coaches. The hordes of riffraff will
make the way difficult as well. Perhaps fate has done
us a fortunate turn in avoiding that squeeze, hmm?"

A smile crooked his thin lips, and Laura found his
attempt at humor distasteful, for there was nothing
about Lady Josephine's calamity that could be termed
fortunate. Then she chided herself. He had been extremely generous with his time, sacrificing this rare
opportunity to attend the crowning of their queen.

"I cannot thank you enough," she said. "If anything

is fortunate, it is only that the accident occurred in front of your home. My husband will be most grateful that you were so helpful in assisting his aunt."

Mr. Stanhope-Jones narrowed his eyes. Rather than responding to her appreciation, he changed the subject. "I understand from Mrs. Samson that you felt unwell this morning. Pray do not take offense, but you're looking rather pale. And you've suffered quite a shock."

He reached down to open a drawer tucked cleverly into the base of his seat. Inside lay a silver flask and two crystal goblets in a bed of white satin. He took out one, uncorked the flask, and poured a measure before pressing the goblet into her hand. "There, that should help."

Laura looked down at the amber liquid. "What is it?"

"A mild sherry. I've found it's an excellent restorative."

She really didn't want anything, but after he'd been so kind, it seemed rude to refuse. Lifting the rim to her lips, she took a tiny sip, but the sweet taste and pungent aroma nearly made her gag.

"Thank you, but I-I simply can't tolerate anything right now."

Laura tried to give the goblet back to him, but he refused to take it. "You'll feel better once you've swallowed it all," he said rather forcefully. "Drink it down, now there's a good girl."

"I truly cannot. Please, I can't even abide the smell." She thrust the goblet at him again, and this time he accepted it, albeit with frowning reluctance. She hesitated to reveal her condition, but felt that some explanation was needed. "I'm still feeling a bit ill, you see."

"Forgive me. I was only trying to help." Turning abruptly, he rapped hard three times on the wall nearest the coachman. "Dratted fellow is taking his time."

His palpable disapproval made Laura uncomfortable. Did Mr. Stanhope-Jones fear she would be sick all over his pristine coach? "I'm fine, really I am," she told him. "And I doubt we can travel much faster in this crowd, anyway."

As the coach swayed, she looked out the window to see a dray full of country folk perched on a bed of hay in the back, the excited children waving handkerchiefs and homemade flags. In spite of her anxiety, Laura smiled and waved back.

"Bumpkins," Mr. Stanhope-Jones said, his lip curling. "They oughtn't to sully the city with their presence."

"I beg to disagree," Laura felt obliged to say. "They're as much the queen's subjects as you and I. We've *all* cause to celebrate Her Majesty's coronation."

His keen blue eyes drilled into her; then his face relaxed with a charming smile. "You're quite right, my dear. At any rate, I shall be going away from London very soon and leaving all this chaos behind."

"Have you an estate in the country, then?"

"Indeed, I do. In Kent, near the coast. I believe you would enjoy the view from the cliffs. Perhaps you'll see it sometime."

Laura thought it doubtful. Even if he planned a house party, she couldn't imagine Alex consenting to attend. On the few occasions when she'd seen the two men together, they'd appeared less than friendly. Of course, her husband jealously guarded her, seeming to view any man who sought out her company as a rival for her affections.

"Ah, here we are at last," Mr. Stanhope-Jones said.

The coach drew to a halt, and in short order Laura found herself stepping into an elegant foyer. She took fleeting note of the rose wallpaper and statuary on pedestals, making straight for the stairway, where she paused with her hand on the newel post. "Is Lady Josephine in one of the bedchambers? Will you show me to her?"

"We shall go upstairs, of course," Mr. Stanhope-Jones said, taking Laura by the arm and propelling her up the marble steps and through a doorway. "But pray wait a moment in this sitting room while I check on her condition."

"But why can I not go to her at once? If she's in great pain, she'll want me with her."

"Patience, my lady. First, do allow me to see if the doctor has arrived. If he's in the middle of an examination, we mustn't interrupt."

Laura didn't see what difference that would make, but this was his house, after all, and since he'd gone out of his way to help, the least she could do was to respect his request. "As you wish, then."

He was still holding the goblet, which he set down on a table. "Should you change your mind," he said in a sympathetic voice, "I shall leave your sherry here. It will do wonders to ease your anxiety."

Then he bowed to her and went out, shutting the door.

Laura removed her bonnet and tossed it onto a cream-upholstered chair. She walked restlessly around the stylish sitting room. The palette of lavender and cream with touches of green was not what one would expect in a man's house. Maybe Mr.

Stanhope-Jones had a mother or a sister who had chosen the furnishings.

She went to the window and glanced down. The black coach with its team of bays was still parked in front of the house. Was the coachman awaiting instruction in case the doctor allowed Lady Josephine to be taken home? Laura hoped so.

The street had begun to clear, the bulk of the crowds surging toward Westminster Abbey. The ceremony would be under way now, the choir singing and the music playing in a rich display of pageantry. Laura wished with all her heart that she could have seen Alex in his crimson robes seated with the other peers . . .

At that moment the coachman looked up at the house. She had a sudden, clear view of his face.

A disbelieving gasp choked her throat. That grizzled visage with the beady black eyes was burned into her memory. Constable Pangborn!

She stepped back from the window, her hand pressed to her madly beating heart. No. It couldn't possibly be him. Why would a police officer be wearing livery and driving a coach? It made no sense at all.

Yet it *was* him; she felt the sinister certainty of that in her bones.

As she was trying to determine a reason for his presence here, the door opened and Mr. Stanhope-Jones entered, followed by a young maidservant carrying a tea tray. At a motion from him, she set it on a table and scuttled from the room, closing the door behind her.

"I thought you might want refreshment, Laura."

She had not given him leave to address her so familiarly, but that consideration seemed minor at the moment. Making haste toward the door, she said,

"That's very kind, but I do wish to see Lady Josephine. I cannot think of my own comfort until I've assured myself of hers."

And she must find out why Pangborn was driving that coach. What could it mean?

Mr. Stanhope-Jones caught hold of her arm. "There's no need to hurry. The poor old dear is sound asleep. The physician has administered laudanum to ease her pain."

Laura couldn't shake the disturbing suspicion that he was delaying her on purpose. "I'll sit at her bed-side, then."

"All in due time. The doctor is still binding her leg. When he's done, I'll take you to her straight-away." He strolled to the tray. "In the meanwhile, might I offer you a cup of tea? It will soothe your nerves."

Laura waited until he picked up the silver pot and began to pour. Then she darted past him and flew to the door. She wrenched it open and hastened out into the passage, making for the upper stairs.

Mr. Stanhope-Jones came after her and grabbed her arm again. "Where are you going?" he said tes-tily. "I want you to drink your tea."

"Not until I've seen Lady Josephine. If you won't take me there, I'll find her myself. One would think she isn't even here."

Something secretive flashed in his pale blue eyes, and Laura felt a bone-deep shock. "Dear God. She truly *isn't* here . . . is she?"

"What nonsense," he said, his tight grip pulling her toward the sitting room. "You'll see her as soon as you've had refreshment."

Laura dug in her heels. "No. You will tell me where Lady Josephine is."

"You're overwrought. Come, sit down before your tea turns cold."

Her mind raced. His insistence first on the sherry, and now on the tea, struck her as peculiar. Was there a sedative in it? Or . . . poison? She controlled a shudder. It was rapidly becoming clear that he'd lured her here for some nefarious purpose. Did he desire revenge for her rejection of his vile offer to be his mistress?

Laura pretended to submit, forcing her body to relax. "As you wish, then," she said in a meek tone. "But just one cup. And please, do loosen your grip on me. You're hurting my arm."

His fingers slackened ever so slightly, though not enough for her to entertain hope of escape. He was stronger than he appeared, and she let him draw her back into the sitting room. When he urged her to a chair, Laura balked. "I fear I'm too distressed to sit," she murmured.

"Perhaps once you've drunk your tea, then." Mr. Stanhope-Jones brought her the porcelain cup and placed it into her hand. "There, my dear. Swallow it all down and you'll be much improved, I promise."

She lifted it to her lips and blew on the steaming liquid, noticing that it had the same sweetish aroma as the sherry. Bile rose in her throat. He was watching her avidly, so she clenched her teeth and forced a disarming smile at him over the rim.

She took a step toward him. Then she flung the hot contents of the cup straight into his face.

He screamed, staggering backward, his hands clutching at his eyes. Laura didn't tarry. She rushed out the door and to the stairs. With the constable waiting out front, she'd have to find a rear exit.

Clutching her skirts, she started down the steps.

But at that moment, the front door opened and Pangborn entered the house. He looked up and spotted
Laura. Uttering an animal growl, he surged toward
the staircase.

Chapter 29

"Where is my wife?" Alex demanded. "My coachman said he's been waiting out front for nearly an hour."

Standing by the staircase, Mrs. Samson lowered her gaze to the floor. "I-I don't know, my lord. She went out the garden gate to look for Lady Josephine some time ago. I haven't seen her since."

The news stabbed into him. He had absconded from the Abbey just as the queen had started up the aisle. There'd be hell to pay for his desertion, but he'd give up his earldom to assure himself of Laura's safety. He'd stolen one of the processional horses and ridden hell-bent for leather, the crowds giving way for the madman in the swirling crimson cape. But by the time he'd reached Copley House and scanned the note sent by Mrs. Samson, Laura had been long gone.

He knew in his gut that she was in danger. However, it wouldn't do any good to go haring off until he had all his facts straight.

"So my aunt is missing, too?"

"Er . . . no, my lord." The housekeeper darted a

quick look at him while clutching convulsively at her white apron. "As it turns out, she wasn't missing at all. I found her a little while ago, up in the attic of all places, poking through a box of trinkets that Lady Copley had put in storage. I'm happy to say, she's napping in her bedchamber now."

The woman's furtive avoidance of his eyes raised suspicion in Alex. "Look at me," he commanded.

Mrs. Samson slowly lifted her head. "Yes, my lord."

"Has Rupert Stanhope-Jones been here this morning?"

Her gaze widened slightly, and then flickered away for an instant. "N-no, my lord."

He seized hold of her sharp chin and forced her to meet his eyes. "You're lying. He was here, and he took Laura when he left, didn't he? My coachman wouldn't have seen them depart because they went out through the mews."

"I . . ."

"Speak up! Or by God I'll see you locked in prison for abetting in the abduction of my wife."

She drew a shuddery breath. Alex could see the woman thinking, calculating, deciding how best to save her own skin. "All right," she burst out, "yes, he did take her. He told her that Lady Josephine had fallen and . . . and hurt herself. I didn't know at the time that he was being deceitful . . . because I hadn't yet found her ladyship in the attic. I'm truly sorry, your lordship. I-I didn't wish to be blamed for asking Lady Copley to come here when it was all just an unfortunate mistake."

Her story was absurdly flimsy. Stanhope-Jones couldn't possibly have known that Laura had stayed home from the coronation unless this woman had sent

word to alert him. She likely had been paid handsomely for her treachery.

But he didn't have time to deal with her now.

"Where did they go?" he asked.

"To his house on Albemarle Street, I believe." Mrs.
Samson fell to her knees, her head bowed, displaying
the lace cap on her graying black hair. "Pray forgive
me, my lord. I never meant to cause harm to anyone, I
swear it!"

Unmoved by the entreaty, Alex yanked open the
front door. He motioned to the footman waiting by
the carriage that had brought Laura here. "Come inside and keep a watch on this woman. Don't let her
out of your sight until I return."

Laura pounded one last time on the door of the dressing chamber before abandoning the useless endeavor.
If there were any servants in the house other than the
one timid maid who'd brought the tea tray to the sitting room, none of them would dare to help her.

Especially not Pangborn. The burly man apparently had quit the police force and was now employed
by Mr. Stanhope-Jones.

Upon seeing her starting down the stairs, Pangborn had rushed toward her with more nimbleness
than when he'd chased her through the slums. Had he
been paid by Mr. Stanhope-Jones even back then?
Instead of Lord Haversham, had Mr. Stanhope-Jones
been the one watching for her return to England?

The very possibility of that shook her. What did it
all mean?

Between Pangborn and Mr. Stanhope-Jones, who'd
emerged from the sitting room drenched in tea and in
a fury, she'd had no chance to escape. The two men had

cornered her. At his employer's instruction, Pangborn had hauled her upstairs to lock her in this dressing room.

She'd been trapped in the dim, stuffy room for at least half an hour, enough time for her to hunt through the empty cupboards and clothes press for anything that might be used as a weapon. To her frustration, there was not so much as a hairbrush on the dressing table.

Daylight came from a small round window fixed high in the wall. Laura dragged over a chair, hitched up her skirts, and climbed onto a chest of drawers. Standing on tiptoes, she could just peer out.

The window faced the rear of the house. Even if she broke the glass, it was unlikely that anyone would hear her cries for help. Especially not with the muffled sounds of celebration all over the city.

What did Mr. Stanhope-Jones intend to do with her?

Chilled by that question, she climbed down and renewed her efforts to find a weapon. This time, she spotted a tiny dull gleam on the carpet beneath the dressing table. Crouching, she reached for it and pricked her finger on something sharp.

A long hatpin. It wasn't much but it would have to do.

At that moment, heavy footsteps sounded outside and a key rattled in the lock. She poked the hatpin through the fabric inside her bodice.

Just in time.

The door swung open to reveal Pangborn's grinning visage with its muttonchop whiskers. He gestured to her to walk forward. "The master will see ye now, m'lady. Come along nicely, and ye won't be hurt."

Laura did as she was told. Nothing could be gained by resisting this heavily muscled man who looked as if he would enjoy subduing her. She had Alex's baby to protect. Above all else, she mustn't invite a battering that could result in a miscarriage.

As Pangborn prodded her through a deserted bed-chamber and into the passageway, Laura said, "My husband will pay you extremely well for my safe return. He's a very wealthy man."

The officer guffawed. "Too late for that. Like as not, I'd end up swinging from a noose."

He brought Laura back to the sitting room, where Mr. Stanhope-Jones sat waiting on a chaise, drumming his fingers on the cream-striped cushion. Upon seeing them enter, he jumped to his feet. He'd changed out of his tea-stained clothing, Laura noted. Vanity must be the reason for the delay in whatever he had planned; he couldn't bear to be seen in disrepair. Now he wore a burgundy coat, tan trousers, and a pristine white cravat. He might have been setting out for a ballroom instead of abducting a woman.

Pangborn took up a stance in the doorway, blocking any hope of escape in that direction.

Nevertheless, Laura refused to quail as she stepped toward her captor. "I demand to know what this is about," she said. "What gives you the right to lie about my husband's aunt and then lock me in a closet? I wish to return home at once!"

Mr. Stanhope-Jones gave her a coldly exultant smile. "Your home is now with me, darling. I've waited ten long years to possess you. I've no intention of giving you up."

Laura stared at him. "Ten years—?"

"I asked you to marry me back then, remember? I went down on my knees before you. But still, you refused me. You wanted a title—you, a mere commoner yourself."

She had refused offers from several ardent gentlemen. Because she had fallen madly in love with Alex.
"You're wrong," she said with a shake of her head. "A
title has never mattered to me."

He curled his lip. "Indeed, *Countess*? I'd have
stopped you from wedding Copley had I not been out
of town making arrangements for us."

"Arrangements? What do you mean?"

"You'll find out soon enough," he said slyly. "In the
meanwhile, I have something for you, something I've
longed to see you wear."

He must be mad, Laura thought in horror. Did he
really intend to take her somewhere away from London? Was that why the coach was still parked out
front? She must stall him, keep him talking.

Even as the thought flitted through her mind, she
despaired at the futility of it. Alex would still be at
Westminster Abbey. After the coronation ceremony,
all the peers would line up to kiss the queen's ring
and pledge fealty. The process would be slow and tedious. With the traffic afterward, it might take him
hours to reach home and realize she was missing.

Mr. Stanhope-Jones went to a table by the window
and picked up a jeweler's box. Opening it, he drew
forth a necklace and brought it to her, holding it rever-
ently in his hands. Sunlight sparkled on a string of diamonds from which dangled an enormous bluish stone.

Laura gasped. "The Blue Moon? Dear God, *you*
stole it."

"Yes. I've kept it all these years just for you."

He stepped behind her and fastened the necklace at
her nape. She was too stunned to object. The Blue
Moon lay cold and heavy against her skin. His hand
at her back, Mr. Stanhope-Jones urged her toward a
gilt-framed mirror on the wall.

She gazed at her reflection, the tawny-gold tendrils that had fallen from her upswept hair, the pale oval of her face, and the spectacular blue diamond that was so enormous it looked almost gaudy.

"Ah," he said softly. "Just as I'd hoped, it's the perfect complement for your blue eyes. You, Laura, are truly the most beautiful woman in the world."

His triumphant face loomed behind her in the mirror. The brush of his fingers on her neck made her skin crawl, snapping her out of the spell of shock. She spun away, stepping behind a chair for protection, her fingers touching the faceted diamond. "I don't understand. How did you manage to steal it? Did *you* have an affair with the Duchess of Knowles?"

He laughed. "That old crow? Hardly! Rather, I seduced her lady's maid. Those of the lower classes can be quite susceptible, you know. Some to charm and some to money."

Laura glanced at Pangborn, who stood impassively in the doorway. It struck her that Mr. Stanhope-Jones must have paid Mrs. Samson, too. Else how had he known Laura had taken ill that morning and wouldn't be attending the coronation?

She'd been horribly wrong about Lord Haversham. And Evelyn, too. Having grown up hearing about the feud between her father and the marquess, Laura had been blindly certain of her conclusion. In her own way, she had been as pigheaded as Alex.

"*You* must have placed the matching earrings in my father's desk."

"Indeed so. I'd intended to send an anonymous tip to the police, but Copley ruined everything." Mr. Stanhope-Jones stared at her, his features hard and cold. "I had it all planned out. Once Martin Falkner was imprisoned, you'd have been ruined, shunned by society, with nowhere to turn. You'd have been quite happy, then, to become my mistress. But instead, you vanished."

The most dreadful realization of all struck Laura. Her father must have come back to England to visit Mr. Stanhope-Jones in the hope of retrieving the diamond and clearing his own name—for Laura's sake. Not wanting his dastardly scheme exposed, Mr. Stanhope-Jones had ordered Pangborn to attack Papa and leave him for dead.

It all made horrible sense. After all, the officer had been the one who'd found Papa lying in an alley. The officer also had sent the note to Laura in Portugal in order to lure her back to England. He'd known that she would come to the police to find out what had happened to her father. Had she not escaped into the slums, no doubt Pangborn would have hauled her straight here to Mr. Stanhope-Jones.

Laura clenched her teeth to stop them from chattering. These two men had conspired to murder her father. And they would not hesitate to do the same to her—and her unborn baby—if she refused to cooperate.

"This is folly," she said forcefully. "I've a husband now."

Mr. Stanhope-Jones eyed her. "Indeed. Copley's been stuck to you like a nettle these past weeks. I'd intended to lure you away this evening during one of the balls. But when this excellent opportunity arose this morning, I seized upon it." He advanced on her. "And now, darling, it's time for us to go."

Laura gripped the back of the chair, but it was no use. He caught firm hold of her arm. "Where are you taking me?"

"First to my estate on the coast, and then to the Continent. If you'd drunk your sherry in the coach, we'd already be on our way. And you'd be happily asleep right now."

Laura was glad she'd thwarted him. Every little delay shortened the time until Alex could find her. "You won't succeed in this," she warned as he tugged her out of the sitting room and toward the staircase. "My husband will come after you. He'll track you down and kill you."

Following them, Pangborn uttered a gravelly chuckle. "He'll have to go past me first."

"It'll be hours before Copley learns you're missing," Mr. Stanhope-Jones said. "Even then he'll be hard-pressed to figure out where we've gone. We'll have ample time to set up and wait for him, Pangborn and I."

"A shot through the earl's heart as he's riding up to the house should do the trick," Pangborn said, pulling back his coat to display a brace of pistols stuck into his leather belt. "I'll make it appear 'twas brigands who done it. We'll be long gone by the time the law arrives."

Laura tried not to panic. Surely Alex would not come alone. He would bring others with him. Unless, of course, he was in a fury and riding ahead at breakneck speed to rescue her.

Yes, Alex would do exactly that. The thought made her tremble.

"Enough," Mr. Stanhope-Jones told Pangborn. "You're frightening the poor girl. Go on ahead of us and see if the way is clear. I don't want any neighbors spying on us as we leave the house."

"Aye, sir." Pangborn started down the stairs.

Laura dragged her feet to put as much distance between the men as possible. She could not allow herself to be spirited away from London, transported to a remote manor house, where these men would lie in hiding to murder her husband.

Alex would be heading straight into a trap.

As Pangborn reached the bottom, she and Mr. Stanhope-Jones were only on the third step down. It was now or never. On a pretext of touching the Blue Moon diamond, she drew out the sturdy hatpin from inside her bodice. She turned to her captor, swung back her arm, and stabbed viciously at him.

Biting out a curse, Mr. Stanhope-Jones jammed up his elbow to block her. Instead of plunging straight into his neck, the hatpin gouged his throat. Blood bloomed in its wake and stained his cravat. His grip on her arm slackened.

Desperate, she used her shoulder to shove him away. He staggered, tumbling down a few steps before catching himself. He sprawled there, gasping, his hand to his throat, his fingers seeping red.

Laura scrambled back up to the landing. Her heart pounded wildly. There had to be a servants' staircase at the rear of the house. The door would be hidden in the paneling of the passageway.

She tripped on her skirts and fell to one knee. Pushing herself upright, she glanced over her shoulder and swallowed a moan. Pangborn was galloping back to the staircase in pursuit of her.

Then, just as he reached the first step, the front door burst open. A man in a crimson cape rushed inside the house. Laura blinked, clinging to the upper railing above the foyer, certain she was dreaming. "Alex?"

He afforded her only the flick of a glance. Then he hurtled forward to seize Pangborn. The two men went down in a crashing flurry of arms and legs, grappling, throwing punches at each other. The constable had the burly build of a pugilist, but Alex had the advantage in height and quickness. He administered a crashing blow to Pangborn's jaw, which Pangborn countered with a hard jab to the abdomen. The two men traded strikes, the sickening thuds resounding in the foyer. Alex appeared to be winning, though Pangborn had the stamina of a bull.

As the battle raged on, Laura kept a fearful eye on Mr. Stanhope-Jones, who had risen to his feet and stood wavering. Blood soaked his cravat, and he kept his hand pressed to his throat. All of a sudden he reached into an inner pocket of his coat and withdrew a small pistol. Apparently waiting for a clear shot, he aimed it at the two thrashing men.

He would shoot Alex.

Laura didn't stop to think. She flew down the stairs and threw herself at Mr. Stanhope-Jones, knocking his arm and wrestling for the weapon. The pistol fell clattering onto the marble steps. But Mr. Stanhope-Jones clamped his arm around her waist. His face a cruel mask, he began hauling her back up the stairs.

She cried out, wriggling in an effort to escape his clutches. Despite his injury, he had an iron grip on her. Laura was afraid to struggle too hard lest they both topple down the stairs.

As they reached the landing, she saw Alex strike out at Pangborn with one final murderous blow. He sent the stocky man sliding across the marble floor to land with a thump against the wall. Then Alex came charging up the staircase to her aid.

Looking past her husband, Laura spied a terrifying sight. Still sprawled on the floor, Pangborn had drawn one of the pistols from his belt. He cocked it and took aim.

"Alex, duck! He has a gun!"

But he didn't duck. Instead, he grabbed her close, flung Stanhope-Jones down the stairs, and shielded Laura with his body. Then a deafening blast of gunfire echoed through the foyer.

His body jerked and he collapsed half on top of her. At the same instant, two men came running through the open front door. One of them was her coachman, a sturdy fellow who seized hold of Mr. Stanhope-Jones as he lay groaning on the stairs. The other man, a constable, used his truncheon to subdue Pangborn with a knock to the head, then divested him of the two pistols and tied his hands behind his back.

Laura frantically wriggled out from beneath Alex's heavy weight. He lay unmoving, his eyes closed. Touching him, she was aghast to see that his back was wet with blood. Dear God, he'd been shot. How badly was he hurt?

"He needs a doctor," she called down to the men. "Quickly!"

The constable went dashing out of the house.

With trembling fingers, she stroked her husband's dear face, battered from the fight, and traced the scar of her own making. He had protected her from being struck by the bullet just now. If only she had known back then how fine a man he was. "Alex. Wake up. Please, you mustn't *die*. I won't let you."

He groaned. His eyes flickered open, and he looked straight at her. His hand lifted as if to caress her, and then dropped as if it were too much effort. "Laura. I must . . ."

Laura caught hold of his hand and brought it to her lips. "Don't try to talk, my love. Save your strength."

Tears blurred her vision. The thought of losing him was a dagger to her heart. She laced her fingers with his and held tightly, determined never to let him go.

What foolishness had caused their quarrel? She couldn't even think of it anymore.

"*Listen,*" he rasped. "I must . . . tell you . . ."

He seemed so resolute that she deemed it best to let him speak. "Yes, darling? I'm listening."

That dark intensity burned in his gaze, revealing a deep river of emotion. "I need to say . . . I love you, Laura. *I love you.*"

Then his eyes closed and he fell still.

Chapter 30

Tucking her gardening gloves into a pocket of her gown, Laura surveyed the new grave site. Lush green grass covered the mound. At the base of the headstone, she had planted white calla lilies, purple gladiolis, and yellow freesias. The tall marble slab had been carved with haloed angels and a loving tribute.

Wrens twittered in the overhanging oak trees. A pleasant summer breeze stirred tendrils of hair around her face. This peaceful resting place in the neatly manicured grounds of London's finest cemetery did much to assuage the sorrow in her heart. Nevertheless, her eyes went misty with unshed tears as she contemplated the past. So much had happened, there were so many memories . . .

An arm slid around her waist, and a kiss brushed her hair. "You've done a fine job, Lady Copley. It's a fitting memorial, indeed."

Her spirits lifting, Laura smiled up at her husband. His arm in a black sling, Alex looked so tall and handsome in his dark blue coat that her heart performed a little dance of joy.

Four weeks ago, she had feared he would die. There had been several agonizing days when the doctors had not been sure how badly Alex had been injured internally. The bullet had entered his lower back at an angle, gone through his chest, and exited to lodge in his upper arm. He'd been insensible with fever for a time, until one morning he'd awakened alert and able to sit up in bed.

Since then, Alex had had a remarkably swift convalescence. Of late he'd been chafing to resume their intimate relations, but Laura would not allow him to exert himself just yet. They'd contented themselves with kissing and caressing—and talking. The long conversations in bed had enriched their closeness. Her husband had opened up more about his difficult youth, his life during the ten years of their separation, and his dreams of a large, happy family full of love.

Laura intended to give him all that, for he had given *her* so much.

"I have *you* to thank for making all the arrangements," she said, laying her head on his shoulder. "Papa deserved a better resting place than a pauper's cemetery. And now at last he can be buried under his true name."

Arm in arm, they gazed at the finely chiseled headstone.

Martin Falkner
Loving husband of Aileen
Beloved father of Laura

Alex's good arm tightened around Laura's waist. "I misjudged him in the worst possible way," he said heavily. "I don't know how you've found it in your heart to forgive me."

She reached up to trace the scar on his cheek. "Oh, darling. We've both made mistakes."

"You?" he said rather grimly. "Quite the contrary, the fault for what happened is entirely mine."

"Nonsense. Rupert Stanhope-Jones placed the earrings in Papa's desk. Yet *I* was all too ready to blame Evelyn and Lord Haversham for the deed."

"That's hardly as reprehensible as forcing you and your father to flee the country, to leave behind everything you'd ever known," Alex persisted. "You were right to despise me, Laura. I courted you under false pretenses. By God, I should never have heeded my godmother."

Careful to avoid his injury, Laura pressed herself to his muscled form. The sight of his tormented eyes touched her heart. "Well, I'm exceedingly *glad* that you courted me, no matter what the circumstances. And at least Her Grace seems happy to have the Blue Moon diamond back. It was decent of her to apologize to me."

"I'm the one who'll be apologizing for the rest of my life," Alex declared. "I was far too calculating—"

"If the queen can pardon you for dashing off from her coronation, then *I* most certainly can forgive you, too. Now, there'll be no more apologies, darling. It's time for both of us to let the past go."

To seal her words, Laura gave him a tender kiss. She slid her fingers into the rough silk of his hair, letting her lips convey just how much he meant to her. Alex might give the appearance of a rogue, but deep down he had a strong sense of integrity that only made her love him all the more.

Presently, she drew back, pleased to see the fire of passion in his eyes. A cocky smile lifting one corner of his mouth, he said, "Does this mean I won't have to